Facing the Wind 2
African Storm

EH Lorenzo

DEDICATION

With love and appreciation to my dear wife,
Dana, for her encouragement and patience over the years.

I am also appreciative to my daughter, Ralae, for the excellent cover
painting.

I am also grateful to our friend, Pam, for her excellent editing.

EH Lorenzo

Contents

AUTHOR'S NOTE

The series, 'Facing the Wind', is anticipated to be a three-part work. However, though connected, each book is intended to stand on its own.

This series is inspired by the lives of real people, but it is a work of fiction. The inspiration for several of the characters comes from ancestors of EH Lorenzo. Other characters, particularly the African leaders, are based on real people, and some references to events are based in fact that is well documented, but the book is fiction.

When I started writing this book, I hadn't anticipated dealing with the brutalities of war or of slavery. As the work progressed, I realized that, due to the time period and locations, the work would be wholly incomplete without doing so. However, I have tried to approach both subjects in a manner that supports the story without overburdening the reader with the horrors of either.

To be sure, I don't have personal experience with either conflict and have relied on the testimonies of others and on my own imagination. I trust that the reader will also rely on their own imagination to fill in details that I have either left out intentionally or due to my own inadequacy.

I will also state that slavery of any kind was and is an abominable practice. I've always known that, but in writing this book, I've come to a much greater understanding of its wickedness. So far as I can determine, it has been perpetrated by all races and on all races at some time during the history of the world. I suspect that at its base is greed. When a people view another people as something less than themselves, or worse yet, less than human, they are in danger of accepting the practice of slavery. We are all children of God, and He must be very disappointed in the behavior of man towards their brothers and sisters.

The horrors of slavery cannot be overstated. Probably more especially, the horrors perpetrated against women slaves are most egregious. I am grateful to those men and women who fought against it, or who endured its brutality. I thank God that I've never known its horrors and pray that my grandchildren will ever be safe from its evil grasp.

Chapter One – Leaving England
May 1841
London, England

Standing on the port-side deck of the ship, Hyrum Prince surveyed London. It seemed to rise out of the River Thames teeming with life. This was only the second time that he had been to London, and its large buildings still filled him with amazement. He wondered how it was possible that so many people lived and worked in such close proximity.

Opulent carriages in seemingly great numbers hurried about, transporting their occupants on important errands. Other coarse wagons loaded with farm goods or housewares slowly made their way to one of the many markets.

Hyrum heard the whistle of a locomotive and saw billowing plumes of smoke rising above the buildings across the river, indicating the route of a train. Trains were very much a marvel to him, and its approach gripped his attention. He had never been on a train and had only seen them occasionally along the road to London. How they managed to propel themselves forward, without the aid of a horse, was a mystery to him. He watched the smoke clouds until the train broke free of the buildings and crossed the river on a recently constructed bridge. *I surely doubt that I'll ever see another train,* he thought to himself.

Hyrum wanted to ensure that he would remember this moment and the scene before him for the rest of his life. He had long anticipated leaving England to venture to a faraway place, and surely there was no land farther than Africa. Not only was the distance great, but he expected that the chasms of culture, wildlife and environment were greater still.

"Lift anchor!" yelled the first mate in a strong voice that reached every corner of the ship's deck. At the command, two men began turning a large wooden spool that lay horizontal to the deck and the anchor's heavy chain began winding about the spool.

After a few rotations, the anchor was free of the river bottom and one of the men yelled, "Anchors aweigh!"

"Release cables!" shouted the first mate and men on the dock quickly removed the thick ropes that secured the ship to the dock.

Hyrum watched with interest as other members of the crew hauled in the thick ropes from the starboard side and coiled them neatly for storage.

As the ship broke free of its tethers and yielded itself to the gentle pull of the river, Hyrum again studied the buildings of London. He had little familiarity with London; nevertheless, this was the famed capital of his homeland, perhaps the most prestigious of all cities, and watching it slip quietly away behind the ship underscored the finality of the decision to leave.

He knew well that this was to be his last visit to London, but that suited him fine, since he found greater comfort in more rural settings.

Hyrum turned his face to the direction of the sea and couldn't restrain himself. "Africa!" he said aloud, as though to inform the other passengers of their own destination. Some of the passengers would undoubtedly share the same ship all the way to Africa, but others were destined for ports along the way.

Julia looked up at him and smiled. It was then that Hyrum saw the moisture in her eyes.

Stroking her face lightly with the back of a hand, he asked, "Are you very sad then to be leaving England?"

Julia looked down at the baby in her arms. Francis was not yet a year old. It pained her to consider that he may never know England. Named after her own father, Francis' ancestors had been in England so long that none were sure where they had come from before their arrival on its green shores. Now this little lad would be the first of his family to leave those shores, having never known them. Looking at Francis also reminded her of the infant son that she was leaving buried in an English churchyard.

Though she had tried to push thoughts of her former life to the recesses of her mind, she couldn't help but occasionally consider the memories. She had been born into a family of some influence and means, but following the deaths of her parents, had been raised at Brentwood Hall, home of Lord and Lady Hammond. As a result of the care and kindness of the Hammond's, she was more associated with the leisure and refinement of life in Society than she was with the toil and uncertainty that often defined a commoner's life. However, it was the life of a commoner that she had so willingly accepted when she chose to marry Hyrum. Regardless of toil or uncertainty, she considered that her love for him ran as constant as the river that so gently carried their ship and as deep as the sea that lay before them.

She felt safe with Hyrum. He was hardworking and determined. She knew that if he said he was going to raise sheep in Africa, he would do it. She didn't think that there was anything or anyone that he feared. She also loved him for his earnestness and honesty. She knew that she could trust her innermost thoughts with him because he was loyal. Above all, she knew that he was loyal to his God and that knowledge gave her confidence to follow him to Africa.

Julia thought of her dear friend, Queen Victoria. Though she would never have personal associations with her again, she wondered whether the Queen would remember her and perhaps send correspondence. She also wondered whether it was possible that such a correspondence would even find her in a far off land. Julia knew, despite her former close associations with the Queen, it would be completely inappropriate for herself to initiate the correspondence. Only the Queen could make the first gestures of familiarity.

Julia silently considered Hyrum's question. Was she sad to be leaving England? She smiled at Hyrum and with tears building in her eyes, replied, "Yes, England's all that I've known and I worry so for Francis."

England was a safe place. Though she knew little about Africa, she knew that safety wasn't its calling card. Wild animals and wild peoples were its population and she wasn't sure which terrified her more. England was refined and there was opportunity for education, even if it was a limited education for commoners. But, Julia considered that, given her connections with the Hammond's and the Queen, if they were to stay in England, her children would likely be afforded greater opportunity than other children of like station. Regardless, she would follow her husband.

Though she felt badly as soon as the words escaped her lips, Julia added, "And you've got Ian." The implication was that she was giving up everything to leave her home and that Hyrum wasn't required to sacrifice as much.

Ian was Hyrum's younger brother and Hyrum was thrilled to have him joining with them to settle in Africa. Hyrum looked about to see where Ian was and saw him in the direction of the bow. Hyrum thought it odd that instead of watching as they drifted out of London, Ian sat at the base of the foremast with a sullen look about him. Hyrum looked back at Julia and replied with a smile, "'Tis true, that I have Ian, but more importantly, I have you and Francis."

Julia smiled and settled into Hyrum's arms thankful that he hadn't taken offense at her thoughtlessness. As she did, Hyrum observed, "Why do you suppose that Ian is so sullen?"

Julia looked in the direction that Hyrum was looking and observed Ian with his head resting on his knees. "Indeed, I don't believe that I've seen him with such a despondent countenance. Perhaps you should speak with him."

"Without a doubt, I will. But he looks as though he would not take kindly to my approach at present. I'll speak with him soon."

Hyrum and Julia directed their attention back to the buildings and docks that they were passing. They both watched as London blended into the countryside and disappeared altogether.

Soon the captain shouted orders to the crew and like several parts of the same organism, they quickly set about to man their assigned stations. A light breeze was blowing from the west and so the order went out to unfurl all the sails. Most passengers had not sailed previously and they watched in amazement as the large sails first dropped and then filled with the breeze that pushed them toward the sea. As the sails filled to capacity, the three-mast ship seemed to leap forward. So much so, that passengers who had not secured themselves with the railing nearly lost their balance. Many laughs and joyous cries went up as the passengers struggled to maintain an upright position.

Julia and Francis were safe in Hyrum's arms, but the sudden movement of the ship caught him unaware and he shifted his weight quickly to maintain his balance and to keep his family upright.

It wasn't long before the gentle movement of the ship on the water caused Francis to start fussing. "I'm going to take Francis below and change his nappy," said Julia. "You should speak with Ian. He appears more distraught about leaving England than do I," she smiled.

"Indeed he does. I'll speak with him," agreed Hyrum as he ruffled his son's hair.

"I shan't be long," Julia assured him.

Hyrum and Julia had been below deck earlier in the day to drop off their trunks and to lay claim to a set of bunks. It had taken several moments for their eyes to get accustomed to the darkness of the lower deck. In retrospect, Julia was grateful for those few moments of darkness. Had she been accosted by the sights, smells and sounds of the lower deck all at the same time, she was sure that she would have removed her family from the ship that instant. Earlier in the day, as she had carefully negotiated the stairs down to the lower deck with Francis in her arms, she was shocked to encounter a thick wall of human stench. The smell hung in the stale air of the lower deck and seemed to have a presence all its own. After gasping and covering her mouth with a handkerchief, she had exclaimed to Hyrum, "If this ship smells so before leaving port, what will it yet smell like?"

Once inside the lower deck, she had noticed that the bunks were much closer than she had imagined. There would surely be no privacy on the ship. They hadn't the funds to purchase lodging in a cabin, but had paid extra for bunks in a corner. Corner bunks provided precious little privacy, but they had felt that it would be worth the extra price.

On her initial decent below deck, Julia had to fight back her tears. Now returning below deck with Francis, it wasn't as shocking, but it was disgusting to her, nonetheless.

After Julia went below with Francis, Hyrum approached Ian who was still sitting at the base of the foremast. Hyrum gently kicked Ian's boot and cheerfully said, "Why the sullen countenance, Brother? This is the day we've waited for. I'd have thought you'd be at the railings watching with the others."

Ian slowly raised his head and looked at Hyrum. It was only then that Hyrum noticed the cut above Ian's right eye and a swollen jaw. Hyrum bent down and turned Ian's head to get a better look and with concern asked, "What happened to you, Ian? Who did this?"

Ian dismissively shook his head loose of Hyrum's grasp and replied quietly, "It's nothing."

Hyrum looked about as though he might find the culprit and then knelt next to his younger brother. "Well, it certainly looks painful regardless. What happened? Has a member of the crew done this?"

"Always the older brother, aren't you?" replied Ian.

"I can't hardly change that now, can I?" replied Hyrum. "Listen, if you don't want to talk about it, suit yourself, but it's a long way to Africa."

"Indeed, it is," agreed Ian in a straight tone and still not looking at Hyrum.

"Well, whatever it was, or whoever it was that did this to you certainly weren't justified in their actions."

"Oh, aye?" replied Ian with a swift glance at Hyrum. "Can you be certain?"

Hyrum noted the slightest upturn in the corners of Ian's mouth and knew that his brother wasn't going to keep the secret much longer. "If you shan't tell me, maybe you'll share it with Julia. She'll be about shortly."

Ian stood and grasped the ship's railing with both hands and leaned against it. Looking down at the river, he said, "Very well then. While you and Julia were taking strolls about the parks of London each day that we waited for the ship, I went to the market."

"Indeed you did. And you got a fine price for the wagon and other wares that we couldn't bring along on the ship."

"Quite right," Ian smiled slightly and looked straight at Hyrum. "But it didn't take long to sell those."

Hyrum was now very intrigued. What else had Ian been doing while in London? Ian was about to continue when Hyrum suddenly smiled and said, "There was a lass at the market, wasn't there?"

Ian looked back at the river and replied with a smile, "Aye, there was a lass at the market." The smile caused his jaw to hurt and he groaned quietly and rubbed it with his left hand.

Hyrum slapped Ian slightly on the shoulder and laughed, "Now, why am I not surprised?" Then feigning great concern, he continued, "Did that little lass do this to you?"

Ian turned to face Hyrum with a slight smile on his face. The thought of the girl injuring him almost caused him to laugh and perhaps would have had the pain in his jaw not discouraged it.

"To be sure, she did not. But, as it turns out, she has a father," Ian replied with a hint of sarcasm, and his countenance seemed much improved as a result of just speaking with Hyrum.

Hyrum laughed aloud and urged, "Please, do tell me more."

"When I went to the market on the second day, I saw a beautiful girl working a stall."

"Like Julia?" interrupted Hyrum.

"Julia?" Ian questioned.

"Yes, beautiful like Julia."

Ian smiled. "Yes, beautiful like Julia, I suppose. Only taller."

"Go on then."

Ian rolled his eyes as though exasperated at the interruption. "I must have watched her for an hour before I mustered the courage to approach her. And of course, I had to wait for her father to leave the stall for a time."

"Of course," Hyrum smiled in agreement.

Julia returned from below deck and approached the two brothers with Francis in her arms. When she saw Ian's face, she grimaced and asked, "Ian, you poor fellow, what happened to you?"

Hyrum took Francis from Julia and said with a light laugh, "He was just relating the story to me. You'll find little amazement to hear that a lass was involved."

Julia pouted her lips gently and replied, "Oh, Ian, how terrible. Do continue."

"I was relating to Hyrum that I met a girl at the market as she was working her father's stall. A beautiful girl to be sure."

"Like you my dear," Hyrum added with a smile at Julia.

Julia smiled at Hyrum and then looked back at Ian to encourage him to continue.

"I've never met a girl as delightful as she. And I might add that she was pleased with me as well. I know it was only a few days, and you'll likely scoff, but we resolved to marry."

"Ian, I know that you're decisive, but don't you think that was rash?" asked Julia with a concerned look.

"Rash indeed," agreed Hyrum. "And marry you? Did she realize that you were bound for Africa?"

"You may believe it was rash, but it didn't feel so to us. And she certainly did agree to go to Africa."

Julia looked about the deck and asked, "But she's not on the ship now, is she?"

Ian looked across the river at the green pastures that they were slowly drifting by. With a tone of discouragement, he replied, "Nay, she is nay on the ship. I went to fetch her this morning. She was supposed to be waiting around a corner near the market. Instead of finding her when I rounded the corner, I discovered her father and he was madder than a shorn ram. He caught me by surprise and inflicted these marks that you see. He informed me with clarity that his daughter would nay be joining me."

"Did you strike him?" asked Hyrum.

Ian looked back at Julia and Hyrum. "Without a doubt, I wanted to, but I did nay do it. As his mind was firm, I had a decision to make. I would either have to stay in London and continue to see her or make my way to the ship and forget her."

"You made the right decision, Ian," replied Hyrum with a hand on his shoulder.

"Did I now? It was nay an easy one. I have little money for lodging in London and the ship was sailing straightway. So, here I am. The right decision though? I'm nay sure."

"How can you say so?" asked Julia.

Ian looked at Hyrum and asked, "How many English women do you suppose are in Africa?"

Hyrum shifted his weight nervously and replied with a glance at Julia, "English women in Africa? I don't know, but probably not many."

"Well spoken, Brother." Then looking at Julia, Ian asked, "How many of those few will be unattached to a man?"

Julia diverted her gaze toward Francis and made motions of straightening his few tufts of hair. When neither Julia nor Hyrum responded to the question, Ian continued. "So, here I am. The right decision? Perhaps. Only time will tell and only God knows."

"Ian, you must have thought about this before coming to London or before making the decision to go to Africa," observed Julia.

"Quite right. I did, but the reality of it didn't quite settle on me until I saw the girl in the market."

"Ian," Hyrum said with an arm about his shoulder, "I'm sure the Good Lord will provide." Then with a slight grin and a twinkle in his eye, he added, "And after all, Africa is a big place and you only need one."

Ian smiled at the notion. "Do you suppose that she'll have a father also?" he said with a grin.

The sun had dropped below the horizon and it was nearly dark before the ship reached the mouth of the River Thames and entered the disturbed waters of the North Sea. By then, a brisk breeze was blowing and the sails were filled to capacity. The ship began to rock forward and back with each wave.

Though Ian and Hyrum had helped hold Francis throughout the day, Julia's back felt the strain of carrying her son for so long. She began to realize that though she detested the smells and the closeness of the lower deck, she would be obliged to spend considerable time there to allow Francis to move about. He wasn't going to be content being held the entire voyage to Africa.

"Hyrum," Julia asked, "how will Francis learn to walk on this ship? This is much more turbulent than I had expected."

"I'm sure that it won't always be so." Then he added with a laugh, "But if it is, I suppose that he'll walk like a drunken sailor."

Chapter Two – Life Aboard Ship
May 1841

The seas were rather turbulent the first few days, and Julia spent much of the time feeling nauseated. Hyrum, Ian and Francis had acclimated to the rocking of the ship much more quickly than she. She had spent much of the time during the daylight hours with her head over the railing, ejecting the contents of her stomach into the sea. She had never expected to perform such a revolting task in public; and though she was joined by several others, doing so caused her much humiliation. Though she was reluctant to admit it to herself, there were several times that she thought about the refinement of the English Society and the comforts of the Royal Court that she had left behind.

She was grateful to have a pail by her bedside at night. Others, not so fortunate, were required to search quickly in the darkness for the stairs. Many groans could be heard as seasick passengers failed in their attempts to reach the upper deck before heaving uncontrollably in the lower deck. The groans were in response to the acknowledgement by the other passengers that the mishap would rend the air all but consumable. It became necessary, almost for very survival, to employ the mop on a continual basis to gain some measure of relief from the offensive odor.

After a few days the seas calmed, and Julia began to feel better. All the passengers cheered when the captain announced that they would take an overnight respite on the Island of Guernsey at the port of Saint Peter.

Hyrum, Julia and Ian had been standing at the railing watching the shoreline of France when they heard the news. "Surely, we are still in the Channel," remarked Hyrum. "I find it astonishing that we would go to port so soon."

"Perhaps the captain keeps a residence there," smiled Ian.

Julia turned to Hyrum and put her hand on his arm. "Hyrum," she said. "Don't you think it a grand idea if we were to stay the night in an inn on the island?"

Hyrum looked astonished and replied, "An inn? Why would we stay in an inn when we've already paid for lodging on the ship?"

Julia turned her head in the direction of the opening to the lower deck. "It smells so, and Francis would surely be benefited by the fresh air."

Hyrum smiled and took Francis in his arms. "We'll stay the night in the inn then. It will be good for all of us. Ian, will you join us?"

Ian smiled and replied, "Indeed not. I'll go ashore with you. That should prove interesting, but I'll return to the ship. Who knows but what all the passengers will leave the ship."

Julia got a distressed look on her face. "Hyrum, let's go to the inn the moment we are allowed off the ship."

Hyrum smiled and hugged Julia with his free arm as Francis looked on. "Without a doubt, my love, we will."

Later that day, the cry went up that the Island of Guernsey had been sighted from the crow's nest. The Princes stood near the bow and watched in anticipation for the first sight of land from the deck of the ship. The Island of Guernsey was sighted on the starboard side at about the same time that a smaller island was seen from the port side.

"I presume the large body is Guernsey," remarked Ian.

"Yes, that's correct," replied Julia. Then looking at Hyrum, she added, "My anticipation surprises me and gives rise to concern in my mind."

"Why should your anticipation concern you?" asked Hyrum.

"We've only been on the ship for a few days and already I'm anticipating debarking. We have such a long voyage ahead of us. Shouldn't that be cause for concern?"

Hyrum placed a hand on Julia's hand as it rested on the ship's railing and looked at her with compassion. "Indeed, we may have underestimated the rigors of ship travel, but it won't last forever. A night on shore will do us good."

Julia looked again in the direction of the island and wondered whether she had the strength to complete such a difficult voyage. *"What makes it so difficult?"* she asked herself. *"All I have to do is stay on the ship and it will convey me to Africa. No physical effort is required."* She thought about the strenuous and urgent ride that she and Lord Hammond had made on horseback from

Warwick to Newmarket in an effort to save Katherine. Though rigorous, the ride had caused her no concern. *"When did I become weak?"* she wondered. *"Did the loss of my child weaken me? Surely it has made me stronger?"*

Still looking across the body of water at the island that was getting closer ever so slowly, Julia shifted Francis from one hip to the other. Francis playfully tugged at his mother's hair and she turned her head and smiled at him. In the same instance, her gaze took in both Hyrum and Ian standing at the railing. A look of anticipation and satisfaction was clearly visible in their countenances. Of a sudden, Julia too was satisfied and the realization gave her strength. *Everything that I have and need is right here,* she thought. *Because of them, I can and will be strong.* She considered that, though emotional contests can sometimes outweigh physical challenges, she had the strength within her because of her family and their faith in the Lord.

Soon the details of the low laying island began to come into view. The port was situated at the southern end of a peaceful bay, protected by a natural barrier formed by smaller islands. One of those tiny islands sitting at the mouth of the bay was Cornet Rock. A stone castle still stood on the diminutive island, protecting the bay as it had for hundreds of years.

As the ship passed Castle Cornet and entered the bay, the buildings of the town were visible. They looked stately as they lined the shoreline, each three or four stories high. The two most prominent buildings of the town were the parish church and the Castle Carey. Each were on a little higher ground than the first row of buildings. The castle had been completed only the year previous and appeared very grand.

The crew set about to furl most of the sails so that the ship drifted slowly into the bay and approached the dock. Soon the ship was adjacent the dock and the thick ropes were thrown ashore and tethered.

The crew was preparing to lower the gangplank when Julia said, "Hyrum, Francis needs his nappy changed before I can go ashore. Please take Ian and go in advance of me."

"I'll not leave you on the ship, my dear. We'll wait for you."

"No, you must go. What if all the rooms are taken?"

"Surely there aren't so many people on this ship. It'll be fine."

Julia reluctantly agreed and hurried downstairs with Francis.

Changing the diaper didn't take long and she and Francis soon joined Hyrum and Ian on deck. A queue had formed to get off the ship and they were soon moving down the gangplank with the other passengers.

Guernsey was a Crown Dependency and though both English and French were spoken in the town, English seemed to be spoken predominantly.

"I don't see any inns," Julia remarked with disappointment.

"I'm sure that there is an inn or a public house nearby," Hyrum assured her as they continued along the docks and rounded a corner. "Ah, there. Just ahead," Hyrum said pointing ahead and to the other side of the street. "The Fox and Hound. They'll surely have a room."

Julia seemed pleased. "Indeed, they will," she replied and walked more quickly in the direction of the public house.

"Will you join us for tea?" Hyrum asked, looking at Ian.

"Nay, I should like to see more of the town and I'll take my tea on the ship."

"Very well then. We'll likely nay see you until tomorrow, on the ship then?"

"Aye. Tomorrow on the ship."

"Jolly good," replied Hyrum as he hurried to catch up with Julia.

The Princes took a moment to get accustomed to the lower light of the public house and then approached the keeper.

"We should like a room for the night," Hyrum stated.

The keeper was a big man with a full beard and a strong accent that Hyrum and Julia expected must be unique to the island. The accent was so strong that neither initially understood what the keeper had said.

"Pardon?" asked Hyrum.

The keeper looked a little perturbed at the request to repeat himself, but he did so slowly. It seemed to Hyrum that the keeper had slowed his speech excessively in a patronizing manner.

"Aye, ye want a room, aye?"

"Yes. For the three of us," Hyrum replied pointing at Julia and Francis.

"Aye, I have a room available, but it is nay much."

Hyrum looked at Julia for confirmation and she smiled slightly at him.

"We'll take it, sir."

"Top of the stairs then. Ye must pay first. It'll be two bob."

"Right then," replied Hyrum and he gave the keeper a few coins.

Julia followed Hyrum as they ascended a narrow staircase that creaked beneath the weight of each step. The staircase had no bannister, but had floor to ceiling walls on either side. After the third flight of stairs, the staircase narrowed still further for one additional flight. Their room would be an attic room.

The room was rather spartan. No bed, only a straw mattress on the floor and one blanket. The floor had no covering over its well-worn wooden floorboards. A few of the planks stuck up slightly on the ends, having ejected the nails intended to keep them anchored. A solitary window faced the bay. It had no covering, but was open, allowing a salty breeze to blow through the room.

Hyrum's initial thought was that Julia would be very disappointed. Though rarely mentioned, he hadn't forgotten the comforts and fine appointments that she had been raised amongst. For her part, Julia would have been pleased with the accommodations of a cave as a substitute for the rudiments of the ship's lodging.

"Well, this is it, my love," announced Hyrum as he stepped into the room and held the door for Julia and Francis. "The keep was right, it isn't much."

Julia quickly surveyed the room and with eyes closed, took in a deep breath of the clean ocean breeze. "Without a doubt, it's the finest room I've ever encountered," she said joyfully as she placed Francis on the floor. Then, while embracing Hyrum, she continued, "Thank you for letting us stay here. Just one night will greatly increase my confidence to face the rest of the voyage."

Hyrum smiled and kissed his brave wife.

After leaving Hyrum and Julia, Ian continued along the street next to the dock. He had only seen the sea for the first time a few days earlier when the ship had left the slow flowing Thames, and he found that it fascinated him. The waters of the bay were clear, with a blue-green tint. He sat on the dock near the south most point of the bay and was fascinated by the several schools of colorful fish that swam beneath his dangling feet. He gasped however and pulled his feet up quickly when he saw a snake swim just beneath the water's surface.

Startled by laughter, Ian spun about and saw a young woman only a few feet away.

"It's a harmless eel. You probably thought it to be a snake," the young woman said with a laugh and a smile. "You've never lived by the sea, have you?"

Ian stood quickly, removed his cap and tried to look unconcerned, but he felt his face was warmed by embarrassment. "Nay, I've not lived next to the sea. What is an eel then?"

Looking at the waters below the dock for signs of the eel, the young woman said, "It's just a type of fish. They are mostly nocturnal you know. You're fortunate indeed to have seen it."

"Nocturnal?"

The young woman smiled and looked back at Ian. "Yes, that means that they mostly are active at night."

"Oh, right," replied Ian knowingly.

Ian surveyed the street and the shops nearest the dock and saw that there were a few people walking about. Then he looked back at the young woman, readily noting that she was pleasing to look at.

"Are you looking for my escort then?" she asked.

Ian was embarrassed that it had been so obvious.

"That's so old fashioned. Don't you think," she added.

"Yes. Quite right," Ian agreed.

"Well, if you must know, those are my parents coming out of the shop just there."

Ian looked in the direction that she was looking. He wasn't accustomed to a young woman being so forward, but he approved.

"Are you from the ship then?" asked Ian.

"Well, I'm actually from Henley-on-Thames," the young woman said. "But yes, we were on the ship," she added with a smile. "I've seen you on the ship, you know."

Ian was taken aback again at her forward manner, but he was intrigued by it also.

"My name is Ian Prince," he said with a slight bow of the head.

"How very nice to meet you, Ian Prince," she replied with an offered hand. "And I am Amanda Barnes."

Ian took her hand gently. It was softer than he would have expected. He also thought that she was a little taller than Julia and quite slender. He noted her brown hair that was wound in a bun on her crown.

"Are you traveling to Africa then?" asked Ian.

"Indeed," Amanda replied, "and I can't imagine what attraction Africa holds for my father. I expect that you are going to Africa also."

"Quite right."

"And you are traveling with someone?"

"Yes, my brother, his wife and child," replied Ian.

"Pray tell, what attraction is Africa for you?"

Ian paused for a moment and said, "A chance to start without the restrictive structure of English Society I suppose. I'd never own land in England, but in Africa it's all but a certainty."

"And what does your brother's wife think of Africa?"

"Julia? She consented, to be sure, but I do expect that it is hard for her. Perhaps hardest of all is living aboard the ship," Ian said with a smile.

"Without a doubt," Amanda agreed with her nose wrinkled. "It's far worse than I had imagined."

"Will you be spending the night on the ship then?" asked Ian.

"Regretfully. My mother so wanted to spend the night in town, but my father wouldn't hear of it."

"May I escort you back to the ship?" asked Ian.

Amanda smiled. "I would like that very much," she replied as she took his offered arm and turned toward the shops.

They met Amanda's parents coming out of a shop and Mr. Barnes looked narrowly at Ian.

"Father, this is Ian Prince. He's traveling to Africa aboard our ship."

Ian offered his hand as he said, "Pleased to meet you, Mr. Barnes."

"Pleased to meet you, I'm sure, Mr. Prince."

"What will you do in Africa?" asked Mr. Barnes.

"I'll ply the cooper's trade and raise sheep with my brother."

"Both will be prosperous, I'm sure," replied Mr. Barnes. "I'll be practicing law."

Ian thought it odd that a lawyer would leave England and stranger still that he didn't purchase better accommodations for his family. He suspected that there was a reason and didn't pursue it further.

"May I accompany your family to the ship?" Ian asked.

"As you wish, sir," Mr. Barnes replied.

Ian and Amanda stayed on the deck after Mr. and Mrs. Barnes went below to have their tea. The sun was setting as they walked along the deck to the foremast and stood at the railing.

"I don't believe that your father approved of me," Ian commented to Amanda.

"Oh, I think that he liked you well enough. That's his reaction to any young man, I assure you."

Ian smiled and ventured to ask Amanda why it was that her father left England.

"He really had little choice after the investments that he was managing for his clients failed to produce. He couldn't get clients after that and since he had heard that lawyers were in short supply in Africa, he decided that we must go."

"Your mother couldn't have been keen on the plan," observed Ian.

"Indeed not. She's lost all her friends and her fine house. All that she has left really are her fine clothes. She hasn't been speaking a great deal to my father since."

"And how have you faired?"

"The announcement that we'd be leaving England was quite a shock, to be sure. I'm not fond of it at all, but what can I do. I've just come of age, but with no means of a dowry, I had no prospect of suitors. I have no means of independent support. So, here I am."

"Do you know anything of Africa?"

Amanda sighed and looked out at the bay. "I only know that there is little refinement, plenty of wild animals and wild people. My prospects have hardly improved. Wouldn't you agree?"

For his part, Ian considered that his prospects had improved greatly.

Chapter Three - Shaka
September 22, 1828
Zulu Kingdom, Africa

Atop a prominent hill, a small group of Zulu captains stood a few paces apart from the king. To approach without invitation could mean instant death, a sentence that they themselves had administered to others on orders of the king many times. At 41 years old, the aging king was still a powerful warrior and his very presence at once commanded respect and fear. Wearing little more than a full-length fur robe and a fur cap crowned with long green and blue feathers, he was a majestic sight.

Shaka Zulu stood silently for several minutes and surveyed his realm. This was his kingdom; his vision and his aggression had built it. The Zulu Kingdom stretched from the hills to the south, to the sea on the east and as far as the eye could see to the north. There was only one way to unite and rule such a vast empire and that was to execute quick and final justice at the first sign of any dissent. The king had inflicted much pain, but he also knew pain. The story of his warring prowess could be read in scars across his body. They told of numerous conflicts, and though each could have ended the king's life, he had always been victorious. He and his well-trained army had subdued scores of tribes into one kingdom united under his rule. People of yet unconquered tribes had no word in their languages to describe the multitudes of people who had died as a direct result of Shaka's unrelenting pursuit of power.

As the king looked over his realm, he remembered that, though he had been born the illegitimate son of a king himself, his path to kingship hadn't been willingly handed to him. Chief of the Zulu tribe, Senzangakona, had accused his mother, Nandi, of having a "shaka" when her abdomen started to protrude. "Shaka," stomach worm, had stuck as the name that the baby boy would carry all of his life. But, instead of causing him to cower, he had become as a devouring "shaka" to his enemies. The very name "Shaka" had become synonymous with fear and power.

Nandi and her young son had been exiled by Senzangakona and after wandering in the countryside, they found refuge amongst the Langeni tribe. Despite the exile, or perhaps more especially because of it, Nandi was careful to instill in her son a sense of his royal heritage, and he was quick to embrace it. Whether planned or by chance, she also conveyed to him a keen sense of the injustice dealt by their banishment and a general distrust of others.

As Shaka grew, he became ever more devoted to his mother. Because of his vigilance in watching for injustice afforded to himself or to his mother, and his emphatic claims of royal descent, he had few friends. These characteristics often raised the angst of the other boys of the tribe, and they in turn, were ruthless in their taunts.

If the other boys did allow Shaka to join them in their play or adventures, he was the first that the group turned on when boredom or disagreement set in. Their taunts on one particular day were not uncommon. The boys had been playing as warriors, and he had successfully captured two "prisoners". One of his prisoners was the brother of the self-appointed leader of the group. An argument ensued and the lead boy managed to push Shaka to the ground. As he did he snarled, "If you're a king, where is your kingdom? Perhaps it's a kingdom of shakas like you." The other boys laughed as Shaka, landed in the dirt with arms and legs outstretch.

Shaka grabbed a stick and was quick to his feet. Though he was younger than most in the group, he stood taller than the others. He knew that they dared to taunt him only because they were banded together.

"I didn't say I was king. I am the son of a king and will be king one day," demanded Shaka defiantly.

The lead boy decided that such a declaration was too arrogant to go unpunished. "Get the shaka!" he demanded as he picked up a nearby stick that he had been using as a makeshift spear.

Shaka turned quickly and burst through the ring of boys and ran quickly through the tall grass. He could hear the others yelling as they also picked up sticks and chased after him. There wasn't a boy there that could outrun him, but Shaka wasn't running out of fear. He was running only to gain the advantage.

After a short distance, he began ascending a small hill. The incline of the hill allowed the group to close some of the distance that Shaka had put between himself and the group. He was now in striking distance of the "spears" and two struck his back almost simultaneously. In his heightened state of excitement, Shaka felt the impacts, but no pain. Then, two "spears" flew over his head. One stuck in the ground and Shaka snatched it up as he ran.

One more spear, he thought to himself knowing that there were five pursuers. No sooner had he the thought than a stick struck the back of his leg. Again, there was no pain.

Five! he thought to himself as he spun about, still gripping his two sticks. The incline that was previously a disadvantage, now put him in a superior position. His taller stature, coupled with the higher ground, created an imposing sight for the boys below, and they were startled. Letting out a loud yell, Shaka ran down the hill toward them. Instinctively, he held onto the sticks and didn't throw them as was the custom for tribal warriors. The other boys stopped their pursuit and turned to run. Shaka began jabbing them with the end of the sticks as they ran. Cries went up from the group as repeated thrusts of Shaka's spears found bare flesh, and the five would-be pursuers dispersed in different directions. Shaka followed after the leader, and again he held to the sticks and did not throw them. It only took a few paces before Shaka was at the boy's back, jabbing him with the sticks. Even when the boy cried for relief, Shaka continued the punishment until they neared the village. Only then did Shaka stop and watch as the "leader" entered the village with tears streaming his face.

As Shaka watched the other boys walk slowly back into the village defeated, something within him took great satisfaction in his victory. He began to realize that he was stronger and faster than his peers. "I'm already the king!" he declared to himself.

His relationship with the boys of the tribe continued to deteriorate until he was never invited to associate with them. He resented the jeers that he heard when he passed near them and he found himself plotting revenge.

Nandi too was embittered by the treatment that her only child received by the tribe. She was in little position to influence a change, but she reinforced in Shaka his feelings of supremacy. "Someday you will cause them to bow at your feet, my son. They aren't worthy of you," she would often say. "If they don't choose to lay at your feet, you'll compel them to."

Shaka found that he was most comfortable when he was alone and away from the village. Though his mother disapproved, he occasionally spent days at a time alone in the bush. Many a night was spent in a tree to avoid prowling lions.

Though ridiculed for it, he wore no sandals. Unlike other boys, he couldn't be bothered by the task of lacing them. Consequently, the skin of his feet became thick as elephant skin and as tough as dried cow hide. He easily ran over rough and thorny ground without pain.

When he was 15 years old, the rains didn't come when expected. One day he noticed that there was a large movement of animals from their valley. He knew that the animals would move to anywhere that they could find water. Initially, the lack of rain was not a concern, because the tribe had cattle. But as the cattle began to die for lack of water, or were eaten by the tribe, the tribal leaders began selectively allocating food. Nandi and her son were not a priority. Eventually, they were no longer welcomed, and Nandi resolved to take her son to the home of her aunt amongst the Mthethwa people.

To Shaka, the exile was an affront to his mother. He didn't much care whether he lived with the tribe or not and felt that he would be fine alone. But to exile his mother caused hatred to grow inside him. "How dare they to exile the mother of a king!" he exclaimed to himself.

He vowed that he'd never forget the laughs from the other boys as he and his mother walked out of the village with only a bladder of water and a few slices of dried meat. "Lions will eat you by nightfall," one boy had whispered as Shaka walked nearby. "Your mother's bones will be consumed by vultures," another remarked. Shaka glared at him and imprinted his face in his mind.

It was a five-day walk to the valley where the Mthethwa lived. Lions were a constant threat, especially at night. Shaka's experience in the bush made him well suited to protect his mother, and he was fiercely devoted to her.

Little was spoken between Shaka and Nandi as they moved quietly through the valleys and across the plains. Shaka knew that predators were about and that they had excellent senses of sound, sight and smell. Grass couldn't be used as cover, since there was little left on the hills and plains. But it also meant that Shaka could see further across the plains. Before crossing an open area, Shaka would climb a tree or a small rise to check their surroundings. Less grass also meant that a lion would be less likely to use it as cover for an attack. Shaka had also insisted that he and his mother rub their bodies with petals of the king protea to mask their scent.

On the morning of the third day, Shaka felt as though they were being watched. "Wait here," he instructed his mother with silent signs, and he climbed a tree. Holding carefully to the limbs, he closely examined the plains in all directions. He and his mother were heading primarily eastward, and there were no dangers in sight. Still he was nervous. He noted a few bushes in the direction that they were traveling and also some bushes and a tree to the north. Between these was a waterhole, or at least what was left of a waterhole. Though there would be more mud than water, there would be water, and they were in need. Pointing in the direction of the hole, Shaka made the sign for water and indicated that they would go there.

There were no other animals at the hole, but they still approached cautiously. The smelly mixture of water and dirt was all that was left of what would have once been a small grassland lake. As the lake had evaporated in the hot sun or as the contents had been consumed by man or beast, what life there was left in the lake would have been concentrated into this small puddle.

Shaka was attentive to the surface of the water, it was perfectly calm. This troubled him. Many small ripples would indicate the presence of fish fighting for their last breath. Perfect calmness could be concealing dangers beneath the surface. As he carefully inched forward, he occasionally glanced about for sign of opportunistic predators who may be waiting for him to be distracted.

All was quiet, almost too quiet, but very near the water's edge, he decided to motion his mother closer. Without taking his eyes from the water, he lifted an arm to motion to her. As he did, the water moved ever so slightly. Instantly, he jumped backward as the water burst with life, and a large crocodile, with mouth agape, sprang from its muddy domain. Shaka thrust a long spear directly into the charging animal, but it slowed him little. Shaka would have willed the spear to enter the beast just behind the front legs, but in his surprise and haste, the spear had entered directly into the mouth and part way down the throat. The crocodile bit the handle off without slowing. Shaka jumped to one side and thrust his second spear, but didn't release it. This spear found its mark behind the left front leg and directly into the heart and lungs. Shaka withdrew it immediately and blood flowed from the wound. The crocodile gave another attempt to reach Shaka, but his life had flowed from him and he lay motionless once again.

After approaching carefully, Shaka stabbed him for finality before withdrawing his shortened spear from the crocodile's mouth.

Shaka looked expectedly at his mother, but to his horror a male lion was nearly upon her. Shaka wheeled about and threw his spear just to the left of Nandi as the lion leapt for his prey. Nandi gasped in surprise and recoiled for fear of the spear. Shaka's spear caught the lion in his soft underbelly and he initially collapsed to the ground. Instantly he was up, but Shaka was upon him with his shortened spear. With a quick and final thrust of his spear, Shaka ensured that the animal was no longer a threat.

Quickly, Shaka retrieved his spear, and uncertain of how many other beasts may be nearby and attacking, he spun about in all directions until he was satisfied that there were no other attackers.

Adrenalin still surged through his body and in its resulting heightened state of physical energy, Shaka held both his spears skyward in a triumphant manner and shook them as he smiled at his mother. The two deadly beasts now lay harmlessly within twenty feet of each other.

Nandi smiled at her son and approached. "Shaka, the great warrior," she said in a quiet tone.

Shaka smiled and again raised his spears triumphantly. He then used the metal tip of the short spear to cut meat from the crocodile and handed the flesh to his mother. He then set about the task of removing the skin. Nandi produced a sharpened stone from her pouch and began skinning the lion.

Two days later as they neared the valley of the Mthethwa, Shaka was particularly alert for a predator of a far more cunning and vicious variety, two-legged predators. The approach to the village was amongst low-laying hills, and he constantly scoured the hills and bush for sign of humans. He suspected that they were being watched, but expected that no harm would likely come to them prior to reaching the village. It would be the chief's pleasure to determine their fate. Shaka anticipated that his heavy load of skins may gain the favor of the chief.

They were within an afternoon's walk of the village when Shaka first noticed slight movement at the top of a hill. Someone was watching them from just over the top of the hill. Shaka watched only with his eye and no movement of his head.

"Keep your head low, Mother," he urged. "We're being watched."

The sun was approaching the horizon when two men stepped out from behind a large rock with spears in hand and motioned that Shaka and Nandi should follow them, but they made no attempt to take Shaka's spears or skins. Shaka took this as a good sign. His mother smiled and whispered, "We'll be well received."

They soon began to pass the Mthethwa cattle. The drought hadn't been as severe in the valley of the Mthethwa as among the Langeni, and their cattle had fared far better. Based on the number of the cattle, Shaka determined that the Mthethwa were led by a powerful chief.

The village was made up of many round huts. The outer walls were plastered with mud and each pointed roof was covered with grass. Many of the huts were painted in designs with bright colors.

Word of their arrival had preceded them and most people of the village were outside their huts and looked on with interest. Shaka met the stares of each young man and didn't avert his eyes until they had. Two young men who appeared to be older than him didn't look away and Shaka locked eyes with each until he had passed by.

"Nandi?!" an old woman called out and stepped from beside a hut.

Nandi recognized the woman as her aunt and greeted her warmly.

"Nandi! Have you come to live amongst us?"

"Yes, if the chief is willing."

Nandi's aunt looked at Shaka and the skins that he bore and smiled. "I think that he will be pleased. Follow me."

The chief's hut stood near the center of the village and was covered in brightly painted geometric designs. The chief was aware of their arrival and stood near the door of the hut in a ceremonial robe of cheetah skin, holding a spear. Shaka was surprised at how young he appeared. The chief was a powerfully built warrior. Shaka averted his eyes as he neared the chief.

When chief, Dingiswayo, saw Shaka walk into the village, he was pleased. The young man was tall and muscular. He stood erect and walked with confidence. Perhaps a welcomed addition to his forces.

A man standing near the chief indicated that they may approach. Shaka suspected that the man was a commander among the chief's warriors. With Nandi's aunt, Shaka and his mother approached the chief with heads lowered. Standing before him, they waited for the command to speak.

"Who are these?" the chief asked Nandi's aunt.

"They are among my people and wish to make Mthethwa their home."

"What are they called?"

"Nandi and Shaka, son of Senzangakona," replied Nandi's aunt with a motion toward Nandi and Shaka.

A few snickers were heard at the reference to shaka. Shaka wasn't surprised by the snickers, but could feel anger rising inside him regardless.

Looking at Shaka, the chief said, "Is this true, they call you 'Stomach Worm'?"

Shaka was well aware that he was standing before the king of the Mthethwa nation. Even his own father, chief of the Zulus, was subject to this great chief.

Having been addressed directly by the chief gave Shaka permission to look at him and respond. "It is true," replied Shaka.

"Do you have a stomach worm?"

Looking the chief directly in the eyes and with straight words borne of the embarrassed anger that he was feeling, Shaka replied, "I have no stomach worm! I am the stomach worm to my enemies!"

A smile formed on the chief's mouth. He was pleased with the response. He then pointed at the bundle of skins that lay at Shaka's feet. Shaka picked up the bundle and lay it before the chief and unrolled the skins.

"A gift for our great king," replied Shaka as he backed away. It was Shaka's desire to impress the king.

King Dingiswayo looked at the skins and then looked at his captain who stood next to him. They were both impressed.

"Who killed these beasts?" asked the great chief.

"Stomach Worm," Shaka responded with a smile.

Again the chief looked at his captain and spoke to him in a dialect that Shaka didn't understand.

"He speaks boldly," said the chief.

"Perhaps too boldly," responded his captain.

"He seems young to have killed these two beasts. Does he lie?"

"He is too young to have killed both these animals. But if he didn't, who did?" replied the commander.

"Perhaps a stomach worm killed them both and he happened upon them," laughed the chief. The commander also laughed, as did a few others standing nearby, and they looked at Shaka.

Shaka looked straight ahead, without reaction. He was slightly embarrassed and a little angered at being the apparent subject of a joke, but he didn't wish to offend the chief or to let weakness known.

Speaking to Shaka and Nandi, the king replied, "You may live amongst us. We need a warrior who can kill such beasts."

Shaka was very pleased and stood more erect. A warrior! He hadn't been invited to join the Langeni forces, and yet, this greater chief had personally invited him!

"It would be a great honor, my king," Shaka responded.

Chapter Four – Gathering Clouds
1841

Julia was surprised but relieved at how refreshed she felt after just one night ashore on the island of Guernsey. Despite having gone ashore, she was able to get accustomed to the rocking of the ship fairly quickly and didn't suffer the motion sickness that she had before stopping on the island.

Julia and Hyrum noticed a change in Ian the moment they came back aboard ship. Whereas he had been somewhat melancholy after leaving England, he had returned to his jovial self.

"Ian, it's grand to see you smiling so," offered Hyrum after Ian had warmly greeted their return to the ship.

"And why should I not be smiling so on a beautiful day as today?" asked Ian with a slap to his brother's back and a smile at Julia.

"Of course, it is a beautiful day, and you should be smiling," agreed Julia and she handed Francis to him. "Your nephew has missed you."

"Come here little man," replied Ian with a big smile as he took Francis from Julia.

"Well, whatever it is that has changed your countenance, I approve," Hyrum said as he put an arm around Julia's shoulders and pulled her in close.

Ian smiled and motioned for Julia and Hyrum to stand closer to him and to look in the direction that he was looking. Hyrum and Julia exchanged glances of bewilderment and did as he beckoned.

"See that girl near the bow?" Ian said without pointing in her direction. "The one in the blue dress."

"Yes," said Julia.

"Oh, I see," replied Hyrum with a grin.

"She's beautiful, isn't she," Ian asserted.

"Indeed, she is," agreed Julia.

Still grinning and looking at Ian, Hyrum continued, "I understand now why you are so jovial. I should have known it was a lass that changed your mood."

"Have you spoken with her?" asked Julia.

Ian stood a little taller and seemed to push out his chest. "Without a doubt," he replied.

"And you like her?" Hyrum asked.

Ian looked back in Amanda's direction. This time, she caught his glance and smiled at him before turning away. "Like her? I love her."

"Of course you do, brother," grinned Hyrum.

"Well, I'd better. I'm going to marry her."

Julia and Hyrum smiled at each other.

"Would you care to meet her?" asked Ian.

"Of course, we'd love to," Julia replied.

The three of them, with Francis in tow, walked to where she was standing with her mother and father. Ian introduced the Barnes's to Hyrum and Julia. Mr. Barnes and Hyrum talked briefly about opportunities in Africa. Amanda and Mrs. Barnes were thrilled to greet Francis.

"By the looks of things, I think that this little man is the youngest person on the ship," observed Mrs. Barnes.

Julia kissed Francis' cheek and replied, "He may well be." Then looking about as though looking for someone, but not finding them, she continued, "To be sure, he may not be for long. I've seen at least two women who are with child."

Mrs. Barnes got a concerned look on her face and replied, "Without a doubt, I would not care to give birth on a ship. Can you even imagine?"

Amanda looked distressed and Julia replied, "Undoubtedly, I don't care to imagine so." Then looking at Amanda, she said, "Perhaps we shouldn't speak of such things."

"Quite right," agreed Mrs. Barnes.

After the Princes had taken their leave, Mr. Barnes turned to Mrs. Barnes and said, "A fine family that. Wouldn't you agree?"

"Quite right," agreed Mrs. Barnes.

From that point on, Ian spent as much time as he could in the company of Amanda and she seemed quite willing to let him.

It was the next day that Julia approached Hyrum with a concerned look on her face.

"What bothers you so, my dear?" asked Hyrum.

"Hyrum, I've been walking with Francis about the deck and I'm troubled."

"What troubles you then?"

"Some of the crew have very frightful appearances and are quite coarse in their speech."

Hyrum brushed her hair away from her face and replied, "I'm sure they're fine, dear. They've probably spent their lives at sea. That would likely give anyone a frightful appearance." Then he smiled and added, "They haven't lived in Society as we have."

Julia smiled dismissively at his playful joking about the life that she once lived and continued in a quieter voice, "I think that it's more than that. I overheard one of them bragging that he was a Barbary pirate."

"A Barbary pirate?"

"Yes, do you know what that is?" asked Julia.

"I of course know what a pirate is, but Barbary pirate? Never heard of such."

"Well, if you had, I assure you that the thought of sailing with one would concern you."

Julia explained briefly to Hyrum that the Barbary pirates were once quite feared. They often plundered coastal towns and villages of Spain, Italy and France and even as far north as England occasionally.

"And our ship will be sailing not far off the Barbary Coast you know," she added.

"I'm certain that our captain will stay far from the coast at that point."

Julia found little relief in Hyrum's assurances. "You know," she added as she looked about to ensure that no one was listening, "their main source of plunder were the peoples of those towns and villages."

Hyrum looked puzzled, so she continued. "They stole them and sold them as slaves!"

"French and Spaniards sold as slaves? Can you be certain?"

"Of course I'm certain. I've heard Queen Victoria speak of it. And it was not only the men that they stole."

"Women?"

"Yes, women. But also boys and girls," Julia continued quietly. "Many coastal towns and villages were nearly completely abandoned to avoid capture."

"How dreadful! To whom were they sold?"

"To traders who took them to many countries, like the Ottoman Empire."

Hyrum was shocked. "How is it that I've never heard of this?"

"To be sure, I couldn't say, but perhaps because you lived away from London."

"I thought that slavery had been abandoned in all its forms."

Hyrum had always hated the very thought of slavery, but had always thought of it in terms of Africans being enslaved. But the revelation that

European Christians had also been enslaved in vast numbers to masters in the Ottoman Empire personalized the tragedy of the practice in a way that he had never considered.

Another passenger walked nearby and Julia waited for them to pass before she continued. "Yes, officially slavery has been abandoned, at least in Europe. But it is still very much practiced in America and in the Ottoman Empire."

Hyrum put his arm around Julia and promised, "We'll be fine, my dear. Pirates were defeated early in this century by the great English navy, and I'm sure that includes the Barbary pirates."

"Perhaps, but just the same, I'm sure that there are still pirates and some may be on this very ship."

"I promise to keep a close eye on you and Francis, my dear," Hyrum assured her.

June - July 1841

Amanda stood at the railings and wiped her brow. The afternoon was clear and the sun was high in the sky. It was reported that they were nearing northern Spain and there was general excitement on the ship, because the captain had announced that they would stop to take on fresh water in Portugal. It would be a short stop, but it would allow passengers an opportunity to get off the ship for a while and to purchase fresh food for themselves.

A light breeze was blowing, but it was a very warm breeze and didn't do much to soften the intensity of the sun's rays.

"Just how long will it take to get to Africa?" she asked Ian who was standing with her.

Ian wore a hat to shade his brow from the sun, but he had never experienced warmth with such intensity outside the cooper's shop.

"I'm told that it could be three months or more, perhaps four months," he replied.

Ian and Amanda had continued to spend each day together and seemed to be falling in love. For Ian's part, there was no doubt and it seemed that Amanda was encouraging him.

"It's so hot! I can't sleep at night, and the day brings no relief," Amanda said, and she fanned herself more vigorously with her small fan.

"I've only known heat like this inside the cooper's shop, never outside," replied Ian. "You do look ever so pretty with your cheeks flushed as they are," he smiled and Amanda tapped him lightly with her fan.

Ian wanted to ask her to marry him, and planned to do so soon enough. He didn't feel an urgency to act on it though, since they were both going to be captive, as it were, on the ship for many more weeks.

With few people to speak with and nowhere to go, Julia and Amanda had also become close friends. Julia deeply missed her association with Queen Victoria and with Lady Hammond, and to have a friend, who might also become a sister, pleased her very much. Julia occasionally thought of Katherine and wondered whether she could have been a better friend and sister to her. Though Hyrum had not been acquainted with Katherine, he assured Julia that she had done all that she could. Having never known a sister, the prospect of having one now, brought joy to Julia.

"Has Ian asked you to marry him?" Julia asked Amanda one evening as they walked along the deck.

Amanda smiled and looked at Julia.

"He has, hasn't he?" Julia coaxed.

Again Amanda smiled. "No, but I do wish that he would," she said.

"Well, I know that he likes you very much indeed. I'm sure that it is only a matter of time."

As they walked arm in arm, Julia noticed that a few members of the crew, who had nothing to do at the present, stared at them as they passed. Their stares made Julia very uncomfortable.

After they passed by the men, Julia leaned in to Amanda and said quietly, "I so dislike the way that they watch us. Have they never seen ladies?"

"Indeed, it troubles me also."

Some of the women on the ship had chosen to be friendly with the crew, but Julia and Amanda had kept aloof.

Cheers went up from the crew and passengers alike a few days later when land was spotted from the crow's nest, and a short time later land could be seen from the deck of the ship.

"How long will we have ashore?" Julia asked Hyrum. "Wouldn't it be grand to spend the night ashore again?" she smiled.

Hyrum laughed. "It would indeed be grand, but the captain has said that this will be a short stop. Perhaps only a few hours."

Julia pouted with disappointment, then smiled and said, "Perhaps the town will have public baths. I would so enjoy a bath."

"Yes, you and perhaps every other person on this ship," Hyrum replied. Then he added with a grin, "the crew aside, I'm sure."

"It is so hot here. Will it be this hot in Africa?"

"We are nearing the equator, it's bound to be warm. But, I don't think that the southern part of Africa is quite so hot," replied Hyrum.

"I do hope not. In England, a weekly bath was quite sufficient, but it would be altogether inadequate here." Then with a wrinkle of her nose, Julia added, "Do I smell as dreadful as the other passengers and crew?"

"Not at all, my dear," replied Hyrum grinning slightly.

Julia looked closely at him, then smiled and replied, "I hope not."

Watching the land draw close was a practice in patience, but after a few hours the ship was docked in the small town of Peniche. It seemed to Julia and Hyrum that the entire town was on the dock to welcome the ship.

Before allowing anyone to go ashore, the captain announced that the passengers weren't to go far afield and that the ship would be leaving promptly within three hours.

"Mark me word as a sailing man, we'll not wait for you. You'll be on the ship, or you'll be left behind. Don't test me on this," he promised. "They won't be speaking English to you either, so you'll be best advised to stay within sight of the ship."

Julia looked at Hyrum. "Perhaps we should stay on the ship."

"It will be fine. You wanted a bath and by the throne of England, you are going to have a bath," he declared with a smile.

Julia smiled with pleasure, but tapped a finger on his chest and said, "Don't you start swearing on my friend's throne. I'll not hear it."

"As you wish, dear," he replied with a smile and a stroke on her cheek.

Ian and Amanda were standing nearby with Mr. and Mrs. Barnes. Mr. Barnes turned to Mrs. Barnes and said, "Perhaps we should stay on the ship."

"We certainly should," agreed Mrs. Barnes.

Amanda looked at Ian with some disappointment in her expression. Ian quickly offered to Mr. and Mrs. Barnes that he would be pleased to escort Amanda ashore to purchase fresh fruit and other items for them.

"Wouldn't it be grand to have some fresh fruit?" Amanda asked her father with expectation.

Mr. Barnes looked at Mrs. Barnes and then back at Ian. "Well sir, do you promise to keep my daughter safe and attend her side at all times while ashore?"

Ian replied emphatically, "Without a doubt, sir."

"Very well then."

The town itself was rather small with only a few cobblestoned streets and several other streets of dirt. Each street had a few stone houses with red-tiled roofs, and some of the houses were plastered and painted. Most of the businesses were centered near the dock.

Determined to locate a public bath, Julia and Hyrum departed from Ian and Amanda soon after they had gone ashore. Ian and Amanda headed directly to the market.

Walking beside Amanda, Ian glanced at her and ventured, "Perhaps it would be best if we were to represent ourselves as husband and wife to the locals should the subject come up. I think that it might be safer for you if they considered you my wife."

Amanda stopped and smiled at Ian. "I'm sure that they have a priest. We could just as easily make it official."

Ian was still not accustomed to her forward nature and was caught by surprise. He studied her face to try and determine whether she was serious. Lacking a different response, he replied, "I haven't asked your father."

"Oh that is so provincial, don't you think?" asked Amanda as she put her arms around his neck and pulled his face close her to own and kissed him on the mouth.

Ian had never kissed a girl and certainly had never been kissed by a girl. The kiss was almost over before he seemed to realize what was happening, but he enjoyed it.

"There!" said Amanda. "Anyone that saw will expect that we are already married," she smiled.

Ian stood in silence for the briefest time and rubbed his fingers across his lips unconsciously. *She's so direct,* he thought to himself as he studied her face. *But, I like that.*

"Indeed," replied Ian. "But, I really should ask your father." Then he thought to himself, *And Hyrum thinks that I'm impetuous! I think that she has offered me a proposal of marriage.*

Amanda smiled and continued walking toward the market, swinging her arms merrily and with her head high. "Very well. He'll agree."

"Can you be certain?"

"He'll agree," was all she offered.

Julia was pleased to find that the village did have one small bath house. It was a stone building with small, separate bathing areas for the men and women. The baths were spring fed, and since it was June, the water temperature was acceptably mild. Julia and Hyrum weren't the only ship's passengers who had anticipated bathing, but the wait wasn't long.

Julia emerged from the bath house completely refreshed. "Thank you, Hyrum," she said. "I'm certain that I shall be able to continue on to Africa now."

"And I as well," smiled Hyrum. Even Francis seemed to be refreshed.

After visiting the market for some fresh food items, the Princes were able to make it back to the ship with plenty of time to spare before the ship lifted anchor. Ian and Amanda had arrived at the ship before they did, and Ian pulled Hyrum aside.

Once they were away from the others, Ian playfully jabbed Hyrum in the stomach and said with a laugh, "Amanda asked me to marry her!"

Hyrum was certain that he had misunderstood his brother. "Pardon?" he asked.

Ian put his arm around Hyrum's shoulder and pulled him close and again playfully punched his stomach and said, "Amanda made a proposal of marriage to me!"

Hyrum pulled away from his brother, and with a surprised looked replied slowly, "Amanda asked you to marry her?"

"Yes! That's what I said."

"Can you be certain?"

With a sweeping motion toward the sea, Ian responded, "I am as certain as the sea that lays before you."

"Not a woman to follow tradition then, I suppose."

"Indeed not."

Hyrum smiled and asked, "Will she be asking me for your hand then?"

"I suspect that would be too provincial for her," replied Ian with a smile.

"Will you be speaking with Mr. Barnes?"

"Without a doubt, and soon."

"God speed, brother," Hyrum offered.

It wasn't long before the captain ordered the anchor lifted and the topsails of the mainmast and foremast lowered. A gentle breeze filled the small sails, and the ship began to slowly move forward until it was safely away from the dock. Once away from the dock, the captain ordered the mainsails unfurled, and the ship was soon back at sea.

"I haven't heard any cries," observed Mr. Barnes. "I trust that everyone made it aboard."

"Quite right, my dear," agreed Mrs. Barnes.

Ian and Amanda were standing nearby watching the port move into the distance. Ian thought to take an opportunity to speak with Mr. Barnes and asked him to step toward the rear of the ship.

"Mr. Barnes," started Ian, with some uncharacteristic nervousness, "I should like to ask for your permission to marry your daughter."

Mr. Barnes eyed Ian closely and replied, "My Amanda?"

"Yes, sir," Ian replied, but thought to himself, *Surely, sir, you've only one daughter aboard ship.*

Mr. Barnes turned his back to Ian and leaned against the railing for a few moments. Ian shifted nervously from one foot to the other. When Mr. Barnes turned to face Ian again, he responded, "Sir, it takes considerable gall for you to request my daughter's hand. I know little of your character, or of your ability to provide properly for my daughter. No, you may not have my daughter's hand!" With that, Mr. Barnes turned and walked back toward Mrs. Barnes and the others.

Ian was taken aback. He hadn't expected such a reaction at all. After all, Mr. Barnes had been able to observe him for the last few weeks. Ian realized that the others probably knew what it was that he had been conversing with

Mr. Barnes about, so in his embarrassment, he didn't walk back to the others right away.

Amanda looked on as Ian walked the other way, and she glared at her father as he approached the group. Nothing was said by Mr. Barnes or the others regarding the conversation with Ian, but Julia exchanged a look to Hyrum that suggested he go and speak with his brother.

"I must take my leave and speak with the captain," Hyrum told the others knowing that it wasn't an entirely truthful statement.

"Yes, dear, do speak with the captain," Julia smiled. "I worry so about those dark clouds on the horizon."

Hyrum located Ian sitting on a coil of rope near the stern and sat beside him. As they both watched Portugal slip away, Hyrum said, "Give him some time. He'll be agreeable."

Ian kicked the end of the rope that lay near his feet and replied, "All I've got is time. I suppose that I've nowhere to go for a few weeks anyway. But, I wish that I had your confidence on the matter."

"In the meantime, he'll get to know you better."

"Yes, but will he be able to make a judgement on my ability to provide for his daughter?"

"Amanda's already made that judgement, and she'll convince him."

Ian looked at Hyrum and asked, "You think that she can convince him?"

"I'm altogether certain of it," replied Hyrum. "Remember, it's the woman who chooses, and once she's made the choice, there's little anyone else can do to deter her."

Ian looked at his brother as though to say, "Go on."

Hyrum continued. "Our society tends to make the men, both the suitor and the father, think that they are in charge, but in reality it is the women," he said with a smile. "What father is there that wants to disappoint his daughter anyway?"

Ian smiled and kicked the rope at his feet again, and Hyrum added for emphasis, "He'll be agreeable."

"Thank you, brother. I feel better. I really do love her," replied Ian with a smile.

"I know you do. Now what do you think of those clouds?"

Ian looked at the darkening clouds. "I think we're about to find out how well this ship rides a storm."

Amanda was walking toward them when Ian and Hyrum had finished speaking. Ian waited for her to approach and Hyrum continued on to find Julia and Francis.

Amanda spoke first. "He rejected your offer, didn't he?" speaking of her father.

Ian took her hands and replied with a tone of disappointment, "Yes, he did. Flatly."

Amanda smiled and used her fingers to curl his lips into a smile. "You leave him to me," she said and then took Ian's arm and turned to walk along the railings.

"Will you be able to change his mind then?"

Amanda smiled, "Of course!" Then she looked out over the sea and continued, "Though the more pressing problem may be those clouds."

It was later that afternoon that Amanda saw her father descending the steep steps into the lower deck. Because of the stench, she and most passengers did all that they could to avoid the lower deck, but this might be the opportunity she was looking for to speak with her father alone, or nearly alone. She placed a handkerchief over her nose and mouth and followed soon after her father.

Mr. Barnes was laying on his cot and looked toward the opening to the upper deck when he noticed a change in lighting that signaled someone had blocked the remaining sunlight by their own descent below deck. All of the other passengers were on the upper deck watching the storm roll in, and he recognized his daughter coming down the steps.

"Father, may I speak with you?" asked Amanda as she approached the cot.

"Of course, child," Mr. Barnes replied. He had an idea what she might want to speak with him about.

"You rejected Ian's offer," she stated in a straight, non-accusatory tone.

"I did indeed."

"On what grounds, may I ask?" Amanda replied with a voice that was clearly hiding some emotion.

The ship was beginning to pitch with the rise and fall of the sea and Amanda nearly fell onto the bunk behind her. Quickly she grasped onto an upright post and held tightly.

"On the grounds that I know little of his character and even less of his ability or willingness to provide for you," replied Mr. Barnes.

"You've known him since we left England."

"Observance of a man on a ship for a few weeks will do little to persuade me."

The ship rolled sideways and Amanda nearly lost her grasp on the post. As the ship finished its sideways roll and before it started to return to center, she quickly sat on the bunk across from her father.

"I remind you, Father that there will likely be few eligible men in Africa," she said in a voice that was raised over the noise that was starting to build from the storm.

Mr. Barnes seemed quite safe laying on his bunk and quite at ease with the conversation. "Now that statement alone tells me something of your naivety, Child."

"Naivety! I am not a child, Father," insisted Amanda loud enough to be heard quite well over the growing storm.

A few passengers were starting to seek the relative safety of the lower deck, and Amanda tried to keep her voice lowered.

"Besides," she continued, "I asked him to marry me!"

Mr. Barnes sat up quickly and stared at his daughter. Then he looked about to see whether the other passengers who were then in the lower deck had heard her declaration.

"You did what?" he asked.

Amanda leaned forward and replied slowly and emphatically, just loudly enough for her father to hear, "I asked him to marry me!"

"You can't have done so. It isn't done!"

"It is done, and I did!" she replied.

Mr. Barnes lay back onto his bunk and shut his eyes. Amanda kneeled next to his bunk and put her hands on his chest. "I love him, Father."

Without opening his eyes, he replied, "Life on a ship for a husband and wife is hard you know. Especially for a young couple. It's a long way yet to Africa."

Suddenly, there was a loud crack of thunder and the steps to the lower deck were clogged with passengers trying to get below before the rain started or before they were electrocuted by the storm.

"I'm sure that it's a long way to Africa regardless of your age, Father."

Mr. Barnes smiled and opened his eyes. Looking into his daughter's eyes, he observed, "It may not matter much how far it is to Africa if this storm gets much worse."

"Then you'll think about it?"

Smiling again, Mr. Barnes promised, "I'll speak with your mother."

Chapter Five – Stomach Worm
1816
Mthethwa Tribe, Africa

While Zulu chief Senzangakona, Shaka's father, yet lay in his gore, a runner was already on his way to the Mthethwa village to inform King Dingiswayo. The Zulu were subject to the Mthethwa alliance and King Dingiswayo would be very interested to learn of the death of a subordinate chief.

It didn't take long for Sigujana, one of Shaka's half-brothers, to claim the right of ascendancy to kingship of the Zulu, and he was in a rage when he learned that the message of the chief's death had already been dispatched to King Dingiswayo. Standing before him were two of his most trusted warriors.

"Find this traitor, and don't bring him back alive!" he screamed. "Feed his carcass to the birds!"

Turning to other warriors that were with him, Sigujana commanded that they find his main rival and bring him bound. He would be summarily killed before he could mount his own claim to leadership. Sigujana's intention was to solidify his rule before informing the superior chief Dingiswayo. If there appeared to be a void in leadership, King Dingiswayo would fill it with one of his own captains.

Hour after hour the messenger ran. He had served in Dingiswayo's army and knew that the great chief would reward him well for bringing news of such importance. It was highly suspected that Sigujana had orchestrated the king's death, though he now vowed to find his father's murderer.

The runner was also aware that, in his urgency to become the new Zulu chief, Sigujana would try and stop him. There was little need to hide his tracks, his pursuers were well aware of his destination and would have little need to try and track him. His best hope lay in running faster than they. He suspected that his window of advantage was small.

Though a trail lay between the two villages, the messenger took a course that lay in as near a straight line as possible. The moon was bright enough to cast shadows, and the light helped him avoid obstacles and to navigate a straight course, but it would also make him more easily seen by his pursuers. Predators were also a threat, but he didn't slow. He carried a spear and a knife and was proficient with both.

He occasionally looked backward to see whether he was alone. Nearly halfway to the Mthethwa village, and on the top of a little rise, he stopped momentarily to survey the plain below that he had crossed several minutes earlier. The grass and bushes of the plain below were tall, but he was sure that he saw two shadows moving rapidly in his direction. Realizing that his advantage was less than he had hoped, he turned and ran with more energy than before.

The sharp edges of grass whipped at his legs and arms, and the branches of trees and bushes tore at the flesh of his chest and face. Suddenly, in the shadow of a tree, he twisted his ankle on an unseen rock. Still, he ran on as best he could. Like hungry predators, he knew that his pursuers would recognize the change in his footing and would increase the pace of their own pursuit. Any advantage that he may have had was going to be erased quickly.

He was well accustomed to pain, but he hadn't gone far before the pain became immense. He would no longer be able to keep the pace that he had set. In his weakened condition, he was also more vulnerable to beasts of prey. Careful to leave little trace, he moved from the straight course that he had set. He would wait and watch to see whether his pursuers passed by, then he could continue by a slightly detoured route.

Crouching beside the trunk of a gnarled tree, he tried to make himself as small as possible. He would feign be glad to blend into the very bark of the tree if only he could. His heart beat so loudly that he almost feared the noise would betray his hiding place. But louder still was his breathing. He tried holding his breath so that he could listen, but his body demanded air like a raging fire demanded fuel.

Exerting the willpower that had become instinctive during his years in the bush, he calmed himself enough that he could listen intently. He could only hear the wind rustling in the trees. Perhaps he was alone after all. Perhaps he had eluded his pursuers.

A drop of moisture landed on his hand and momentarily distracted him. Then he realized that it was from his own face. Until then he had been unaware that lacerations from the grass and branches covered much of his unprotected skin.

Under the soft glow of the moon, he caught a glimpse of slight movement a short distance away. Or had he? Night shadows can deceive, wind could move branches. Still, there it was again in nearly the same location. Something had stirred.

Daring to only move his eyes, he followed the direction that the movement suggested, but nothing was there. Perhaps he hadn't seen anything after all. His breathing calmed a bit and he began to relax. After several more minutes, he decided that he was alone and arose from his crouched position. Still moving only his eyes, he studied the darkness again. The same darkness that shielded him, may also be hiding danger. He had to be certain that he was alone. A mistake could be deadly. If he had alluded his pursuers, he intended to alter his route and drop down into the small valley before continuing.

Satisfied that he was alone, he started to move away from the tree. Suddenly, he saw the dark form of a warrior, holding a spear, move out from amongst the shadows of a nearby tree. The hair on the back of his neck bristled, and his heartbeat quicken. Had he been seen? Most likely not, since if he had, he would have a spear in his chest already.

"Where's the other one?" he silently wondered, then he became aware of a presence near him. He was certain that he heard soft breathing. He wasn't alone! He moved his head and eyes to the right and realized that the other warrior was a spear's length away and yet hadn't seen him! Controlling his urge to flee required all his concentration. Neither warrior was aware of his presence and yet each seemed to be unaware of the other's position. Quietly, he made a series of clicking sounds only loud enough to be heard very close by. The warrior nearest him moved his head quickly and looked directly at him. Initially startled, the warrior relaxed, thinking that it was his companion.
The runner then motioned to where the other warrior stood, partially outside the protective cover of the shadows.

The warrior nearest the runner slowly raised his spear and in one quick motion threw it at his companion. The spear found its mark and the shadowy figure fell to the ground without a sound.

As soon as the spear had been thrown, the runner lunged forward and thrust his spear into the chest of the warrior. The warrior looked startled, and realizing his mistake, terror filled his eyes. He grasped the spear with both hands, and with a groan, removed it in one swift motion. With the spear raised above his head, he prepared to thrust it at the runner.

Time seemed to slow for the runner, and he waited with knife in hand for the inevitable. As the warrior stepped forward to throw the spear, life flowed out of him and he landed first on his knees, and then his face hit the dirt.

The runner let out a relieved breath and without hesitation, retrieved his spear. Knowing that the predators of the night would soon enough pick up the scent of blood, he left the area with haste in a straight line again toward the Mthethwa village. He hadn't gone far before he heard hyenas fighting over their find. Stopping only momentarily to look back in the direction of the noise, he continued on as quickly as he could.

Because of his injured ankle, it took the remainder of the night for the runner to reach the Mthethwa village.

Shaka was sitting with King Dingiswayo when the runner was brought before him. After the runner had bowed before the chief, he was commanded to speak.

"Chief Senzangakona is dead!" declared the runner.

Shaka stood quickly at this declaration, but Dingiswayo held out his hand instructing him to sit.

"Did you witness this?" asked Dingiswayo.

"No, my king."

"Did you see the dead chief?"

"Yes."

"Who did this thing?"

The runner looked hesitantly at Shaka and then back to the chief. "Sigujana! The chief's son."

Shaka leapt to his feet again at the pronouncement that his half-brother had killed his father. He didn't share any love for his father, but the confirmation that the killer was a son underscored his expectation that his half-brother was trying to usurp the throne from himself.

Looking at King Dingiswayo, Shaka declared in a loud voice, "I am the rightful heir! I'll spill the blood of Sigujana before the lions have their prey tonight!"

Without a word King Dingiswayo ordered the runner to be taken away and Shaka to sit, then he turned to Shaka and said, "You've waited long, with the patience of an alligator. You'll have your throne, but you must not run off as a young lion among elephants."

Shaka bristled at the comparison to a young lion who would run among elephants without discipline. Shaka knew discipline and he knew cunning strategy. Nevertheless, he listened to his king.

"Take my banner and as many men as you think necessary," Dingiswayo smiled, "and you shall be king of the Zulu before the next rain."

This pleased Shaka very much. He stood and pointed his spear to the sky and, with head raised, declared, "Shaka! King of the Zulu!"

Dingiswayo was pleased that the time had come for Shaka to be king of the Zulu. He had watched Shaka closely since he had come to live amongst the Mthethwa. Shaka was a strong and arrogant young man when he had arrived. Little had changed since then, other than he was stronger and his arrogance was backed with experience and skill as a warrior. Now, as the 29 year-old warrior and captain of the army stood before Dingiswayo, he looked like a chief. He stood erect, with his feet firmly planted and arms raised to the sky. The muscles of his arms and legs were well defined and flexed as though meeting an enemy in battle. A leopard skin draped over one shoulder left much of his powerful chest and abdomen bare. Dingiswayo, who was well acquainted with battle and knew little of fear, was surprised that the very sight of this powerful warrior before him stirred something in him that made him glad that his own guards were near.

Thirteen years earlier - 1803

Life amongst the Mthethwa was generally good for Nandi. She enjoyed her associations with her aunt, and she was often a welcomed guest in the court of King Dingiswayo. The chief had appointed a hut for her and Shaka, and there was ample food and water. Like the other women, her life was one of continual toil with little time for relaxation. She had long ago aligned her expectations with the realities of life, so the constant work didn't cause her concern. She enjoyed the time that she spent cultivating the village garden, but she found little enjoyment in hauling the water to nourish it. When she did haul the water she went with other women for protection against beasts and men from other tribes. Her main concerns were the jealousies of the other women due to her acceptance by Dingiswayo.

Life wasn't easy for Shaka. It wasn't long before the other boys started taunting him about his claims of royalty, and he carefully logged in his mind the faces of the boys that were most vicious in their ridicule.

At 16, he was a member of the chief's army and learned the art of war. It wasn't long before he began to excel as a warrior, aided by his tall stature and physical abilities. He also learned that he enjoyed being a warrior very much. The "games" that the warriors used in training provided him opportunity to punish the other young men who had taunted him. It wasn't long before he had asserted his dominance over all but one young man, one of the same young men that had locked eyes with him on his first day in the village. During the "games", the warriors used spears with animal skins covering the point.

As the training games were beginning on one particular day in the late afternoon, Shaka walked past the other young man and heard him tell his companions that he would be "eradicating the stomach worm." Shaka locked eyes with the young man and continued to his position on the opposing team.

The two teams stood apart, farther than a man could throw a spear. As the two groups moved closer together, the warriors began throwing their spears, or blocking the throws from the opposing side. Shaka held his spear and watched carefully. When the other young man had thrown his spear, Shaka cried out his own name and rushed forward. The other young man was shocked to see Shaka running at him with spear in hand. Their training was to throw their spear at their enemy. The young man was apart from the group and ran back toward the group, hoping to gather a spear. Shaka's approach was so swift, that he realized this was impossible and he turned and ran for the bush.

The young man ran up a small hill and Shaka was able to close some of the gap between them. Without a weapon, the young man had little choice than to continue running. He ran for over an hour, only looking backward occasionally to see that Shaka had not slowed. He was surprised that, though Shaka carried a spear and shield, he continued closing the gap. The young man wondered why it was that Shaka didn't throw his spear. He finally decided to take a stand and he stopped and picked up a large rock.

Shaka didn't slow and didn't raise his spear for a throw either. He again let out a yell and called out his own name loudly. He could see terror in the young man's eyes and it gave him immense satisfaction.

With only yards between them, the young man threw his rock with great accuracy, but Shaka easily deflected it with his shield. Shaka was upon him as the young man turned to run, and Shaka's first thrust was into the middle of his back.

Though the tip of the spear was covered with skins, sharp pain shot through his back and into his abdomen. The pain was so severe that he was sure that Shaka had removed the skins. He let out a yell and ran faster.

The next thrust of Shaka's spear caught him in the base of his skull behind his ear. The impact caused his head to lurch forward violently and he nearly lost his balance. Darkness started to close in on him, but didn't completely.

Shaka had tossed aside his shield and now used both arms to swing the spear at his opponent. The heavy end of the spear struck the young man just below the hip and he suddenly went down face first. He came to a stop after sliding in the dirt with arms outstretched.

The young man rolled over and saw Shaka standing over him, spear raised. The young man yelled out for mercy as Shaka yelled loudly and made a motion as though he would drive the spear through him. Instead, he lowered the spear and laughed as he walked away.

Pain as he had never before felt, radiated from the young man's hip. When he tried to rise the pain intensified, and he fell again in a heap in the dirt. Shaka looked back at the young man and laughed again.

"Don't leave me!" begged the young man. The sun was getting low in the sky and he knew that left alone, without a weapon and in a weakened condition, he wouldn't last long enough to see the moon rise.

"Shaka!" yelled the young man.

This was the first time that Shaka could recall that the young man had used his name, rather than "Stomach Worm". Shaka turned and replied, "Stomach Worm," with a strange smile and then walked on.

Shaka had just gone over the top of a small hill when he heard hyena's barking and running toward where he had left the young man.

"Shaka! Shaka!" The urgency in the voice and the sheer terror behind it, gave Shaka great pleasure. He turned back and looked down on the young man just as the hyenas closed in and began fighting violently over their find.

Shaka picked up his shield and continued on to the village. The moon was rising just as he entered the village and he looked up at it and smiled.

Over the course of the next year Shaka's skill in battle continued to increase as did the pleasure that he derived from war fighting. Word of his expertise as a warrior soon came to the attention of King Dingiswayo, and he was called before the great chief.

Shaka leaned his spear and shield near the entrance of the chief's hut and ducked at the door to enter. The chief was seated at the far side of the hut, with his lead captain standing beside him. Shaka didn't approach until invited to do so, and then he kneeled before the king until ordered to rise.

"I'm told that you are a powerful warrior," declared the chief.

Shaka wasn't certain how he should respond. He briefly thought to himself, *He's right, but would an acknowledgement be an afront to the king? But shouldn't the most powerful warrior in the tribe state so?*

A slight smile crossed Shaka's lips. "I am as you say, my king."

Dingiswayo seemed pleased. "And have you learned the art of war? Are you a strategist in battle?"

Again, Shaka considered a proper response. "I've learned the strategy of war," responded Shaka. But to himself he thought, *Surprise with an overpowering force. How's that for strategy?*

Dingiswayo smiled and looked at his captain and then back at Shaka. "Chief Abasi didn't send his tribute. Many days have past and still no tribute. You will teach the chief a lesson in war making and will bring me the tribute."

Shaka smiled and bowed his head in agreement. This would be a great opportunity for him to display his military skill and his loyalty to Dingiswayo.

"You'll leave tomorrow and will have 200 men," the captain said.

Shaka was aware Chief Abasi had at least twice that number of men and also suspected that he would be expecting an attack. He wouldn't know when the attack would come, but he would be expecting it. He would have guards posted.

Shaka considered why his chief would send so few men in the face of a larger army. *Surely the king could send an overpowering force,* thought Shaka. *Perhaps this is more than about a tribute. He will prove my abilities to lead an army into battle.*

Knowing that rejection of the assignment was not an option without instant death, but also willing to please his chief, Shaka smiled and bowed in agreement.

"Chief Abasi is to remain unharmed," declared Dingiswayo. "You will bring him to me. And bring me his strongest young men and young women. They will bring a handsome price from the Dutch. That should satisfy Abasi's obligation for tribute."

Again Shaka bowed his head in acknowledgement.

"Now go and gather your men. Take whomever you will. Two hundred, no more."

With a nod in the direction of the chief's captain, Shaka ventured, "I will take him as my first choice."

The captain said nothing, but glared at Shaka before looking expectedly at Dingiswayo. The chief hadn't taken his eyes off Shaka, but seemed to be studying him before making a decision. After looking up at the captain, a smile grew on Dingiswayo's mouth and he replied, "You may take the captain. He will be my eyes and ears." Then to the captain, he said, "You'll go as a warrior, nothing more. Report back to me regarding the campaign."

The captain glared again at Shaka, but remained silent, not daring to question the authority of the king. The captain's countenance suggested to Shaka that the captain would do what he could to bring about Shaka's death.

Shaka was smiling as he left the king's hut and gathered his spear and shield. This would be his great opportunity to become a trusted captain of the king's army. "I'll be in charge of his entire force soon enough," he said to himself.

The sun was high in the sky the next day as Shaka led his men out of camp. He heard whispers about leaving so late in the day, and complaints that they would be required to sleep with the beasts. Shaka didn't acknowledge the complaints, but a slight smile formed on his lips as he considered the ignorance of strategy amongst the warriors.

Shaka led his men in a wide half circle approach to the village. They would approach from the opposite side. Knowing that Abasi may suspect an attack and would possibly anticipate such a strategy, Shaka also sent a few men directly to the village as messengers. They were to inform Abasi that Dingiswayo desired him to visit and to bring his tribute. Shaka hoped that this stratagem would placate Abasi and cause him to relax his guard. The possibility that Abasi may kill the messengers gave him no concern.

Shaka caused that his men move at a very fast pace all afternoon and into the evening. He planned to attack the village in the early morning hours before daybreak. Nearly two hundred men running across the plain and through the bush would create some dust, and they would disturb animals who would in turn move out of their path. Shaka would use the cloak of darkness in his final approach to the village.

Shaka looked on with scorn when the strap of a sandal that was worn by of one his warriors broke, and the warrior stopped to re-tie the leather thong. In all likelihood, the warrior would fall behind and would spend considerable time and energy trying to catch up. If he did manage to catch the group, he would be weakened from his haste. If he wasn't able to make up the lost time, he may miss the battle. "What good is a warrior who misses the battle," thought Shaka. As was his practice, Shaka ran without sandals. The soles of his feet were as thick as rhinoceros hide from years of running across the thorn-strewn ground.

The moon would not rise until very late in the evening, but Shaka was able to use the stars and the faint outline of hills as his guide. Though they were two hundred strong, they moved silently across the tall grass plain. After hours of running, Shaka knew that they were nearing the village. He looked over his left shoulder and saw that the moon was beginning to rise. His timing was perfect. The village would be asleep and he would have just enough light from the moon to accomplish his task.

Just short of the village, he halted his warriors, but sent eight ahead with instructions to approach in pairs on each side of the village, find the guards and kill them. Shaka only gave them a short while before he divided the remainder of his warriors into four groups and instructed them to surround the village. The village was comprised of well over 100 huts standing in a circular fashion around the center. The chief's hut would be in the center of the village. Once the village had been surrounded, Shaka would make the sound of a night bird, and the warriors were to enter the huts quickly and destroy anything that moved. Shaka was counting on the surprise of an attack in the dark of night to give him the advantage over such a vast force.

Subria lay on the dirt floor of her family's hut and listened to her father's breathing. The tall, slender 12 year old girl was the oldest in her family that consisted of father, mother and two younger brothers. She was often given the responsibility of watching over her brothers as her parents were either hunting or doing other domestic chores. The fact that she lay awake and couldn't sleep frustrated her. "Patience," she repeated to herself. Sometimes her very name frustrated her, because it meant 'patience', and she didn't feel that she had enough patience. If she couldn't go back to sleep, she knew that she would struggle the next day in her chores. She had recently started training with her grandmother in the medicinal uses of plants and herbs. She was excited to continue her training. Perhaps my excitement is keeping me awake, she thought.

It had been a very quiet night in the village. Subria wondered whether the late rising of the moon had kept the animals quiet. No dogs barked, no cattle rustled. She hadn't even heard the noise of wild beasts that was generally so common.

If it's so quiet, I should be able to sleep, she tried to convince herself. *Patience.*

At one point, she was almost asleep and her father's breathing changed and it woke her again. Out of frustration, she arose and stood at the doorway to the hut. A thick skin covered the doorway and she held it aside letting in a fresh breeze.

How much longer to morning? she wondered.

Subria's family hut was near the outside of the village. Perhaps three other rings of huts were closer to the edge of the village. As she stood at the doorway, she could hardly make out the silhouettes of the nearby huts. When she heard the distant call of a night bird, she looked in the direction of the noise.

Bat Hawk, she thought to herself, then she looked more closely and realized that there was a shadowy figure that moved between the huts. Her heart raced. *What was that? Who was that?* she wondered.

Subria was just about to step outside the hut to get a better look when she nearly gasped in shock. It wasn't one shadowy figure, it was many, and they were men. Clearly they were warriors!

Subria hurried to her father's side and touched him. "Father, wake up," she urgently whispered.

Her father sat up quickly, startled from his sleep by her touch. "Warriors! Attacking!" Her breathing was quick and shallow and her heart pounded as though someone was beating a war drum. She felt that she could hardly get the words out.

"Attacking?" asked her father quietly, and he was up in an instant. "Quiet! Wake your mother and brothers!" he urged as he started lacing his sandals.

It was then that Subria heard the first cry go up in a hut near the outer ring.

At Shaka's signal, the warriors had begun entering the huts nearest the edge of the village. As the work of destruction began, cries went up throughout the village, yet there was little resistance. Shaka himself saw many warriors of the village die with their spears and shields laying against the walls of their hut while they themselves were tying sandals to their feet.

Subria woke her mother and brothers and then thought of her grandmother. Grandmother lived in a hut one row closer to the village center. Throwing the skin back from the doorway, she ran out into the night.

"Subria!" her father called after her, but she didn't stop.

Shaka ran to the middle of the village and located King Abasi's ornately painted hut. Though they were without shields, two guards had managed to get to the door of the hut before Shaka, but Shaka's advance was so quick and his strength so great, that they were only able to put up a momentary resistance before one was killed and the other fled.

Shaka quickly entered the hut and took hold of the surprised king. With his spear snuggly pressed beneath the king's chin, Shaka ordered, "Command your people to resist no further."

If left unchecked, the destruction would leave the village empty except for the dogs.

"Who are you?" Abasi asked defiantly.

Shaka pressed the spear a little harder against the king's flesh for emphasis and replied, "I am Shaka, captain of King Dingiswayo's warriors! Order your people to submit or you will die."

Even in the dim light of the hut, it was obvious to Shaka that Abasi was visibly shaken at the very mention of King Dingiswayo's name. Shaka was almost surprised at the surge of excitement that swept through him when he saw the effect that just speaking a name would have on someone. And it wasn't respect that he saw in Abasi's eyes, it was fear. His first thought was that his own name would one day elicit even more fear.

Abasi carefully reached for a hollowed out antler that leaned against the wall, and Shaka lightened his grip so that the chief could press the horn to his lips and blow. Three blows of the horn in quick succession signaled his warriors to cease resisting.

Shaka shifted his spear and held it with the same hand that was holding his shield. He was about to escort Abasi outside the hut when the low light within the hut suddenly dimmed signaling a person in the doorway. Releasing his grip on Abasi, he spun about to face the intruder as he also shifted his spear to his right hand. In the low light it would take a moment to identify whether it was one of his men. It would be easier to thrust his spear and make identification later, but he held still.

"I'll take the prisoner," came the voice of Dingiswayo's captain.

"You'll do as I say," replied Shaka. "Step aside."

"You're nothing! I am the King's captain. You step aside."

Abasi saw this argument as an opportunity to make an escape and he started moving along the wall toward his weapons. With his feet firmly planted, Shaka pushed the butt of his spear backward against the wall and stopped Abasi's movement.

"I am captain of this campaign and you'll do as I say," Shaka retorted.

"Who are you to threaten me?" snarled the captain.

Shaka smiled. "I'm a stomach worm and you are a dog."

With that, Dingiswayo's captain let out a yell and raised his spear above his head leaving his midsection unguarded. He didn't get the chance to thrust before Shaka's own spear pierced his ribcage and entered a lung. The captain gasped for breath and fell to his knees. Shaka placed a foot on the captain's chest and pulled on his spear.

"I am a stomach worm, Dog," Shaka said as he pushed the captain to one side. He then grabbed Abasi and pushed him toward the door.

Her grandmother was already awake when Subria entered her hut. "Grandmother, we're under attack!" she declared urgently in a hushed tone.

Her grandmother was shocked to see her. "I know, child. Why have you come here? It's dangerous to leave the hut!"

"I know," replied Subria. "I had to wake you."

"You can't go back to your hut now. You must stay here."

The village was full of cries and commotion. Subria could hear the fear in her grandmother's voice as she demanded, "Hide here." Subria lay down by some pots near the wall farthest from the doorway just as a warrior threw aside the skin.

Subria's grandmother raised her arms and cried, "Stop! It's just an old…"

Subria put her hands over her mouth to muffle her cry when she heard her grandmother gasp and fall to the floor. Her grandmother landed very near where she lay, and the old woman's face was only a small gourd's distance from Subria's face. Subria wanted to jump up and run, but her grandmother whispered, "Shhh. Patience, child. Stay put, little one." Then her grandmother's eyes closed, and she was gone. Subria didn't move, and it seemed that she didn't breathe, but the tears flowed and wet the dirt floor beneath her face. She felt paralyzed with fear and just lay and stared at her grandmother's lifeless face. After several minutes, when she was sure that she was alone, she reached out with a shaking hand and touched her grandmother's face.

"What's happening?" she cried to herself. Then her thoughts turned to her family, and she wanted to run to her own hut.

Shaka pushed Abasi from his hut and declared, "King Dingiswayo said to bring you back alive, otherwise you'd feel my spear also."

The eastern sky was just beginning to glow, and Shaka could see that his warriors were in total control of the village.

"Command your young men to come forward without weapons," ordered Shaka.

Following the order of Abasi, the young men of the village began appearing in the doorway of many huts, and they slowly made their way forward and to the center of the village. As they did, Shaka ordered them to prostrate themselves on the ground. Either out of their training to obey, or in recognition that to run would be fruitless, the young men came forward without resistance and lay on the ground. Shaka's warriors tied each young man's hands behind his back and also tied a short piece of leather between their ankles.

Subria very carefully pulled aside the skin slightly from over the doorway. She was shocked to see many warriors with shields and spears. From her grandmother's hut, she could see many of the young men of the village lying facedown and tied. She was frightened, but she was worried about her family, and she wanted to run to their hut, but didn't dare. Tears began to fill her eyes, and her chest hurt.

"Command your young women to come now," ordered Shaka.

Still standing in the doorway, Subria heard her king yell out that all the young women must come forward. At twelve, she was considered a woman, but she wasn't going to leave the hut. She quickly released the skin and sank back into the hut. Suddenly, the skin was thrown back and a warrior stepped inside and grabbed her by the arm. With great force, he pulled her outside and pushed her toward the village center.

Subria was terrified. She gasped for air, but couldn't seem to fill her lungs. She turned her head toward her family's hut. Horrified, she saw her mother and father laying just outside the hut. Her mother lay atop her father as though she had been cut down while mourning the loss of her husband. One of her brothers lay partway outside the doorway. He too was lifeless.

She started to run toward her family, but was hit with the end of a spear across her face and pushed back toward the village center. Shocked and thrown off balance, she landed hard in the dirt. A warrior hit her again with the spear handle and commanded her to stand. She quickly stood as ordered, but couldn't help crying. Dirt streaked her face where the tears were flowing.

She didn't look back, but walked slowly in the direction of the king's hut. *"Where is my brother?"* she wondered. Just knowing that he may yet be alive gave her great hope.

Subria hardly noticed the other young women who began to appear in doorways, and others who were moving forward to the center of the village.

As Shaka watched the young women walking slowly, but directly toward him, he could see that fear was visible on the face of each one, and it pleased him. One young woman, taller than most, caught his attention. She kept her head facing straight ahead, but her eyes darted about in a searching manner. Shaka watched her closely.

"I'm going to be a slave!" Subria realized. *"I'd rather be dead!"* she thought.

Subria realized that her only chance was to act decisively and right then. Without further thought, she turned and ran toward the bush. When she did, many other young women, almost in one accord, also turned and ran.

Chaos had erupted, and Shaka was displeased. Pointing to some of his warriors, he ordered, "After them, and if they resist, kill them!"

When the young men, with hands tied and feet shackled, saw the commotion caused when the young women ran, many of them also tried to rise up and run. Not one of them made it to their feet before, at Shaka's command, they were run through with spears.

"Why do you do this?" asked Abasi. "They are not my tribute. Cattle are my tribute." By this time, Abasi's hands were also tied behind his own back.

"Chief Dingiswayo doesn't want your cattle," hissed Shaka with a snarled face. "Your tribute this time will bring a fine price from the Dutch," grinned Shaka.

"He would sell my people?"

Shaka was losing patience. Taller than Abasi, he stood directly in front of him and yelled at his face, "Your lack of a tribute has sold your people!" Such treatment, even of a disgraced chief, was an affront to custom and declared Shaka's arrogance.

Soon the young women had been rounded up and they too were prostrated on the ground and hands and feet tied. Shaka then ordered the older women of the village to bring food and water for his warriors. As they ate, Shaka studied the prisoners and realized that the first young woman who had run was not among the captives.

"Where is the first girl who ran?" he asked one of the warriors he had sent to catch the young women.

"She couldn't be found, captain," he responded.

"Fool!" Shaka declared as he walked to the edge of the village and looked out on the bush in the direction that she had run. He knew that the girl would have gone too far to be easily located. *She'll be dead by tomorrow,* he declared to himself as he walked back to his prisoners. *What's one sparrow amongst so many?* he thought. But still the fact that he had lost her displeased him greatly. *One girl out of a whole village gets away?* he said to himself, and he looked up at the sky and yelled out, "No sparrows will get away!"

After his warriors had eaten their fill, Shaka stood and said in a loud voice to those remaining in the village, "The great King Dingiswayo will decide whether your chief returns. No one will be chief of this village unless declared so by Dingiswayo!" Before he turned to lead his warriors and prisoners from the village, he added, "Don't try and follow. If you do, they'll all die, everyone! But whoever brings me the girl can have released one prisoner of their choice."

Shaka commanded his men to assist their prisoners to their feet and for all to start the walk back to Dingiswayo's village. Before they left the village, Shaka turned and declared in a loud voice to all who had gathered, "I am Shaka. Remember my name!"

When Subria darted from the village she barely managed to elude capture by several warriors. Holding their shields and spears made them less agile than she. Still, she could hear their footsteps and breathing behind her as she broke free of the village. She expected to be pierced by a spear, but it never came. She ran faster than she had ever run and didn't notice the sharp rocks and thorns on her bare feet.

There was tall grass between the village edge and a stand of trees. *If I can reach the trees, I can hide,* she thought to herself, and she ran on.

The grass reached past her waist, but she gave no thought to the wild beasts that might be hiding. Soon she was at the trees, and only then did she pause and look behind her. No one was following! She climbed a tree and hid as best she could in its branches. A few tops of huts were visible from her hiding place, but she could see little else of the village.

Only after she was satisfied that no one was following her, or seemed to notice where she had gone, did she allow herself to think about her family. Her eyes filled with tears and, she fought to hold back her cries. She wanted to scream, but she didn't dare to give away her location. She thought of her family and cried inside, *"Dead! All of them dead!"* It seemed that it was not possible. Just the day before, they had worked together and shared an evening meal. And now she was alone! She wondered who this evil captain was that would kill so ruthlessly, and she hated him!

Subria didn't know how long she would stay in the tree, but she was prepared to spend the rest of the day and night. Then she might venture back to the village to see whether the warriors had gone. She lay her head against a branch, and in her exhausted state, fell asleep.

"Subria! Subria!"

Subria slowly opened her eyes. She couldn't determine how long she had been asleep and she wondered whether she was dreaming. She thought that she had heard her young brother calling her name.

"Subria!"

Subria sat upright on the branch and excitedly looked out over the grassy plain. She had definitely heard her brother's voice.

"Subria!"

He's still alive! she excitedly thought to herself, and her eyes searched the area from where the sound came.

A man and woman from the village where searching about the grassy area. She recognized them right away as the parents of her friend. Subria was so excited to know that they must have her little brother with them, but he was too small to be seen in the grass.

Her excitement was only slightly subdued by the thought that the couple must have lost their daughter, her friend, along with the other young women.

"I'm here!" Subria called out. With that, the man and woman turned and rushed to the tree where she was hiding. When they cleared the grass, she caught sight of her little brother. The joy that it caused her was almost too much for her, and tears of joy rolled down her cheeks.

Subria lighted from the tree and greeted her little brother warmly. "Are you unharmed?" she asked him. He seemed too traumatized to speak and held her very tightly.

"We've been so worried for you, Subria," the woman stated.

"That was a brave thing that you did," observed the man solemnly.

Subria didn't look at them, she was so happy to see her brother that she couldn't take her eyes off him. Tears coursed down her cheeks as she considered the awful scenes that he must have witnessed. *Did he see our parents killed?* she wondered.

She didn't notice that the man was standing behind her. She was startled when he suddenly grabbed her foot, and almost before she realized it he had slipped a rope around her ankle.

"Get up!" he said gruffly.

Subria, in surprise, looked at her ankle and then up at the man. "What?" she asked in surprise.

"Get up! And don't try running!" Turning to his wife, he added, "Leave now! Take the boy!"

His wife grabbed the young lad by the arm and spun him about and headed for the village.

Her little brother, who to this point hadn't said a word other than to call her name, cried out, "Don't leave me sister! Don't leave me!"

Subria couldn't comprehend what was happening or why her friend's parents were treating them so.

"Where are you taking my brother?" she cried and called out his name. She tried to run after him, but the man pulled up on the rope, making it impossible to run. She could only hop on one foot, until he pulled more firmly, and she fell to the ground.

Subria looked up from the dirt and saw her brother disappear into the tall grass, still being pulled along by the woman. He had a frightened look on his face, and he was crying her name.

"Don't take my brother!" she cried.

"He isn't your brother any longer. I lost a son, and now he'll be my son."

Subria knelt before the man and grabbed his ankles. Between sobs, she declared, "And I'll be your daughter."

"I have a daughter. Dingiswayo's warriors took her. I'll be trading you for her!" he replied with a grin. "Let's go get her."

Subria tried to run again, but it was no use. She sat in the dirt to remove the rope, but the man lowered his spear and pressed the point against her chest.

"Get up!" he ordered.

Subria slowly arose. Her head was spinning. She couldn't fathom how her life had changed so completely in just one morning.

"What do I have to do with getting your daughter?" she cried out. She had no basis in her short life to measure the treachery that was about to befall her.

"Shaka took our daughters and sons. He said that whoever brings you could have another prisoner in exchange. You become Dingiswayo's slave, and I get my daughter back. Now start moving!"

Subria still could not make sense of why Shaka would want her so badly. *"I'm just one small girl,"* she thought. *"Why would he care?"*

The man led Subria away from the trail and in a straight line toward Dingiswayo's village. They walked the rest of the morning and late into the afternoon. Then as they stood atop a small hill, they could look down and see the line of warriors and prisoners.

Subria felt an urge to run. The man must have sensed her intentions, because no sooner had she the thought then she felt the spear pressing between her shoulder blades.

"Don't give any thought to running!" the man ordered. "I lose nothing by running my spear through you."

With that, the man led her down the hillside and toward a point where they would soon intersect Shaka's caravan. It wasn't long before they were spotted and two runners were sent to bring them to Shaka. The entire group stopped when they stood before Shaka.

"What do you want?" demanded Shaka.

Subria didn't look up at the man that had killed her father, mother and brother. The man that had destroyed her family and life. She found herself wishing that she was a man herself so that she could exact justice.

"I have brought the girl that ran from the village. You said that you would release a prisoner in exchange for her," declared the man boldly.

Shaka walked about Subria and studied her closely. Standing directly in front of her, he replied, "Yes, this is the girl that ran. You thought to escape the Stomach Worm?"

Subria raised her head and looked defiantly into his eyes. His eyes looked cold and shallow to her. Though she trembled, and with tears in her own eyes, she calmly and deliberately stated, "You killed my father and my mother. And you killed my brother. You won't be so fortunate as to succumb to a stomach worm, but you'll die by a knife."

Shaka was taken aback by her directness, and it infuriated him. Turning back to the man that had brought Subria, he asked, "What prisoner do you want?"

The man and Shaka walked to the rear of the large group. Then standing near the young women, he pointed to one and said, "That one."

Shaka laughed aloud and said, "You want that one! So do I!" With that, he drove his spear into the man and laughed as he fell to the ground.

Subria gasped, and the man's daughter burst out crying. The girl tried to go to her father's side, but was stopped by a warrior.

Subria's own hands were bound, and a short rope was tied between her ankles. Along with the others, she was forced to march toward Dingiswayo's village.

The next day Dingiswayo was told that Shaka was approaching the village, and he dressed in his finest cloth and skins and went out to meet them. He was pleased when he saw Shaka marching into the village at the head of the large group of warriors and prisoners. Shaka caused the group to stop short of the king, and Shaka approached with only Abasi.

Kneeling before the king, Shaka said, "My king, here is your tribute."

Dingiswayo looked at Abasi and then at the large group of prisoners and then back at Shaka. "You've done well Shaka. How many of my warriors did you lose?"

"One, my king?"

"Only one? You've done very well."

"Who did you lose?"

"Your chief captain, my king."

Without emotion Dingiswayo declared, "You are now my chief captain."

Dingiswayo stood in front of Abasi and said, "You don't kneel before your king?"

Abasi fell to his knees and lowered his head.

In a voice dripping with accusation, Dingiswayo added, "You didn't send your tribute. Did you forget to send your tribute?"

"Yes, my king," replied Abasi with head still lowered.

Dingiswayo was angered by Abasi's response, knowing that it was a lie. He placed a foot on Abasi's head and pushed hard. Abasi fell to the dirt.

"Your village had many fine young men and young women," Dingiswayo observed after he had turned back to study the group of prisoners. "They will bring a fine price. Then I will have my tribute." Looking back at Abasi laying in the dirt, he added, "What price will you bring?"

From that day, Shaka was Dingiswayo's head captain and engaged in many successful campaigns for him. Dingiswayo was very pleased with Shaka and over time began to treat him almost as a son. So it was natural that after hearing of the death of Shaka's father, Dingiswayo said, "Take my banner and as many men as you think necessary. You shall be king of the Zulu before the next rain."

Chapter Six – Storm at Sea
July 1841

Julia looked out over the ocean that was becoming increasingly violent. She had never seen such large waves and they frightened her. She held Francis tightly in her arms and decided that it was best to move away from the railing. She looked about for Hyrum and saw him speaking with Ian several yards away. He seemed unaware of the swelling sea.

"Hyrum!" Julia cried out as the ship started to pitch with a sudden gust of wind and a large wave. Hyrum hadn't heard her over the wind, but he was now acutely aware of the storm and was looking in her direction.

Still holding Francis tightly with one arm and frantically searching for anything stationary to support herself with her other arm, Julia began to make her way to the entrance of the lower deck.

Suddenly, there was simultaneously a flash of light and an incredibly loud pop. Julia was so startled that she lost her balance and fell. Instinctively, she wrapped both arms about Francis to protect him. She fell full force on the deck, landing on her right side and shoulder. She let out a cry of fright and pain. The ship was pitching so much that she couldn't rise to her feet. Then she felt two strong arms wrapped around her and lifting her.

"Hyrum!" Julia exclaimed with relief.

"Let's get below deck quickly!" Hyrum yelled above the wind.

With Hyrum's arms wrapped about her and with her arms around Francis, they began to carefully pick their way to the hatch. Before they reached the opening, the skies opened and great drops of water began pounding them and the deck. Many other passengers were trying to get below deck and soon they were all soaked through with rain.

Hyrum looked up and saw that most of the sails had been furled against the storm, but some smaller sails were unfurled to assist the captain in keeping the ship perpendicular to the waves. He then looked in the direction of the ship's stern and saw the captain standing at the wheel along with a sailor. They were both holding the wheel against the rise and fall of each wave. Hyrum noticed that they were both attached to the base of the wheel with ropes.

"If they've taken such precautions," thought Hyrum, *"this is surely going to be a dangerous storm."*

With the pitch and roll of the ship increasing by the moment, and with the passengers still struggling to get through the hatch, Hyrum said loudly to Julia, "Get on your knees!"

Julia looked incredulously at Hyrum. "What? Why?"

Hyrum was already pulling her and Francis down to the deck. "Look at the waves! If the captain can't keep the ship directly into the waves, we might end up over the railings!"

Julia looked out at the sea and saw a wave approaching from directly in front of the ship. It was taller than the bow of the ship! Almost as soon as she saw the wave, it was over the ship and crashing down upon it like a mighty hammer. A wall of water smashed into her and Francis and pushed them hard against Hyrum. Julia screamed and held tightly to Francis. Only then did she realize that Francis was screaming.

"Hyrum!" Julia yelled frantically.

All the passengers who remained on the deck were now on their knees. Because the others had been standing, the wall of water had hit them with great force and most were pushed farther from the hatch, presenting Hyrum and Julia a better opportunity to get below deck. Hyrum scurried toward the hatch on his knees and pulled Julia and Francis along with him. Julia was unable to remain on her knees and slid across the deck on her back, being pulled by Hyrum with the collar of her dress. Almost of an instant, she was at the hatch, and Hyrum spun her about and almost pushed her down the stairway feet first.

With Julia and Francis safely below deck, Hyrum swung his feet into the hatch and started to descend. Just before he lowered his head below deck, he looked out again over the ocean and saw a wave coming at the ship from the side. The wave hit the ship with great force causing it to roll sideways. Many screams of men and women pierced the air as they slid across the deck, all the while trying to hold fast to something stationary. In horror, Hyrum watched as a woman hit the railings and broke through a weakened section, disappearing over the ship's edge. He wanted to run to her aid, but he knew it would be useless. She was lost.

Not content to flee into the safety of the lower deck without at least trying to help his fellow passengers, Hyrum hurried back outside the hatch.

When Julia reached the lower deck, she turned around expecting to see Hyrum directly behind her, instead she saw him go back outside.

"Hyrum!" she yelled, but he was gone.

Other passengers crowded the hatch and Julia was obliged to move out of their way.

"Julia!" Amanda called with relief and rushed to her side.

Julia looked up and grabbed onto Amanda and hugged her. They supported each other against the pitch and roll of the ship for a few moments before Amanda asked where Hyrum was.

"He went back out to the deck," Julia cried urgently. "I'm so scared." Then looking about, she asked, "Where's Ian?"

"I thought that he was with you!"

"He's surely on deck also," cried Julia. "He was speaking with Hyrum before the waves started."

The surroundings of the lower deck were chaotic. The sound of thunder, the creaking and groaning of the ship against the waves and the incessant wind all served as a backdrop to the screaming of the passengers.

The lighting below deck was low. Two lanterns hung from wooden beams and swung side to side with each pitch and roll of the ship, causing a violent dance of ever moving shadows. The movement of the ship and the dancing shadows combined to make walking all but impossible.

The two women supported each other and carefully made their way to the Princes' bunks and lay down.

"I'm so worried for Hyrum and Ian!" cried Julia above the noise of the creaking ship and the cries of the other passengers.

"As am I!" cried Amanda and hugged Julia. "Why wouldn't they come below deck?"

71

"They can't, or at least they won't, until they've done all that they can do to rescue others. That's just the way they are," responded Julia loudly.

All the while, Julia caressed and hugged Francis, but he was inconsolable.

When Hyrum had left from speaking with Ian above deck to rush to Julia's aid, Ian had started for the lower deck himself. He hadn't gone far before he noticed passengers in peril. He immediately began assisting the frailest passengers to safely move below deck. He hadn't noticed the rogue wave that crashed over the side of the ship causing it to roll. The wave had washed his feet from beneath him and pushed him against the railing. Before he could get to his feet, a barrel rolled and smashed against him, hitting his head. Ian grasped the railing and held it with all his strength. His head reeled from the impact with the barrel and darkness began to cover him like a cold blanket. He shook his head in an effort to remain conscious. Still he was in a mental fog.

Holding firmly to any stationary object that he could grasp, Hyrum slowly made his way to the back of the ship. He had seen a rope coiled there earlier in the day, and he planned to tether himself to the ship in a fashion similar to the way he had observed the captain at the wheel. Stepping over or around passengers, who were struggling desperately to get below deck, made his progress difficult. The thick clouds had cast an impenetrable layer of darkness on the sky, and Hyrum could see very little between each lightning flash.

He was dismayed when he didn't find the rope coiled where he expected. Being on deck without the aid of a tether would be very dangerous. He fell to his hands and knees and felt about for the rope, then in a flash of lightning, he saw it bunched up against the railing. Having seen the woman bust through the railing, he wanted to avoid it altogether, but with no obvious choice, he made his way cautiously to the rope. Still on his hands and knees, he pulled the rope to the mast nearest the hatch and tied one end about himself and the other to the base of the mast.

Mountainous waves rose and fell without pattern and rolled across the sea. Many crashed over the deck. The captain fought desperately to keep the ship pointed directly into the waves, but they came from all angles. The wind also blew water horizontally from the crest of the waves. The salty spray stung Hyrum's eyes as he searched for passengers in need of help.

With the security of the rope, Hyrum started pulling passengers to the hatch. On his third trip he found a little girl huddled next to the foremast.

Hyrum reached out a hand and yelled, "Come with me! I'll take you below deck."

The girl looked up. She was crying, but didn't respond or reach for his hand. Hyrum moved closer.

"Take my hand and I'll take you to the hatch," he cried.

"I want my mum!" she cried out.

"I'll take you to your mum!" Hyrum promised and took her by the hand and pulled her close to himself. The girl grabbed him about the neck so tightly that Hyrum thought he might not breathe, but he turned and headed toward the hatch.

As he was making his way to the hatch, lightning lit up the sky, and in the flash he saw a man clinging to the railing.

"Ian?" he cried.

There was no response. Holding the little girl, Hyrum made his way to the railing where Ian lay and shook Ian firmly.

"Ian!"

Ian raised his head. "Hyrum," he said weakly.

"Ian, I'm going to get you below deck. I'll come back for you."

Ian smiled weakly and nodded.

Hyrum sat the little girl beside Ian next to the railing and removed the rope from about himself and tied it to Ian.

"Don't move! I'll be right back! I promise," he commanded Ian.

Ian only nodded.

Hyrum wrapped an arm about the little girl, but didn't dare stand. In a crawling position, he moved along the deck slowly toward the hatch. When they neared the hatch, Hyrum saw that a woman was standing on the steps to the lower deck. She was struggling to hold the hatch open against the force of the wind. With only her head visible, she was screaming above the sound of the wind and waves for her little girl. She was overcome with joy when she saw that Hyrum had a girl under his arm.

"My baby! My baby!" she cried over and over. "Thank you! Thank you! Oh my child!"

Hyrum felt a surge of joyful energy rush through him as he handed the little girl to her mother and shut the hatch. Without hesitation, he turned and headed back for Ian.

Below deck, the woman was shouting and crying for joy at the return of her little girl. Julia and Amanda, who had been anxiously watching the hatch for any sign of Hyrum and Ian, hurried to the woman and asked who had brought her child to safety.

"To be sure, I don't know," cried the woman as she repeatedly kissed her crying child.

"Where is he now?" asked Julia urgently.

Julia could see tears flowing down the woman's face, but she was smiling broadly. The smile disappeared when she responded.

"He went back out."

Julia turned to Amanda and said reassuringly, "Surely it's Hyrum or Ian. I know they'll be okay. Let's pray just the same."

The two women held each other and Julia prayed aloud for both of them.

After the prayer, Amanda wiped the tears from her eyes. "If something dreadful has happened to Ian, I don't think that I can go on living," she sniffled.

Julia wiped Amanda's tears gently from her face and replied, "I know the Prince men. They are stronger than one storm." She tried to feign a smile and continued, "Trust God." Though the words were hers, she wasn't certain that she had full confidence in them. She realized that if something had happened to Hyrum, she would have to return to England. The thought of losing Hyrum was frightening, but the thought of completing this voyage without him and Ian, or the thought of sailing back to England alone terrified her. Both would be dangerous journeys for a woman traveling only with a small child. She didn't even know whether she would have enough money for a return trip. *"What if I am obliged to stay in Africa?"* she thought. She forced the thoughts from her mind and chose instead to think of Hyrum and Ian fighting the storm. She continued to pray silently for their safety.

"Ian," yelled Hyrum above the noise of the storm when he reached his brother. "I'm going to get you below deck."

Ian looked up at Hyrum and struggled to smile. "Jolly good," was all that he uttered, but even that was lost to the wind.

It was quite dark, so Hyrum felt for the knotted rope and untied it from Ian. He then tied it about his own waist, leaving a generous length that he tied around Ian's waist. He ensured that the rope was tight by pulling on it securely.

"Can you crawl?" asked Hyrum.

Ian nodded and struggled to his hands and knees.

So far as Hyrum could determine, they were the only ones left on deck other than the crew. Salty spray had made the deck quite slippery and both men struggled to make progress. Hyrum moved along in front of Ian. Each time the ship rolled in the direction of the hatch, Hyrum allowed himself to slide freely and then attempted to latch onto a stationary object to prevent sliding backward. Because of his injury, Ian was not strong enough to stay on his knees and fight the rolling ship. Hyrum was obliged to pull him along with the rope.

At one point, Hyrum used a mast to secure himself from sliding backward after a wave caused the ship to pitch. He had moved to one side of the mast and left Ian on the other with the rope around the mast. As the ship rolled back to center and then compensated to the other side, Ian slid past, and Hyrum suddenly found himself the one being pulled.

Progress was slow and Hyrum's strength was waning. At some point, he considered lashing both he and Ian to a mast and waiting out the storm. Considering that the storm may last for many hours and that they would be at greater risk of lightning strikes, he decided against it. Instead, he determined to take advantage of the pitches of the ship. When a roll moved them in the direction of the hatch, they slid along with it and made every effort to not slide backward.

After what seemed a very long time, they were at the hatch. Hyrum secured the rope about the hatch and lifted it open. Only after helping Ian into the hatch did he remove the rope from Ian's waist. As soon as Ian was inside the lower deck, Hyrum removed the rope from his own waist and lowered himself onto the steps and closed the hatch.

Julia and Amanda were holding each other and watching anxiously for any sign that the hatch was opening. They were distressed that the hatch hadn't opened in several minutes.

A man in a nearby bunk had overheard their cries and worries. He finally offered, "Ladies, I'm sorry to say that there ain't nobody coming through that hatch tonight. It's been too long. No one could survive out there so long. This isn't my first time at sea and I barely made it below."

Amanda cried the more when she heard the man, and Julia cradled Amanda's head on her own shoulder.

"Don't listen to him, Amanda. He doesn't know Hyrum and Ian."

Suddenly, the hatch opened and Julia and Amanda both arose quickly from the bunk and hurried as best they could to the steps. Ian grasped onto the steps and carefully made his way down. As soon as she recognized him, Amanda grabbed him about the waist and helped him off the steps. Amanda and Julia both burst with joyous cries.

"Ian," cried Amanda. "Ian, you're safe. I was so worried."

Ian collapsed in her arms and Julia helped her get him to the bunk. As she did, she kept looking over her shoulder for signs that Hyrum was also coming down the hatch. In the dim light, she saw another person coming through the opening and her heart leapt.

"Hyrum!" she cried and after Ian was safely on the bunk she rushed to the steps just as Hyrum stepped onto the floor of the lower deck. "Hyrum! I was so worried!" she said as she wrapped her arms around his neck and cried.

Hyrum firmly planted his feet against the constant movement of the ship and held Julia close.

"Everything's fine now, my dear," he said just loud enough for her to hear.

"I thought that you'd gone overboard!"

"No. I'm fine. I assure you that I stayed far from the railings."

"Please don't do that again," Julia implored him. "I just don't know what I'd do without you."

"I'll not leave you. I promise," replied Hyrum.

Hyrum helped Julia to the bunk where Ian lay. Amanda was already dressing his wounded head. Blood mixed with rain and salty spray had covered his face and was staining his shirt.

"You're a frightful sight," Hyrum smiled as he looked at his brother.

"Without a doubt, I am," Ian agreed and closed his eyes. "Thank you, brother."

Amanda's father, Mr. Barnes, watched as his daughter cared for Ian. Turning to his wife, he said, "Those Prince boys are without a lick of common sense, putting themselves at risk in such a manner."

"I thought they were very brave," replied Mrs. Barnes.

"Very brave? Indeed!" scoffed Mr. Barnes. "Fools I'd say. Did you know that the younger one asked if he could marry our Amanda?"

Mrs. Barnes smiled. "No, of course not. How wonderful!" Of course she did know, but considered there would be no benefit to letting on that she did.

"Wonderful? I think not!" scolded Mr. Barnes. "Africa can be a dangerous place without putting one's self at risk by helping others in such a foolhardy manner. Each to their own in Africa I say." Laying back onto his bunk with his eyes closed, he added, "I'll not be giving my consent to any such marriage."

Mrs. Barnes had been sitting on her own bunk and she leaned close to Mr. Barnes ear so that no one would hear. With a voice dripping in sacasim, she whispered in his ear, "A dangerous place indeed! Perhaps Amanda would be best served by a man that leaves her to find her own way to safety in a storm. Every person for himself! Indeed!"

Mr. Barnes opened his eyes and turned his head in the direction of his wife. "I'll remind you that I was below deck before the storm started. It would have been altogether impossible for me to get above deck, what with all the passengers trying to negotiate the steps to the lower deck. Clogging the hatch entrance and all. To be sure!"

"Nonetheless, I'm pleased that there was a Prince boy on deck. Otherwise, I may be halfway to the bottom of the ocean by now."

Mr. Barnes closed his eyes and said, "Melodramatic to be sure."

Chapter Seven – Shaka, King of the Zulu
1816

Following the death of Shaka's father, King Dingiswayo gave Shaka charge of a sizable force, and Shaka set out to capture the kingdom from his brother, Sigujana. Though it was a relatively insignificant kingdom, and was subject to Dingiswayo, Shaka felt that the right to the Zulu kingdom was his own. He had no intention of destroying the kingdom, but to only destroy Sigujana.

He hadn't been in the village since he was a young lad when he and his mother had been driven into exile by his father. He felt little compassion for the people who had treated his mother with such contempt, and he had long desired to exact revenge against them, especially his own family members. He planned to satisfy his revenge against the leadership, and as much as possible preserve the people. *After all, what is a king without a kingdom?* he thought.

Shaka's forces entered Sigujana's village under the cloak of darkness, and using the same strategies of surprise and overwhelming force that he had used against Abasi, the village was soon his, and Sigujana was his captive.

After securing the village, Shaka donned the royal headwear and ordered that Sigujana be brought to him.

"Do you know who I am?" Shaka asked a defiant Sigujana.

"I presume you to be Dingiswayo's captain," Sigujana responded with a voice of contempt. "He will be displeased that you've treated one of his chiefs with such disgrace."

"I am now the chief and you will bow before me."

"I'll not bow before an imposter."

"And I ask again, do you know who I am?"

Sigujana studied Shaka's face. "You are a traitor."

Shaka stood and stepped close to Sigujana. He stood taller than his half-brother, and looking him in the eye, he declared, "I am Shaka, king of the Zulu!"

"Shaka?!" Sigujana repeated in almost a whisper.

Shaka smiled and leaned in for emphasis and replied, "Yes, Shaka! Bow before me."

"Never!" replied Sigujana.

"You yet will," smiled Shaka.

With a motion toward two warriors who stood nearby, Shaka ordered that Sigujana be removed from the royal hut. He was taken to the center of the village and forced to kneel. All of the villagers were ordered to gather. Shaka soon appeared wearing skins and headwear that signaled his ascendancy to kingship. He sat in the royal seat that had been placed where all could see. Nearest Shaka was a strong force of warriors, and others of his faithful warriors were behind the gathered villagers.

"I am Shaka, son of Senzangakona, captain of King Dingiswayo's warriors. By his authority, I am king of the Zulu tribe." Pointing at Sigujana, he continued. "This man presumed to be king. He had no authority of Dingiswayo. That makes him a traitor, and traitors must suffer with their lives."

Shaka nodded almost imperceptibly to one of his guards, and the guard quickly stepped forward and drove a spear through Sigujana's chest. Sigujana slumped forward without a sound and fell face first into the dirt.

Shaka stood and declared loudly, "If there are other traitors, they will be treated in like manner."

The villagers averted their eyes and Shaka continued. "If there are no other traitors, your village will be punished no further. Join with Shaka and your village will prosper. No army will prevail against your village while Shaka is your king."

There was a hush over the assembled village, and Shaka was satisfied that he had established his supremacy. Regardless, he retained Dingiswayo's warriors for two months to ensure that his rule was fixed. He systematically sought out those who were friendly with Sigujana and executed them publicly, while at the same time rewarding those who clearly swore allegiance to himself. He selected a few of the village warriors that he could trust and gave them control of a portion of his new warriors. After two months, he sent all but a few of Dingiswayo's loaned warriors back, along with a generous tribute of cattle.

Shaka immediately began to alter the affairs of warfare amongst his Zulu warriors. He had well developed plans of strategy that he had kept to himself, waiting for the right time when they could be best used to his own advantage.

Young warriors would be separated from the village. They would eat together, train together and live together, all under the watchful eye of Shaka's captains. Those who showed promise would be rewarded.

Gone were the traditional sandals worn by warriors of other tribes. Shaka's warriors would have bare feet, and would toughen their feet by long runs over thorny ground. Shaka had seen too many warriors die after losing a sandal in battle. He would turn toughened feet to his advantage.

Shaka's new warriors were most shocked when they were commanded to cut their spears in half. They knew well that a short spear was useless as a throwing weapon. Shaka armed each warrior with a full length shield made of cowhide and taught his warriors to protect themselves with their shields until their enemies had thrown their own spears. Only then were they to move forward as one tight body. When in close proximity, they were to use their shortened spears as stabbing instruments.

Shaka also demanded complete obedience and discipline. He trained his warriors to follow the command of captains quickly and without descent.

He assigned cattle to the village of young men and fed his warriors well.

Shaka altered the affairs of the young women as well. They were formed into villages of their own, separate and apart from their home village, but near to and assigned to a village of young warriors. They would learn the ways of cooking, dancing and other domestic chores.

Shaka planned that when a village of young men had sufficiently proved themselves in many battles, they would be allowed to marry the young women of these villages. Until then, they were not to socialize. The promise of wives and cattle would become strong motivators for his warriors.

81

Shaka knew that the Ndwandwe tribe of the north presented a growing challenge, and he planned to become strong enough to meet that challenge. There were only two options available for Shaka to counter the Ndwandwe, either form alliances with neighboring chiefs or conquer those neighboring villages and assimilate them. To that end, he sent emissaries to several of the villages nearby to know their disposition on forming an alliance. All of the nearby chiefs were already subject to King Dingiswayo, and Shaka knew that they would have little impetus to form an alliance with himself. Still he sent his emissaries.

When one of the nearby chiefs received Shaka's messengers and learned that to form an alliance with Shaka, he would have to be subject to Shaka's command, he refused.

"Who is Shaka that I should be subjected to him?" demanded the chief. "I am subject only to Dingiswayo. No other!"

"Shaka is also subject to Dingiswayo, but if you want Shaka's protection from the Ndwandwe, you will form an alliance with him," instructed the messenger.

"Form an alliance with a weak tribe as the Zulu?" laughed the chief. "Never!"

It was soon after this that the chief was found dead, and very soon following the death, Shaka's warriors were in the village before new leadership could be established. There was no surprise when the village aligned with Shaka.

When still other villages resisted forming alliance with the Zulu, Shaka marched his warriors against them. Forming a tight crest in the shape of bull's horns, his warriors moved deliberately and in formation toward the opposing camp. The captains of the opposing tribes didn't know what to think of this strange approach to battle.

"They hide like women behind their shields," laughed a chief when he watched Shaka's warriors slowly approaching. Then on command his own warriors ran toward Shaka's Zulus, and when within distance, cast their spears. The Zulus stopped and lowered their heads beneath the level of their shields. Not one of the Zulus was visible until the spears had hit their shields or had fallen harmlessly to the ground. The spears that had penetrated shields were removed and cast aside, then on command the Zulu warriors shouted in one accord and moved forward quickly, still in a tight crescent formation. The opposing chief was shocked to witness the pointy ends of the "bull horn" formation wrap about his forces and pull them into the crescent until there was no escape.

Only when they were in tight proximity to the opposing force did Shaka's warriors begin the work of death with their short stabbing spears. If left unchecked, they would have completely destroyed the warriors of the opposing tribe. It wasn't long before the defenseless warriors surrendered to Shaka's forces and the work of destruction ceased.

With a few warriors by his side, Shaka walked to the opposing chief. Fear was clearly evident in the chief's eyes as Shaka stood before him.

"Will you now form an alliance with the Zulu and be subject to Shaka?" asked Shaka.

"Yes, great chief," replied the opposing chief.

Shaka smiled and lifted his spear slightly off the ground and let it back down. On that signal, the warriors with him destroyed the opposing chief and his captains.

After taking control of the village, Shaka incorporated the young men and young women into the villages that he had established and began training them.

1817

It wasn't long before some of the chiefs complained to Dingiswayo about Shaka's aggression. Dingiswayo, who considered Shaka almost as a son, only smiled and dismissed the concerns.

"So long as he remains subject to myself, it is of no concern to me," he said. "He forms a strong force with me against the Ndwandwe."

Even at that time Dingiswayo was preparing an attack against Zwide, the powerful chief of the Ndwandwe, and he sent word to Shaka to join his forces at Ngome. Word didn't reach Shaka in time, and before Shaka could join his forces to those of Dingiswayo's, Zwide had captured and beheaded Dingiswayo.

Shaka was very wroth at news of his mentor's death and vowed to take revenge on Zwide. Before doing so he marched quickly and forcibly against

Dingiswayo's village. Because he had until recently been Dingiswayo's chief captain, he met little resistance.

In less than two years he had become the most powerful king of the area and had established the Zulus as a most fearsome war machine. Time was right that he march against Zwide. For his part, Zwide was anxious to destroy his latest rival. He knew well that Shaka had taken control of Dingiswayo's territory and that Shaka was intent on his own conquest of neighboring tribes. Zwide knew that it would be best to destroy the stomach worm before he grew stronger.

1818

In his first attempt, Zwide sent an expedition and encountered Shaka's forces at Gqokoli Hill. For the first time, Zwide's forces came into direct contact with the superior warring strategies of Shaka, and they were repelled.

Desiring to take no chances, Zwide sent his entire force into Zululand. Shaka's warriors were shocked and their spirits weakened when they saw the vast numbers marching against them. Shaka also knew that Zwide would not be easily conquered using regular tactics. He knew that Zwide would not command his warriors to throw their spears as they had been accustomed. So, Shaka employed a different strategy.

Commanding his men to retreat, they led Zwide's forces deep into Zululand. Zwide and his warriors were joyous at the apparent fear that they had instilled in Shaka and his warriors, and they gave strong pursuit.

As the pursuit continued at an exhaustive pace hour after hour, Zwide began to be concerned that he may have been lured into a trap. He observed that his warriors were weakening as a result of the pace and length of the pursuit. After many hours, he began to consider calling off the pursuit and returning to his own lands. As he considered this, it appeared that Shaka's warriors were slowing.

"Surely we've weakened them by the pace of our pursuit. They'll soon fall into our hands," Zwide thought, and he urged his men forward.

What Zwide couldn't have known was that Shaka had trained his men with many such runs and they hadn't weakened in the least. Shaka had only slowed their pace when he realized that Zwide's pace had slowed, and he didn't wish for Zwide to call off his own pursuit. Shaka decided that the time was right to engage Zwide.

At Shaka's command, his warriors in one accord turned and created their attack formation in the shape of a crescent. Before he realized his error, Zwide had run his men into the crescent, and Shaka's warriors quickly began the work of destruction. So intense was the attack of Shaka's warriors that Zwide's forces began to retreat in any direction that they were able. Though it was a great victory for Shaka and a near total devastation of Zwide's forces, Shaka was in a rage that Zwide had escaped. He rejoiced that he was left with no rival in southeastern Africa, but he vowed to hunt Zwide down like a dog and avenge the death of Dungiswayo.

With no meaningful rival in the area, Shaka's quest for domination intensified as he forced submission of increasing numbers of smaller chiefdoms. Fear of the stomach worm spread and mass migrations ensued to avoid an encounter with his forces. His cruel domination and the mass migrations caused widespread starvation and suffering. With the migrations and lack of food came large numbers of deaths and the very name "Shaka" caused fear to all that heard.

His personal hunt for Zwide was often a consideration in deciding who to attack. If Shaka heard that Zwide was in a village, he attacked without mercy. Soon, he received credible information that Zwide was hiding in his mother's village. His mother, Ntombazi, was reportedly a seer. To combat her power, Shaka consulted his own seer who told him to attack at night.

Shaka quickly assembled a large force and began the quick march toward the village. It would take three days to get there and speed was important if he were to have any chance of a surprise attack. Yet he knew that they would be traveling through territory of a subject tribe that was still suffering the wounds of a defeat to Shaka. He would skirt around the villages of the tribe as much as possible and would only move his forces at night while in the vicinity. Even with the cloak of darkness, spies could be expected to send word ahead if Shaka's destination were known.

Zwide was asleep in his mother's hut when he was awaken by a trusted captain of his depleted forces.

"My king, Shaka is approaching!" declared the captain with some urgency.

Despite being aroused from a deep sleep, it only took Zwide a brief moment to process the information and to jump to his feet.

"How many warriors does he bring?"

"As many as the spring migration of wildebeests, my king."

Zwide had already grabbed his shield and spear. "From which direction does he come?"

"From the east."

Zwide thought for a moment and replied, "Give command of our warriors to one of your captains. Have them meet Shaka quickly." Then with a snarl he added, "It will give time for you and I to escape the stomach worm."

"Yes, my king," replied the captain as he turned to leave the hut.

"Meet me at the base of the large hill to the west of the village."

The captain nodded and left the hut.

Zwide's mother was awake and spoke to her son. "You will elude the stomach worm this time, my son, but not always."

Zwide didn't respond, but only looked briefly at his mother and left the hut. Suddenly he heard yelling and realized that it was the battle cry of Shaka and his warriors. They were already entering the village! He tossed aside his shield and ran from the village. He wouldn't wait for his captain at the base of the large hill as planned, as he was sure that Shaka would kill all the warriors and more especially the captains.

The ferocity of the warriors of the village surprised Shaka, but ultimately the victory was his. He had complete control of the village by sunrise, and he lined up the warriors and demanded to know whether Zwide had been there. The warriors wouldn't say, so he started killing each warrior in turn that wouldn't speak.

"My king," said one of his captains.

Shaka turned and saw his captain approaching with an ornate shield.

"My king, surely this belongs to Zwide."

Shaka was furious to know that he had been so close to capturing Zwide, but had failed.

"Where is this dog?" Shaka yelled at the still assembled prisoners.

Shaka grabbed the shield and was about to destroy it when he stopped and looked about. "Which hut is the seer's, Zwide's mother?" he asked.

A warrior pointed to the center of the village. Shaka walked to the hut and demanded that Ntombazi stand before him.

"Where is your son, the dog?" Shaka demanded.

Ntombazi said nothing.

Shaka was the more furious and yelled again, "Where is your son, the dog?"

Again, Ntombazi said nothing.

Shaka smiled and said, "Perhaps my dogs will help you to remember."

With that he ordered Ntombazi back into the hut and placed guards about it. He then sent warriors out to kill a beast and to use it to bait hyenas. After the warriors had lured the hyenas with the fresh kill, they surrounded the wild animals and with pointed spears, moved them into the village. The ferocity of the hyenas was increased by repeated jabs of the spears.

It was near nightfall before the hunters had successfully moved three hyenas into the village. The people of the village hid themselves in huts and watched as the wild beasts fought against their captors, each one barking loudly and snarling menacingly. The hyenas were forced to Ntombazi's hut. Villagers who dared looked on in horror as Shaka gave the order to force the hyenas inside and covered the entry with strong skins.

Immediately, Ntombazi's screams could be heard throughout the village. The agonized screams were chilling, but didn't last long before there was an eerie silence. Still, Shaka didn't allow the hyenas released.

The next morning, the village was quiet except the occasional growling of the hyenas inside the hut. After he arose, Shaka walked to the hut and stood outside the door.

"This is what happens when dogs are protected!" he yelled. Then he turned and ordered his captain to set fire to the hut. The frantic howling and barking of the hyenas pitched as the fire consumed the hut. The hut went up in flames quickly and soon all was quiet.

With his appetite for revenge momentarily satisfied, Shaka and his warriors left the village. This would be one village that he wouldn't try and assimilate into the Zulus. The village had been left with no warriors of its own, and without protection, Shaka didn't expect them to last long anyway.

Shaka's reign of terror continued as his appetite for power and revenge grew. The only person that he allowed to get close to him was his mother, Nandi, and when she died in 1827, he was extremely distraught. Putting on his royal robes and carrying his shield and spear, he cried his anguish throughout the royal village. Dissatisfied and angered that others did not display the same level of grief as he did, he took measures to ensure that all felt that same anguish. He immediately ordered the execution of many individuals, including women and children. In response, the royal village erupted in a sea of killing. Old grievances were settled under the cloak of royal anguish. Still others took part in the destruction only for the sport.

Such terror and primal release of brutality had scarcely been witnessed since the beginning of man. Before the orgy of killing ceased, nearly one half of the royal village of 15000 were dead. There was not a household that didn't feel the pain and anguish that Shaka felt, and in the end, that pleased him very much. But he knew that there were many other villages who had yet to feel the pain of Nandi's death.

Calling his captains together, he sent out his armies with one instruction, inflict pain on the Zulus, his own tribal members, so that they would know that Nandi had died. All tribal villages were to experience the pain of death. With no other chief to rival his majesty, he was free to inflict terror and death on his own people. By this point, he only had one enemy, Europeans who he referred to as "Swallows".

Shaka had gone too far. The Zulu language had no word to describe the number of those dead at his hands. His two half-brothers and captains had seen enough.

"The dead of our people are as vast as the migrating herds," one brother observed. "If Shaka does not go, we will all be dead."

"What do you propose?" asked the other brother.

"He has left himself vulnerable. He has sent out his armies and remains here. He has become weak in his grief."

September 22, 1828

Atop a prominent hill, a small group of Zulu captains stood a few paces apart from the king. Included in the group were Shaka's two half-brothers and his bodyguard. Shaka had become particularly unapproachable since his mother's death.

Though he hadn't been on a warring campaign in months, Shaka still carried his shield and spear every day. Since his mother's death, he had rarely been seen without his royal furs and headdress.

Shaka stood silently for several minutes and surveyed his realm, his kingdom. He had known much pain and grief in his 41 years, but had inflicted greater on others. He was still a powerful warrior, but dissatisfied in all things.

As he looked over his kingdom, he resolved to lead a campaign against the encroaching Swallows. Though they had purchased many of his captives, he was angry that they continued to push their settlements deeper into his kingdom. It was time to eradicate them.

As Shaka turned to declare his intent to his brothers, he felt a searing pain in his side. His eyes widened when he saw a spear with its head completely embedded in his abdomen. Shaka grabbed the spear and looked into the eyes of his brother. At first he was shocked, and then he was angered.

His other brother quickly stepped forward and thrust a knife into his shoulder. Shaka only grinned.

"Hey, Brother!" Shaka laughed. "You kill me, thinking you will rule, but the Swallows will do that."

Even in his wounded condition, or perhaps more especially because of it, Shaka was a terrifying foe. It had taken all their courage to mount the attack and now the brothers and bodyguard determined to finish it. In an accord, they pressed on Shaka with their knives and spears.

"Are you stabbing me, kings of the earth?" Shaka fell to his knees and gasped for air. "You will come to an end through killing one another," he yelled with his last breath.

Those were the last words spoken by the king, and the life of a tyrant ebbed away. Word of his demise spread quickly, and one of his brothers assumed power. Few expected that the reign of terror begun by Shaka would end though, and in this they were right.

Chapter Eight - Casablanca
July 1841

The Princes' ship struggled against the storm, rising with the swells and then falling into the troughs. The passengers were obliged to stay below deck as the storm raged all night and into the next day. There were times that they were certain the ship wouldn't hold together.

The ship was constructed such that the great timber of the main mast passed through the lower deck and connected to the hull of the ship. When the ship was hit with fierce wind or crashed upon by waves, vibrations from the movement of the mast caused the entire ship to shake and groan loudly.

The captain wouldn't allow fire in the ovens while the storm continued, but owing to the stop in port just before the storm, there was plenty of bread and fresh vegetables. The only meat was cold meat, but because of the recent marvel of preserving food in cans, the meat was tolerable.

As the storm persisted into the second day, most of the passengers had resigned themselves to their bunks. Some passengers cried and moaned incessantly that neither they nor the ship would survive.

In the mist of all this commotion, Julia asked Hyrum with some trepidation, "Do you suppose we will meet with a watery grave?"

Hyrum was laying next to Julia on the small bunk, and he held her more tightly. "No, dear. We shan't meet a watery grave," he replied with confidence. "Have you prayed?"

"Yes," replied Julia.

"Then all will be well," he smiled.

After three days the storm began to moderate enough that passengers who were surefooted could again go on deck. Hyrum and Ian were among the first. They were pleasantly surprised that the ship had held together so well. Because neither had been on a ship in a storm, they had assumed the worst. Nevertheless, damage was obvious.

"Regardless of what Julia might think of the crew, they certainly managed to see us through the storm," Hyrum commented to Ian.

"Indeed," replied Ian. Then pointing to a broken cross member on a mast and to some tattered sails, he asked, "Do you suppose that we can continue on with sails in such a state?"

"I'd think not. But can a ship be repaired at sea?"

"You think that we'll be forced to port then?"

"Yes, I do," replied Hyrum.

Ian looked over the sea that still rolled and swelled like a spoiled child refusing to be pacified.

"Surely, we wouldn't go back to Portugal."

"Perhaps we were driven back already," observed Hyrum. "Or, perhaps we were driven forward."

"Ah, now to be driven forward would be capital. Would it not?"

Hyrum looked again at the torn sails and the broken cross member. Then he looked over the sea and said, "Not so capital I'd say."

"How so?"

"Julia was telling me of the Barbary Coast and pirates that troll the waters."

"Pirates? Surely the imagination of a woman."

"I think not," replied Hyrum. "But regardless, you and I are powerless to influence what the captain decides to do with the ship."

By the evening, the seas had calmed considerably and Julia was able to go on deck with Francis. She and Hyrum noticed the captain studying the skies, but there were too many clouds for navigation.

Hyrum waited until the captain had seemed to satisfy himself that navigation was not possible, and then he approached.

"Excuse me, sir."

The captain turned and studied Hyrum's face.

"Yes, young man."

"May I ask how we faired in the storm?"

The captain smiled and spit on the deck. He was missing several teeth, which seemed to Hyrum an undesirable condition, yet a convenience for spitting, nonetheless.

Looking at the broken cross member and the tattered sails, he replied, "She was a mighty angry storm to be sure. Just like a woman I knew in Spain." And he laughed aloud.

Hyrum laughed politely and asked, "Have we been blown off course, or backward perhaps?"

The captain looked at Julia and Francis. "Little lady, you have a brave young husband here."

Julia smiled and put an arm around Hyrum's waist. "I do indeed," she replied.

"Though it were dark, and I was battling that angry lady of a storm, I saw that he saved plenty of our passengers." Then he added, "Brave or foolhardy? Perhaps I'm not certain. Maybe there's little difference."

Hyrum smiled but seemed a little embarrassed.

The captain looked at Hyrum and continued, "I'm sure that the clouds will be thin enough tomorrow that I'll be able to determine our position. Until then, it's impossible to say how far we've been blown off course with any certainty. Without a doubt, we'll have to put in at a port to repair this lady."

"How long might a repair require?" asked Hyrum.

The captain looked at the ship and spit again. "Well, I've seen worse, to be sure. But, she'll be a few days in port. That sail over there can nay be repaired, but the others can. If there are other ships in the same port for repair, it could be weeks. But, with any luck, it will be a few days."

Hyrum's brow furrowed and he looked at Julia, then back at the captain. "Well, we'll hope for the best then."

"That we will," replied the captain as he turned to leave. "That we will."

The next day at about noon, Hyrum saw the captain and two of his crew near the wheel of the ship studying the horizon and the sun. The captain held up a short metal tube to his eye and marked the height of the sun above the horizon. As he did, his crew members wrote the measurements down. After several minutes and several measurements, the sun had reached its high point, and the captain called, "Mark."

Hyrum had seen this same routine many times while they were at sea. He hadn't initially known what the captain was doing, but Julia had explained that they were taking measurements of the sun against the horizon so that the ship's position could be estimated.

With their measurements in hand, the captain and his two crew members disappeared below deck to calculate their position. It seemed to Hyrum that they were gone a very long time, but eventually they returned to the deck.

"All gather for an announcement from the captain," one of the crew yelled out.

Hyrum and Julia gathered with the other passengers, along with Ian, Amanda and the Barnes. There was general anticipation on the part of the passengers to know whether they had been blown backward during the storm and where they might be putting in to port.

Soon the captain appeared and stood near the wheel. The wheel was on the quarter deck, above the captain's quarters and afforded a good raised platform from which to speak to the passengers.

"I know that you've been wondering how the ship faired in the storm and whether we will be required to put in at port. It should be obvious to even a greenhorn that she needs repair," the captain said in a loud voice.

Julia looked at Hyrum and smiled nervously. She knew that whatever the captain said was going to have some impact on their lives. If he said that they had been blown backward, or that the damage to the ship was extensive, it would lengthen their voyage and possibly cause them to arrive in Africa too late in the African summer to plant a garden. If they had been blown toward Africa, but still needed to put in at port, it could mean that they would have to put in at an unfriendly port.

"Well, as nasty as the storm was, she didn't blow us back toward England."

When the passengers heard that they hadn't been pushed backward, a general, but subdued sigh of relief went up from the crowd.

Julia, however, didn't make a sound. This was about the worst that she had expected.

The captain raised his arms to silence the group and continued.

"With the damaged sails and cross member, it wouldn't be prudent to continue on without making repairs. If given a choice, I'd rather have been pushed backward clear to Mother England, but we weren't, and it would nay be prudent to go on without repairs."

The passengers seemed confused and started speaking quietly amongst themselves trying to guess the captain's intent. The crowd hushed as the captain raised his arms again and continued.

"If we were to continue on in present state, and a storm arose, we'd find a resting place at the bottom of the ocean. Our singular best option is to put in at a Moroccan port."

Most of the other passengers seemed to have little understanding of the import of the captain's declaration. Instead, they seemed excited at the prospect of visiting a Moroccan port. Julia understood, and she squeezed Hyrum's arm in response.

Another passenger also understood and asked, "Morocco? Isn't the sea safer?" Then to his fellow passengers, he declared, "Morocco is full of thieves and pirates. We'd be safer at sea!"

"If there be pirates," shouted the captain, "they be at sea also! Not just in port! I do nay care to try and outrun a pirate ship with tattered sails."

The passenger who complained about putting in at a Moroccan port continued to grumble to those nearby, and there was general chatter among the passengers. In response, the captain declared to the most vocal passenger, "Best to keep your opinions to yourself sir. Mutineers will nay be tolerated!"

Hyrum looked at Julia and could see concern on her expression. "What does this mean, Julia?"

With an earnest look on her face, Julia replied, "Morocco is at the northern part of the Barbary coast! There may well be pirates in port. These are a dangerous people. They are without law, and we mustn't go ashore while in port!"

In an attempt to calm the passengers, the captain said, "The threat of pirates has been greatly exaggerated. Our own great English navy, with the help of the American navy has largely destroyed the pirates' ability to terrorize the seas. Do you think that I would venture in these waters at all if that were nay the case?"

Most of the passengers seemed pacified, but Julia was undeterred in her reservations. Still gripping Hyrum's arm, she looked at him and said, "Indeed, the seas may be safer, but that only renders the ports more dangerous still! Promise me that we won't go ashore."

Hyrum smiled and stroked her face. "I promise," he replied.

It took nearly three days on relatively calm seas for the ship to reach Morocco. The captain determined that it was necessary to put in at the Casablanca port, rather than at a smaller port. The larger port would afford the best opportunity of repairing the ship, but also had increased likelihood of an undesirable element amongst the populace.

When the port was in sight, the captain called the passengers together to warn them to stay within sight of the ship.

Julia stood next to Hyrum and held Francis. He had been getting less and less content to be held and so he squirmed in her arms to be free. The calmer seas had allowed him to be down long enough that he had learned to crawl about.

"This is nay jolly olde England," he warned. "You may think well that Africa is a dangerous place, but in comparison to Morocco, Africa is an English gentleman."

Julia turned and walked away from the crowd with Francis in her arms. Hyrum followed and when they had passed by the main mast, she put Francis on the deck and he immediately crawled to some coiled rope and started to climb the small pile.

"Julia," said Hyrum, "I know you're troubled. We won't go ashore. I promise."

Julia kept her eyes on Francis, but quickly glanced at Hyrum. Though she smiled and didn't speak, Hyrum could see the tears in her eyes and the concern on her face.

Ian was standing with Amanda when the captain had instructed them to stay within sight of the ship if they chose to go ashore.

After walking a little away from the group, Amanda asked, "Wouldn't it be grand to see Casablanca? Shall we go ashore?"

Ian, the impetuous one, always ready for an adventure, hesitated. "I'm not certain that is altogether a good idea," he responded.

Amanda was surprised. She studied his face and smiled. "You surprise me, Mr. Prince. It's Casablanca! When will you ever get the opportunity of seeing Morocco again? Never."

Ian smiled and looked briefly in the direction of Hyrum and Julia. He then looked at Amanda and replied, "Julia seemed genuinely concerned about even being in port, not to mention that your father wouldn't allow me to escort you ashore."

Amanda took Ian's arm and pulled him closer. "Oh I think he would. He'll likely wish to go ashore also. He and mum would love to feel land again."

Ian loved Amanda's forwardness and sense of adventure. "You're right," he said. "When will we ever get to see Morocco again? Never!"

"Wonderful!" Amanda exclaimed with a smile. "It will be so much fun!" Then she leaned close to Ian and whispered, "Maybe if we go ashore with my father and mother, you can speak with my father again, and we could be married in Casablanca!"

Ian smiled and touched Amanda's nose lightly with a finger. "Hmm, a capital idea. But to marry in Morocco may not be an option. I don't believe that it's a Christian country."

"Surely, there is a priest somewhere in Casablanca," insisted Amanda.

"Well, if there is, we'll find him!" Ian assured her. "Your father willing, of course," he smiled.

Mr. and Mrs. Barnes approached at that moment, and Amanda kissed her father's cheek. "Ian and I should like very much to go ashore in Casablanca, will you join us?"

Mr. Barnes looked stern. "Shouldn't the father of a young lady be consulted, before such plans are made?"

"Quite right, sir," Ian agreed.

Amanda smiled and patted her father's arm. "Mr. Prince was going to consult you, Father, but I was so excited. The words just burst from my mouth."

Mr. Barnes' face relaxed and he smiled at Amanda. "Of course, my dear." Then he looked at Mrs. Barnes and asked, "Do you care to go ashore?"

"If we stay within sight of the ship as the captain has recommended," Mrs. Barnes replied. Then added, "Perhaps we shouldn't be the first off the ship. Let's wait and see the experience of others."

"Capital idea, my dear," observed Mr. Barnes.

Ian and Amanda exchanged glances and replied simultaneously, "Indeed."

"Let's go and tell Julia and Hyrum," exclaimed Amanda.

"Please excuse us, sir and madam," Ian said to Mr. and Mrs. Barnes as he turned to follow Amanda.

"We can tell Julia our plans, but to be sure, she'll discourage it," replied Ian.

Ian and Amanda found Julia and Hyrum still near the main mast watching Francis play on the coiled rope.

Amanda was nearly bursting with excitement when she exclaimed, "Julia, Hyrum! Ian and I are going to visit Casablanca with my mum and father. Will you join us?"

Julia looked at Hyrum and he replied, "No, Julia and I won't be joining you, and we offer caution to you not to go ashore."

Amanda smiled and grabbed Ian's arm. "Oh our minds are quite firm on the matter." Then she looked about to ensure that no one was listening.

Satisfied, she said in almost a whisper, "We're hoping to be married in Casablanca."

"Married!" exclaimed Julia quietly as she looked about to see whether anyone was listening. "In Casablanca? It isn't even a Christian country. You'll not find a priest." Then she relaxed a bit and asked with a smile, "Does that mean that your father has agreed then?"

"Not exactly," Amanda smiled while glancing at Ian.

"Not exactly?" Hyrum asked.

"I haven't actually asked him again," admitted Ian. "But, I hope to while we're ashore."

"Well, to be sure, going ashore is a bad plan. Hyrum and I will remain on the ship," Julia said.

Amanda pouted. "It would be so much more fun if you were to accompany us."

Excitement was high among the passengers as the ship sailed slowly into port. It was clear that Casablanca was a busy port. Two other ships were already in port, and their tattered sails had been removed for mending. It seemed to Julia as they neared the two other ships that there were no passengers aboard.

"Could they all be ashore?" she wondered.

The shops nearest the dock were busy, and Julia could see many people amongst the shops that appeared to be English.

Hyrum was apparently wondering the same. "Perhaps Casablanca's reputation is undeserved," he observed. Then he saw that Julia glared at him and he said with a smile, "We'll remain on the ship, just the same."

Several of the passengers were standing at the ropes, ready to be allowed onto the dock even as the ship dropped anchor. Julia stood at the railing on the quarter deck and marveled at the passengers' anticipation. From the raised position of the deck she could see many Moroccan men sitting in the shade of the buildings, most on the dirt street, watching the English move amongst the shops. There were open air shops as well as shops indoors. The buildings were all white stucco with flat roofs. Most were single story and connected in long rows with an occasional alleyway or street in between. A large structure stood near the center of the town. It appeared to be a church. It had a steeple of sorts, but it didn't appear to be of Christian design.

"Perhaps I've overreacted," she thought. *"The town looks peaceful."*

Hyrum joined her, and they watched the people on the dock together for a couple of hours before Ian and Amanda approached.

"We'll be going ashore now," announced Ian.

"Won't you reconsider?" asked Amanda.

"As you can see, it's a peaceful town," insisted Ian.

Julia and Hyrum exchanged glances and Julia's expression told Hyrum that she was uncertain, but hadn't changed her mind.

"No, we'll remain on the ship," Hyrum said. "But, perhaps you'll be good enough to bring some fresh fruit or vegetables back for us."

"Without a doubt," agreed Ian.

"Miss Barnes!" Amanda's father's called from below.

"We must be off," Amanda said, and she and Ian rushed to meet her parents.

As she watched them depart the ship, Julia said to Hyrum, "I do hope that they are safe."

"They're in God's care, my dear. I'm sure they'll be safe," Hyrum assured her.

Hyrum and Julia watched from the quarter deck as Ian and Amanda and the Barnes moved amongst the shops. Each time that they disappeared inside a shop, Julia watched intently until they were again in sight. Eventually they disappeared around a corner.

"Hyrum, it worries me so that they've gone so far into the town," she said.

"Perhaps we should busy ourselves. I'm sure that they'll be safe, and our watching for them isn't going to assure it," replied Hyrum.

"Yes, indeed," Julia agreed, and they left the quarter deck and took Francis to the other side of the ship to watch the sea birds.

It was a couple hours later that they heard Ian call their names, and they turned about and were glad to see Amanda and Ian approaching.

"Amanda! Ian!" Julia called and held her arms out. "You're safe!"

"Indeed we are!" replied Ian with a broad smile.

"Was it frightful?" asked Julia.

"It wasn't so much frightful," replied Amanda, "but the men kept watching us and speaking about us. Of course, we couldn't understand them. Their stares were unnerving."

Ian smiled. "I'm sure she exaggerates," he laughed.

Amanda playfully punched his side, and Julia frowned at him.

"If a lady says that she was unnerved, then she was without a doubt unnerved," Julia scolded.

Ian looked down and acted remorseful.

"Well?" said Hyrum expectedly.

Amanda and Ian looked at him with bewilderment.

"Did you find a Christian church and priest?"

Amanda and Ian laughed and responded simultaneously, "No, there wasn't one Christian church."

"Did you at least speak with Mr. Barnes then," asked Julia.

"There was nary an opportunity," Ian stated with a glance at Amanda.

Amanda smiled and held Ian's arm. Patting his chest, she observed, "What he means is, opportunity didn't hit him straight on."

They all laughed, and then Julia asked earnestly, "Why did you not stay within sight of the ship?"

Ian looked at Amanda and then said, "The town didn't seem altogether unsafe, and with so many new things to see, it's easy enough to lose track, and soon enough the ship is no longer in sight."

Amanda agreed and reached out and held Julia's hand. "You'd so much enjoy the shops. To be sure, they aren't like the fine shops of London, but they are different than any sort of shop that you've likely seen. Come with us tomorrow!"

Julia smiled politely and then glanced at Hyrum. "No, I think not," she replied.

"Our minds are quite firm," Hyrum insisted.

"Well, here's the vegetables that we promised for you," said Ian as he held the vegetables out to Hyrum. "And there's plenty more for a fine price."

The next day even more passengers departed the ship than had the first day in port. Again, Ian, Amanda and the Barnes went ashore, as Julia and Hyrum watched from the quarter deck. On their return to the ship, Ian and Amanda brought descriptions of the exotic wares in shops and assurances of safety. On this trip in the town, they had deliberately left sight of the ship to see even more exotic and fine wares. Other passengers had done the same.

Except for the Lord's Day, this scene repeated itself several more days, until the captain announced that the ship repairs would be completed the next day.

"Won't you go with us tomorrow?" begged Amanda.

"It would be capital if you did," promised Ian.

Hyrum and Julia exchanged looks and Hyrum responded, "Very well then. Julia and I have discussed it, and we will go ashore for a small bit."

Amanda and Ian were pleased. "Now that is capital, indeed, Brother!" responded Ian with a slap to Hyrum's back.

"I'm ever so pleased," agreed Amanda.

"I suppose that a person can only stay aboard ship so long when the opportunity to debark, even for a time, is presented," observed Hyrum.

Julia smiled politely, but didn't join in wholeheartedly.

Ian and Amanda were especially enthusiastic the next day as they gathered with Hyrum and Julia and other passengers to debark.

"Where's Mr. and Mrs. Barnes?" Julia asked as they started down the ramp to the dock.

"They've seen quite enough of the town and won't be joining us," replied Amanda. "But that's quite alright. It will be just us! We'll have a lovely time!" she said with a smile.

"Perhaps you should leave Francis with them," Hyrum offered.

"Yes, do," agreed Amanda.

Julia only briefly considered it before replying, "No, I'd like to take him along."

They had no sooner stepped from the dock and onto the first dusty street of the town before Julia began to question her decision to come ashore and of bringing Francis. The town was busier than it had appeared from the ship. Near the port were bundles of wool that were bound for England and many workers moved about the bundles preparing to load them onto ships that were due to arrive in the coming days. The men wore full beards and long hair. They also wore turbans on their heads.

As Julia passed by, she was keenly aware of their stares and comments. Though she couldn't understand the words, the look about the men and their tone frightened her. She was glad to move away from the docks and on to the shops.

The women of the town wore long robes and most were completely covered with the exception of their eyes. It was impossible to determine whether they were smiling or scowling.

Merchants called out loudly and pressed on them as they moved among the stalls. Some merchants knew a little English and declared the virtues of their merchandise. All the merchants wore knives on their sides.

"Look at the beautiful color of this cloth," Amanda said excitedly as she held it up for Julia to see.

Julia smiled and nodded. She couldn't relax enough to enjoy looking at the wares. She looked about to satisfy herself that Hyrum and Ian were close by and saw them looking at knives in the adjacent stall.

Moving from stall to stall, Julia would occasionally look toward the port to ensure that she could still see the ship. The stares of the many men that sat in the dirt near the shops disturbed her. At one point a man stood and approached. Julia stepped close to Hyrum and nudged his side. The man came directly up to Julia before Hyrum noticed. Reaching up to touch Francis' head, the man spoke and laughed while glancing back at his companions. It seemed that he was not accustomed to seeing young children with light colored hair. As soon as Hyrum noticed the intrusion, he gently moved Julia and Francis behind himself. Hyrum smiled, but held up a hand to gesture that any further intrusion would not be welcomed. The man walked back to his companions laughing.

"Hyrum," Julia said with a concerned tone, "I'm not comfortable being here."

Amanda had seemed unaware of the exchange with the man and turned away from the merchandise to speak with Julia.

"There is a shop with the most beautiful glass figurines just around this corner," Amanda said excitedly. "We must show them to you. Don't you agree, Ian?"

"Quite right," agreed Ian as they moved around the corner.

"I don't know," said Julia hesitantly, and then looked at Hyrum.

"It should be okay," Hyrum said. "We won't go far or be long." Then glancing at the men sitting near the shops, he observed, "There may also be fewer onlookers."

The group moved around the corner and into a nearby shop. Julia agreed that the glass figurines were beautiful. The merchant seemed somewhat perturbed that Amanda and Ian were back, but not making a purchase.

In broken English, the merchant said, "You buy today, no look."

"Only look," replied Ian.

"Out!" demanded the shopkeeper.

Ian, Amanda, Hyrum and Julia, with Francis in her arms exited the shop quickly. Outside the shop, Ian told Hyrum about a shop on the next street that sold an interesting assortment of wool combs.

"That really must be the last shop though," Hyrum replied with a glance at Julia.

"I don't know Hyrum, we agreed that we wouldn't leave sight of the ship," she said hesitantly. "And these shopkeepers don't seem humored by our presence."

"It will be quick, I assure you," offered Ian.

"Very well then," Hyrum replied.

Julia pursed her lips and Hyrum was certain that she glared at him.

On the way to the shop, Julia noticed piles of rubble where buildings once stood. Ian observed her looking at them and offered, "An earthquake destroyed this town almost a hundred years ago. Can you imagine that almost one hundred years later, some buildings still remain where they fell?"

"An earthquake?" asked Julia.

"Yes, one of the merchants told me of it," replied Ian. "And if you care to go a little farther, the remains of a Christian church can still be seen."

"No, thank you," replied Julia straightly.

Amanda smiled. "There were so few Christians in the town at the time, that following the earthquake, the church was never rebuilt," she said.

"Hence, no priest," observed Julia.

"Evidently," agreed Amanda.

Julia's uneasiness increased when she realized that there were absolutely no other passengers venturing as far into the town as they. In fact, there were fewer town residents on the dusty streets as well. Whereas she had been uncomfortable with the crowds around the dock, the unease caused by the realization that few people were about was greater still.

"Hyrum, where is everyone?" she asked.

Hyrum looked about and replied, "To be sure, I don't know."

"Let's not stay," Julia whispered.

"Ian, where's this shop then?" Hyrum asked.

"We're all but there. I assure you," Ian replied.

"We'd better be!" Julia said quietly.

Francis was getting discontent with being carried, so Julia offered him to Hyrum, who put the young lad on his shoulders. Francis was placated.

When Julia turned her attention back to the street and the nearby buildings, she was startled to catch a glimpse inside a building and was sure that she saw many people crowded together and sitting on the floor. It was only an instant, and she initially thought that she was mistaken, but there was no mistake.

"Why would so many people be crowded together?" she wondered, and then with shocked realization, she grabbed Hyrum's arm and increased her pace. With urgency in her voice, she whispered, "Hyrum, we must go now!"

Hyrum was bewildered by her quickened pace, and as she nearly pushed him along, he looked at her and said, "We're almost there, my dear."

"No! Hurry! We must go now!"

Hyrum studied Julia's face and saw a look of fear that he had never seen in her eyes, "What is it?"

"I'm sure that I saw a group of people being held for slavery!"

"Slavery? Are you certain?"

By now their conversation and quickened pace had captured the attention of Ian and Amanda.

"What is it?" asked Ian quietly as he surveyed the street. "Why are we walking at such a pace?"

"Julia said that there is a group of people being held in a building that we passed by," replied Hyrum.

"Held? For what?" asked Amanda looking backward as though to observe for herself.

"Slavery!" replied Hyrum.

Turning her attention back to Hyrum, Amanda asked, "Slavery? Can you be certain?"

"Yes, I'm certain!" Julia insisted. "They were sitting on the floor and crowded very closely."

"How peculiar!" remarked Amanda. "But slavery?" Then looking backward, she asked, "Where?"

"Don't look back!" insisted Julia. "Yes, slavery! They were in the building near the corner on the right."

"I thought that had been done away," replied Amanda.

"Yes, in England, but not everywhere. Now keep walking," Julia insisted quietly. "This whole area was once very much involved in slave trade! It must still continue, but not openly!"

"We'd best be getting back to the ship," Hyrum suggested.

Julia looked up and down the street.

"We can't return by the same route," insisted Julia.

Hyrum took Francis from his shoulders and asked Ian, "Can we get back to the ship by another way?"

"Let's continue on this street and the next corner will take us toward the docks," Ian replied.

Before reaching the next corner, the group discovered an alleyway. Though narrow, the group quickly turned into it. Just before doing so, Hyrum looked back at the building where Julia had seen the slaves. He saw two men exit the building and look in their direction. One of the men pointed at them and yelled.

"Quickly!" Hyrum ordered.

The group hurried through the passageway to the next street. Before exiting onto the next street, Julia looked back and saw the two men running toward them through the same passage.

The street wouldn't take them straight to the docks, but ended, forcing them to take yet another passage to another street.

"Are we still headed toward the ship?" Julia asked, nearly out of breath.

With long dresses, Julia and Amanda were finding it difficult to go very fast at all. A group of four English adults hurrying and carrying a young child was bound to draw attention, and Moroccan's stared and called out to them as they passed by. Julia was concerned that their pursuers would attract the attention of the men nearby, and that they would also take up the pursuit.

"There's the ship," Hyrum called out. "Hurry!"

With the ship in sight, Julia took courage. She didn't look backward again until they were at the dock. When she did glance backward, their pursuers were no longer in sight. Suddenly, a cry went up from the street nearest the docks.

"My daughter! Help! My daughter! They've taken my daughter!" a woman was yelling and crying.

The four companions were at the ramp to their ship when they heard the cries, and they all stopped and looked toward the town. There were still several passengers on the street, but the street was in commotion. The passengers were huddled about the woman who had cried out and the Moroccan's were starting to gather around them as well.

Julia saw Hyrum looking back at the crowd and she knew what he was thinking. "Please, Hyrum, don't go back!" she pled.

Hyrum looked at Julia and handed Francis to her. "Take Francis. You'll be safe on the ship."

Julia's face showed her worry, and tears started running down her cheeks. "Please, Hyrum, don't go!"

"I must, Julia. The men following us probably took the girl when they didn't catch us."

Ian was already heading back toward the town, and Amanda cried, "Ian, please be careful!"

"Hyrum, these are lawless people. They'd be happy to kill you. Don't leave us," Julia cried.

"Julia, I love you. If Ian and I hurry now, we might be able to find the girl. If we wait, she'll never be found. At least we know where the others were being held."

Julia's cries had upset Francis and he was also crying. With tears coursing down her cheeks, Julia relented. "Yes, hurry," she sobbed. "You're right, but please come back to us."

"I promise," replied Hyrum, and he turned to catch up with Ian.

Standing on the ramp of the ship, Julia quietly cried and bounced Francis to settle him. "Please come back," she said quietly.

Amanda too was crying. The two women hurried up the ramp and watched from the railing. The cries from the woman who had lost her daughter had attracted much attention and many passengers also watched from the railings. Julia overheard some say that the woman should have known better than to go ashore in such a lawless place. "Where's her husband?" they asked.

Julia also heard some comment that Hyrum and Ian were without sense for going back to look for the girl. "Every one of those Moroccan's have a knife on their side." someone said.

Julia overheard more than one person postulate that Hyrum and Ian would never be seen again.

The comments hurt Julia deeply and frightened her. "Here, hold Francis, please," Julia tearfully asked Amanda. Amanda took Francis and watched Julia disappear amongst the other passengers.

Tears made it difficult to see as Julia searched for a place where she could be alone. It seemed that every portion of the upper deck was occupied.

"Mrs. Prince!" she heard the captain yell out.

Julia stopped and faced the captain.

"Where's your husband?" he demanded.

Julia sniffled and through her sobs, she replied, "He went to search for the girl."

"Didn't I advise to not go ashore?"

"Indeed, sir."

"We may never see him, or his brother, or the girl again," the captain said sternly. "Furthermore, the Moroccan's may try and board the ship."

Julia gasped. "Board the ship? Why?"

"They don't need a reason! They're without law. They'll do it out of sheer boredom. Besides, look around woman! If you think that one little girl will bring a fine price, what would an entire ship full of women, men and children bring? Of course, they would only keep the healthy ones, or the ones old enough to care for themselves. I can't even speak of what they would do with the rest."

"I'm sorry," Julia sobbed.

The captain turned to leave, but stopped and turned back to Julia. "I can only give them an hour. If they aren't back, and if the Moroccan's appear to be pressing on the ship, I'll pull up the anchor and push away from the dock. Mark my word!"

"You'd leave Hyrum and Ian?" Julia cried.

"No, they left us! My first priority is the ship and the remaining passengers. Don't think that I won't do it. This ship is seaworthy, and I'll put her out to sea if I must!"

With that, the captain turned and left. Julia fell to her knees sobbing and watched as the captain went up to the quarter deck to watch the town.

Julia's heart beat wildly and her breathing was labored. Without a private place on deck, she resorted below deck to her bunk. There she kneeled. Praying hadn't been a frequent part of her life and praying aloud was even more foreign to her, yet in her anguish the words spilled out without concern that someone might hear.

"Dear God of Heaven," she cried, "please care for Hyrum and Ian. Please bring Hyrum back to me. I can't go on without him. I can't go on to Africa without him, and I can't go back to England. Please...for Francis if not for me. I'll never forget you if you'll bring him back to me."

She didn't know what else to pray, so she just stayed on her knees and sobbed. As she tried to calm herself, her breathing slowed, and her heart didn't race. Though the tears still flowed, she felt a peace settle over her. The peace allowed her thoughts to turn to the girl who was missing. The girl must be terrified, she thought, and she's in danger. Suddenly, her heart went out to the girl and to the others that she had seen crowded together. She realized that the look that she had briefly seen in their eyes was a mixture of fear and despair. Suddenly, she realized that no one was looking for them, and they knew it. No one cared whether they lived or died. No one cared whether they had food or shelter. And if they were women, the dangers multiplied. Suddenly her heart was drawn out to them.

"Dear God of Heaven, please care for the girl and all those that I saw. Please if possible, free them. Please dear God."

She stayed on her knees for several more minutes. Her heart was heavy, not for Hyrum and Ian, but for all the others who had no hope.

Hyrum and Ian ran across the dock and toward the town. The mother of the missing girl was crying out loudly and was being supported physically by other passengers so that she wouldn't collapse. One appeared to be her husband.

The entire street had seemed to erupt into commotion. Many Moroccan's were cheering and yelling and starting to encircle the couple and other passengers as those same passengers about the woman started moving her toward the ship. Other Moroccan's seemed to want to escape any ensuing trouble and started to clear from the area or off the streets.

"Would you nay think that the girl's father would be searching for her?" asked Ian incredulously.

"Perhaps his plan is to get his wife to the ship first," replied Hyrum.

"It will be too late!"

The two gave plenty of clearance to the gathering crowd as they passed by them.

"Let's go to the building where Julia saw the slaves," Ian called to Hyrum over the din of the crowd.

"Don't you think that they would have been moved already?" asked Hyrum.

"They wouldn't have had time."

Hyrum thought about it momentarily and replied, "Indeed. There were too many of them to move so quickly. If the men we saw took the girl, she'll likely be there with the others. You know the way best. Lead out."

With Ian leading, the two ran straight toward an alleyway. Just prior to entering the alley, a Moroccan stepped in front of them with hands outstretched. Ian nearly ran into him and turned suddenly to the left to avoid the man. Hyrum was unable to react and ran directly into the man, nearly knocking him down. With feet firmly planted and ready for a struggle, Hyrum and Ian faced the Moroccan.

"I help you," offered the man quickly in a strong accent.

"What?" demanded Ian loudly.

"I help you find girl."

Ian and Hyrum exchanged glances, and Hyrum responded, "Why should we trust you?"

"I Christian. I see man take girl."

Hyrum looked at Ian and back at the man. "Christian? I didn't think that there were any in this town."

"Few," responded the man.

"We don't need your help," Ian declared. "We've seen where the slaves are being held."

The Moroccan's smile showed several gaps where teeth once were lodged. "White slaves not held there. I take you to white slaves."

Ian turned to Hyrum. "Can we trust him?"

Hyrum was studying the Moroccan's face and, without taking his eyes off the man, replied, "I think that we have little choice."

"Good," replied the man. "Follow now."

With that the man turned and ran down the alleyway and through a door. Hyrum hesitated and his heart began to race the more. *"Is this a trap?"* he asked himself. Without good alternative, he also burst through the door with Ian directly behind. The building seemed to be vacant. By then the man had exited through a door into another alleyway, and Hyrum was relieved to follow him. The route had saved them the several minutes that would have been required to go around the building.

Still Hyrum wasn't certain that they weren't being led into a trap, but they had already committed to following the Moroccan and had little choice now.

There were still few people on the streets, yet the man that they were following seemed intent on covering his face when they were near others.

After running through a couple more secluded streets, the man stopped at the end of an alley and pointed at a building across the street.

"Well, where are they," demanded Ian.

The man remained silent and pointed again at the building.

"How do you know this?" Hyrum asked.

The man turned and started walking away, returning in the direction that they had come. As he did, he replied, "Not first time."

Hyrum studied the building and then looked at Ian. "Do you suppose it's a trap?"

"To be sure, I don't know. The building that Julia saw the others in isn't far. Why would they have not taken her there?"

"Perhaps we should check that building first," Hyrum suggested.

"We'd lose precious time. Let's check this one first, and then we can still check the other."

"Very well then, but it will likely be dimly lit inside," Hyrum observed. "Cover your right eye for a moment and leave it covered until we're inside. It will help with the adjustment."

"We don't have time for this," Ian insisted.

"Just do it. It may just save your life."

Ian frowned at his brother, but covered his right eye as did Hyrum. After a few moments, with right eyes still covered, they stepped from the alleyway. As they did, Hyrum noticed that the door of the building started to open, and he quickly nudged Ian back into the narrow alley.

As Hyrum peered around the corner, he observed a Moroccan man step from the building. The man hurried down the dusty street in the opposite direction.

Hyrum let out a deep breath and said to Ian, "Well, there's one less person in the building now."

"Indeed," replied Ian. "Let's go before he comes back."

Without further hesitation, the two left the alley, hurried across the street and burst through the door. The small room that the door opened to was empty, and the brothers quickly searched each room of the first floor. A narrow, steep stairway in the back room led to the second floor, and Hyrum motioned for Ian to follow him. The stairway had no banister, but was opened to the room below.

As the brothers ascended, the door at the top of the stairs opened, and a Moroccan stepped out with a large knife in hand. Hyrum hesitated, knowing that from his elevated position, the man potentially had the advantage.

The man yelled something that the brothers didn't understand, and rushed down the stairs toward them. With his full turban, full beard and flying robes, the man was a frightful sight, but Hyrum held his ground. Though it was only a moment, the scene before him seemed to slow, and Hyrum could clearly see that the lower position of the stairs gave him the advantage. Hyrum quickly crouched on the stairs and waited. With knife raised above his head, it would be almost useless against a crouched opponent.

The man leaned forward to make use of his knife, and as he did, Hyrum grabbed his robes about his knees and pulled hard. The motion threw the man off balance, and he started to fall toward Hyrum and Ian. Hyrum threw his own body against the wall and pushed the man outward. The man yelled as he fell from the stairs, and he hit the stone floor hard. The man struggled to rise, but Ian was on him and struck him aside the head, and the man lay still.

Hyrum was already ascending the remaining stairs, uncertain whether someone was waiting in the room above to ambush. He burst through the doorway and was relieved to find no attacker there. Ian was soon behind him. The room had a bed and a table and one chair and appeared to be empty. Hyrum looked about the room and around the bed and found no one.

"I don't understand," Hyrum said.

"We've been tricked!" Ian responded. "It was a setup."

"We need to get out of here," responded Hyrum.

Then the two heard a noise from under the bed. Startled, they both moved backward and then squatted to look beneath. There they saw a young English girl. She was lying on her side and holding her knees close to her chest, crying softly. She recoiled when she initially saw them, backing away from them.

"We're English!" Ian said reassuringly. "We've come for you."

The girl pushed farther away still, and her face plainly showed her fright.

"Come lass," Hyrum urged gently. "We must get back to the ship. We're here to take you to your mum and dad."

With that, the girl's face relaxed, and she let go of her knees and moved from under the bed. She was taller than Hyrum expected, and he thought that she might be 12 years old.

"Come with us, you'll be safe," Hyrum promised, and he led the way.

"Wait, what happened to?" Ian asked as he carefully held Hyrum's arm and moved him so that he could get a closer look at Hyrum's shoulder.

Hyrum looked at his left shoulder and saw that blood was oozing from a tear in his shirt. In the excitement, he hadn't noticed the wound.

"It must have been the knife. I hadn't noticed it, but it does hurt now," Hyrum said.

"We've got to get you back to the ship quickly," replied Ian.

Hyrum led the way down the stairs, and they saw that the Moroccan man was still laying unconscious.

"Do you suppose he's dead?" asked Ian.

"I don't think so, but let's not wait to find out."

Hyrum peered out the door and didn't see anyone in the street, so the three of them stepped from the building and headed quickly for the alley. As they did, they heard a yell and saw two men running toward them. One appeared to be the man who had left the building earlier.

"Run!" Ian called urgently, and the three ran up the alley with the girl protected between the two brothers.

They had made it to the next street before the two men chasing them entered the alley. By the time that they turned the next corner it appeared that the men were gaining on them, and the men were still yelling and drawing attention.

"Ian, we must get to the ship soon. We'll have the entire city after us soon," Hyrum declared breathlessly.

Several Moroccan men were starting to pay attention to the yelling of those chasing Hyrum, Ian and the girl, and the three quickly turned onto another street. The street didn't lead directly to the ship, but put the three on a street that was out of earshot of the commotion.

"You realize that they know we're headed for the ship," the girl said. "They'll be waiting at the dock."

Hyrum looked at Ian. "She's right, you know."

Ian glanced at Hyrum and the girl. Without slowing, he said, "Indeed. Keep running. We've got little choice."

Julia was standing at the railing of the ship watching the docks and the town. The mother and father of the girl were nearby, and the mother couldn't be consoled.

"You should have gone for our daughter!" the mother had cried to her husband.

"It would have done little good. I didn't see her taken," he had responded. "And all the Moroccans look the same."

Amanda had stayed at Julia's side, helping to hold Francis. She too was beside herself with worry.

Julia put her arm around Amanda, and the two women held each other with Francis in between.

"Don't give up, Amanda," Julia urged. "I know these men. They'll be back."

"I wish I could be as certain," Amanda said through her tears.

"I've prayed for them, and I'm at peace," Julia offered. "Whatever happens, God will sustain us."

Amanda tried to choke back her sobs. "I wish we would have married yesterday."

Julia took Amanda's head and lay it on her own shoulder and held her.

The captain approached and waited for a few moments before he interrupted, then he cleared his throat. Julia and Amanda looked up at him. Julia pursed her lips at the sight of him.

"I'll not wait much longer. It's nearly been an hour," he declared.

"Please, sir," Amanda started.

Julia interrupted. "Before you pull anchor, tell that mum over there that you've left her child," she demanded.

The captain looked at the woman and her husband. "To be sure, I feel for them. But I'll not wait. Look at these passengers. Do you think that they want to be boarded by a hoard of Moroccans?"

"You don't know that would happen," insisted Julia.

"And you don't know that it won't. I've been in these waters enough times to know that it could."

With that the captain turned and walked away.

"I hate him," Amanda insisted.

Julia didn't respond, but looked back toward the docks and town.

"Amanda! Look!" Julia exclaimed. "It's Hyrum and Ian! And there's a girl with them!"

Julia clapped her hands and covered her mouth.

"They're coming! They're coming!" yelled Amanda with excitement.

When the mother and father saw their daughter, they started to cry and hug each other. Another passenger called to the captain that the three were coming. Julia was horrified to see a small group of Moroccans following closely behind Hyrum and Ian. Her joy was consumed by fear when she realized that the Moroccans were so close behind them.

The ramp to the ship was 50 feet long and ran at a steep angle from the dock. The captain observed the Moroccans following the three, and he ordered his men to pull anchor and unfurl sails. His orders also went out to be prepared to cut the ramp loose.

Julia felt the force of the sails pull at the ship and heard the anchor rising. She realized that the ship was now only held in place by the ropes holding the ramp, and she gasped and covered her mouth with her hands in anticipation.

Ian looked over his shoulder and realized that the girl seemed to be slowing. He cried out, "Run! They're gaining on us."

"I can't!" the young girl yelled back.

Hyrum grabbed her hand and replied, "Come on! You must!"

Julia's heart sank when she saw the left shoulder of Hyrum's shirt red with blood. Francis started to cry, and Julia realized that in her anxiety she was holding him tightly.

Suddenly, Julia saw that one of the Moroccans had pulled out a knife and appeared to be preparing to throw it.

"Run, Run!" Julia and Amanda cried out simultaneously. Then Ian was on the ramp, followed immediately by the girl and Hyrum. The man threw his knife in desperation, but it fell harmlessly into the sea.

Ian, Hyrum and the girl burst onto the deck, and the crew immediately started cutting the ropes. Several Moroccans charged up the ramp, but it collapsed into the sea as the ship broke free.

Hyrum looked about anxiously for Julia, but in the press of the crowd couldn't immediately find her.

The girl's parents pushed through the crowd and embraced her and cried joyously.

"Hyrum! Hyrum!"

Hyrum looked about expectedly and saw Julia, Francis and Amanda trying to push through the crowd.

"Julia!" Hyrum yelled.

"Amanda!" Ian called out.

Hyrum grabbed Julia and Francis into his arms and held them tightly. The excitement of the reunion frightened Francis and he cried. Julia shed tears of joy.

Julia's tears of joy turned to concern. "You're bleeding!"

Hyrum looked at his shirt. "It isn't so terrible as it seems," he replied reassuringly.

"Still, we need to clean the wound," Julia insisted. Then she reached up and pulled his face close to her own and kissed him firmly on the mouth. Then she smiled, and with joy written on her face and in her eyes, she said, "I'm so glad you're safe! I prayed for your safety." Then she closed her eyes and laid her head on his chest.

Amanda was overjoyed to embrace Ian again. "I was so frightened! Don't leave me again!"

"Marry me!" Ian replied with a smile. "Marry me now!"

"Yes, I will," Amanda smiled and kissed him. "Speak with my father again. Come with me."

Ian and Amanda found her father. Ian walked right up to Mr. Barnes, offered his hand and said, "Sir, I desire your approval to marry your daughter."

Mr. Barnes took Ian's hand and replied with a smile, "I've never met a more brave man. My daughter will be well cared for. You have my permission."

Amanda and Ian were thrilled and hugged for joy. Mrs. Barnes seemed pleased also, but cautioned, "Life won't be easy aboard ship for a young couple. You'll have no privacy."

"But we'll still be married and that's enough," Amanda beamed.

Amanda and Ian went to find Julia and Hyrum to share with them their news. Julia and Hyrum were thrilled to hear that Mr. Barnes had granted permission for the marriage. Julia bounced Francis excitedly on her hip and hugged him close. Then she and Hyrum hugged and spun about as though dancing.

Hyrum and Julia were still embracing when the parents of the girl approached with broad smiles. It seemed that they couldn't express enough thanks.

"Sir," the father said, "we could never adequately express our thanks and joy. Our daughter is everything to us, and we had thought to have lost her."

The young girl stayed close to her mother's side and didn't speak. She still seemed traumatized by her experience.

The ship was soon out to sea, and the captain found Hyrum and Julia with Ian and Amanda.

"Sirs, while I don't understand your motivation, I will say that you've performed a great service." Then looking at Ian and Amanda, the captain continued, "I understand that you are to be married."

Amanda hugged Ian and smiled while Ian replied, "Yes, sir. We'd like to be married right away."

"I'm authorized by Her Majesty to perform marriages. Would you like for me to marry the two of you?"

"We would like that very much," replied Amanda as she wrapped both her arms about Ian's neck and smiled.

Julia and Hyrum were so excited for Ian and Amanda. Julia insisted on combing and dressing Amanda's hair. Another passenger loaned her a ribbon to lace through Amanda's hair as well.

It didn't take long before news of the planned marriage spread about the ship, and people started gathering. Despite his earlier protestations, Amanda's father seemed quite satisfied as his daughter stood beside him when the captain began the ceremony.

Julia's eyes were moist as she watched Ian take Amanda in his arms and kiss her after the captain pronounced them husband and wife. Hyrum smiled when the captain announced that he was giving Ian and Amanda use of his quarters for their first night together.

The remainder of the voyage to Africa proceeded without incident. The winds were favorable, and the greatest challenge amongst the passengers was overcoming boredom. Finally, 115 days after leaving London, the ship docked in Port Elizabeth. The passengers were thrilled to arrive at their new home, though they knew little about it. Most debarked the ship with anticipation of a better life than the one that they had left behind. They knew little of the people, the climate or the animals of this vast land. But they had been given opportunity, and they felt that they were serving their Queen by extending the influence of her realm. This filled them with hope and confidence.

For Julia's part, she had no expectation that the quality of her life in Africa would be measured in luxury or ease. From the ship's railing, she looked over the ramshackle buildings of Port Elizabeth and its dusty streets. She realized that this was probably the best that this part of the country had to offer. Hyrum intended to move inland from the coast, and any town that they might encounter beyond the boundaries of Port Elizabeth were sure to be less accommodating still.

Africa was a wild country, and it wouldn't be easily tamed. If countries had opposites, Africa was England's opposite, and Julia knew it. She felt a slight pang in her stomach as she thought about Brentwood Hall, and Lord and Lady Hammond. She supposed that they would be having tea in the garden right about then. *Do they think of me?* she wondered. *I so miss them.*

She also thought about the palace and her friend, Queen Victoria. As she did, she instinctively placed her hand on the broach that she kept pinned to her dress, and thought about the day in London when the Queen gave it to her.

As Julia thought about her life in England, Francis squirmed in her arms, bringing her thoughts back to the present. Julia looked into his beautiful eyes and held his head against her breast. Looking up, she immediately caught sight of Hyrum. He looked so confident, so full of anticipation, so strong and handsome. Suddenly, in an instant, the pang in her stomach was gone, replaced with joy in her breast. *All that I've ever wanted or needed is on this ship,* she thought. *Africa is my home. It may be different from England as the night is from the day, but it's my home. Its people are my people. This is where I'll be buried someday.*

Chapter Nine - Subria
November 1817

Subria struggled to place one foot before the other as she ascended a small hill. The heat of the day was intense, and her thirst intolerable. Though she thought that she would rather be anywhere than where she was at the moment, little did she know that her present condition was far better than her future.

A thin cloud of dust hung in the air, kicked up by a multitude of shuffling feet. As though it had its own thirst, the dust pulled any remaining moisture from Subria's throat and made breathing almost intolerable. The dust brought on an occasional cough, and the dryness of her throat felt as though she had swallowed sand.

As she struggled up the hill, all she could see was the shuffling of the feet directly in front of her. She had watched those feet for days. How much longer she would have to watch them, she didn't know. Because one of her own feet was roped to a foot in front of her and the other was roped to a foot behind, she had no choice but to follow. Her hands were also bound. She was only one of a long caravan of humans, roped together, moving methodically, without veering to the right or to the left. In this condition, any thought of escape had long since fled Subria's mind.

The ropes that bound her were made of dried and woven plant fibers. Their coarseness dug into her legs just above the ankles. Each painful step was a reminder of the indignity of being bound as an animal.

Only her feeling of hatred toward Shaka for killing her family burned hotter than the incessant cutting of the ropes. This wasn't the first time she had been treated as an animal. It was only a few seasons earlier that she had been bound by Shaka.

1816
After Subria had been delivered with the other captives, bound hand and foot, to Dingiswayo by Shaka, the young men and young women had been confined in separate huts. The huts were guarded day and night, and the only visitors to the hut housing the young women were a few old men who were allowed to select wives. Each time the skin across the doorway had parted, Subria's heart raced for fear that she would be chosen. She stayed in

the darkest part of the hut to avoid eye contact with any visitor. Her friend that had also been captured didn't share the same concerns.

"Why don't you hide when the old men come into the hut," Subria had asked her.

Her friend looked at Subria with a surprised expression. "Better to be the wife of an old man, than the slave of a Swallow," she replied.

"The slave of a Swallow?" asked Subria.

"You don't know what Dingiswayo intends to do with you, do you?"

"No," replied Subria tentatively.

"He is going to sell you to the swallows because our chief didn't pay him a tribute."

Subria was shocked. She had never seen a Swallow, but she had heard that they were hideous. They had hairy faces and arms, and the hair on their heads was long like a rope. She had also heard that they had magic sticks that sounded like thunder and could kill from great distances. Worse still, they ate people like her. Though they had the resemblance of being human, she had been told that they may not be. Suddenly, the thought of being wife to an old man seemed almost tolerable. Still she wasn't going to volunteer.

After several days, Subria's friend was chosen by an old man, and she left the hut. Subria didn't see her very often after that.

Subria and the other young women were given tasks in support of the village. Subria's main task was to carry water for the village gardens. She had been carrying water since she was a child, so the task suited her, but after carrying water all day for several days, her back, legs and neck were in constant pain. She was initially under the watchful eye of a guard, and she detested being forced to work. As she labored under the heavy load of the water, she thought of little else than how she might escape. But with little opportunity of putting a plan into action, and with no idea of how to return to her village, she eventually abandoned the idea.

Most detestable to Subria was Shaka. When he wasn't on a military campaign, he walked about the village in a state of great arrogance. After he became king of the Zulus, she was glad that she wouldn't have to see him again.

Subria occasionally saw her friend, but they rarely had opportunity to speak. Her friend's plight didn't seem much better than her own. She also worked hard, but wasn't guarded. After several months, Subria saw that her friend was growing big with child.

November 1817

As the weeks had turned into months, Subria was growing accustomed to her life as a slave. She was given increasing freedom to move about the village. Still, a day didn't go by that she didn't think about the horrors of losing her family. She thought about her little brother and wondered whether he would remember her.

She noticed that a young man from her own village, also now a slave, watched her each day as she went for water, and she liked the attention.

"You have caught the attentions of Maarku."

Subria recognized the voice of her friend, and she spun about. Subria smiled, but was embarrassed when she felt her face flush.

"Maarku?" Subria asked.

"Yes, Maarku," replied her friend with a smile.

Subria looked about to ensure that Maarku wasn't nearby. "How do you know his name?" she asked.

"I knew him in our village. I'm surprised that you didn't know him."

At the mention of their home village, Subria's smile disappeared, and she looked at the ground. "Our village is such a distant memory to me," sighed Subria. "I'm not sure who I knew sometimes."

"Make this your home, Subria," urged her friend.

Subria looked in surprise at her friend. "How can you suggest that? You have a mother in our village. You shouldn't forget that it is your home."

"I haven't forgotten," her friend said. Then she held her abdomen and replied, "I'm going to have a child, and this is the only village he will know. This village is my future."

"It isn't mine!" insisted Subria.

Her friend turned to walk away, and as she did, she said, "Really, your only choice is to accept it. It will only be more difficult if you don't."

As Subria considered the advice of her friend, she noticed Maarku walking toward her. Embarrassed that he saw her look at him, she turned and walked away.

"Subria," Maarku called, but she kept walking.

"Subria," Maarku called more boldly.

Subria stopped and smiled briefly making certain that she wasn't smiling when she turned to face Maarku.

"Are you going for water?" Maarku asked.

Subria smiled and held out her empty hands. "Without a pot? I don't think so."

Maarku seemed embarrassed as he looked down and kicked the dirt. "Shall I walk with you?" he asked.

"If you wish," responded Subria.

They walked in silence for a short while, and it made Subria uncomfortable.

"I've heard that you lost your family in our village," Maarku finally said.

"Yes, but I still have a brother there," replied Subria, but she was slightly perturbed that he had started a conversation in that way.

Maarku looked briefly at Subria as they walked. "I don't even have a brother left in our village."

Subria stopped and turned to Maarku. She noticed moisture in his eyes for a brief moment before he looked away. "Shaka killed your entire family?" she asked in a concerned voice.

Maarku didn't answer right away, but continued along the path. Subria stepped quickly to his side and accompanied him. When he did speak, he said, "Shaka took everything from me. Do you wish to return to the village?"

"I will return," Subria asserted. "I think of little else."

Maarku smiled and replied eagerly, "I'll help."

"How do I know that I can trust you?"

"It's a difficult journey. Who else can you trust?"

Subria sat on a rock and looked at Maarku. "Why do I need your help?"

"Do you know the way?"

"I have a general idea."

Maarku sat beside her. "Do you know how to avoid lions and hyenas?"

The rock that she sat upon was beneath a tree at the edge of a grass covered plain. Subria looked over the large expanse of grass. She knew that if she were to try and reach her village, she would likely encounter lions and hyena. Turning back to Maarku, she asked, "And you know the way?"

Maarku smiled, "I have a general idea. After all, I've made the trip once."

That didn't seem to impress Subria much. "Do you know how to avoid lions and hyenas?" she asked.

Maarku smiled broadly and pointed toward the grassy plain. "Of course. Lions are out mostly at night, so travel mostly in daylight. Of course, if you are being pursued, darkness provides the best cover. Avoid tall grasses. Don't walk beneath trees without first observing their branches. Climb a tree and watch grassy areas for signs of movement before crossing. Always..."

"Yes, yes," Subria interrupted him with a push to his shoulder and a smile. "You know how to avoid beasts."

Maarku was pleased that she seemed to appreciate his skills. "We'll travel together then," he offered.

Subria looked over the plain again and then back at Maarku. "Yes. Yes, we'll travel together," she replied with some initial hesitation and then with building excitement and confidence. "Yes."

"When will we leave?"

"Dingiswayo will have a celebration in two days hence," Subria said.

"Yes," agreed Maarku, "and we'll leave just as it begins."

"No, I'll be expected to help prepare and serve the food. But with that food there will be plenty of pito drinking."

"Yes. When the warriors are full of pito, we'll leave," offered Maarku.

Subria sighed with exasperation. "No, Dingiswayo will be giving wives to some of the warriors. All girls of the village will be accounted for, and I'll be missed if I'm not there."

"If you get chosen, I'll wait in his hut and will put a spear through his heart."

"Then you'll be no better than Shaka."

"And no worse," Maarku grinned.

"If I'm chosen, I'll bring more pito with me to the hut. The sun will be high in the sky before he comes to himself," Subria smiled.

Maarku also smiled and replied, "You've given your plan a lot of thought."

Subria smiled and her face flushed. Continuing, she said, "There will also be lots of drumming and dancing. We'll leave after the wives are granted and during the dancing and drumming. Also, the moon will be bright, so we will be able to see well."

"True, a bright moon will help us to see, but a darker sky would make the stars more visible. I'm familiar with the sky near our village," observed Maarku.

The day of the celebration was spent intensively preparing for the feast. Subria worked alongside the other slave girls to prepare great quantities of food. The amount of food surprised Subria, until she saw that many warriors had come from other villages. The presence of the additional warriors concerned Maarku also. Subria had a brief moment to speak with him during the afternoon, and he suggested that they not follow through with their plans.

Subria glared at him. "Do as you wish, but I'll not be here tomorrow," she said quietly, but firmly.

Maarku seemed conflicted. "With so many warriors in the village, our departure may be observed."

"They will be too occupied by the dancing and drinking pito to notice."

"Even if they don't notice, there will be just that many more to look for us," insisted Maarku.

"Why would they care to look for us?"

"They would if Dingiswayo offers a reward to them," Maarku replied.

"Maybe you'll help them for the reward," Subria sneered.

Maarku seemed hurt. "I'll not help them. I'll be with you," he said quietly.

Subria smiled faintly and walked away.

That evening, Subria watched from the shadows as the dancers moved energetically to the beat of the drums. She had served food and drink to the guests for hours but tried to be unnoticeable.

The first groups of dancers were girls, followed by boys. They were followed by young women dancing in celebration of rains. Young men followed, displaying their future prowess as warriors.

The sound of the drums and rhythmic yells raised an excitement within Subria, and she wanted to join the dancing. She refrained for fear that a warrior would desire her to wife.

Drums grew louder as great quantities of pito were consumed. After the young men and young women danced, the village women began displaying their skills. Dressed in brightly colored skirts and headbands, and carrying dried stalks of corn, they danced in anticipation of bountiful harvests.

Finally, the warriors, with tufts of fur tied to each leg, danced with shield and spear. The line between dancer and spectator was erased as the women and the young men and young women joined in the aggressive display.

Subria felt a hand on her shoulder. Startled, she turned to face Maarku, his face illuminated by the flicker of the fire's light. Subria was surprised at how strong he looked with a spear in hand.

"Let's go," Maarku urged.

"No. Let's wait for Dingiswayo to grant wives," insisted Subria.

"That could be hours. We'd be able to go a great distance by then."

"If I'm not here when wives are granted, my absence may be noticed."

"Your absence will be notice eventually regardless," observed Maarku. Then he smiled and continued, "You want to see whether you'd be chosen. You want to be chosen, don't you?"

Subria pushed him backward. "I do not!" she said firmly. "Let's go then!"

Subria looked back at the dancing throng and about the shadows. She and Maarku seemed to be unnoticed, so they slipped into the shadows and hurried to the edge of the village.

Just outside the village, she stopped near a large rock and removed a smaller rock that leaned against it. She then reached into the cavity and pulled out a small skin bag. Maarku smiled to think that she had hidden food for them. After retrieving the bundle, they hurried on.

The moon was even brighter than they had expected, and once away from the light of the fire, they could plainly make out the hills and the trees.

"Let's stay in the shadows of the trees until we're beyond the hill," Maarku urged.

Subria was happy to follow his lead since she had little experience beyond the edge of a village.

A large grass plain lay beyond the hill. Though it would be quickest to cross the plain, Maarku insisted that they skirt the edge and stay in a dry creek bed.

"The tall grass may be hiding lions," he said. "Also, if we pass through it, we'll leave an obvious trail."

As they walked in the creek bed, the occasional sound of a distant lion could be heard. Each time she heard a roar, Subria's heart seemed to skip, and she felt the hair stand up on the back of her neck. She felt safer walking very close to Maarku.

When they approached a large boulder, Maarku suddenly stopped and held out a hand against Subria. Without saying a word, he pointed to the base of the boulder. There, peering about the boulder was the dark, but distinctive form of a jackal's head. The nose was pointed and delicate, and the large ears were silhouetted against the lighter colored sand of the creek bed.

Subria's heart raced and she grabbed Maarku's arm. Maarku gently nudged her to the side as he slowly raised his spear. A lone jackal, or even two together, posed little danger, but Maarku knew that jackals rarely hunted alone.

With his spear raised to the ready, Maarku waited for the jackal to make the first move. Subria looked about to see whether there were others, but didn't see any. After several seconds the jackal turned and trotted away. Subria sighed with relief, and only then did she realize how fast her heart was beating.

With his spear still raised, Maarku carefully approached the boulder to be certain that no other beasts were lingering. He then motioned for Subria to follow.

Subria felt something inside her stir as her appreciation of Maarku's strength and bravery grew. He had seemed to be yet a boy while still in the village, but here, with spear in hand and standing forward to protect her, he was not a boy at all. She felt safer with him than she had felt since she was a little girl in the presence of her father.

Thinking of her father and of his loss saddened her, but being with Maarku was beginning to fill the void that he had left, and it felt good.

Subria followed Maarku along the dry creek in silence, paying little attention to the route that they followed. She realized that she could never have made the trip to their village without him.

Just before sunrise, Maarku stopped to listen.

"What is it?" asked Subria nervously as she looked about.

Maarku didn't respond, but held a hand to his ear. Subria's heart began to race.

"Listen!" Maarku whispered. "Hyenas."

"Hyena?!" Subria repeated in a whisper that didn't mask her concern.

Hyenas hunted in packs, and they were particularly vicious. While they would generally kill most of their own food, they were known to drive lionesses and leopards from their own kills. Subria expected that if there were hyenas, there were also evil spirits about.

"We shouldn't have left the village," Subria whispered. Her eyes began to fill with tears. "The spirits have led the hyenas to us."

"Hurry," whispered Maarku. He was already running, and Subria quickly followed him. "Climb that tree."

The sound of the hyenas was closing fast when Subria reached the tree. Maarku was tall enough to jump and reach a branch, and lifted himself up. Subria looked behind herself and saw several hyenas running at her.

"Grab my hand!" yelled Maarku.

Subria frantically jumped and grabbed for Maarku's hand, but missed.

"Subria! Jump!" yelled Maarku.

Subria jumped again and clasped Maarku's hand. Maarku easily pulled her into the tree as the hyenas jumped and snapped at her feet.

Subria screamed with fright as she grasped a branch and held tightly. Still trying to catch her breath from the run and the fright, she gasped, "It's the evil spirits!"

Maarku only took his eyes off the hyenas momentarily to look at her and reply, "It's not evil spirits." Studying the hyenas again, he said with certainty, "It's the food in your bag. Throw it to them."

Subria felt the bag at her side with one hand, and replied incredulously, "I'm sure they want more than the food in my bag."

"Perhaps, but it might pacify them. Throw it to them."

Subria removed the bag and looked at it for a moment and then threw it to the ground. The hyenas fought viciously over it, and the contents were soon gone.

"How do you know that they won't stay here and wait for us to fall out of this tree?" asked Subria.

"I don't," replied Maarku. "All we can do is wait."

"And while we wait for them to tire of waiting for us, their noise will surely attract a lion."

"Or perhaps it will attract anyone sent from the village to find us," replied Maarku with some concern.

After several minutes the hyenas were distracted and ran from the tree. Maarku and Subria stayed in the tree for several more minutes before venturing down.

They were quite hungry by the time they reached the village in the early evening. After having been taken prisoner by Shaka, and after having been gone from the village so long, they had anticipated a warm welcome on their return.

Subria immediately recognized the first person they met as they approached the village. It was an elderly woman who had been a friend of her grandmother. Subria hadn't liked the woman very much and thought that she was grouchy. Still, she had been her grandmother's friend, and being the first person of the village that they had seen, Subria was glad to see her.

"Subria? Maarku?" the old woman said in surprise as the two walked up to her.

"Yes, it's me," Subria replied with a smile.

The woman smiled and touched Subria's face and then glanced at Maarku. "Maarku," she said with a smile. Subria noticed a tear forming in the corner of the old woman's eye and wondered whether she had misjudged her.

Suddenly, the old woman's countenance changed. "What are you doing here?" she demanded.

Subria was shocked at the abrupt change and hesitated. Maarku replied in an almost triumphant tone, "We've escaped Dingiswayo."

"You've escaped Dingiswayo?" the old woman snarled. "No one escapes Dingiswayo! You've brought dishonor to this village! Do you not know that he'll send Shaka back to us and kill us all?"

Subria looked at Maarku with a puzzled expression.

"Did you think that you could just walk away, and that they wouldn't find you? Did you think that they'd look for you in the savannah or in some other village? No! They know exactly where you'd go, and are probably even now approaching the village."

Subria looked toward the grassy plain that they had come from as though to see whether they had been followed.

The old woman grabbed Subria's arm. "Come with me," she demanded.

Subria instinctively pulled away. She had intended no disrespect to the woman, it was just a reflex reaction.

The old woman was surprised that Subria had pulled away and it seemed to cause her more irritation.

"Don't think to run! I'll call out and there'll be warriors enough after you."

Subria apologized, and said, "No, please don't call out." Then looking at Maarku, she continued, "We'll come with you."

Maarku had a distressed look, but he followed Subria and the old woman.

The old woman walked surprisingly quickly and with a look of determination. When they entered the village, villagers stared and pointed with surprise to see a young man and young woman. Because of Shaka, their village was otherwise devoid of young people. Some villagers seemed very happy to see them. A few called out their names as they passed by, but others clearly had the same fears as the old woman.

The warrior who had been left in charge of the village stood waiting near the village center. He had been alerted by a warrior who had seen the trio walk into the village. Subria was frightened when she saw the chief warrior. He was a big man with powerful arms and legs. He stood with feet firmly planted and with arms crossed over his chest. When Subria and Maarku approached, a nearby warrior stepped forward and pushed them both to the ground.

"Kneel before the chief," he demanded.

Subria hit the ground hard on her hands and knees. The soldier kicked her hands out from under her and she felt gravel pierce her cheek bone just below her right eye.

Subria was shocked at the treatment that she was receiving in her own village, and tears began to form in her eyes. She fought to control her emotions for fear of appearing weak.

"Who are you?" demanded the chief.

"I'm Subria. This is my village."

"Then you were amongst those taken by Shaka to Dingiswayo?"

Maarku glanced at Subria waiting for her reply. Regardless of her answer, the result wouldn't likely be good.

"Yes. This is our village."

The chief laughed. "This was your village. You have no village now. You belong to Dingiswayo."

Turning to the warriors nearby, the chief continued, "Take them back. It will please Dingiswayo that I returned them before his warriors find them."

"No, Great Chief!" begged Subria. "Please don't send us back."

Two warriors quickly came forward and pushed Subria and Maarku back to the ground until they were both prostrate. They then tied their hands behind their backs before pulling them to their feet. Without hesitation, the warriors led them from the village and soon they were headed back toward Dingiswayo.

As they left the village, Subria heard a young boy calling her name. "Subria! Subria!"

She instantly knew the voice and turned to see her brother running toward her. Subria stopped and called to him, but their warrior escort pulled hard on her arm and kept her moving forward.

Looking over her shoulder, Subria called out to him again and saw that he was being restrained by others. Being so close to her brother, but also being treated so harshly caused emotion greater than she could contain and her tears began to flow freely. She started to cry aloud. She couldn't remember ever having cried aloud, but great gasping sobs escaped her mouth. She cried for her dead mother and father. She cried for her dead brother and her dead grandmother. She cried for her living brother who was now dead to her. She cried for herself and the injustice that she was forced to endure.

The anger that she had known since the raid on her own village began to well up inside her. She wished that she were a man so that she could kill Shaka for what he had done to her family. She imagined meeting him in combat and driving a spear into his side. She thought of little else as she trudged silently along. Soon, there were no tears, just numbing anger.

Darkness encompassed them as they marched toward Dingiswayo's village and neither Maarku nor Subria uttered a word. After Subria had nearly exhausted herself with her cries, she recognized that her stomach was aching. She had eaten little since they had left Dingiswayo's village the day before, and she expected that they wouldn't eat again until well after their return. Despite the hunger and growing fatigue, her hatred of Shaka kept her moving forward.

At the village, Dingiswayo rewarded the warriors for the return of the runaways and also sent them back with gifts for the warrior who had been left in charge of the village. Subria and Maarku were returned to the huts that housed the other young men and young women taken from Abasi's village, but they were kept tied most of the time.

The other young women were angry with Subria, because since her attempted escape, they had been guarded more closely and tied at night.

It was only a few nights after Subria had been returned to Dingiswayo's village that she noticed the other young women were visibly shaken. Some were crying. Since her return, she had spoken but little to the other girls. The distress of the other young women caused her to speak to one of them.

The other young women looked at Subria in surprise. Through tears, she responded, "We are to be sold to the Swallows!"

"Sold to the Swallows!" Subria repeated with disbelief. "When?"

"We don't know, but soon."

Subria sat on the floor of the hut and leaned her back against the wall and stared at the dirt. *Sold to the Swallows*, she thought. *Could it be any more dreadful than being slave to Dingiswayo?*

Two days later, Subria was carrying water when she saw a group entering the village. They walked on two feet, but she wasn't initially certain that they were human at all. If they were human, they were the most grotesque that she had seen. More cloth covered their bodies than she had ever seen on anyone, but their skin that did show was pale and sickly looking. Their skin that wasn't covered with cloth was mostly covered with hair. Some had dark hair and some orange. Their heads were mostly covered, but their hair hung down in long, straight strands below the head covering. The hair of their face also hung down in loose curls. She assumed that they were men because of the hair on their faces.

"Swallows!" Subria exclaimed aloud though no one was nearby. Just looking at them struck her at once with fear and disgust. *I'm going to be sold to the Swallows!* she thought to herself. The thought nearly paralyzed her with fear, but she dropped the water and ran away from the village. She wanted to look back and see whether anyone was following, but she didn't. *Run!* she thought. *If I can only make it to the trees!*

Though she didn't realize it, adrenaline surged through her body and she ran faster than she had ever before. She didn't feel the tall grass whipping her thighs, or the sharp pebbles on her feet. Through her tear-filled eyes she focused on the trees ahead. She knew that she could not return to her village, or to any village, but she would rather die with the beasts than be sold to the Swallows.

Subria was breathing hard, but over her labored breath she could hear footsteps close behind. She hoped that it was Maarku running away from the village also, but she didn't look back.

Just before the trees, Subria felt a rock hit her between her shoulder blades. It was a solid hit and she felt the pain despite her heightened state of excitement. The force sent her to the ground face first, and as she struggled to get back to her feet she was grasped by a strong hand and yanked back toward the village. As Subria struggled in vain to escape, she was pulled ever closer to the village.

"The Swallows have come for you," her captor taunted with a laugh.

"Please, no! Don't force me to the village! Let me go!" Subria pled, but her pleas weren't effective. Her captor seemed to enjoy her pleas and her struggles. Though he didn't speak again, he smirked and laughed at her efforts to escape.

A large fire burned in the center of the village that night. The drums and singing were loud. And, though she couldn't see from inside the hut where she was tied, Subria knew that there was much dancing and much drinking of pito.

Several other girls were tied inside the hut with Subria. Little was said, but there were plenty of tears. Subria cried little because she was sustained by her anger toward Shaka and Dingiswayo.

The drums and the dancing lasted most of the night, and the next morning the village was quiet long after the sun arose.

"Will we be sold to the Swallows today?" one of the younger girls asked aloud to no one in particular.

"Of course we will," replied another girl. "Why do you think that we are tied?"

"Don't tell her that," whispered another girl.

"Why not? It's true," said the second girl. "Whether I state it or not, changes little."

The younger girl began to cry.

After what seemed a very long time, the skin covering the doorway of the hut was thrown aside and two warriors entered and demanded that all of the girls arise and leave the hut. The girls slowly filed through the doorway and into the bright sunlight. They were led to the village center where Dingiswayo and the Swallows waited. They were commanded to line up opposite of the Swallows. All of the girls kept their eyes to the ground, but

Subria looked up briefly. She was still horrified at the site of the Swallows, but she saw that they were staring at the girls and it made her very uncomfortable.

As the girls stood side by side opposite the Swallows, a man that was apparently the leader of the Swallows moved slowly along the line of girls, stopping before each. Occasionally, he would look into a girl's mouth, or spin her about to study her from all sides. A few were pushed aside by him and they were taken away. Each time he pushed one aside, Dingiswayo complained aloud to him that the girl was valuable, but that he would accept a lower price.

Subria's heart raced and her breathing became rapid and shallow as the Swallow drew closer to her. She had a strong impulse to run, but knew that it was of little use. Suddenly, she saw his feet directly in front of her as she looked at the ground. Like the feet of the other Swallows, his feet were covered with one solid mass of hide. Subria had never seen anyone that kept their toes completely covered. The hide disappeared inside the cloth that covered his legs.

Though she didn't intend to, she looked up and into his eyes. They were terrifying! Each eye was a ball of yellow membrane with a dark center. Thin red lines ran through the yellow membrane like frozen lightning against a yellow sky.

The Swallow seemed to sense Subria's shock and he smiled and laughed. He had few teeth, and the teeth that he did have were yellow and crooked. His breath smelled like a stagnant pond after the summer rains had disappeared.

Subria quickly averted her eyes.

The Swallow made noises with his mouth that Subria couldn't understand, but another Swallow nearby seemed to understand, and he turned to Dingiswayo and said, "What is her name?"

Dingiswayo looked at Subria and demanded, "What is your name?"

"Subria," she repeated quietly.

With that the Swallow in front of her spoke again, and the second Swallow asked Dingiswayo, "What does Subria mean?"

"Patience!" replied Dingiswayo.

The second Swallow spoke incomprehensible words again to tell the first Swallow what Dingiswayo had said. When he did, they both laughed and the second Swallow said to Dingiswayo, "Patience indeed!"

The Swallow standing in front of Subria spun her about. Subria hoped that he would push her out of the line, but he didn't.

Again, he spun her about to face him. Then grabbing her hair at the top of her head with one hand and also grabbing her chin with the other, he forced her mouth open. With her mouth fully open, he moved his face close and looked inside. At that proximity, his breath was intense. He then released her chin and she was shocked that he stuck a finger in her mouth. Subria nearly gagged. The finger tasted awful and it was rough like the hide of a beast. She could barely restrain herself from biting down on the finger. Then when he stuck it far back in her mouth, she nearly regurgitated, and she couldn't control the urge to bite down any longer. When she did, the Swallow quickly withdrew his finger and yelled. Then he hit her hard across the face.

Subria held her face, and she felt tears fill her eyes and roll down her cheeks. She had never been so humiliated. But then she realized something. If the Swallow felt the pain of her bite, these Swallows were definitely human! That meant that additional pain could be inflicted on them. The thought brought a slight smile to her lips.

After the Swallow had inspected all of the young women and the young men, and had selected many, he and the second Swallow sat in front of Dingiswayo. Subria couldn't hear what Dingiswayo was saying, but eventually the Swallows gave Dingiswayo something and he seemed satisfied.

At the realization that they had been sold to the Swallows, there was great agitation among young men and young women. Many of the young women began to cry out, and many of the young men and young women appeared as though they would run. To keep them from running, all of the Swallows along with Dingiswayo's warriors rush forward, and hit them with sticks and prodded them with spears until they were all in a tight group.

Subria had given up on the idea of running, and ended up in the middle of the group, pressed on all sides by the bodies of the others who were trying to avoid the sticks and pointed spear tips.

Her heart raced. A cloud of dust had been kicked up by the struggle, and Subria gasped for each breath as she was pushed about by the pulsating throng. She felt that she would surely faint.

After the Swallows and the warriors had the group controlled, Swallows stepped forward and began tying rope about the hands of each youth. The youth were then forced into a long line and the Swallows tied ropes about their ankles. Each young man or young woman was tied to both the person in front and to the person behind, until they formed a long line bound together.

With their prize bound hand and foot and sufficiently under control, the Swallows began whipping the youth with small sticks until they began marching obediently out of the village. Subria felt the sting of several strikes against her legs, arms and back. How she wanted to run. She didn't care where she would run, but she wanted to run until she were away from every other living human. None could be trusted.

For days, the group trudged along, roped in the same fashion. Initially uncomfortable, the rough ropes soon began to cut into any flesh that they touched. The pain was almost as intolerable as the thirst that was caused by the long dusty marches. The group of bound youth were fed little and offered even less to drink. The only time that they were allowed to drink was when a small creek or stagnant pond was encountered. Initially, the ponds were refused by the group, but soon even putrid water seemed a welcomed relief to the otherwise parched, cracked throats.

The youth remained tied at all times. They slept in their bound state and were obliged to relieve their bodily waste while either marching or while bedded for the night. Initially humiliating, it soon began to seem normal and lost its disgust as fatigue, hunger and thirst took over all mental functions.

After several days, some of the youth began to grow sick and to collapse. With little hesitation the Swallows removed the ropes from their feet and bound the ropes to those who had been in front and behind the youth. The sick youth was left at the side of the trail and the crowd moved on.

As they marched up a small hill, Subria's thoughts turned to her mother, father, brothers and grandmother. How she missed the warm days working by their sides. She remembered the last night that she spent in the hut sleeping beside her family and she longed to hear their soft breathing as they slept. Subria didn't know how long she could last, or whether she wanted to survive. But the thoughts of her family gave her strength, and she felt as though they were nearby holding her up.

At the top of the hill, Subria saw a scene that she had heard about, but never expected to see herself. Before them lay a body of water as vast as the grasslands of her home. No, it was larger. It was as vast as the entire earth. It seemed to encompass the entire earth. It was deep blue in color and stretched beyond the horizon. The wonderful sight momentarily distracted Subria from her own desperate situation.

A ship was docked in the bay and Subria had never seen anything like it. Sitting on the water, like a leaf on a pond, it appeared larger than a village. She couldn't fathom what kept it afloat and concluded that it must be magic.

As the pitiful human caravan approached the town, great numbers of Swallows came into sight. They were all covered in cloth from head to foot. The long, full dresses that the women wore covered their legs and feet and made it seem that they floated when they walked.

The people of the town stopped and stared as the horrible train passed by. Subria was angered when a young boy threw rocks at the slaves. She was also shocked to see people with dark skin dressed in a fashion similar to the Swallows. It confused her, and she wondered whether they were Swallows, or whether they were her own kind. *If they were of her own kind, why would they be dressed so?* she wondered.

There were no familiar hut structures in this large village. Subria hadn't realized that it was possible to build huts so large, and she wondered what kind of people required such large structures.

The caravan of slaves were marched into one of the large structures. Once inside, the ropes were removed from their feet and hands, and they were allowed to sit. The relief and the feeling of freedom brought unspeakable joy to Subria. Still the open sores were painful.

They hadn't been in the building long before another Swallow came into the room and spoke to the Swallows who had brought the slaves from the village. Subria couldn't understand him, but could tell that he was angry.

"Fools! Did you not feed or water these slaves?" demanded the Dutch man who had just entered the room. "A dead slave is worthless to me."

Before long, food and water were brought into the room, and the young men and young women pressed upon it almost in one body. Subria went first for the water. She quickly raised the gourd to her lips and sucked in the fresh water. The relief it brought to her parched throat was instant. She could have drank all the contents of the gourd, but other young men and young women were pulling it from her. It was finally pulled from her hands and she turned her attention to the food. She managed to secure two small, crusty cakes, and they were soon devoured.

With her stomach somewhat satisfied and her thirst quenched, she began to consider how she might escape. She was surprised to realize that it was the first time in days that she had thought about escape. Her thirst, hunger and fatigue had been demanding companions and had left little energy for other thoughts.

Chapter Ten – Slave Ship
November 1817

For the next several days, Subria and the other young men and young women were confined in the building. The boredom was intense, but with food in their bellies, some of the boys and girls were feeling strong enough to make jokes and play mindless games. Subria didn't join in with them. *Have they forgotten that we are slaves?* she wondered. *Don't they care what will become of us? They act as though we will go home again. We aren't ever going home. Where is home?*

The only windows in the room were high above the floor, making it impossible to look out. Because there were no guards inside the room, some of the young men had stood atop other young men's shoulders and were just able to peer through the window. They described the immediate area around the building that confined them. They spoke of men, women and children, with pale skin, walking about the streets. The Swallows often entered buildings and came out bearing bundles. They wondered why anyone would want such bundles. They also described a building directly across the street that had dead animals hanging in the window. It was astounding to them that a great hunter would give away his prey so readily. But more astounding was the appearance of the great hunter. He didn't look like a hunter at all. He was fat and old. *How could he have killed so many animals?* they wondered.

Each boy was bewildered by the invisible barrier that separated them from the outside. They could peer through it, but if they pressed their face against it, something stopped them from passing through. Finally, one boy pounded his fist against it, and the barrier shattered. Pieces of it fell outside and some inside. The startled boy also sustained a cut on his fist. The disturbance of the pieces falling to the ground outside caught the attention of the Swallows and soon the head Swallow arrived. He was none too pleased. No one ate that night.

The next day, several Swallows returned with rope, and there was great agitation amongst the young men and young women when they realized that they were to be bound again. The young men and young women ran about the room trying to avoid being caught by a Swallow, but it was futile. There were enough Swallows that they slowly moved in upon the youth and herded them into a corner of the room. The young men recognized the tactic as one they had used while hunting with their fathers, and now it was being used effectively on themselves.

Subria was alert, and her heart raced. Despite a great deal of pushing and shoving, she avoided being knocked to the floor. Other young women were toppled to the floor and were stepped upon, each crying out loudly. While keeping an eye on her captors, Subria tried to avoid the fallen girls. Soon, despite their efforts, all were pressed as one body into a corner of the room, and Subria, in the middle of the press, felt as though she would suffocate. Over and over she gasped for air, but couldn't fill her lungs. Relief only came when the Swallows used short whips to break up the group, and to peel a few off at a time. Only then was Subria able to fill her lungs.

As they were separated from the group, each young man and young woman was bound hand and foot as before. Because the press of the group was less, Subria's heart calmed somewhat. But then it was her turn to be separated from the group. She resisted until she felt the sharp stings of the whip on her legs and back. Soon, even she was bound.

It was mid-afternoon when the group was led from the building into the warm summer sun. Many Swallows gathered and watched as they passed. Some yelled or spit at them. Subria couldn't understand their taunts, but it angered her regardless.

They were led along the dusty street, past many shops. Despite the ropes, the shops became a momentary distraction. Subria peered as best she could into the windows. She couldn't see much, but it did appear that Swallow women were admiring great amounts of cloth in one shop. She thought that the shopkeeper must be very wealthy to have so much cloth.

After a short while the group was turned onto another street that ran perpendicular to the bay. The street descended sharply toward the water, and at the water's edge was the large ship, floating as a leaf on the water.

Subria hoped that they would get close enough that she could get a better look. As she considered this she noticed that a few of the young men were getting very agitated and were holding back as though they would go no further. The Swallows began whipping them, forcing them forward. The young men were yelling something, but Subria couldn't initially make out what they were saying. Soon many were yelling the same thing and fighting against the ropes.

"Death ship! Death ship!" they yelled.

Subria's heart raced and she too fought against the ropes. *Of course, I should have known!* she thought. She had vague memories of being told about a death ship by her grandmother. Her grandmother had learned of such awful ships from someone who had escaped from the Swallows. The person had never actually been on a ship, but had heard tales about the horrors of such floating villages. Their language had no words to describe the sufferings endured on such ships, they only knew that there were many deaths. Until this moment, Subria had supposed that they were going to be transported by land caravan to their final destination. The thought of the death ship filled her with terror.

She felt the sting of the whips against her back as she pulled back on the rope with the others. She didn't count the strikes, but the pain screamed through her body. The sting was so sharp that she initially thought that she was on fire. Soon, neither she nor the other young men or young women could resist against the constant onslaught of leather scorpions, and they fell back into line.

Though they continued marching toward the ship, the air was rent with their cries of anguish and fear. As they neared the ship, however, a hush fell over the group. It was as though the ship was a beast that they didn't want to awaken.

The stench of the ship was evident before they had even boarded. To Subria, it smelled like death and human waste mixed together. She felt as though she couldn't breathe.

The pitiful caravan was marched up the gangplank and onto the ship. Only then did the full impact of the smell become evident. The smell made the air seem thick and heavy, as though it could be cut asunder with a knife. Hordes of flies had also found the ship, and the warm air buzzed with the sound of their wings. The smell alone was torturous, but multitudes of flies crawled on Subria's skin, trying to enter her mouth, her ears and her eyes. Without the full use of her hands to wipe them away, their persistent humming and crawling was maddening.

Once on the ship, the Swallows began separating the young men from the young women. They would untie a young man or young woman from the group and lead them away below deck by a short length of rope. Subria was anxious to get out of the sun and away from the flies, and she welcomed being untied when it came her turn.

It took a few moments for her eyes to adjust to the low lighting after she was led below deck. Relief from the flies was almost instantaneous, but if she had anticipated relief from the smell, she was mistaken. The dreadful smell was intense. Subria placed a hand over her nose and mouth, with no relief.

As she descended the stairs she became aware of moans and cries, and as her eyes became accustomed to the light, she saw a most horrifying sight. Before her were rows of racks, each about a forearm's length from top to bottom. The racks were stacked six high, and the only visible thing sticking from the racks were the soles of feet! Initially, she thought that the feet belonged to dead bodies, but then she saw that many were moving occasionally. She realized that the moans and cries were coming from deep inside the racks.

Subria gasped and pulled against her rope when she began to comprehend the awfulness of the scene before her. When she gasped, a great breath of the putrid air flowed into her lungs. *The Swallows really aren't human!* She cried within herself. *No human would treat another human in this manner!*

The Swallow leading her pulled so firmly on the rope that she was compelled to move forward, nearly toppling to the deck.

"Please, don't put me in the 'death hole'," she pled over and over, but the Swallow showed no comprehension of what she was saying, and he led her deeper into the bowels of the ship.

After descending another set of stairs the chamber was completely dark, save for the single candle carried by the Swallow. Subria could see a myriad of eyes reflecting the soft yellow glow of the candlelight, and she realized that many, many slaves were watching her every move. Initially frightened, her fear turned to pity when she saw that they were crowded together like animals in a stall. Still their situation was far better than those chained to the racks of the death hole.

The Swallow motioned for Subria to join some others in a holding cell. To do so would require that she crouch on all fours and squeeze into a confined area that was already crowded. When she hesitated, the Swallow pushed Subria forward, and she sustained a bump on her head as she fell headlong into the cell, landing atop another girl. The girl pushed Subria from off her leg. The Swallow attempted to close the grated door of the cell, but Subria wasn't yet in far enough to allow the door to swing freely. The Swallow kicked the door and yelled something at Subria and kicked the door again. She moved away from the door as best she could, and the Swallow shut the door.

The confines of the cell were such that it was impossible for any person to keep from being pressed closely to one or more others. Subria sat for a time in shocked silence other than her occasional soft cries. Tears flowed freely down her cheeks. She considered her condition most dreadful, though not so dreadful as those in the death hole.

"Crying will do you no good," a voice whispered.

It was the voice of an older woman, and though it was a whisper, barely audible, it startled Subria. The source of the whisper was so close to her that it almost seemed to have originated within her own head.

"You'll need to save your strength," the voice whispered again.

Subria's right arm was pressed against the wire door of the cell, but with effort, she was able to use her right hand to dry her eyes.

The voice had a calming influence on her. Subria imagined that the voice was that of her grandmother.

From her seated position on the floor, Subria could tell that the confining cell was just higher than her head. She couldn't determine how many people were in the cell with her, but she knew that they were packed so tightly as to nearly be sitting atop one another.

She became aware of others whispering in nearby cells.

Subria carefully turned her head toward the direction of the voice and whispered, "Where are they taking us?"

"I'm not sure, but you'll never see your home again."

Subria was already numb to the notion that she'd never see home again. "Why are they doing this?" she asked.

Just then the flicker of a candle could be seen in the direction of the stairs, and a hush fell over the occupants of the deck. A slave was roughly pushed down the steps and a Swallow followed close behind, holding a rope that secured the slave.

Subria's eyes were fully accustomed to the dark, and though faint, the glow of the candle initially stung her eyes. In the glow of the candle, she studied the face of the Swallow, memorizing its every disgusting feature. The Swallow was young, but she felt nothing but contempt for him and imagined that she were thrusting a spear into his chest.

She would have felt sorrow for the poor slave, but her condition was no better.

Subria followed the flickering light as it pushed back the blackness. With her eyes adjusted to the dark, she was amazed at how much she could see by the light of the candle. She was shocked to see at least ten such cells on either side of an aisle, with two cells stacked atop each other. In each cell were packed five or six slaves, each pressed tightly against one another. The scene at once filled her with horror and disgust.

She wanted to cry out in rage, but was afraid of the Swallow's whips. So, instead she drew her knees to her chest, rested her head on her knees, wrapped her arms about her legs and cowered.

Subria was surprised that she was able to fall asleep, but when she awoke the ship was gently swaying back and forth.

"What's happening?" she whispered to the older woman.

"The ship has pushed out to sea."

"Are we going to die?"

"You'll desire to die before you do," came the reply from the older woman.

Subria sat for a long time in silence. Her back hurt, she wanted to stretch her legs and arms. The hard wooden floor was painful on her buttocks. Many hours passed and Subria lost all sense of time. She decided that the woman was right, maybe she would want the relief of death.

It wasn't silent in the lower deck any longer. Many cries were heard. Cries of men and women, boys and girls. Crying out in pain from the rigidly cramped quarters. Some of the stronger had taken to pushing against the weaker in an attempt to get enough space to stretch, and in the darkness many fits of anger broke out amongst the slaves. Subria felt glad that her cell was free of fights.

Just at the point that she could bear no more, a light was seen at the steps. The deck grew silent out of anticipation and fear. Several Swallows came down the steps, each holding a lantern. The light was intense, and the occupants' fear of the Swallows was palpable. But when the Swallows began opening cells and leading the occupants out, cell by cell, the slaves couldn't resist, but cheered out in anticipation and joy.

When Subria's cell was opened, she struggled to exit and to stand. Though it was difficult to straighten her legs and back, she felt more joy and relief in doing so than in anything that she had experienced.

Slowly, she with the other occupants shuffled across the wooden deck and up the first flight of stairs. The racks of the death hole were bare when they passed. Ascending the next stairs they burst into the full brilliance of daylight. A fresh breeze wafted away the stench of the ship. It seemed to dance on Subria's skin, offering relief from the heat of the lower deck.

When full realization of their temporary freedom settled on them, many of the slaves took to spontaneous dancing borne of great pleasure. When her own limbs had gained their strength, Subria joined in the dancing with a joyous smile on her face.

After dancing for a short time, Subria realized that the Swallows were feeding the slaves. Her own stomach had been empty for hours, so she hurried to get some for herself. The crowd was aggressively pushing toward the food, but Subria was able to secure a small bowl. It was horrible, but she ate it anyway.

"Subria!" a male voice called out nearby.

Subria turned and was overjoyed to see Maarku. He didn't look good and had obviously been beaten.

"Maarku? What happened to you?" she asked.

Maarku lowered his eyes as though in shame. "The Swallows put me in a rack, for resisting."

Subria put her hands gently on his face. "The death hole?" she asked. "I'm so sorry."

"If they put me back in the death hole, I'll die. I'd be glad to jump into the water right now if the Swallows weren't watching so closely."

"Do you think they are going to put us back below deck?" asked Subria.

Maarku looked up in surprise. "Of course they are. They can't have us prancing and dancing about the deck all night. There's too many of us. We would eventually get the upper hand." Then turning his head about as though to point, he continued. "Look. This is only a fraction of the people that they brought aboard. The others are still below. After you've had a chance to stretch your legs and eat something, they are going to put you back below deck."

Subria was distressed. In her naiveté, she hadn't considered that their time on deck was only a reprieve.

"I can't go back there!" she managed between gasps. "I'll die!"

"The Swallows don't want you to die. You're worth nothing if you are dead. They'll keep you just this side of death. Just enough alive that you'll cause no problems for them."

"I don't think I want to be alive then."

At that moment, the Swallows had begun herding the slaves below deck. At the realization that she must be caged again, Subria began to cry.

"I can't go down there again," she cried out as she looked on in horror.

Nearly all the others were beginning to cry out similarly and the whole ship seemed to erupt in commotion. The Swallows began using their whips freely to bring the salves into line and to herd them like animals below deck.

Subria considered jumping over the ships railings. *A watery grave is better than a living death*, she thought. The Swallows had anticipated the possibility and had stationed several men to guard the railings.

Just then, she felt the lightning sting of the whip, and she moved forward toward the lower deck. Soon she was back in a dark, damp cage. She was crammed in so tightly with others that she felt she couldn't breathe. She would rather have not breathed at all, for to do so was to suck in a mixture of air and foul stench that seemed so thick that it would surely choke any living thing.

Whereas the bowels of the lower deck had been relatively quiet on her first incarceration, now due to the fear of the inmates, it was filled with the howls and shrieks of the damned. They cried out for their families who were either lost to them entirely, or who were caged elsewhere on the ship. They cried out in pain from the whippings they had endured. They cried out from the crush of the other bodies, and they cried out in sheer terror of the dark.

Though it was late in the day and the sun would be setting soon, the heat was sufficient to cause each person to perspire significantly. And with no alternative, there were many who were forced to endure the dehumanizing effect of relieving themselves within the confines of the cages.

Each day brought the same routine, with the exception that the slaves resisted less and less to the demands of the Swallows. They quit resisting because they knew it was futile, and also because they had not the energy or the health to resist.

It wasn't long before some of the weaker slaves began to die, and Subria noticed that sometimes the cages were less crowded because there were fewer bodies.

In these deplorable conditions, Subria would have welcomed death, but it didn't come. She rarely saw Maarku, and when she did, he looked weak and ghostlike. He had once been strong and confident, but now his eyes were hollow and his cheeks gaunt.

Chapter Eleven – Beyond Port Elizabeth
1844
Grahamstown, Africa

Hyrum and Julia stood outside the door of their small adobe home. Hyrum hugged Julia and kissed her as their eight month old daughter squirmed in her arms, and four year old Francis clung to his father's leg.

"I'll only be a few days, my dear, and I'll travel as quickly as the oxen will pull the wagon," he smiled.

Julia forced a smile. She knew that he had to go and that he would be back soon enough, but still she didn't enjoy being without him.

"I know," she replied, as her eyes began to moisten. "God speed, but hurry back."

After nearly three years in Africa, Julia was still frightened by its wildness and felt vulnerable when Hyrum was away. There was also extra work to do when Hyrum was gone. Someone had to tend to the garden, while also caring for the children and the house. Fortunately, Hyrum was able to hire a few natives that helped with the livestock.

"Someday we'll be able to afford domestic help for you," Hyrum promised.

Julia smiled. She would welcome the help, and she knew that Hyrum meant well, but also knew that it would probably be years before the luxury of extra help could be afforded. And with Francis growing up, would also come the extra responsibility of teaching him to read and write.

Hyrum kneeled beside Francis and put a hand on his shoulder. Francis' blond hair was nearly over his ears, and it drew much attention amongst the natives.

"Will you be my little man while I'm away?" asked Hyrum with a smile.

"I mummy's lit'le man," insisted Francis with a stern look and a pout.

"Yes, you're mommy's little man, aren't you?" replied Hyrum with a chuckle.

Then standing and kissing Julia again, Hyrum said, "Ian is nearby, and Amanda. Let them know if you need anything."

Julia smiled. "Amanda needs 'my' help. Being large with child as she is."

"Aye, indeed," agreed Hyrum. "Nonetheless, call for Ian if you need anything."

"I will," promised Julia.

With that, Hyrum turned and walked to the wagon where one of his hired men waited with the oxen hitched and ready. Hyrum needed to make the trip to Port Elizabeth once every six months or so to either sell wool or to purchase supplies that they couldn't grow or make for themselves. Julia had gone with him on a few occasions, but that became too difficult when she was pregnant and the difficulty was compounded with the new baby. It would take Hyrum four days to reach Port Elizabeth, one or two days to conduct his business, it would then be another four days home. A week and a half against the wildness of Africa would seem like a month to Julia.

Three years earlier
Port Elizabeth
1841

"Goodbye, dear child," exclaimed Amanda's mother, Mrs. Barnes, as Ian and Amanda's wagon began moving alongside that of Hyrum and Julia's own wagon. Mr. Barnes stood nearby and fought to hold back his tears as their only child departed in the care of another man. It would be the first time that they would be separated from her.

"Goodbye, mother. Goodbye father," cried Amanda. "We'll visit within a year's time. I promise."

Julia looked on with a sense of longing. She wasn't entirely emotionally connected to the immediate farewells, but the scene before her cast her mind back to a similar scene, not so long before, outside Brentwood Hall. How she still missed Lord and Lady Hammond!

Amanda may be able to visit within a year, she thought. *But I'll never see Lord and Lady Hammond again!*

Hyrum seemed to sense how she felt, and he placed an arm gently across her shoulders and pulled her closer. He realized that Ian and he would never see their mother or sisters again either, but he also knew that Julia would feel her loss more deeply than he could possibly feel his own. Adding to the weight of concern for his wife was the knowledge that she had followed his dream, and he loved her for striving every day to make it her dream.

She's never once expressed regret, he thought. *I'm sure she must feel it sometimes, but I'm afraid to ask.*

Hyrum thought that he had seen a look of shock or regret on Julia's face as their ship had approached the harbor, and she had gotten her first look at Port Elizabeth. He wondered whether she had observed a similar look of shock on his own face, for truly he had never seen a more miserable looking place than the weather-beaten, dry rotted buildings that constituted Port Elizabeth. *Surely,* he thought, *the town was named more out of disdain for Elizabeth, than for honor.*

Though small, Port Elizabeth had come to some prominence being the only location suitable as a port on the southeastern tip of Africa. It was strategically placed to benefit the Queen's need to move soldiers and equipment inland to fight the natives.

After finding temporary lodgings in Port Elizabeth upon their arrival, Hyrum had lost little time in securing a wagon and other supplies. He was not only anxious to remove his family from the town, but he was anxious to push on to their land grant near Grahamstown.

Their arrival in Port Elizabeth had been warmly welcomed by the people of the town, most of whom genuinely anticipated the arrival of each ship and the additional settlers. The new arrivals were often the closest connection that they had with England, and they questioned at length anyone who would allow them regarding the politics and happenings of the homeland. They had particular interest in their new queen Victoria. Julia had urged Hyrum and the others to remain silent about her own relationship with the Queen as she didn't want to appear boastful or to expose herself and her family to possible requests for favors that she was powerless to fill. *To be sure,* she thought, *who would believe me were I to tell them? Their curiosity would surely demand to know how and why I came to Africa, and why I didn't stay at court. The constant retelling would undoubtedly bring sadness to Hyrum.*

The new arrivals were often seen as insurance of sorts by other settlers. The fresh arrivals helped to secure their own safety and a continuance in the untamed land. The additional settlers brought with them a perceived strength in standing against native rebellions.

There was also an undesirable class of residents in Port Elizabeth that anticipated preying on the naivety of new settlers. They would try and sell them deeds to land that didn't exist, or unneeded supplies. They would fill settlers' minds with fears of beasts and natives and then offer their own services as a guide and protector to the settlers' final destination.

The ship's captain had issued a general warning to the passengers to be wary of anyone that seemed too anxious to meet them, or who offered flattery on a grand scale. Such were likely not to be trusted.

It was under these circumstances that Hyrum approached Port Elizabeth with friendly caution. Mr. Barnes, on the other hand, displayed little caution. He immediately set about securing accommodations for a law practice, and he made it a point to view everyone that he met as a potential client.

Hyrum observed that too many people of the town were anxious to know his business, and word travelled quickly that he was headed for Grahamstown to raise sheep. There were many offers to sell him sheep, supposedly at a lower price than could be obtained in Grahamstown. Though Julia thought it a good idea to take advantage of a lower price, Hyrum opted to wait and purchase in Grahamstown.

"It's four days to Grahamstown," Hyrum told Julia. "I've no desire to herd sheep all that way. Surely, you don't wish to drive the wagon four days running."

"Indeed not," Julia replied.

"Surely, there will be an ample supply of sheep in Grahamstown," Hyrum said with confidence. "And we may not be getting the best information regarding the prices in Grahamstown."

Julia smiled and hugged Hyrum. "You're a brilliant man!"

Hyrum seemed to enjoy the compliment and continued. "Undoubtedly, there is the chance of meeting a lion on the way. I have little interest in feeding sheep to lions."

At the mention of lions, Julia's brow furrowed.

Hyrum smiled. Having raised Julia's concern of lions gave him the opportunity of being her protector, and he relished the role.

"Don't let it concern you, my dear. I'll be purchasing a gun before we leave Port Elizabeth. If we see a lion, we'll soon enough have a pelt."

Julia pursed her lips. "I do hate guns!" Then she added with a smile, "Do you even know how to use one?"

"Of course, my dear," Hyrum replied with confidence.

With the final goodbyes exchanged between Amanda and her parents, the two wagons slowly made their way along the dusty streets and out of Port Elizabeth.

"Have you ever seen a more miserable looking town?" Ian asked Hyrum with a chuckle.

"Indeed not, my good man," Hyrum replied with a smile and in his best high-society accent.

"I notice that you reserved your judgement until we left the town," smiled Amanda.

"There's little point in raising the ire of the residents, now is there?" Ian replied.

Julia certainly agreed with the assessment of Port Elizabeth and its surrounding locale. There were few trees and the grass was a brown color that she had rarely seen in England. Only a few of the buildings had been constructed of stone and none were of brick. There also seemed to be a serious scarcity of painting supplies.

Looking straight ahead and in almost a whisper, Julia said, "And that may be the best that this land has to offer."

Hyrum heard her comment and knew that she only expressed what he too was thinking. He looked at Julia and saw the track of a tear on her face.

"I'll figure out a way to grow some flowers at Grahamstown, Julia," Hyrum promised.

Julia looked at him and smiled.

"In fact, I'll grow some bushes and keep them trimmed. It will be like Brentwood Hall," he smiled.

"It will be lovely," Julia smiled and kissed him.

They hadn't traveled far from Port Elizabeth before they started seeing animals that they had only heard about.

"Look," gasped Amanda, pointing to small stand of trees. "You can just see the head of a giraffe above the trees."

As the wagons moved a little closer to the trees, the giraffe's entire body came into view as well as two other giraffes that were also feeding on the trees.

"Well I never…" exclaimed Ian.

As the group admired the giraffes, their approach disturbed several zebra that they hadn't yet noticed. They were startled when the zebra dashed from the trees and ran as a group across their path and on to another stand of trees.

The group was cautious as they approached a rhinoceros that was directly in their path in the later afternoon.

"I've heard that these old chaps have bad attitudes," said Hyrum. "We'd best keep our distance."

"If he expresses his bad attitude, I'll answer with my gun," Ian replied with a hand reaching beneath his seat to feel for his new gun.

Hyrum laughed. "I'm not sure that you know how to use it. I think that Julia is the only person here with shooting experience."

"And I dislike guns very much," Julia insisted.

"But you did go on fox hunts, did you not?" asked Amanda.

"Well a fox is a fine sight different than a rhinoceros, I assure you," Julia smiled. "And indeed, I have been on a fox hunt, but I enjoyed it a good measure less than the others, and no fox came to harm as a result of my actions."

"Aye, but you would kill a threatening beast, would you not?" asked Ian.

Julia looked at the rhinoceros and then back at Ian. "I don't see a threatening beast," she smiled.

"Aye, but were he running in this direction, would he not be threatening?" pressed Ian.

"He would indeed be threatening," Julia conceded.

"Aye," smiled Ian. "And you would shoot him?"

Julia smiled and touched Hyrum's arm. "Indeed not! I have Hyrum with me."

Ian smiled and looked at Amanda. "Amanda might well grab the gun before I had opportunity."

"I very well might," smiled Amanda.

Hyrum pulled the wagon to a stop. "I'm not entirely certain that our guns would stop a rhinoceros regardless. And until he decides to let us pass, we'd best wait here."

"This could take hours," observed Ian.

"Indeed, it could," replied Hyrum.

After a few moments, Ian inched his wagon closer to the rhinoceros.

"I don't think that's wise," called Hyrum.

Ignoring his brother's warnings, Ian continued in the direction of the beast.

"That isn't wise," repeated Hyrum to Julia. "Especially with Amanda aboard."

Julia looked at Hyrum and smiled. "I dare say that Amanda encouraged it. Neither he nor she is as cautious as you and I."

Still watching Ian's wagon, Hyrum replied, "Certainly not. But we have Francis to care for. He'll surely become more cautious when they have a child."

"We'll see," replied Julia.

As Ian and Amanda's wagon inched closer to the waiting beast, it lifted its head and looked directly at them. Hyrum's heart raced as he watched the standoff.

"Ian," he said quietly, "don't go any closer."

From their wagon, they could see that Ian had pulled his gun out from beneath the seat and was pointing in the direction of the rhinoceros. Suddenly, there was a puff of smoke and the crack of a gunshot. Julia flinched at the sound.

The shot had been aimed directly over the top of the oxen heads startling them, and they began to run toward the rhinoceros. Whether the shot hit the rhinoceros or not wasn't clear, but it began to run also.

As Ian fought to control the oxen before they upset the wagon, he dropped his rifle to the ground. Amanda held tightly to Ian and her hair flew behind her. Julia and Hyrum could hear her screams, but weren't sure whether they were screams of fright or delight.

"Ian!" called Hyrum. "Pull up on the reins! Apply the brake!"

They were beyond hearing range, and Ian was apparently attempting those things with little success.

Hyrum held his wagon steady and seemed to hold his breath for a long time until Ian's wagon finally slowed and stopped.

Hyrum looked with relief at Julia. "That's why we don't approach rhinoceros," he said with relief.

"Indeed," agreed Julia. "Thank you for being cautious."

Hyrum retrieved Ian's gun and pulled his wagon up close to Ian and Amanda's wagon. If he expected to find them in a terrified condition, he was disappointed. Ian and Amanda both had broad smiles on their faces and were laughing.

"Did you see that beast run?" Ian called out as Hyrum and Julia approached. "Do you think I hit him?"

"If you did, I don't think he noticed," replied Hyrum.

"You certainly gave the oxen a fright," observed Julia.

"Yes, but perhaps they will grow accustomed to it," Ian said.

"Perhaps a bit more caution is in order until we understand this land," Hyrum suggested.

Ian and Amanda exchanged grins. "Quite right, Brother," Ian replied, though he wasn't committed to change.

Though it offered little protection, they kept a fire lit all night and slept inside the wagon beds for concern of prowling lions. The group had no trouble with beasts the remainder of the trip to Grahamstown and arrived there on the fourth day. Their arrival had been anticipated and they were well received. Because of struggles against the natives, and the general desire to be surrounded by their own countrymen, the residents of Grahamstown welcomed them warmly.

Chapter Twelve – Settling Elephant Hook
1841
Grahamstown, Africa

Grahamstown was not much of a town at all. By comparison, Port Elizabeth was a metropolis. The town consisted of a small dry goods store, a pub, and a stable. One dirt trail, that fancied itself a road, passed through the village.

A few houses were scattered nearby.

"Well, it's not much to look at," Ian remarked as the wagons neared the village.

Julia looked about at the adobe and wood structures and observed, "There's no church, Hyrum."

"And apparently no school," Hyrum added.

"There's no church," repeated Julia in a tone mixed with surprise and disappointment.

"Where are we?" asked Amanda.

"Grahamstown," replied Ian with a look at her that reflected his surprise that she would ask.

Amanda looked at Ian. She had tears in her eyes. "I know where we are. Where is everyone else?"

"I think this is it," Ian said.

Trying to reassure the group and to strike a positive tone, Hyrum offered, "Most people in these parts are sheep farmers and that requires large tracts of land. There's certainly more people about than it appears."

Julia smiled faintly.

There were only a few people visible near the buildings, most appeared to be English, and some were native. As the wagons drew near the store, it seemed that all the occupants of the store, the pub and the stable vacated to become an informal greeting committee. It was obvious that none of those vacating the buildings were native.

"Welcome to Grahamstown! Welcome!" shouted several of the gathered people. They seemed genuinely pleased to see new residents.

Julia studied the faces of the people. They looked quite different from the paleness of those she was accustomed to in England. She had really never given it much consideration that the sun and the wind would effect such a change of appearance. These faces appeared to have spent a great deal of time in those elements of change. She then looked at Hyrum. *When had his skin become so brown?* she wondered. She noted the same on the faces of Ian and Amanda. She looked at her own hands and Francis' arms and legs and realized that somewhere on the voyage from England the sun had worked its magic on all of them. It had been accomplished so slowly that they had scarcely noticed. *If I were to see the Queen this instant, she'd think me her subject from India,* she thought with a smile. The smile faded from her face when she considered that in a few short years the wind and the sun would sculpt her face in a fashion similar to those before her now.

"Come in and rest yourselves," offered a man from the pub.

"We have little money," replied Hyrum.

"The women and the child need a meal," insisted the man. "You'll have money enough soon. You can pay me then."

Hyrum and Ian exchanged looks, and Hyrum looked at Julia for approval. "Very well. We could use a meal."

Julia suddenly felt uncomfortable when she realized that of the assembled group, there were only three women, and they were of middle age. The men seemed to be staring at Amanda and herself.

"Where are all the women?" she whispered to Hyrum as he lighted from the wagon and turned back to help her down.

Hyrum looked about as though he hadn't noticed, and replied to Julia through an expression on his face of bewilderment.

Many of the group followed them into the pub, but one of them acted as the self-appointed leader and spoke for the group.

"I'm Jacob Spalding. What might you be called?"

"Oh, pardon my rudeness. I'm Hyrum Prince and this is my brother Ian. These are our wives," he said while motioning toward Julia and Amanda.

The men nodded at Julia and Amanda while Jacob continued.

"Do you have land grants near here then?"

"Aye, near Elephant Hook."

"Good country that. The natives aren't very welcoming though."

Hyrum looked at Julia, then back at Jacob. "The Queen's regiment is stationed nearby I understand."

"Oh aye. They keep the natives suppressed for the most part, but regardless, what with stealing sheep or cows, the natives can make life difficult."

"Can't they be reasoned with, or controlled?" asked Ian.

With that, the group laughed and someone called out, "You can nay reason with someone what no speaks your tongue."

"Or them that doesn't have reasoning powers," another called out.

The group laughed again, and Jacob said, "The regiment does a good job of keeping the natives under control, but you'll want to keep close eye on your animals." Then looking at Julia, Amanda and Francis, he added, "And your women and children."

Most of the group began to disperse shortly thereafter, but Jacob remained and continued to share his advice with the newcomers.

"You'll want to see Matthew Crawford about purchasing your sheep. He'll have the most to choose from and the best prices," he assured them. He also instructed them on how best to prepare for the coming summer months.

How odd, summer in January, thought Julia. But, being south of the equator, she knew that would be the case.

His last piece of advice came as a shock to Julia.

"Because of the drought and the success of the English regiment, there are many of the natives that have become 'domesticated' shall we say," Jacob said. Then he lowered his voice a little and looked about before continuing a little more discretely. "We can't keep them as slaves, but because of the drought, they are hungry and many will work for near nothing. They don't understand wages in any event. So, what I'm getting at is that you can hire them and, because you pay them so little, you can hire several. You can live like kings."

Hyrum looked at Ian and smiled and then said to Julia, "Perhaps we'll have as many servants as does Lord Hammond."

Amanda and Ian seemed quite pleased at the prospect.

After their meal, they were soon back in the wagons and headed to Elephant Hook. Julia was extraordinarily quiet. Hyrum looked at her occasionally and tried to make conversation about the surroundings and the unusual animals. He was rather chipper. Eventually, he said, "Isn't it grand that we'll be able to hire so much help for so little! We'll have at least one domestic help for you and several farmer workers for me. Don't you love Africa? You can live like a king here."

Julia turned to Hyrum and said emphatically, "I had little understanding previously, but I now understand that Lord Hammond could hire many servants at a low wage because the villagers had little other opportunity. Even now you might be little more than a servant if we were still in England. We left because we had opportunity to do so, but surely that didn't include taking advantage of others' misfortune."

Hyrum was silent for a moment before responding. When he did respond, he asked, "What would you have me do?"

"Pay your workers a decent wage or don't have workers."

Again, Hyrum was silent for a moment before he looked at Julia and replied, "You're right, my dear. We won't take advantage of the natives for their lack of opportunity. We didn't come here to do such a thing."

Julia was pleased with his decision and laid her head on his shoulder as the wagon creaked along. His honesty and bravery were exactly the reasons that she was drawn to him in England, and she was pleased that he hadn't abandoned them.

It took the group an additional day to reach Elephant Hook. It looked much like Grahamstown and Julia noticed right away that it also had no church.

"Hyrum, have you noticed that neither Grahamstown, nor Elephant Hook has a church?" she asked.

Hyrum looked about and replied, "I hadn't noticed."

"I may not have been as attentive to my church attendance in Exning, but how are we going to raise our children with no church?"

Hyrum thought for a moment and replied, "We brought the Bible with us, we can teach them of God."

"Yes, but who will christen them?"

"Surely there's a minister somewhere in Africa," Hyrum smiled. "We'll find him when the time comes."

The full impact of life outside England was beginning to settle in more deeply on Julia. She knew that this was a wild land, but now she was beginning to realize that if her children were to be taught to read and write, she and Hyrum would have to teach them. If their children were to learn of God, she and Hyrum would have to teach them. If clothing were needed, she may need to learn to provide it. She would need to learn to garden, to sew, and any number of other tasks that she hadn't considered. As she considered on the complexities of life away from civilization, her mind began to race and her head to spin. Soon she recognized that her heart was beating quickly and she was short of breath.

"Are you quite fine, my dear?" asked Hyrum.

Julie smiled briefly and replied, "Yes, quite."

She knew that she wasn't completely fine though and it troubled her. *I mustn't be overwhelmed. I must accept one day at a time and trust in God*, she repeated in her mind several times. *Other women have gone before me. Surely they had fears and struggles.*

Julia looked at Hyrum. There was no sense of fear or concern in his expression. Julia thought that, instead of fear, his expression was of anticipation. Knowing that Hyrum was with her and that he didn't know fear gave her strength and hope.

Julia glanced at Amanda and wondered whether she was experiencing any of the same thoughts. *Amanda looks so young. I wonder whether she's prepared for this life. At least I lived for a time away from the coddling of Lord and Lady Hammond, but she's never been far from the watch and care of her parents.* Julia decided then that she'd need to be sister and mother to Amanda.

Hyrum had been advised that it would be most important to build a shelter for his family when they reached Elephant Hook. After finding their land grant Hyrum and Ian worked together to build shelters. They were simply constructed from upright tree limbs covered with mud in much the same manner as the natives' huts. The roofs of the shelters were covered with long grasses. Once constructed, they provided cool relief from the heat of the day.

"I present to you, my lady, your castle," Hyrum said with a bow and a smile after the structure was completed.

Julia curtsied and told Francis to bow and then they entered.

"It's lovely," Julia said before hugging and kissing Hyrum.

"Well, it's not Brentwood Hall to be sure, but it should keep us dry and away from marauding animals until I can build a proper home."

"It'll do just fine," Julia replied with a smile.

It wasn't long before Hyrum had purchased 100 head of sheep and a couple cows. Julia enjoyed witnessing the satisfaction that he received from being the creator of his own destiny.

For her part, Julia busied herself planting a garden, learning to sew and caring for Francis. With such a small home and a dirt floor, there was little effort required in actually caring for the house.

Her days were pleasant, but she missed regular interaction with other women. Amanda and Ian were the closest neighbors, but their home was a 30-minute walk. Hyrum made certain to take Julia and Francis at least weekly to visit Ian and Amanda, sometimes leaving Julia and Francis there the entire day before collecting them before dusk. Still Julia would have been pleased to make the walk daily with Francis if doing so was safe for a woman and child. She knew that she was not aware of all the dangers of this wild land, but she did know that there were occasionally lions and leopards about, and she was frightened by the natives. She and Hyrum owned a single gun that he usually kept with him. He promised that they would eventually own another, but Julia still hadn't warmed to the thought of using it for its intended purpose. However, if doing so were in defense of her child, she was certain that she wouldn't hesitate.

About once each month, the settlers nearby would congregate at a central location to share a meal, share news from England, and other conversation. The women often discussed their children and their longings for the civility of England. The men often spoke of the weather, their farms and any trouble with the natives.

"Three of my sheep went missing a fortnight ago," one man declared.

"Lions?" another man asked.

"No. Lions would've eaten their fill and would've left the carcass for the vultures. It was the Xhosa," the first man declared.

"That's the second occurrence in as many weeks," a Mr. Richards replied.

Hyrum and Ian listened intently, but as newcomers, they didn't feel it was their place to comment.

Shaking a finger toward the northeast and looking at Mr. Crawford, Mr. Richards continued, "There's another group of natives that've squatted near your place, down by the river. I seen 'em there two days ago." Then looking at the rest of the group, he declared, "My guess is that you'll find at least three nice sheep hides in their squatter village."

"I've not seen them, but I haven't been to that section for a while," replied Mr. Crawford.

"Well, they're there, I assure you," declared Mr. Richards.

"Let's drive them out!" someone called out.

Hyrum looked about to see who said it.

"Aye," agreed Mr. Crawford. "I'll not have squatters on my land. Who'll help me?"

When several men voiced their support loudly, Hyrum looked in astonishment at Ian.

"Well, what will it be Prince?" asked Mr. Richards. "Will you help drive the squatters out?"

Hyrum looked again at Ian. Mr. Richards was clearly addressing both, but Hyrum felt obligated to respond for both he and his brother.

"What exactly do you intend?" asked Hyrum.

Mr. Richards looked at the others as he spoke and back to Hyrum and Ian. "It's clear. We'll use any means necessary to drive them off."

"Does that mean that you'll speak with them first and ask them to leave?" asked Hyrum.

The group laughed at the thought, and Mr. Richards addressed the others. "He's fresh off the boat lads." Then to Hyrum and Ian he added, "Is that what they do in England then? If the farmer don't pay the rent, does the lord ask him to leave kindly? No, he sends the sheriff."

"Surely, the regiment is the sheriff in these parts. Perhaps they should be sent for," offered Hyrum.

"There's no time for that," replied Mr. Crawford in a tone that underscored his growing impatience. "Sometimes, you have to shoot a crocodile to teach the others to stay away from the boat."

"Surely, you wouldn't consider shooting a native?" declared Hyrum.

"Any means," replied Mr. Richards slowly and firmly as he locked eyes with Hyrum.

Hyrum met his glare and replied steadily, "We'll have no part of it." With that, he placed a hand on Ian's shoulder and squeezed as a signal that it was time to leave.

Hyrum and Ian found Julia and Amanda and left the gathering. Julia and Amanda were surprised that the men would insist that they leave so soon. It was obvious to Julia and Amanda that their husbands were troubled. After they were in the wagon, Julia stated, "You seem upset. Did something happen?"

Hyrum explained that there were squatters on Mr. Crawford's land and that the group wanted to drive them out 'with any means'.

"What do they mean 'with any means'?" asked Amanda.

"Just as it sounds," replied Ian.

"Surely they don't mean to use force," replied Julia.

Hyrum looked at Julia and stated, "Indeed they do. In fact, I suspect that there are some that would delight in bloodshed."

Julia and Amanda gasped. "What will you do?" asked Julia.

Hyrum looked at Ian and replied, "We're going to warn the natives."

"You don't speak their tongue," observed Amanda. "How will you communicate with them?"

"I don't know yet," replied Hyrum.

"Some of them do speak, or at least seem to understand, rudimentary English," Ian offered. "Or perhaps we can compel one of the native workers from another farm to go with us."

Hyrum thought for a moment, then replied, "Yes, perhaps. But, would that be safe for them, if their employer discovered it I mean?"

"Is it safe for the two of you?" asked Julia. "Are the natives to welcome you into their village so easily?"

"Yes, it would be best if you took a native with you," agreed Amanda.

"Who would you recommend?" asked Ian to no one in particular.

All looked at Hyrum, and after a moment's consideration, he responded, "We'll be on Mr. Crawford's land, will we not? If we hurry, we can deliver Julia and Amanda to our home and you and I can go directly to Crawfords'.

We won't go too near the house, and perhaps we can find and compel a worker to accompany us."

"Let's be off then," replied Ian.

"Please hurry, while you still have the light of day," Amanda urged.

"And before the others discover your plans," Julia advised.

As Hyrum tried to coax a faster pace from the beast pulling the wagon, Julia expressed her concerns. "Hyrum, we've not been in Grahamstown a year, and discord's already wedged itself between us and our neighbors."

Hyrum smiled at Julia in an attempt to calm her fears. "Nay, we needn't have discord. The farmers want the natives off their land and that's what Ian and I will attempt to accomplish. The rest needn't care that it is accomplished without violence."

Julia was quiet for a moment before she responded, "I hope you're right."

As the wagon rolled along, Julia prayed for Hyrum and Ian's safety and thought how different Africa was from England. *Will this land ever be tamed?* she wondered. *Is this really my new home?* At that moment, Hyrum pointed with some excitement to the hillside. Coming over the crest of the hill was a group of female elephants, some with calves in tow.

"What a glorious sight!" Hyrum declared.

As she watched the group work their way slowly down the hill and toward a stand of trees, she noticed the female elephants helped their calves around obstacles. She gasped when one small calf fell over a downed tree trunk, but smiled with pleasure when two of the nearest adult females rushed to the small one and gently lifted it back to its feet.

What a glorious sight indeed, Julia thought. *There's only one way to see such wonders, and they aren't found by staying safe in England.* Her next thought surprised her, and she found that her eyes began to moisten. *Hyrum and Ian are like the female elephants rushing to the aid of their young. The natives will fall prey to predators without their assistance.* When she thought this, she glanced at Hyrum and then at Ian. Both seemed fearless, both true to their convictions. *Would they ever have opportunity to stand for the weak in England as they do here in this wild land? I think not.* Turning her attention back to the elephants, she thought, *May this land always stay wild and free.*

Julia, Amanda and Francis were left at the small home of Hyrum and Julia, and Ian left with Hyrum for the natives' makeshift village. They weren't entirely certain where to find the village and knew that Mr. Richards and his men would have the advantage in that regard.

"If we can find a native working for Mr. Crawford that will assist us, he'll undoubtedly know where the village is," observed Ian.

"A capital idea, Ian," replied Hyrum. "And we've likely gotten the jump on them. Wouldn't you suspect that they'll wait for the social to end before they set out?"

"Without a doubt."

"Then let's make haste," urged Hyrum.

The sun was uncomfortably low in the western sky before Hyrum and Ian reached Mr. Crawford's ranch.

"We'd better find an English-speaking native soon," observed Hyrum. "I'm not keen on approaching the natives' village after dark."

"Well said, brother," agreed Ian.

Anticipating that they'd find a farm worker near the barn, and with the barn providing cover from others who might be in the house, Hyrum and Ian left their wagon and hurried toward the barn. The door of the barn was on the side opposite their approach. They stopped short at the edge of the barn and moved quickly along the barn wall until they reached the corner. Little did they realize that a native farmhand had exited the barn and was coming around the barn in their direction. As Hyrum stepped around the corner, he ran directly into the farmhand. The surprise was great for both of them, and though they resisted, yells of fright escaped both their mouths.

Reacting with the speed he learned in the bush, the farmhand picked up a stone and in an instant had cocked his arm back ready to throw.

Hyrum held up both hands. "Wait, no. Don't throw," he urged desperately as he stepped backward. "We're friends."

The farmhand seemed to relax ever so slightly.

"We need help," offered Ian.

The farmhand jerked his arm backward again as though he would throw the rock.

"No! Please!" Hyrum said. Then he motioned to Ian and himself and the native and said, "Friends."

"How I know you friends?" asked the farmhand.

"We have no weapons," Ian said as he held out his hands, palms up. Hyrum followed suit and the farmhand was pacified.

"What you want, friends?" he asked.

"We need your help," Hyrum repeated.

"Why?"

"Is there an Xhaso village on Mr. Crawford's land?" asked Hyrum.

The farmhand remained silent.

"Some sheep were killed," Ian told him. "And there are men determined to place the blame on the Xhosa."

"The men will be coming to drive the Xhosa away with force," Hyrum said.

"Why you need me?"

"We need you to speak with the Xhosa and tell them that they must leave," replied Hyrum. He then held his hands up as though he were holding a gun. "It would be very bad if the Xhosa stay where they are."

"How I trust you?"

"We have nothing to offer you, but our promise," Hyrum stated.

The native studied them for several moments, and finally said, "We go."

Hyrum and Ian breathed a sigh of relief and walked back with the farmhand to the wagon. The farmhand led them a short way on a narrow trail. They then walked for some time before they came near to the village.

"You stay," he said pointing to the ground, he then left the wagon and disappeared into the trees.

It was soon dark and the brothers began to feel a little vulnerable being in the bush without weapons.

"Do you think he'll come back?" Ian whispered.

"Aye, he'll be back," whispered Hyrum in return. "My concern is who he'll bring with him, or who may find us before he does come back."

Ian looked about and replied quietly, "Or what will find us."

"Let's give it a few more moments. If he isn't back, I think that we can get into that tree," Hyrum whispered with a nod toward a tree with a gnarled trunk that would allow for good climbing grip.

"If he isn't back, let's get out of here," urged Ian.

Hyrum's white teeth pierced the darkness as he said with a smile, "Do you think you could find your way in this blackness?"

"Quite right," Ian whispered.

Hyrum held up a hand to silence Ian and motioned toward a soft noise that sounded like a bird. Ian slowly turned his head in the direction that Hyrum pointed. They both listened intently. Suddenly, Hyrum felt a hand on his shoulder, and he gasped and jerked away from it. His heart raced madly, but he didn't see anyone.

"You come," a voice whispered in the darkness right next to him.

Hyrum recognized the voice of the farmhand, and his heart slowed just a little. *How did he get so close without us hearing him?* Hyrum wondered. *How long had he been there? Had he heard us talking?*

Hyrum looked at Ian and could see nothing but a toothy smile that had formed on Ian's mouth. *My little brother thinks my fright quite humorous.*

They hadn't walked far before Hyrum sensed others about him. *How many are there?* he wondered. His heart raced again to know how completely they were at the disposal of the natives.

A small fire burned in the center of the makeshift village, and near the fire sat several men. The men looked up as Hyrum and Ian were escorted into the ring of firelight. One of the group, without a doubt the oldest, motioned for them to sit. Hyrum and Ian exchanged looks and sat on the ground.

As Hyrum looked about the group, he noticed that the farmhand who had led them there had shed his English clothing and wore only the traditional cloth about the loins.

Soon, the man who had directed them to sit started speaking, and the farmhand began interpreting in broken English.

"What you called?"

Hyrum put his hand on his chest and said, "Hyrum Prince." Then motioning to his brother, "Ian Prince."

"Why you come here?"

Hyrum glanced beyond the chief and saw the unmistakable hide of a sheep hanging against a tree. The chief caught his glance and slowly turned his head in the direction of the hide and then back to Hyrum and Ian.

"The English aren't happy that some of their sheep are missing," replied Hyrum.

"The Xhosa not happy. Many animals gone. Xhosa are hungry."

"The English will come soon and drive you from this place," Hyrum warned.

"This Xhosa land. Drive Xhosa from their home?"

"The English own the land now," replied Hyrum "And they will drive you from it."

The chief laughed and the other natives also laughed. Then the interpreter said, "No one owns land. Do elephants own land?"

Hyrum looked at the farmhand and said, "Tell the chief that the English will come soon and will force them from this land. He should take his people and leave before the English do this."

After a few moments the chief replied through the interpreter, "Why you tell us this? English not like the Xhosa."

"We have no desire to see harm come to you," replied Hyrum.

The chief thought for a few moments before he stated, "We leave Hyrum Prince. You friend of Xhosa."

Hyrum and Ian nodded approval and stood to leave, but the old chief held up a hand and spoke. Hyrum and Ian looked at the farmhand for interpretation.

"You no spear. Not safe in bush. Many lion." Then motioning to the farmhand, the chief continued, "Good warrior with you. You be safe."

Hyrum and Ian nodded their appreciation, and the farmhand grabbed a spear and led them from the safety of the fire.

At the wagon, the farmhand stated, "You go now. No lion in wagon. You be safe."

"Thank you. Please encourage them to leave Mr. Crawford's land," Hyrum replied.

"You go now," the warrior-turned-farmhand repeated.

Hyrum turned the wagon toward home, and they slowly made their way in the darkness.

"That was easy," offered Ian.

"Aye. They knew why we were there," replied Hyrum.

"What do you mean?" asked Ian.

"While we waited in the dark outside the camp, our guide had already negotiated for us."

"Oh, aye," agreed Ian. "We're probably lucky that our ox wasn't eaten while we were there."

"Perhaps," agreed Hyrum. "Or maybe there aren't so many lion about as the Xhosa say there is."

Julia and Amanda were relieved when Hyrum and Ian pulled up to the small home.

"We were so worried," Amanda cried when they entered the house.

Julia and Amanda greeted their husbands with hugs and kisses.

"Was everything quite alright then?" asked Julia.

"Yes, quite right," replied Hyrum as he hung his hat on a hook.

"We spoke with the Xhosa, and they agreed to leave," Ian said.

"Oh, I'm so glad," Amanda smiled.

"Where will they go?" asked Julia.

"It's hard to say, but they must get off Mr. Crawford's land, to be sure," Hyrum replied.

"Will they go tonight then?" asked Amanda.

"Indeed, we think they will," replied Ian. "They aren't entirely pleased with the prospect, but they will leave."

Hyrum looked about with concern. "You'll stay here tonight," he said to Ian and Amanda. "It's much too late to be out."

"We'll be quite alright," Ian offered.

But Julia wouldn't hear of it. "No, of course you'll stay here with us," she said.

Ian looked at Amanda, but it was clear that she had no desire to venture out into the African countryside at such an hour.

"Very well then, we'll stay," Ian agreed.

Julia retrieved some spare blankets and made a quick bed for Ian and Amanda. "I'm sorry that it isn't a feather bed," she smiled. There wasn't a feather bed in the house, but at least she and Hyrum had a straw mattress.

"We'll be fine," offered Amanda. "Thank you for having us."

They had soon blown out the single candle and retired for the night. The first rays of light had just begun to find their way through the cracks in the door when the four were awakened by shouts outside the home.

"Mr. Prince, you in there?"

Hyrum rolled over and looked at the door, not certain whether he had actually heard his name.

"Mr. Prince!"

There it was again, and both Hyrum and Ian were on their feet and pulling on their trousers. Julia and Amanda were also aroused from their sleep by the commotion.

"Hyrum, who is it?" asked Julia sleepily.

"It sounds like Mr. Richards," Hyrum responded as he reached for his hat.

"What does he want at this hour?"

"I'm sure I don't know, but it must be urgent."

Hyrum and Ian walked outside to find Mr. Richards and several of the men that had been at the gathering the previous day. The men had various weapons with them, including some guns.

Hyrum and Ian exchanged looks, and Hyrum called out "Good day, gentlemen."

Without the cordiality of a greeting, Mr. Richards declared, "The natives are gone!"

"Aye?" asked Hyrum.

With more emphasis, Mr. Richards again declared, "The natives are gone!" And added, "We think that you may know something of their departure?"

"The natives are gone? That's well," declared Hyrum.

"And what do you know of it?" asked another man in the group.

Hyrum looked at Ian and back at the group before he responded. "Aye, we invited them to leave."

"And did you invite them to stay on your land also then?" asked Mr. Richards loudly.

Inside the house, Francis was awaken by the disturbance and started to cry. Julia picked him up and cradled him in her arms.

"What do these men want?" asked Amanda. "Why do they want to cause trouble?"

Julia peered through the doorway. Her stomach ached to see Hyrum and Ian standing in front of the angry crowd.

"The English have been fighting to take this land from the natives for a long time. Some of these men may have lost family members in the struggle. I suppose that they don't want to give an inch of the land back for fear of encouraging the natives to seek for more," replied Julia.

"What will they do?" asked Amanda.

"I don't know."

Outside, Hyrum responded to Mr. Richards' pointed question. "No sir, there was no invitation extended."

Mr. Richards smiled and replied, "Well said. We were concerned as to where your loyalties lay. It would be concerning if a new settler, such as yourself, appeared to side with the natives." Many in the crowd voiced their agreement, and turning to the other men, Mr. Richards exclaimed, "Mr. Prince is with us."

Hyrum and Ian looked at each other, and Ian whispered, "What are you going to do?"

Before Hyrum had a chance to respond, Mr. Richards ordered, "Get your gun, Prince. We got some Xhosa to drive off."

The group of men shouted with joy and some turned to leave, but Hyrum raised his hands high and called out to them. "Hold up. Hold."

The group stopped and turned to face Hyrum and Ian.

"What is it, Prince?" Mr. Richards demanded.

"I'll have no part of this!" Hyrum declared.

Many of the men protested loudly, and Mr. Richards held up his hand to silence them.

"Pardon me, Mr. Prince, I don't think that I heard you correctly," snarled Mr. Richards.

"Without a doubt, you heard me. I'll have no part of violence."

"Perhaps your brother will go for you then," replied Mr. Richards.

Hyrum and the group looked at Ian, but Ian didn't respond.

Hyrum whispered to Ian, "What are you going to do, old man?" but Ian looked at the ground.

"He stays here," Hyrum called to the group.

The displeasure of many in the group was evident on their faces, and again they vocalized their protestations.

"Very well then," smirked Mr. Richards. "Let's go men," he called out to the others.

"Not so fast!" called Hyrum.

The group stopped and faced Hyrum again. Ian was surprised as well.

"I remind you that this land was granted by virtue of the Queen. So long as a Xhosa is on the land, they are subjects of the Queen and under her protection. Only the regiment can drive them off and they aren't likely to do so if the Xhosa have caused no problem."

Mr. Richards' face grew bright red as his anger began to show. After a moment, he declared, "Very well, Prince, but time will demonstrate that you're on the wrong side of this conflict. What will you do when the Xhosa steal your sheep, or your neighbors' sheep, or ravage your house?"

"My mind is firm on this, Richards," Hyrum declared. "Now, good day to you all."

With that, Mr. Richards and the others stormed away, and left Hyrum and Ian standing together outside the small home.

Hyrum looked at Ian and smiled, but he noticed that Ian didn't look happy. Before he could speak, Ian said, "You may have gone too far, Hyrum." Hyrum gave Ian a puzzled look, and Ian continued. "These are our neighbors! We must get along with them if we wish to survive here."

"Should I have granted my approval for violence then?"

Julia and Amanda listened through the door that was opened slightly.

"What if it comes down to violence on the natives, or violence upon us? How would you react then? Would the Queen or her regiment be here to protect you?"

"Ian, your imagination knows no bounds," Hyrum smiled.

With a stern look on his face, Ian responded, "Imagination has little to do with it, you saw those men."

Amanda turned to Julia and said, "I've never seen them disagree so."

"Nor have I," agreed Julia.

The brothers stood silently for a time and both seemed to be looking at nothing in particular somewhere in the distance.

Ian was the first to speak, and in a lowered voice, he said, "Some say that they aren't even human."

Hyrum looked at him in surprise. "Not human?" he asked in more of a declarative tone. "Who?"

"The natives," replied Ian.

"Who declares such a thing?"

"I've heard people talking. Surely, you've heard the same, even before we left England."

"To be sure, I have not," declared Hyrum emphatically. "Perhaps we hear what we want to hear." Then almost as quickly, he added, "Forgive me, old man. That was ungentlemanly of me."

Ian turned and walked a pace or two away.

Hyrum searched for something to say, and offered, "We mustn't listen to all that others say. Of course they'll say that the Xhosa aren't human. Doing so justifies their actions. Of course, the natives are human. They walk and talk. We've seen them laugh. And evidently, they can learn English." Then in an effort to lighten the mood, he added, "Not good English, as we've heard."

Ian turned back to face Hyrum and smiled. "You're right. We have no argument with the Xhosa. Nothing good can come of mob violence."

Hyrum smiled and lightly slapped the back of his brother and said, "Good. Let's have some breakfast."

"Another time perhaps. Amanda and I need to be off."

After Ian and Amanda had left, Julia asked Hyrum, "Do you think that Ian believes that the Xhosa aren't human?"

"Nay, he doesn't believe such absurdity. Mr. Richards just had him upset."

Little else was said on the subject. Rains came several days later, and the Xhosa moved off the land on their own accord. Julia was outside their home when the Xhosa passed by on their way out of the valley. One of the men left the group and walked toward Julia. Her heart raced as the native drew near. She wanted to run, but didn't want to display her fear. Her heart raced, but she held her ground. The native stopped several paces from her and laid a small bundle on the ground and motioned to it. As he walked back to the moving group of Xhosa, Julia retrieved the bundle and unwrapped it. Inside was a string made of sinew, and on the string were several glass beads. *Where would they have gotten the beads?* she wondered. *They must be of great value to them.*

Julia smiled and put the strand around her neck.

Chapter Thirteen - Shipwrecked
November 1817

Subria couldn't be sure how long she had been on the ship. She and the other slaves were forced to spend so much time in the darkness of the lower deck that to ascertain whether it was day or night became impossible. At first, it seemed that she could distinguish days by the hunger pangs in her stomach. But, according to her reckoning, by the third day, the food smelled so putrid Subria and many others refused to eat. *I'll never eat again,* she vowed. *If I die, all the better.*

One day, while on the upper deck, Subria heard one of the Swallows yelling at other Swallows. She expected that he was one of the chief Swallows, because he seemed to be very demanding. Though she didn't understand, she knew by his gestures he was angry with the other Swallows regarding something to do with the slaves.

"If they don't eat, whip them until they do," the lieutenant ordered. "If they still don't eat, whip them dead."

The young crewman receiving the orders looked hesitantly at the slaves and then back at the lieutenant.

"They'll eat or they'll die by the whip," yelled the lieutenant. "If you hesitate, I'll whip them meself and then finish with you," the lieutenant yelled. "They aren't worth spit if they don't eat."

"They're nay worth spit if they're dead," the young crewman muttered softly, but not so softly that the lieutenant didn't hear.

"Would you defy me order, boy?" barked the lieutenant. "Would ye?"

The lieutenant was now standing chin to chin with the young crewman. Even in the early days of the voyage, especially in the early days of the voyage, the lieutenant was determined to exert his dominance. With other crewman and slaves looking on, the lieutenant felt it particularly necessary to demonstrate his superiority to a young crewman.

The young crewman would have feign been glad to have been able to retract his words, but it was too late. His heart raced and his knees grew weak as he stood so close to his lieutenant. It was clear that the lieutenant was intent on setting an example.

"Aye, aye, sir," replied the young crewman weakly, but he hesitated.

At the moment of hesitation, the lieutenant snatched the whip from the hand of the young crewman and raised it to strike him. Just as the whip began its descent toward its target, an older crewman, with knife in hand, stepped in front of the cowering younger shipmate.

"You'll not lay a hand on the lad," ordered the older crewman.

"Aye?" responded the lieutenant with surprise and lowered the whip. In an instant the lieutenant grabbed his own knife from his side and engaged the knife-wielding crewman. "Aye, not until I've fed your bloodied carcass to the sea."

Until that moment, Subria had felt too weak to pay attention to the arguments of the Swallows. Suddenly cries went up amongst the Swallows as the two men began to circle slowly about each other, occasionally lunging in with the point of their knife and then jumping backward out of reach of the other.

Subria looked about the deck of the ship and saw the other Swallows yelling and cheering with seeming delight. *Surely, these are not human, but devils,* she thought. With all the commotion and attention on the two Swallows, Subria looked at the ship's railing. *While they battle, a person could easily jump into the sea,* she considered. Keeping an eye on the Swallows, she made her way to the railing and looked over. The ocean was fairly calm. Only gentle waves lapped against the sides of the ship. The water was clear and she could see well below the surface to see groups of fish swimming together. Slowly, hesitantly, she placed one foot on the horizontal rope that ran between the upright posts of the railing. The rope tightened under her foot as she shifted her weight onto it.

Just then, a cry went up amongst the Swallows and Subria looked at the fighting men just as the older crewman finished striking a blow across the forehead of the lieutenant. Blood rushed down the lieutenant's forehead and into his eyes. With the swipe of his left sleeve across his brow, he cleared his vision. His sleeve of crimson waving in the air reminded Subria of the war banners that her tribe made of hide dipped in blood before going to battle.

The cut to his forehead seemed to spur a new rage within the lieutenant, and he sprang forward, sinking his blade to the hilt into the older crewman's chest. The knife penetrated the heart and the crewman fell to the deck instantly.

Subria was shocked at the display of aggression and utter cruelty. Though the Swallows weren't human, the terrible scene caused emotions to pour from her. She fell back onto the deck with her face buried in her hands and cried.

The lieutenant stood in the middle of the deck and yelled out loudly as a conquering chieftain would have done. He seemed satisfied that he had established his dominance. Still, taking the whip in hand, he struck the young crewman several times as he cowered before him. After he had sufficiently beat the young crewman, he ordered him to throw the body of the older crewman overboard.

From her prone position, Subria watched as the young crewman dragged the body past her and pushed it under the lower rope of the railing. She jerked involuntarily when she heard the splash moments later.

Whether as punishment for not eating or for fear of trouble, all the slaves were forced below deck. Subria turned her head away as she passed by the lieutenant, but he grabbed her and jerked her back to face him. He was frightfully ugly with the streaks of red oozing from the cut across his forehead.

Subria didn't understand, but he motioned to the railing and said, "I'll throw you to the sharks meself if ye get near the railing again." With that, he pushed her down the stairs into the lower deck.

Tears coursed down her cheeks as she sat with legs curled close to her chest in the dark confinements of the lower deck. Though she tried, she couldn't control the convulsions that rocked her body as she sobbed quietly. She didn't cry for the loss of her parents, or her brothers. She didn't cry because of her capture and separation from her village, or the prospect that she would never be free to know the open spaces of Africa again. Instead, she cried only for want of relief from the darkness, the hunger and the cramped cage.

She wasn't startled when she heard the familiar whisper of an older woman next to her. "You must eat and save your strength, or you won't live to see very many more days."

"I don't want to live."

"Are you very certain?"

"Yes, aren't you?"

There was silence a few moments before the old woman whispered again. "I've known many seasons, some good, some bad, and some very bad. This season is very bad. I've learned that seasons change. The good turn to bad and the bad turn to good."

"How could this turn to good?" Subria asked with a strong sense of anger in her voice. "We'll never be free again!"

"You're always free in your mind if you choose to be."

The words were quiet and simple, but they pierced Subria's mind and heart with great force. *Free in my own mind?*

The old woman continued. "You've a choice to make, but the choice is yours alone. You can choose captivity in your mind, or freedom. If you choose freedom, you can do all things and be happy."

"How do I choose freedom in my mind when my body is bound?" Subria asked incredulously, but the old woman sensed a spark of sincerity.

"You must start with forgiveness."

"Forgiveness?!" Subria asked in a firm whisper. "Forgiveness of who?"

"All beings and all creatures. Especially those who cause you harm."

"Swallows? Never!"

"Then you'll never be free, nor happy."

Subria was quiet for several minutes. *Forgiveness never made a chief strong or a warrior brave.*

"You speak of forgiveness, but do you forgive these Swallows?" Subria asked her cellmate.

"I didn't say it would be easy," came the response.

"Maybe not easy, but do you forgive these Swallows?"

The answer was simple, direct and quietly given. "Yes."

"How can you forgive them?" Subria asked.

"Because I love them."

Though it was completely dark, Subria turned her face in shock toward the old woman. *Love them? I hate them*, Subria thought.

"That's not possible. You lie." As soon as she said it, Subria felt badly and wanted to retract her words. *How have I come to be so disrespectful?* she wondered. "I'm sorry, please forgive me," she quickly added.

"Of course I forgive you," came the quiet response. "Still you doubt my ability to forgive the Swallows."

Subria was quiet for several moments. "Yes," she whispered.

"When you're ready…" whispered the old woman.

"How has your forgiveness made you free?" Subria asked.

"I'm free to forgive."

"I'm free to forgive also," whispered Subria.

"Then do it."

"I have no desire."

The old woman let Subria's comment linger in silence for a few moments for impact before she responded. "Then you aren't free."

"Suppose that I wanted to have desire, how would I gain it?" Subria asked.

"From God. He died for you so that you could have the desire and the power to forgive."

"God? Who is God?"

Over the course of the next couple of hours, the old woman told Subria of her conversion to Christianity while living and serving as a slave in the house of Christians. Though it seemed odd to the old woman that those who professed a belief in the God of Christianity would own slaves, the power of their story and a feeling inside her was enough to overcome her doubts. She also forgave them.

Subria felt an unusual peace inside as the old woman spoke of her conversion. Nonetheless, she remained firm in her hatred of the Swallows.

Though she had listened intently to the old woman, Subria also noticed that the ship had begun to pitch and roll with vigor. Obviously, a storm was engulfing the ship. The old timbers of the ship creaked and groaned angrily against the force of the wind and waves as though having been awakened suddenly from a peaceful sleep. As the movement of the ship continued to grow more violent, Subria and the old woman stopped trying to speak over the rage. The increasing intensity of the storm also increased the intensity of the fearful cries of the caged slaves. Having never experienced anything like an angry sea, they cried out in terror for deliverance from their dark bondage. The constant motion caused many to vomit repeatedly, and the stench was overpowering.

It seemed that nature itself was aware of the unholy business engaged in by this ship and was intent on its destruction. The ship that presented such a majestic image on a placid sea was now tiny and impotent against the power of the wind and the waves.

Above deck, the captain and his crew were doing all that they could to keep the ship afloat and straight with the waves. The storm had been observed in the distance, but had engulfed the ship rapidly, and with surprising force. The captain had called initially for the main sails to be lowered to keep them from being torn to shreds in the torrential wind and rain, and to keep the mast from being broken.

As the wind continued to gain strength, the captain called for additional sails to be furled. Still, enough sails were in place that he was able to hold the wheel against the force of the wind and keep the ship into the waves.

The storm raged the remainder of the day and night and into the next day. Though weak from hunger and the lack of sleep, Subria gave thought to little else than hoping for the storm to pass. She and the other slaves cried out loudly when water began raining down through the planks of the deck above. The cool moisture was initially a relief from the heat of the lower deck, though the increased humidity made breathing even more difficult than usual.

Subria cried out to the old woman, "We're going to die! Not even your God can save us!"

Subria expected a calming response and encouragement from the old woman, but there was none. "We're going to die!" Subria called out again, but again there was no response. The ship pitched toward Subria and she felt the full weight of the old woman against herself, pushing her more heavily against the cage door. The old woman was limp, and her head lay motionless on Subria's arm. The ship rolled the opposite direction and the old woman's limp body fell on another woman in the cage, but the other woman pushed her away. Subria was horrified to realize that she was caged with a dead person! Her chest tightened and she was short of breath. In the near total darkness, Subria carefully touched the old woman. She was dead, overcome by the stench, hunger, heat and fatigue. A tear rolled down Subria's cheek, but a part of her envied the old woman.

It wasn't long before Subria heard the large, wooden door covering the entry to the lower deck slam shut against the flood of water that was crashing over the sides of the ship. The blackness of the lower deck was now complete, and the fear intensified. The fear had an energy all its own, and could be felt in the constancy of screams.

Subria could tell that the ship was pitching and rolling more slowly, though the distance traveled with each movement had increased. She couldn't know that the slowed pace of the rolling was caused by water filling the hull. She did feel the crush of the other slaves who were confined with her as they pressed against her with each roll toward her. She was horrified and cried out each time the old woman's body fell on her, and she only gained relief as the ship rolled back the other direction, but then she was pressed involuntarily on the old woman.

The ship was creaking loudly, as though it would break apart. The creaking and groaning of the ship even exceeded the screams of the slaves.

It wasn't long before Subria felt water lap against her side as the ship rolled to the right. Bewildered, she moved her foot about and realized that this water was growing from below and not pouring in from above.

"The ship's filling with water!" she cried out as though someone would be able to do something about it. But her cries blended with the other sounds of distress and were lost.

It wasn't long before the water was above her hip as she sat in the cage. *We're going to die!* she thought. Others were realizing that they were also being buried in water and their cries filled the chambers of the lower deck.

The door covering the latch to the lower deck soon flew open and several Swallows rushed in, each carrying buckets. Subria could see faint outlines of their bodies forming a line as they filled buckets and passed them along to the person behind them. Already the Swallows stood in waist deep water.

It was obvious to Subria that their efforts were useless against the rage of the storm. The water continued to climb higher on Subria until she was chest deep and had to hold her breath as the water completely submerged her with each new roll of the ship.

"The captain's going to lose the ship," a crewman yelled from above, and those that were bailing dropped their buckets and left the lower deck.

Subria looked on in horror as the Swallows hurried up the stairs.

The captain strained against the wheel to keep the ship straight with the waves.

"She's gonna break apart, Capt'n," the lieutenant called out, but the captain gave no indication that he heard or that he would alter his course. If the ship went down, he'd go down with it.

"We should release the slaves," yelled the young sailor who had hesitated with the whip.

"We'll do no such thing," yelled the lieutenant. "The weight of their bodies is helping to keep the ship aright. If they come above deck, the ship will surely roll."

"It will surely roll regardless," the young sailor yelled back above the howl of the wind.

"Man your post, boy," ordered the lieutenant. "Before I throw you overboard!"

Holding tightly to any stationary object, the young sailor hurried away from the lieutenant and disappeared, and the lieutenant's attention was averted elsewhere. Moments later, the young sailor disappeared below deck without catching the notice of the lieutenant.

Subria was surprised to see the dark, shadowy figure of a Swallow descend the stairs. Using a hammer, the Swallow moved quickly, in water to his chest, from cage to cage, stopping only momentarily at each to swing the hammer against the lock. Most locks broke free with one swift stroke, and the slaves fell or climbed out of the cages and into the deepening water. With only the thought of escaping the confines of the cages, many with frenzied minds pushed violently against other slaves causing them to fall into the water between the cages. Many slaves were too weak, or too stiff from sitting in the confines of the cages to immediately stand and move toward the stairs. Their bodies began to clog the passage to the stairs.

Those in Subria's cage were madly pushing against her before the Swallow even neared, and by the time he struck the lock and removed it, she was pressed against the cage door. When the door gave way, she fell from the cage headfirst and into the water. As she struggled to stand, she felt the feet of other slaves pressing on her. Using all her strength, and pushing down on other bodies in the water, she was able to stand just before she gave up all hope of the next breath.

The mass of bodies pressed on each other toward and up the stairs, until finally Subria broke free of the lower deck. The rocking of the lower deck had made it difficult to stand, but with little to hold to, standing on the upper deck was next to impossible. Subria moved as quickly as she could on her hands and knees until she could grasp a stationary object. She sat next to an anchored barrel and held tightly to an attached rope. Others were also trying to negotiate the constantly moving deck on their hands and knees, and Subria looked on in horror as several were washed over the side and into the unhappy sea by a large wave. She wasn't sure why she held on so tightly, other than the look of the raging sea was terrifying. Whereas only hours before she had considered the placid sea a welcomed respite from her bondage, the placidity had given way to a monster, and it terrified her.

"Maarku!" Subria yelled over the strong wind. She hadn't seen him for several days, and just the sight of him filled her with hope and elation. "Maarku!" she yelled again just as the wind blew stinging salt water into her eyes. Squinting against the spray, she could see that he was crawling carefully along the deck. Subria's joy was tempered by Maarku's appearance.

He should have been strong and confident, but he looked weak and appeared to tremble.

"Maarku!" With that, he recognized her voice and looked in her direction. She was sure that she saw a smile cross his face, and he raised his head with more energy. "Maarku," she cried and motioned to the barrel, inviting him to seize its security. As he started to move in her direction, she saw a large wave raise up behind him. Instinctively, she held to the rope with both hands and stretched out her leg toward Maarku. The wave pushed against the side of the ship with the strength of ten elephants, and the ship started to roll in the direction of Subria. The rolling motion put Maarku higher than Subria and he lay outstretched, reaching for her foot. Water crashed onto the deck and hit Maarku, pushing him toward the other side of the ship. Subria could see terror in his eyes as he helplessly began to wash past her. Reaching with all of his strength, he managed to grab and hold fast to her foot. Without premeditation, Subria cried out to the old woman's god for the strength to hold on. It seemed like an eternity before the wave passed over the ship and the ship began its slow roll back to the other side. Only then was Subria certain that there was still a grip on her foot. "Maarku!" she gasped in relief.

Subria pulled her foot close to her, helping Maarku to the relative safety of the anchored barrel. Maarku held fast to the rope about the barrel and Subria momentarily released her own grip and held him tightly.

"Maarku! I thought you'd be washed into the sea!" she cried as she hugged and kissed him repeatedly.

Maarku smiled faintly, and released his grip of the rope with one hand long enough to wrap it about Subria. Then he held tightly to the rope and anchored them both to the barrel.

In exhausted silence, they held on, anticipating each new wave. More slaves were making their way to the deck of the ship and scrambling for something to hold. Soon there were so many slaves on the deck that many were holding the very railings on the sides of the ship for lack of other less treacherous locations.

"Capt'n, if we take another wave like that, she'll surely roll over onto her back!" the lieutenant yelled. For his own safety, he was lashed to the ship near the wheel. The captain had refused to leave the wheel except for brief periods as the storm had raged. In his exhausted condition, he appeared to have not heard the dire prediction.

"Capt'n! She's gonna roll!" the lieutenant yelled again.

The declaration broke the captain from an almost trance-like state, and he glanced at his lieutenant.

"She's nay gonna roll! Get me another forward sail, you blaggard!"

"Aye, Capt'n!"

With that the lieutenant released his lashing and carefully braced himself against the wind and the rocking of the boat to traverse the narrow steps leading down to the main deck. It was only then that he realized that the slaves had been freed. His anger grew as he looked about at the slaves holding to any stationary object. *What in the name of heaven? This is why she's gonna roll!* he thought as he looked about. It was then that he observed the young sailor carefully making his way from the lower deck with hammer still in hand.

"You, boy!" he screamed. "You did this!"

The young sailor looked up in shock. The lieutenant's face was red with anger and his fists were clenched. His wet hair and beard were whipped by the fierce wind like a flag on a pole. The terrifying sight seemed to cause time itself to stall for the young sailor.

"Aaaarh!" the lieutenant screamed as he moved forward toward the young sailor.

Bracing himself against the pitching ship, the young sailor raised the hammer as a defense. But the lieutenant, more experienced in fighting, quickly seized the raised arm of the sailor, while at the same time striking his fist across the young sailor's face. Both men lost their balance and fell to the unsteady deck and were momentarily helpless against the forces of the wind and sea.

More concerned with exacting punishment on the young sailor, the lieutenant was oblivious to the stresses on the ship caused by the high waves and intensifying winds. The ship rolled so far to the starboard side that Subria thought it would roll into the sea. She let out a scream and held more tightly to Maarku. The lieutenant had managed to grab a rope, while the young sailor had only managed to grab fast to the lieutenant's boot. And thus both men lay in their prone positions on the slippery deck. The lieutenant shook his foot vigorously in an unsuccessful attempt to shake the young sailor into the sea.

Suddenly, a loud crack was heard and Subria and Maarku looked up to see a large section of a mast break off and fall, stopping short of hitting the deck as it was tangled in its own rigging.

The ship rolled back to the port side, and the young sailor released his grip on the lieutenant and attempted to stand. The ship rolled so quickly as to render it impossible for the young sailor to maintain his balance before he fell directly into the lieutenant's grasp.

A strange expression of satisfaction, mixed with rage settled on the lieutenant's face as he held tight to the young sailor. The young sailor struggled and yelled out, surely knowing the lieutenant's intention. While the ship continued its port-side roll, the lieutenant grinned a grin of satisfied anticipation. Then just before the ship reached its highest point on the starboard side, he pushed the young sailor downward toward port side. The young sailor let out a yell of desperation, and tried to grab anything stationary. He hit the ropes of the railing and passed right through them and into the sea.

The ship continued its port-side roll past any point of returning, and the internal framework of the ship began to fall apart with thunderous cracking sounds. Shuddering vibrations ran through ship.

The lieutenant looked about in apparent surprise, and grasped on to a mast that was still anchored. It was too late. A gaping hole had ripped open in the upper deck, letting the sea rush in. The ship continued its slow roll into the sea. Slaves and seamen alike were treated with the same merciless anger by the sea without respect to persons. In a rush of adrenaline Maarku held tightly to the barrel despite his weakened condition. Subria tightened her grip on Maarku and watched in an almost surreal fashion as many individuals were swept into the sea, each screaming until their screams were drowned in the sea with them.

Subria screamed until just before she hit the water, then instinctively, she held her breath. The shock of being submersed caused her to lose her grip on Maarku, and she began to panic. She had not been taught to swim, but she kicked her legs vigorously and flailed her arms about in an attempt to reach the surface. All about her was darkness, and it was very disorienting, making it impossible to determine which way was up.

Having deposited much of its cargo into the sea, the ship began to right itself, but broke apart completely under the stresses of the waves. Subria miraculously managed to break above the surface and took in a great breath of air, but also some sea water. Despite the sting of the salted water, she saw a piece of the ship floating next to her and she tried desperately to grasp it.

Maarku had surfaced before Subria, and he had grabbed onto the nearest piece of wood that he could get to. It seemed like an eternity before Subria surfaced, and when she did, he called out to her.

"Subria! Subria!"

She gave no indication that she had heard him, but he reached for her and managed to grasp her hand and pulled her to the relative safety of the wood that he was holding.

"Subria!" Maarku said when she was safely within his grasp. "Are you injured?"

Subria gave no response, and there was no time for conversation. Even then another wave was upon them, as the sea was intent on ripping from them their sole means of survival.

Riding each new wave up and then down again required their constant diligence and required all their energies. Occasionally, their small piece of wood bumped violently into a piece of the ship occupied by others, but they were otherwise unaware and unconcerned whether there was another soul on the sea. The ship was no longer in view, whether it had completely broken up, or whether it had drifted out of their sight, being pushed by the wind and the current, couldn't be determined.

After enduring the wrath of the sea for well over an hour, Subria suddenly realized that the piece of wood nearest their own was occupied by none other than the Swallow who had killed the young crewman. He was a frightful sight. His head wound had reopened and blood streaked his face. He looked weak and scared. She immediately felt the flush of her face as a hatred boiled up inside her. *We must kill this Swallow!* she thought. Diverting her attentions momentarily from the sea and the wind, Subria carefully nodded to Maarku for him to look. Maarku recognized the Swallow instantly.

"Push him into the sea," urged Subria.

Maarku hesitated, looked at the Swallow and back at Subria again.

The rolling sea was pushing the lieutenant's wooden life raft farther from Subria and Maarku.

"Quickly! Push him into the sea," Subria said again with greater emphasis.

Maarku released his grip with one hand from their own wooden float and reached out for the Swallow. The Swallow was just beyond his reach, and he stretched as far as he could, but was still just shy of the Swallow. Relaxing his grip ever so slightly with the other hand he was able to touch, but not grasp the Swallow's shirt. In that instant the Swallow raised his head and looked directly at Maarku. Realizing Maarku's intent, the Swallow gripped more firmly to his wooden float, but grinned eerily at Maarku and Subria. Startled and frightened, Maarku completely lost his grip on his own float and instinctively reached out and grabbed ahold of the Swallow's float. With a quick motion, the lieutenant struck Maarku across the face with an elbow. Despite his fatigue, the force was so great as to render Maarku incapable of maintaining a grip on the Swallow's float. Falling back into the rolling sea, Maarku turned and reached for Subria.

"Maarku!" Subria screamed as she reached a hand out for him.

Maarku frantically struggled to reach Subria.

"Maarku!" cried Subria.

In an instant, he was gone, descended beneath the waves that quickly buried him.

"No!" cried Subria. "Maarku!" Holding tightly to the wood, she buried her face in her arms and cried aloud with great sobs.

"Maaaarkuu!" came a taunting cry and laugh over the sound of the wind and waves. Subria looked up to see the Swallow laughing as his float drifted farther from her own.

Subria knew that she would never forget the face or the voice of this Swallow. She was sure that it would haunt her forever. Subria cried until she didn't have energy to cry more.

As the seas began to calm she was afforded a better view of her surroundings. There was not a soul in sight. Not a slave, not a Swallow. By appearances, they had all joined Maarku in the sea. She was now truly alone. No kinsmen, no friends, no tribe, no home.

Subria cried softly until darkness had gathered around her. The seas had calmed to a gentle rolling and stars shined through the parted clouds. All desire to go on living seemed to leave her, but she still held to the wood float. Perhaps it was the hatred of the Swallows that caused her to hold on, or perhaps it was a fear of a watery grave, she didn't know. Regardless, she held on through the lonely night.

Chapter Fourteen – Rocking Chair and Domestic Help
1844
Elephant Hook, Africa

Julia stopped hoeing the garden row and looked up with a start. She had felt for several minutes that she was being watched, and now she was certain that she had heard a noise coming from the direction of the nearby stand of trees. It may have been her imagination, but she wasn't taking any chances. Her baby was asleep in the house and Francis played nearby. The noise could have been anything, maybe it was the wind. Regardless, she immediately dropped the hoe and ran to her son.

"Francis," she said urgently, but quietly. "Come with mommy."

"Why?" asked Francis.

Grabbing her son's hand, Julia said with emphasis, "Don't ask why."

Francis pulled back against her grip. "My horse!" he cried while reaching for the toy on the ground.

Without relaxing her grip, Julia gave him a little slack to reach to the ground for the toy horse. As Francis reached for the toy, Julia looked again in the direction of the trees and then in the direction of the house. The house was still perhaps 100 feet away. Though she had never used it, there was a gun inside, and she was determined that she could use it in defense of her children.

With the toy retrieved, she and Francis hurried for the house.

Maybe it's a lion she thought, *or a native.* She wasn't sure which instilled greater fear.

Why isn't Hyrum home? she cried within her heart.

Hyrum should have been home the day before. She knew that he was aware of her anxieties concerning beasts, and natives, and that he would not delay without necessity.

If there were trouble with either beast or native this close to the house, it was nearly always because of drought and its associated hunger-induced tensions. Hyrum had insured their own reasonable protection against drought by digging a well soon after their arrival and also by forming several basins to catch and hold rain water. It was these basins that were largely responsible for keeping their sheep watered. These same lifesaving basins had to be guarded more closely during times of drought, as they also attracted beasts.

"I don't want to go inside," Francis insisted while leaning backward against his mother's grip, causing her to pull firmly on his arm in response.

Just before Julia reached the door, a dark figure stepped from around the corner of the house. Julia froze in fear, and Francis buried his face inside the folds of her skirt. After nearly three years amongst the natives, Julia spoke almost none of their language, and their very presence frightened her.

The native was tall and muscular. He was wearing little more than a colorful cloth about his loins, a decorative headband and a ring of white fur just beneath each knee. He also carried a single spear and shield.

Instinctively, Julia reached down and felt for Francis' head and drew him close against her leg. Though terrified, her only thought was to get to her baby girl. It had been rumored that natives occasionally stole settlers' children, but Julia had long ago resolved that it would not happen to her children so long as she still had breath.

Though it was an instant, it seemed like an eternity that she and the native stared at each other. The entrance to the house was between them, and Julia knew that she could not possibly get inside. Julia's heart raced and it felt as though she couldn't breathe.

Perhaps I can lure him away from the house, she thought. *But where? I'm completely at his mercy. Natives have no mercy.*

At that moment, the native reached for the door handle, and Julia screamed. Startled, the native looked at her intently and raised his spear.

"Go away!" Julia said firmly and loudly.

The native seemed surprised and hesitated. Julia heard the voice of another native yelling. The yelling caused the first native to hesitate and look in the direction of the person who was shouting.

Though she understood none of the words, Julia recognized the voice of one of Hyrum's workers. With some relief, she watched as he cautiously approached the spear-wielding native. The two men exchanged angry words for several moments before the intruder turned and walked back into the trees. When he did, Julia ran into the house and snatched her sleeping baby into her arms and held her tightly and cried. Her legs felt weak and her stomach ached.

"He mean no harm, only hungry," Julia heard Hyrum's helper say as he stood just outside the door of her small home.

Julia looked up only briefly and nodded her head. She heard the footsteps of the worker as he turned to leave and she called out to him to wait.

"Thank you ever so much," Julia said tearfully.

The worker nodded and turned to leave.

"Wait!" called Julia. She then grabbed what was left of the bread that she had made a few days earlier and handed it to the worker. "Please, give this to him," she said.

"You no should do," cautioned the worker. "Many more come."

"Please, give it to him," Julia insisted.

The worker nodded and left with the bread. Julia knew that he was right, but she couldn't help but think of the poor, hungry children that she had seen in her own country while she traveled with Princess Victoria. *Should I eat, when they don't,* she wondered.

Exhausted, Julia sat in a nearby chair and cradled her daughter. Francis, who had remained quiet stood beside her. He looked terrified and started to climb onto her lap. Holding the baby with one arm, Julia helped pull him up onto the chair and onto her lap. Her only desire was to rock her babies and sing to them. In her heart, she whispered, *"Dear God, these babies are everything to me. Please protect them. And bring Hyrum home safely."*

When she had finished her prayer, she became aware that the doorway had darkened. Someone was there! Startled again, she looked up quickly. The light coming through the doorway was brighter than the light of the room, and it took a brief moment for her eyes to adjust. In that briefest of moments, her heart seemed to fail her. Then, to her joy, she recognized the outline of the figure.

"Hyrum!" she called with unparalleled joy, and with a child in each arm, she nearly bounded from the chair and collapsed into his outstretched arms.

"Julia, my love, I'm so glad you're safe."

"I've tried to be brave," Julia said with a catch in her voice, "but I've missed you so."

"You've been very brave," Hyrum replied with a smile and a kiss on Julia's forehead. "Even now, word of you standing against a warrior is spreading about Grahamstown."

Julia seemed embarrassed.

Francis was getting heavy in her arms, so Julia put him down, and then she settled into Hyrum's arms again and laid her head on his chest. "Don't leave me again, Hyrum," she pled.

"I wish I could promise to never leave you alone, but we know the day will come when I must if even for a short time."

"Indeed. I know," replied Julia quietly.

Hyrum relaxed his embrace and leaned back so that he could look at Julia's face. He had a big smile and after a few moments, Julia asked, "What is it then? Why the smile?"

"I have a couple of surprises for you."

Julia smiled broadly. "Surprises! As in more than one?"

"More than one to be sure," grinned Hyrum as he took her by the hand and led her through the door. "Now don't look," he cautioned.

Julia smiled and placed a hand over her eyes, but Francis had already seen one of the surprises and started squealing, "A puppy! A puppy!"

Julia looked down and saw that Francis was already running and playing with the pup. "He's so adorable!" Julia said.

"He may be adorable now, but he'll make a great watch dog for you when he's older. You'll not have beast or man surprise you again."

Julia smiled and kissed Hyrum. "What's my other surprise then?"

"Come to the wagon and see," Hyrum grinned.

When Julia saw a beautiful rocking chair in the wagon she gasped. "Hyrum! We can't afford a piece of furniture like that!"

Hyrum was already in the wagon lifting the chair out and handing it to his worker.

"You're right, we can't!" he agreed. "But we didn't."

"You're teasing me, Hyrum," smiled Julia. "Where did you get the chair?"

Hyrum pulled an ornate envelop from his pocket and held it out to Julia. It was instantly recognizable as Queen Victoria's own. Tears began to well up in Julia's eyes as she took the letter. This was the first letter that she had received from the Queen since leaving England. She had thought of her friend often, but hadn't been at liberty to initiate correspondence. Now that the Queen had written, Julia would be free to respond.

Julia's hands were shaking with excitement as she read the letter. After she had finished reading, Julia held the letter close to her breast and smiled at Hyrum.

"The Queen is well," Julia said as she carefully ran her fingers over the smooth finish of the chair. "Her subjects love her, and she loves them."

"I'm sure she's a most excellent queen," replied Hyrum. "It was very kind of her to send the chair."

"It was indeed," agreed Julia. "It must have cost her dearly to send it."

"Without a doubt," replied Hyrum. Then he added with a smile, "She has the means though."

Julia clapped her hands together excitedly and said, "Do take it to the house where I may try it."

Hyrum carried the chair to the house and placed it next to the small hearth. Julia immediately sat and began to gently rock, holding her baby. When she did, Francis quickly climbed to her lap. The floor was a little uneven, and the rocking of the chair reflected the pattern of the floor creating a soothing rhythm that soon had both children quietly resting.

"It's absolutely delightful," whispered Julia with a smile.

As Hyrum looked on, he couldn't help but think about the grand chairs that Julia could be sitting in every day had she not chosen to marry him. Despite his best efforts, he knew that he could never give her comparable comforts.

In a tone that suggested his feelings of momentary inadequacy, Hyrum said, "You would have enjoyed many grand chairs if you had stayed at the Royal Court."

Julia stopped rocking and looked at Hyrum. Then, putting Francis on the floor, she stood and wrapped an arm about Hyrum's neck while still holding the little one. "Please don't ever suggest that I would have been better to remain at Court," she said quietly while looking him directly in his eyes. "I chose you over the Court knowing clearly that there would be few grand chairs in my future. Life with you is worth more than all the grand chairs of England! I'll never look back."

Hyrum smiled and kissed Julia, but she wasn't convinced of his confidence in her declaration. "Take the chair to Grahamstown and sell it the next time you go. I'll get along quite fine without it."

Hyrum stood a little taller and smiled. "Forgive my insensitivity. The chair stays and I'll not mention the Court again," he replied.

Hyrum then pulled back with a start. "I nearly forgot!" he declared. "You have another surprise! Perhaps the finest!"

Julia looked surprised. "Another surprise? Hyrum Prince, what will I ever do with you? What is it then?"

"Follow me," Hyrum said as he took Julia by the hand and led her outside to the garden.

In the garden a native woman was bent over using the hoe with great skill and efficiency. Julia looked at Hyrum with an inquisitive look on her face.

Hyrum put his arm around Julia and said with great pride, "I said that we would have domestic help for you and now we do!"

"Hyrum, that isn't necessary! I can get along just fine," Julia protested.

"No doubt you can and you will, but with the drought and all, she needed the work. And with the passel of children that we'll have, you'll need the help," Hyrum confidently stated with a smile.

Julia looked at the woman and then at Hyrum and asked, "Should she be doing such hard work? How old is she?"

"To be sure, I don't know, but I'd say at least 40 years old. But, she's strong."

"And she needed the work?" asked Julia for reassurance.

"Indeed, she did," Hyrum assured her.

Julia smiled and hugged Hyrum, "I approve then."

Chapter Fifteen – The Red Dress
November 1817

Just before first light, Subria was knocked off the wooden float. Startled, she let out a cry, but instead of sinking into the sea she realized that she was being pushed by the sea onto a sandy beach. She struggled to stand, but was overpowered by a fresh wave. Then as she struggled to stand again, the sea wrapped its fingers around her in a desperate attempt to pull her back toward a watery grave. With all her remaining energy, she crawled crying and screaming away from the sea until she had escaped its grasp.

Subria lay exhausted on the beach and was soon overcome with sleep. The sun was high in the sky before she awoke with a start. Her stomach ached for hunger, and her throat felt as dry as elephant hide. She looked about fearing that she might have been discovered, but there was no one in sight. Pieces of the ship were moving up onto the beach and back out as pushed by the waves. She let out a startled cry when she realized that one of the pieces of wood was actually the body of a Swallow laying face down in the water near her, being pushed about by the waves. The body was already bloated by its overnight immersion in the sea. Assuming it to be the body of the lieutenant, Subria jumped to her feet and ran. She had no idea where to run except to run from the sea, vowing that she'd never see it again.

She hadn't the strength to run far before she was exhausted for want of food and water. She slowly climbed a gentle rise where she could see into the distance. It was only then that she realized that she not only no longer smelled the stench of the ship, but that the stench had been washed from her own body by the sea. She took a deep breath and for a moment didn't think that she had ever experienced anything so satisfying.

From the hill she observed foliage that evidenced a stream nearby, and she sat her course in that direction. Soon she reached the stream. Falling on her hands and knees, she drank until she was satisfied. It didn't take long before her search of the plants growing alongside the stream yielded several roots that began to satisfy the pangs in her stomach.

With her hunger and thirst partially satisfied, Subria determined that she would find her village. She had little comprehension of where her village might be, but she knew that it had to be in the direction away from the sea, so she continued distancing herself from the awful body of water. She walked the remainder of the day, but fearing the beasts of the night, she climbed as high into a tree as she could manage. *How will I ever sleep and not fall to the ground?* she wondered. Hurrying back to the ground, she quickly gathered long strands of grass and braided a short rope. Back in the tree, she secured herself firmly to a branch and tried to fall asleep. Though it was slow in coming and then only in brief durations, Subria did sleep.

The next morning, she continued her general northeastern direction. It was in the late afternoon that she first saw signs of a settlement, but it was a Swallow settlement and not native. Subria watched for quite some time from the safety of a stand of trees, but she didn't see anyone. Also, importantly, she didn't see a dog. She did see something that she very much wanted and needed. There was Swallow clothing hanging on a thin line stretched between two poles. Clothing had been removed from all the slaves when they had boarded the ship, and Subria very much wanted to be covered again.

With no one in sight, Subria ran to the line and removed a piece of bright red cloth and ran back to the trees. She didn't examine the cloth, but bundled it tightly and continued her course. As soon as she felt it was safe, she unbundled the cloth and studied it. The cloth was similar to the long robes that she had seen the Swallow women wearing. Subria was surprised at how easily the cloth could be torn. She carefully tore it into a shape that could be fashioned about her waist. She was overjoyed to once again be covered, even though it was with Swallow cloth.

"How very strange," Mrs. Coburn said as the wagon carrying her and her husband approached the house.

"What is so very strange, my dear?" asked Mr. Coburn.

"My red dress, it should be on the line. Did you remove it then?" Mrs. Coburn asked.

"Remove it? My goodness no. Why would I remove it?"

Mrs. Coburn was very concerned. "That's my best dress. I should be very distressed if it were stolen."

"And who would steal it? Our nearest neighbors are miles away, and it's not as though we get visitors."

Mrs. Coburn looked at her husband with some agitation. "Of course our neighbors wouldn't do such a thing. Can you even imagine one of them wearing it into town? I think not."

"Are you suggesting an animal has taken it then?"

"To be sure, I don't know, but such oddities have occurred."

Their wagon was approaching the house, and it was clear that the dress was not on the line.

"Do you suppose natives have passed through?" asked Mrs. Coburn.

"Oh good heavens no woman," replied Mr. Coburn. "There haven't been natives in this area for quite some time. No, it wasn't natives."

Mr. Coburn began to unhitch the horse from the wagon, but their dog had bounded from the wagon and was soon sniffing the ground near the line.

"Look!" exclaimed Mrs. Coburn pointing to the dog. "Surely, he's discovered a scent."

Mr. Coburn observed his dog and replied, "Indeed, he has. I'll put him on it and we'll soon discover whether it's beast or human."

The dog was moving very quickly beneath the line with his nose to the ground. Soon he was moving away from the line and toward the trees.

Mr. Coburn called to his dog to halt while he removed his gun and a lead from the wagon. The dog waited obediently, but tensely while Mr. Coburn attached a lead to his collar.

"Do be careful," urged Mrs. Coburn. "Perhaps you should go for help."

The dog was pulling hard on the leash, and Mr. Coburn called back to Mrs. Coburn, "I'll not be waiting for help. The trail will grow cold soon."

"Now you listen to me, Mr. Coburn," insisted Mrs. Coburn. "I love that dress, but after all, it's only a dress. There's really no need to rush off to find it."

Mr. Coburn didn't reply. He and the dog were half way to the stand of trees.

Mr. and Mrs. Coburn had emigrated from England several years earlier and had enjoyed success as sheep farmers. Despite their success, they had to endure the disappointment of remaining childless. They had initially blamed each other for their lack of conception, but eventually came to understand that placing blame did nothing to change their situation and only served to cause a wedge to grow between them. Once they had learned this lesson, they were free to love each other more deeply. Though they at times seemed to speak to each other with unflattering terms, the expressions had become almost terms of endearment.

The muscular dog pulled hard on the lead that Mr. Coburn had secured about his neck, and they hadn't gone far before Mr. Coburn found the remains of Mrs. Coburn's dress. He hadn't expected to find it torn so, and the surprise caused the hair on the back of his neck to bristle. *Who, or what would have done this?* he wondered. *Is it man or beast, and why?*

His dog only paused momentarily before he pulled hard again, but stopped short at the base of a tree. The dog placed his front paws on the tree as though he would climb, and he looked intently at the high branches.

Mr. Coburn looked upward and studied the tree. It only took a moment for him to discover a native girl grasping a large branch high in the tree. She wore only a red cloth about her waist.

"What's this then?" Mr. Coburn asked aloud, perhaps to his dog. "A native girl? Why would she need the covering? And what's she doing in these parts?"

"You'll come down this instant if you know what's best for you," he yelled to Subria.

Subria couldn't understand what the Swallow was saying and she wasn't about to leave the tree.

"You'll have to answer to Mrs. Coburn for the dress," he yelled. "She'll not be fond of seeing you in half her dress."

Mr. Coburn waited for a few moments, but Subria didn't respond and didn't move.

The dog started barking at Subria. Mr. Coburn looked at the dog and back up into the tree. He knew that a dog that trees a prey expects to have the prey removed from the tree.

"You'll come down, or I'll cut this tree down."

Again, Mr. Coburn waited, and there was no response from Subria.

"I don't think you understand a word I say, girl. Still you leave me no choice."

With that, Mr. Coburn ordered his dog to remain and watch the tree, and he headed back to the house for an axe.

Mrs. Coburn was waiting anxiously by the house. She knew that Mr. Coburn still thought of himself as a young man, though his advancing years made him vulnerable to injury. He had always been and still was her protector. Still she worried that despite his age he took risks that weren't always necessary.

"I found your dress, mum. Or rather, what is left of your dress."

At word that he had found the dress, Mrs. Coburn initially clapped her hands together with pleasure, but her delight was dashed at the realization the dress was in ruins.

"Is it altogether lost then?" she asked.

"Not altogether I suppose."

Mrs. Coburn looked confused.

"A native girl has altered it to cover herself from the waist down."

"Altered it?" Mrs. Coburn gasped.

"Indeed. Beyond any hope of restoration."

"What will we do? Where is she then?"

Mr. Coburn smiled and disappeared into a shed and reappeared almost immediately with an axe in one hand.

Mrs. Coburn gasped. "I don't want the dress as bad as all that!"

Mr. Coburn laughed. "What do you fancy that I planned to do then?"

"I don't know," Mrs. Coburn said hesitantly. "It appears that you're going to cut the dress from her."

Mr. Coburn laughed again. He enjoyed teasing Mrs. Coburn.

"I shan't cut the dress from her, there isn't enough of the dress that remains."

Mrs. Coburn's anxiety was causing her some impatience. "Right then, Mr. Coburn. What is your intent?"

Mr. Coburn held up the axe and said with a smile, "The native girl is in a tree."

"You'll not cut her out of the tree? You could injure her."

Mr. Coburn laughed again. "No, love, I won't cut her out of the tree, but she doesn't know that."

"What will we do with her then?"

"I don't rightly know," replied Mr. Coburn. "She is a thief. She should pay for her crime. We'll put her to work for you."

"Put her to work for me?" asked Mrs. Coburn incredulously. "We shan't have a slave here. You know we're not favorable to slavery, Mr. Coburn."

"Well said, my dear," agreed Mr. Coburn. "But suppose we keep her for a month, until she's paid off the dress."

Mrs. Coburn considered for a moment and replied, "One month then. But see that you don't harm her."

"Right-o then," agreed Mr. Coburn, and he was off with his axe and gun.

Subria hadn't moved from the branch that she was hugging and Mr. Coburn's dog was vigilantly guarding the base of the tree.

"Come down, girl, or I'll cut this tree down," called Mr. Coburn.

Subria didn't move, but seemed to glare at him.

To Subria's surprise, the Swallow began striking the base of the tree with the implement that he had been holding. It was only then that she comprehended his intentions.

The based of the tree wasn't large, and each strike of the axe sent vibrations running up the tree and into the branch that Subria was grasping.

Subria's heart raced, and she looked about as though to discover a way out of the tree before it fell and without descending to the dog and the Swallow. There was no other tree in proximity of her grasp.

Mr. Coburn slowed his work when he heard the base of the tree crack loudly. He had no intention of actually felling the tree. He only wanted to scare the girl, thereby dislodging her from her lofty retreat. Now he was fearful that he had gone too far, and that he might be responsible for her injury or death if the tree actually fell.

Mr. Coburn quickly grabbed the dog's lead and pulled him away from the tree and backed away from the trunk. He hoped that this would be enough to entice the girl out of the tree.

The crack of the tree trunk sent fear into Subria's heart. As soon as she saw that the Swallow and the dog were away from the trunk, she climbed down quickly, hoping to make her escape. It was a desperate plan with little chance of success. As soon as she was on the ground, the dog was unleashed and herded her like the sheep he was accustomed to herding.

Subria screamed with each gentle nip on her heels. Soon she was running directly back to the house.

Mrs. Coburn heard the commotion and stepped outside and watched in alarm as the young girl was herded like an animal.

"Mr. Coburn," Mrs. Coburn demanded, "stop this at once!"

"I'm not going to harm her," Mr. Coburn assured her.

"I don't question your intentions, but she is a girl, not a sheep! Must I remind you?"

Mr. Coburn called to his dog, and Subria fell in a heap to the earth exhausted at the feet of Mrs. Coburn. Mrs. Coburn immediately kneeled beside the girl and put an arm about her to steady and comfort her.

Glancing briefly at Mr. Coburn, she ordered, "Make haste and fetch a covering for the child. I'll not have her remaining half naked."

Mr. Coburn disappeared inside the house and soon returned with a table cloth. Mrs. Coburn gently wrapped the cloth about the girl and helped her to her feet.

"Come inside, my dear," Mrs. Coburn said gently.

Mr. Coburn looked on with some surprise. "You're taking a native into our house?"

Mrs. Coburn didn't respond directly to the question. "Child, you must be starved. I don't think you've eaten for days. Come inside."

Other than the temporary holding building and the death ship, Subria had never been inside a Swallow structure. She feared the worst and pulled back as Mrs. Coburn urged her forward. Her every urge was to run, but she was without energy, and there was something reassuring in Mrs. Coburn's tone. Subria ceased resisting and moved forward into the house.

Inside the house, Subria's senses were accosted by many things that bewildered her. There were several flat surfaces that stood above the ground at various heights on legs as slender as an antelope's. The house also seemed to have the same invisible barriers in some sections of the wall, similar to the building that first housed the group of slaves that she was amongst.

Most overpowering to her senses was the smell of food. Though it was an unfamiliar scent, she recognized it as food, and she was drawn to it.

"Look. I knew she was starving. Poor child," Mrs. Coburn said with great concern. Then to Mr. Coburn, she added, "Hurry, fetch her some bread. Also, there's some stew over the fire."

Subria didn't know what to do when Mrs. Coburn moved her to one of the flat surfaces on skinny legs. She initially resisted when Mrs. Coburn pushed her gently downward, but then Subria settled onto the flat surface and sat. It made her feel good.

Mrs. Coburn took the bowl of stew from Mr. Coburn and placed it before Subria. Subria immediately grabbed the bowl and lifted it to her lips.

Mrs. Coburn started to correct her, and to give her a spoon, but Mr. Coburn stopped her.

"There's plenty of time for instruction in manners. Let the poor girl eat."

Mr. and Mrs. Coburn watched in amazement as Subria quickly drained the bowl and held it out for more. Twice more they filled the bowl and watched it quickly drained. Only then did Subria seem to relax.

"Keep an eye on the child," ordered Mrs. Coburn. "I'm going to fetch an old dress for her. Running around half-naked will never do."

Subria was surprised to see the woman Swallow return with another length of cloth similar to the one that she had torn and wrapped about her waist. This new cloth was the color of sky. Subria reached out to touch the cloth admiringly, but drew back quickly and stood from the chair when the Swallow women attempted to put the cloth on her head.

Mrs. Coburn backed off and spoke softly and reassuringly to the native girl. "I mean you no harm, love. We just need to cover you properly."

The Swallow woman put the cloth on the flat surface and was speaking words that Subria couldn't understand, but by the gestures, Subria determined that she was speaking her own name and wanted to know Subria's name.

"I Mrs. Ko burn," Subria heard the Swallow woman say.

"I Mrs. Ko burn," repeated Subria.

Mrs. Coburn laughed and tried again.

"Mrs. Coburn," she said while touching her chest.

Subria repeated, "Mrs. Coburn," while touching her own chest.

Mr. Coburn laughed from near the fireplace where he was watching with amusement.

Mrs. Coburn gave him an icy look, followed by a chuckle. It made Subria grin as well.

Mrs. Coburn repeated her own name while touching her own chest again. Then she reached out toward Subria and waited expectedly. Subria smiled and touched her chest and said, "Subria."

Mr. and Mrs. Coburn both laughed and smiled and repeated, "Subria."

"Subria," repeated Mrs. Coburn. "Such a pretty name for a pretty girl. Wouldn't you agree Mr. Coburn?"

"Oh, aye," agreed Mr. Coburn.

Mrs. Coburn held the dress up to herself and ran a hand down its length, smoothing it against her own body. "See how pretty?" she asked.

Subria reached out and touched the cloth and let the table cloth fall to the floor. Mrs. Coburn gently lifted the dress over Subria's head and let it fall over her head and onto her shoulders.

Subria had never experienced the feel of cloth or any other covering over her entire body. It made her feel wealthy to have so much cloth. Slowly, she ran her own hands over the smooth textile. The cloth was soft to her touch, and she felt its smoothness when her fingers moved over the cloth and her body. Suddenly, she had a realization that she felt beautiful.

Subria looked at Mrs. Coburn, and with tears in her eyes, said, "I like this very much. It's a great treasure to me."

Mr. and Mrs. Coburn looked on and smiled, not understanding a word that Subria said.

Mr. Coburn laughed and said, "You've managed to lose two dresses in a single day, my dear."

"Indeed I have," smiled Mrs. Coburn. "I suppose that she'll have to stay with us for two months."

Subria was initially resistant to everything and couldn't be trusted to not runaway. Mr. Coburn's dog was given the task of watching her day and night. Subria was afraid of and disliked the dog very much.

Mrs. Coburn was exceedingly surprised at how bright Subria was, and how quickly she started to pick up the English language and the nature of completing household tasks.

Most surprising to Mrs. Coburn was how quickly she had developed an affinity for the girl. Despite the difference in the color of their skins, she was learning to love the native girl and believed that Subria felt the same. Mrs. Coburn began to wonder whether it would be possible that she could love Subria as the daughter that she never had.

One evening, near the end of the two months, as they lay awake in their bed, Mrs. Coburn ventured to say to Mr. Coburn, "The appointed time has nearly arrived."

Mr. Coburn feigned that he didn't understand, so Mrs. Coburn said, "Subria will leave us soon."

Mr. Coburn seemed sleepy when he replied, "Indeed. I wonder where she'll go. She must have a tribe."

"She never speaks of it. Even with her limited English, I'd think that she'd try and mention it."

Mr. Coburn was awake now, and said, "To be sure, I don't think that she's mentioned anything about her past. Has she?"

"Not so much as a word."

"Have you asked her?"

"I've asked where her home is and what her mother's name is, but she always acts as though she didn't hear or doesn't understand."

Mr. Coburn thought for a moment. "Perhaps she really doesn't understand. Does she know that she'll be free to leave soon?"

"I think so."

"How old do you make her out to be?" Asked Mr.Coburn.

"Fourteen, maybe 15," replied Mrs Coburn.

"Oh, I take her to be older. She must be 16 or 17."

"No, I believe not. Regardless, she's much too young to be turned out on her own."

"Agreed." Replied Mr. Coburn.

That same evening as Subria lay in her bed, she also thought about her new life. She didn't even know that beds existed just a few weeks before, and now this was the most comfortable rest she had ever received.

She thought about the death ship. It seemed as though it was in the distant past, almost nothing more than a bad dream. And yet, it was much more than a bad dream. She hadn't been certain that the Swallows on the ship were even human, but these Swallows seemed very human. Beside her own mother and father, and grandmother, she had never known anyone so kind. When she had first realized this, it had disturbed her. She wanted to hate Swallows, all Swallows. And now, she not only didn't hate these Swallows, but she loved them and wondered whether they could in some way heal the hurt that she still felt in her heart at the loss of her parents, and grandmother and brothers. If she could love these Swallows, was it possible that she could love other Swallows. However, she did know that she would always hate the lieutenant on the ship. Nothing would change that. She also hated Shaka.

The moonlight coming through the invisible barrier in the wall allowed Subria to make out the outline of the attic room that she occupied. She naturally contrasted this room to the cage on the death ship. *This is surely the most grand of all Swallow rooms,* she thought. There were no putrid smells, and no other persons crammed tightly against herself. She thought about the indignity of being without her waist cloth on the ship, and how wonderful it was to have the blue dress. In the low light she could just make out the outline of the dress hanging in the corner. *Truly, it's the most wonderful dress of all Swallow dresses,* she thought. And as she thought this, her heart began to burn and tears began to fill her eyes. *I don't want to leave these Swallows,* she cried in her heart.

A few days later, Subria accompanied Mrs. Coburn to the nearby settlement. It was her first experience being in a Swallow village since being held prior to entering the slave ship. Mrs. Coburn noticed that Subria seemed anxious as the wagon neared the settlement.

"Are you quite alright, Subria?" Mrs. Coburn asked.

Subria stared straight ahead and kept her hands gripped to the wooden seat of the wagon.

"I'll be beside you the entire time," Mrs. Coburn assured her.

"Me no like sluk (Swallow) village," Subria responded.

"Sluk?" Mrs. Coburn asked with a smile. "Not sluk, English. And I'll stay near you."

Subria looked at Mrs. Coburn and asked her to repeat English.

"English?" Subria ventured. "Not sluk?"

"Yes, English," repeated Mrs. Coburn.

"English have death ship."

"No, dear. Not these English."

Mrs. Coburn and Subria went directly to the dry goods store and selected some needed food items. Subria noticed that the other few English women in the store watched her closely and whispered to each other. One had two small children that followed her and mimicked her movements. Subria felt very uncomfortable.

After selecting their food items, Mrs. Coburn stopped at a table that contained several bolts of beautiful cloth.

"Look, Subria, isn't this lovely cloth? It would make a beautiful dress."

Subria touched the cloth and agreed that it was lovely.

The shopkeeper, who had been watching closely, said, "Please don't touch the cloth unless you're going to purchase it."

Mrs. Coburn's head turned quickly in the direction of the shopkeeper. "To be sure, I couldn't possibly make a determination of whether to purchase without touching the cloth."

"Pardon me, Mrs. Coburn." replied the shopkeeper with some embarrassment. "I certainly wasn't speaking to you, but to your slave girl. I beg your pardon."

"I have no slave girl, sir," Mrs. Coburn replied indignantly.

"Please forgive me, I just assumed."

"You've assumed incorrectly, sir. She is a guest and is free to leave at her will," Mrs. Coburn responded.

Subria understood little of the conversation, but did know that it concerned herself. She also understood the word "free", and "leave".

Later in the wagon, Subria was quiet and it troubled Mrs. Colburn.

"Are you quite alright, Subria?"

Subria didn't respond directly, but Mrs. Coburn could see that her eyes were moist, so she placed an arm about Subria's shoulder.

"You want Subria leave?" Subria finally ventured.

Mrs. Coburn gripped gently on Subria's shoulder to pull her closer. "Of course not. Who do you think I purchased the cloth for? Does Subria wish to leave?" she asked.

Subria laid her head on Mrs. Coburn's shoulder. "Subria no leave."

"It's settled then," Mrs. Coburn smiled. "Subria will stay."

Subria smiled. It had been a long time since she felt that she belonged and was wanted for more then a slave.

The designated two months came and went, and Subria became a regular member of the family. It was a different life than her life had been with her own family, and not necessarily a better life, but it was a good life. Life in her village had been structured around the social standing of the members of the village. The chief ruled firmly and sometimes violently. Life with the Coburns seemed more peaceful. If there was a chief, Subria didn't know who it was. If there were enemy tribes, it wasn't evident. In her 13 years she had seen enough turmoil and hatred to last a lifetime. She found that she could finally relax.

Each evening, the Coburns would sit next to the hearth and read out of a large book that they referred to as the Bible. Subria always sat on the floor nearby, and though she initially understood little, she knew that she liked the way that she felt as it was being read. As the months turned into first a year, and then another, Subria began to grasp the meaning of the words that made her feel so warm inside when the book was read. The message of the book had a familiar feel about it as they read about forgiving others. Subria thought of the old lady on the death ship and how she spoke of forgiveness and of a Savior. At the time, none of it made sense to Subria, now she felt the need to forgive. As she learned to pray, she prayed that she could somehow forgive Shaka and the slave traders. She wanted to feel that because God forgave them, so could she, but it was hard.

One evening after Subria had taken her turn reading, she started to cry. She hung her head and sobbed great tears. Mr. and Mrs. Coburn looked at each other with wonder. They had never seen Subria show such emotion.

"What is it, my dear?" asked Mrs. Coburn.

After a few moments, Subria caught her breath and slowed her crying enough to speak. She began by telling her English mother and father about life in her village with her family. She told them about the morning Shaka had raided and killed many and had taken the young men and young women captive. She told them about the march to the slave ship. Then she related to them in the best words that were available to her the horrors of life, if it could be called such, on the death ship. She told them about her hatred of Shaka and the lieutenant. She related to them how frightened she was when the ship had fallen apart, but how she also was hoping for a watery grave. Then she hesitated.

Mr. and Mrs. Coburn had listened intently and Mrs. Coburn had sat on the floor beside Subria so that she could cradle the child in her arms. Mrs. Coburn kissed Subria on the forehead, and she and her husband waited patiently for Subria to continue the awful tail.

Subria raised her head and looked at her adopted parents, and then lowered her head before she spoke.

"I killed someone, and will now go to hell," she said.

Startled by the admission, Mr. and Mrs. Coburn exchanged a surprised look. *How is it possible that this little girl could have killed anyone?* wondered Mrs. Coburn.

After a moment, Subria continued. She told them about the meanness of the ship's lieutenant and how he floated next to her and Maarku in the sea. She admitted to them that her hatred drove her to urge Maarku to push the man into the sea. He didn't want to do it, but she had insisted to the point that he had lost his own grasp on their float and had sunk into the sea. He was dead because of her hatred and now she would be consigned to hell.

Tears filled the eyes of Mr. Coburn as he listened to the sad tail. *No wonder the child has told us nothing of her life. Who would have believed it?* he thought.

"Subria," Mrs. Coburn said gently as she stroked the child's head. "You'll not go to hell. God forgives and he has forgiven you."

"It's true, my dear," Mr. Coburn agreed quietly. "You knew nothing of the Lord. He'll forgive you if you ask him. He's already borne your pains and grief. Turn them over to him."

Subria looked up and dried her eyes on her dress.

"But there is a price to be paid for his forgiveness, Child," Mrs. Coburn cautioned. "You must find it in your heart to forgive Shaka, the slave man and yourself."

Subria nodded her understanding.

"Can you do that?" asked Mr. Coburn.

"I will try," promised Subria.

That night Subria prayed as she had been taught to pray by the Coburns. As she did, a great peace entered her heart. It was a peace unlike any other she had felt before. Her heart burned with joy and tears flowed down her cheeks. She felt lighter and felt more hope than she had ever known. An image of the old lady on the ship came to her mind along with the words that she had whispered to her about forgiveness. *Is this what the old lady on the ship felt and meant?* she thought. *Is this the source of her strength?*

Subria wanted to shout for joy, true joy as she had never known. Suddenly, the thought came to her that without knowing the awfulness of her life's experiences, she may never have come to know God. With this new found realization burning in her heart, she knelt and gave thanks for all her sorrows and trials that had led her to the Coburns and to God.

The Coburns noticed a marked difference in Subria from that day forward. She was bright and cheerful. She was confident and optimistic. The Coburns marveled with each other regarding the miracle that a red dress, or rather that God had worked in their lives through a red dress.

As they watched Subria feeding a small lamb, Mr. Coburn looked at his wife and smiled. Then with a twinkle in his eye, he said to her, "You know, I nearly cut the tree down from beneath her."

"You cruel, cruel man," Mrs. Coburn said with a smile and gently punched his side.

Chapter Sixteen – Alone Again
1844

Subria sat near the head of the bed and watched Mr. Coburn rest. His eyes were closed and his breathing shallow. Subria reached out and stroked the hair of his head. After 27 years with the Coburns, he was the only father she really remembered, and now her heart felt as though it would burst at the thought of losing him. He had always been a strong man, but laying in bed as he was he looked weaker than he ever had. He had been declining in health for some time. He went through bouts when he felt better than at other times. Though he had tried to continue to care for the farm, he tired easily and was often short of breath.

The only doctor in the vicinity had stopped by several weeks previous and had said that Mr. Coburn's condition was likely due to a weakened heart, and that he could do nothing for him. The doctor had said that the best option for Mr. Coburn was for him to return to England for a proper diagnosis and care.

"I understand that great strides have been made in the field of medicine," the doctor had told the Coburns. "They understand things now that we can scarcely imagine. But, we are so far removed from England that it will take years before we have the advantages of care that they enjoy. My recommendation, Mrs. Coburn, is that you take him to England."

Mr. Coburn frowned and slapped the table. "I'll not be going to England," he huffed. "When I left that cold, dreary place, it was permanent."

"Now Mr. Coburn," Mrs. Coburn said calmly with a hand on his arm, "it's not as bad as all that." Then to the doctor she added, "How can he possibly go to England? Would the trip not be too difficult?"

The doctor smiled at Mr. Coburn and said, "He isn't as young as he once was to be sure, but he'll survive the trip."

"I'll be buried in Africa," insisted Mr. Coburn.

Before the doctor left, he instructed Mrs. Coburn to keep Mr. Coburn rested. Initially, that had been impossible since he had always been an independent man and expected that he could go on in his accustomed fashion of working long days on his sheep farm. But as time went on, even

Mr. Coburn had to admit that he was not well and needed more medical care.

One evening as Mr. And Mrs. Coburn lay in bed, Mr. Coburn coughed in a manner that he sometimes did as a means of controlling his emotions and whispered, "I'm sorry that I'm not the man I once was."

Mrs. Coburn put a finger to his lips and quietly said, "Don't say such a thing. You're every bit the man I married."

Mr. Coburn was quiet for a time and said, "I can no longer care for you. What kind of a man is that?"

"You care for me just fine, my love. When we left England we must have known that one day we wouldn't be able to care for the farm ourselves."

"Aye, 'tis true. But I don't think we expected it so soon." He hesitated before adding, "And we had hopes of a large family to care for us in our old age."

Mrs. Coburn didn't respond. She knew it was true, but their dashed hopes of a large family with plenty of sons was a sensitive subject that brought strong emotions to the surface.

Mr. Coburn coughed again quietly and said, "We need to return to England."

Mrs. Coburn sighed with relief to hear him say it.

Mr. Coburn continued, "We can get a good price for the farm that will cover passage, and maybe leave us enough to buy a bungalow in England. And we have family there that will surely help as we age."

"Do you suppose that Subria will come with us?" asked Mrs. Coburn quietly.

"Of course she will."

"I do hope so," replied Mrs. Coburn. "I don't think I could bear it if she didn't."

"She's got no one here. Surely she'll accompany us."

"England is so different than Africa," observed Mrs. Coburn. "People may not be kind to her."

"She's had to deal with such attitudes here as well. She's strong. She'll do fine."

Mr. Coburn remained in bed the next day, and Subria noticed that Mrs. Coburn seemed more subdued than usual. She suspected that Mrs. Coburn was concerned for Mr. Coburn.

"Is he any better today," asked Subria.

"Somewhat, but he's tired."

Both women continued with the chores of washing clothing and preparing the evening meal. Subria had been on the farm long enough that she knew the sheep would be ready for sheering in the coming weeks, and while she had long helped with the task, she also knew that the bulk of the work had always fallen on Mr. Coburn. She wondered whether they would be hiring help this season.

"Will Mr. Coburn be well enough to sheer the sheep then?" she asked.

Mrs. Coburn didn't look up when she replied, "No, I suspect that the sheep will have to get on without him this year."

Subria could hear the emotion in Mrs. Coburn's voice. She wanted to ask what Mrs. Coburn meant by the statement, but didn't. Mrs. Coburn continued with her work in silence for a few minutes before sitting at the table and asking Subria to sit as well.

Mrs. Coburn took Subria's hands and looked her in the eyes and said, "My dear child, the only hope for Mr. Coburn lies in England. It's only there that he can receive the care he needs. He'll either stay here and die, or he'll go to England with the hope of many more years."

Tears filled Subria's eyes. "You will return?"

Mrs. Coburn smiled gently and said, "No dear, but surely you'll come with us."

Subria averted her eyes. *I love me mum and papa, but I'll not enter into a death ship, or any ship again.*

Mrs. Coburn studied Subria's expression and got a concerned look on her face. "Subria, you will come with us, will you not?" she asked.

Subria smiled weakly and replied, "Yes, of course." The words surprised her as soon as they were said.

Mrs. Coburn clapped her hands for joy and then squeezed Subria's hands. "Oh Subria, I'm ever so glad. Mr. Coburn will be so pleased. I'm sure that just knowing this will rally his spirits."

Mr. Coburn's spirits were rallied and he had the strength to negotiate the sale of the farm. Within a few weeks they had disposed of all their belongs except for the wagon, a horse to pull it, and as many clothes and household items as would fit into four large trunks. The wagon and horse would be sold in Port Elizabeth before boarding the ship for England.

The day for departure arrived, and each were filled with melancholy as they looked about their home one last time.

Mrs. Coburn slipped her fingers around Mr. Coburn's elbow and held it close as he stood in the doorway preparing to close it, but still looking inside.

"I always thought that the only way I would leave this place was 'feet first, face up' in a box," Mr. Coburn said.

Tears had formed in Mrs. Coburn's eyes and were starting down her cheek, but she grinned and replied, "I hope that you're not 'feet first, face up' for a very long time."

"Indeed," replied Mr. Coburn quietly.

Mr. Coburn noticed Subria looking at the nearby stand of trees, and he observed, "They've grown substantially since you came into our lives, have they not?"

"Indeed, they have," agreed Subria. She smiled and continued, "I was thinking about Mrs. Coburn's red dress. It really was quite a lovely dress, was it not?"

"Her favorite," replied Mr. Coburn with a smile as he wrapped an arm about her shoulder.

"I'd give it up in a moment again," Mrs. Coburn said as she wiped a tear with her handkerchief.

"Well, it's two-days to Port Elizabeth," Mr. Coburn announced. "We're not going to get there by gawking about the place." As the three settled into the wagon, he said, "With good fortune we'll have a roof over our heads tonight."

"And without good fortune?" asked Mrs. Coburn with a smile.

"The wagon makes a very good roof," grinned Mr. Coburn.

On the second day, as the wagon neared Port Elizabeth, Subria moved from the seat to the bed of the wagon.

"What are you doing my dear?" asked Mrs. Coburn.

"Many will be offended if I am seen sitting next to you," Subria replied matter-of-factly.

"Yes, I suppose you're right," replied Mrs. Coburn. "I would that it weren't so, but it is," she sighed.

"I'll also be in the lowest hold of the ship," Subria observed.

Mr. and Mrs. Coburn exchanged looks. "I hadn't considered such a thing. Won't you just stay in the berth near our own?" asked Mrs. Coburn.

"That wouldn't be proper and would never be allowed. I have my place," replied Subria.

The ship wasn't due to set sail from Port Elizabeth for several days, so the Coburns took temporary lodging at the only inn. The innkeeper wouldn't allow Subria to stay in the main portion of the inn, but rather in a ramshackle room in the back of the building. Still, the days were spent pleasantly enough meandering about the shops and visiting with other soon-to-be passengers. Conversation inevitably focused on the lingering effects of the last drought and whether a new drought was encroaching, and whether the drought would damage already fragile relations with the native population. Whenever conversation shifted to the fragile relations with the native population, Subria always felt the stares of the settlers on herself. Though she traveled with the Coburns, who she considered as her parents and they considered her as their daughter, and though she wore English-styled dresses that were often finer than those worn by other women, she felt generally invisible to the other settlers, especially the women. Only when conversation focused on natives, or when the settlers determined that she was overstepping her place in society, did she feel that she wasn't invisible. Then she could feel the intensity of scrutinizing eyes, and she hated it.

Subria was proud of her native background; that's who she was. Though she wore English clothing, spoke English better than most settlers and loved her English parents, she felt that she could just as easily return to the native dress and the native ways of her youth. Even now, in her fortieth year, she often thought of her family although her days in their care seemed a world away. Though she felt that she had long since forgiven the lieutenant and the other slave traders, still she wondered how it was that the horrors of the death ship could remain so vivid while the memories of her youth so distant.

Occasionally during the few days at Port Elizabeth, Subria was left to wander the streets alone. While living with the Coburns she had occasional interactions with groups of native women, but usually it was an intermittent association with one or two women at a time. While walking about Port Elizabeth with the Coburns, Subria had noticed groups of native women who gathered while attending to their daily chores. Her curiosity was aroused and she determined to attempt to interact with them. She approached a group and asked what village they were from. They looked at her with disdain and laughed amongst themselves at her accent and poor usage of the native tongue.

"She speaks like a Swallow," one laughed to the others.

"She dresses like a Swallow," another laughed.

"Perhaps she is a Swallow," laughed the first.

Subria lowered her head and walked away in embarrassment. *I'm caught between two worlds and don't fit into either,* she thought. This wasn't new to her, but now it was more clearly understood.

Most of Port Elizabeth sat on a small hill that overlooked the sea, and the street that led to the inn had a clear view of the port. From that street it was also possible to gaze far out into the sea to the point where the sea met the horizon. On the way to the inn, Subria noticed a ship in the distance that was approaching the harbor. Out of curiosity she walked to the pier and watched as it slowly grew larger. A favorable breeze was filling the sails and the three-mast ship glided effortlessly across the water toward Port Elizabeth.

Subria watched the ship's approach for at least an hour before the ship was close enough to the dock to start furling its sails to slow its approach. When the ship was yet at some distance from the dock, Subria's breathing became shallow and rapid, and her heart raced. She also started feeling sick to her stomach and wanted to run, but her feet seemed frozen. Memories of the death ship flooded her mind.

The putrid smell of the death ship was etched so completely into the very fabric of her being that it seemed to transport her back to the ship. Suddenly, she was a little girl again, locked in a cage and forced to eat rotten food. All around her was death or the smell of death.

The awfulness of the memories paralyzed her and she felt weak and helpless.

"Subria? Are you alright?"

Mrs. Coburn's voice penetrated the dark shadows that clouded her mind, and Subria took a deep breath, turned and wrapped her arms about Mrs. Coburn's neck.

"What is it, my dear?" asked Mrs. Coburn, but Subria didn't answer. Mrs. Coburn wiped Subria's tears and the two women walked silently back to the inn, Subria supported by Mrs. Coburn.

During the next several days, the ship was made ready for sailing back to England. Mr. and Mrs. Coburn noticed a marked change in Subria's countenance, and though concerned, nothing more was said between the three regarding the cause.

Finally, the appointed day had arrived, and the trunks were repacked and readied for the ship. Mr. Coburn had sold the wagon and horse, so arrangements were made with a hired driver and wagon to deliver them to the port.

"I never expected this day to arrive," Mr. Coburn commented. "I expected surely to be buried in Africa."

"Do you remember how I hated this land when we initially arrived?" asked Mrs. Coburn. "Leaving now is almost as hard as leaving England proved to be." Then looking at Subria, she smiled and continued, "Having Subria with us will make the leaving all the easier."

Subria smiled.

"My poor dear," continued Mrs. Coburn, "leaving your home land must be difficult indeed. Surely, I know how you must feel."

"Difficult to be sure," replied Subria with a forced smile.

"Without a doubt, you'll love England," promised Mr. Coburn. "It is as green there as Africa ever was following the summer rains."

The Coburns room was on the upper floor of the inn and faced the port. Subria stood at the window as though watching for the driver, but she was actually studying the ship. Subria smiled and replied without turning from the window, "Quite lovely, I'm sure."

"Indeed, quite lovely," agreed Mrs. Coburn.

The wagon and driver had arrived at the inn, and the three left the room and went downstairs to meet the driver.

Mr. Coburn explained where to find the trunks, and he, Mrs. Coburn and Subria walked to the wagon.

"Very good, sir," the driver stated. "I won't be but a minute."

The trunks were soon loaded, and the wagon began the short trip to the port. The anxiety that Subria had felt while standing near the port returned and increased in intensity as the wagon worked its way slowly toward the ship. The usually quiet port was bustling with workers loading final articles of cargo and trunks onto the ship and with passengers waiting for the call to board.

Women wore their finest apparel, complete with hat, gloves and umbrellas. Men sported walking canes and pipes. The sights and sounds blended together to create an air of excitement, but it wasn't exciting for Subria. Her stomach ached. She wished that she were 12 so that she could blend into the crowd and run away. Exactly where she didn't know. All she wanted was to be far from the ship.

It wasn't long before the call came to board and the crowd at once moved forward. Soon an orderly queue was formed, and passengers began to slowly move up the ramp and onto the ship.

Walking up the ramp, Subria remembered the flies that greeted her to the death ship and was grateful that this ship had few. She noted the mood of the passengers on this ship was one of excitement, almost as though attending a party. Despite the jovial atmosphere, she couldn't help but feel insecure and despondent.

"This is indeed a grand ship," observed Mr. Coburn as he studied the three masts and the size of the deck. "I'd say it's much larger than the single mast ship that brought us to Africa."

Whether Mrs. Coburn had taken notice of the comment or the size of the ship wasn't clear. Her attention was focused on Subria.

"My dear, you seem altogether distracted. Are you quite alright?"

"Yes, quite," Subria assured her, but she wasn't convincing.

"This ship isn't the slave ship that you experienced so many years ago," Mrs. Coburn ventured. "You'll be well fed on this ship, and you'll have comfortable quarters."

Subria had been trying to be brave, but the observation by Mrs. Coburn penetrated her emotions and the tears flowed.

Mrs. Coburn placed a hand on her shoulder and said, "Let's go below to our quarters. Perhaps you'll feel better after settling in."

Mr. Coburn told the two women to go on without him. He was engrossed in studying the ship.

The two women descended the few steps into the first of the lower decks. The ceiling was low, and the room was divided by supporting beams that stood as pillars throughout the deck. There was some light coming through the opening to the deck above, and there were a few oil lanterns hanging from the ceiling. The berth for each family was small and little space existed between them.

"Here is ours," announced Mrs. Coburn as she located their berth. Its location was favorable because it was near the opening to the upper deck. They would get more light and more fresh air at that location than others might. Their berth was just wide enough for the two of them to lay down side by side and to store a few articles of clothing and perhaps some books.

After satisfying herself with the location and condition of their berth, Mrs. Coburn offered, "Perhaps we should see your accommodations."

Subria was less than enthusiastic about the prospect of seeing her own berth anytime soon, but Mrs. Coburn seemed determined. As the two women descended the stairs to the lower deck, the light became dimmer as fewer lanterns were utilized in the lower deck. The air was quite stale and heavy. An offensive odor hung in the air, and Subria noticed that Mrs. Coburn held her sleeve to her nose and mouth. The berths were very close, tightly placed and afforded no privacy. Mrs. Coburn looked about in surprise.

After her eyes adjusted to the low light, Subria noticed odd marks in vertical rows at regular intervals along the walls behind the berths. Initially she took little notice, but after seeing several it suddenly occurred to her that the marks were small holes left when cages had been removed. *This is a death ship!* The thought at once filled her with fear and loathing. Without a word to Mrs. Coburn, Subria turned abruptly and rushed up both sets of stairs and onto the deck. She was short of breath and everything about her seemed to be spinning. Holding onto anything that she could grasp, she half walked, half stumbled off the ship.

Once off the ship, she hurried to the shade of a building, collapsed onto a nearby bench, buried her face in her hands and cried.

Mr. and Mrs. Coburn were close behind.

"What is it, my dear?" asked Mrs. Coburn with great concern.

"What happened? Are you quite alright?" asked Mr. Coburn.

Mrs. Coburn sat next to Subria and placed an arm about her shoulders. Mr. Coburn looked on a little uncertain how to respond and also very much out of breath from the rush down the ramp of the ship.

Subria laid her head onto Mrs. Coburn's shoulder and continued crying for several moments. Eventually, she wiped her eyes and caught her breath long enough to say, "I can't go back on that ship. I won't go back on that ship."

Mrs. Coburn looked up at Mr. Coburn and replied to Subria, "I know that your berth is dark and uncomfortable, but the voyage won't last long."

"It isn't the berth. Being uncomfortable doesn't frighten me."

"What is it that concerns you so?" asked Mrs. Coburn.

"You've got to go back on the ship to go to England," said Mr. Coburn, stating the obvious.

Subria looked up and replied with tears in her eyes, "It's a death ship! I can't go back on it, or any other ship!"

Mr. Coburn looked at Mrs. Coburn and asked, "A death ship?"

"A slave ship!" replied Mrs. Coburn.

"But we've paid the passage," urged Mr. Coburn.

Mrs. Coburn gave Mr. Coburn a stern look.

"I'm truly sorry," replied Subria. "I can't go to England."

"Can't go to England?" asked Mr. Coburn with some frustration evident in his tone.

"Subria," Mrs. Coburn said quietly, "are you quite certain of this?"

Subria had calmed herself, but tears still ran down her cheeks. Wiping her tears, she replied, "Quite certain."

"What will you do?" asked Mrs. Coburn.

"Yes, what will you do if you stay?" asked Mr. Coburn.

Subria was quiet for a moment before she replied, "To be sure, I don't know."

"What will we do without you?" asked Mrs. Coburn.

"This is a considerable disappointment for us," Mr. Coburn stated. "We are quite sure that you'll love England, and we need you."

"I can't go with you. I'm truly sorry," Subria stated, her voice faltering with emotion.

The call had gone out from the ship several times for the passengers to complete boarding, and with reluctance, Mr. Coburn took Mrs. Coburn by the arm and urged her toward the ship.

"We must go, Mrs. Coburn," he urged.

Mrs. Coburn gave Subria a firm hug. Subria felt safe in her arms, and tears began to flow when Mrs. Coburn finally released her grip. Mrs. Coburn put her hands on Subria's cheek and looked into her eyes. "We'll not forget you," she said with a smile. "You've brought us more joy than you know."

Subria smiled faintly and held Mrs. Coburn's hands. Mr. Coburn relaxed his grip on Mrs. Coburn's arm and stepped close to Subria. "You're the best thing that has happened to us," he said. "I praise God everyday that he brought you into our lives."

Mr. Coburn didn't easily express himself so freely, and when Subria heard the sincere expression of his love, she wept. She wanted more than anything to walk up the ramp and onto the ship, but her legs wouldn't move.

"Come," urged Mr. Coburn with a gentle tug on Mrs. Coburn's arm. Mrs. Coburn stepped backward still holding Subria's hands until their fingertips could no longer touch.

Mr. and Mrs. Coburn walked slowly to the ramp, both still looking over their shoulders at Subria. On the ship, they found a free place at the railing and waved to Subria. The ropes were released from the dock, and with the sails unfurled, the ship began to be pushed by the wind toward the open waters of the sea.

Standing on the dock, Subria continued to wave until her arm ached. Tears coursed down her cheeks and blurred her vision. Her heart ached and felt as though it would burst. *How can I go on without them?* she wondered. Eventually, the ship was a small object on the horizon and then it was out of sight. How long she stood at the dock, she couldn't say, but when she turned to leave, the sun was well past its highest point in the sky.

When Subria turned away from the dock she realized that her stomach ached, not only from sadness, but for want of food. With no money, no lodging and no means of support, the reality of staying behind began to fill her mind. She realized that she had never provided her own food or lodging, and the prospect of doing so now frightened her. She thought about the brief period of her life when she was held captive and realized that, as dehumanizing and disgusting as it was, even then food and shelter were provided. For the briefest of moments, she considered the security of that situation desirable. But then the repulsiveness of the thought caused her skin to crawl and a shiver up her spine shook her entire body. With renewed determination, she faced Port Elizabeth and walked back up the dusty street and into the town.

Chapter Seventeen – A New Start
March 1846
Elephant Hook, Africa

With strong lungs, the baby let out a cry as it drew its first breath. The sound was joyous to Julia who had labored for hours to deliver her fourth child. With a mixture of tears and sweat covering her brow and face, she half cried and half laughed as she asked the midwife whether it was a boy or a girl.

"It's a fine boy, miss," replied the native midwife who had been summoned from Port Elizabeth. "He do his father proud. Mr. Prince be very happy to have two fine sons."

"Three," Julia corrected her despite, her exhaustion.

"Three?" asked the midwife. "One boy and one girl outside."

The baby continued to cry as the midwife wrapped him in a small blanket and handed him to Julia.

"There's a grave in England that holds my other son," replied Julia as she held her new son and caressed his cheek lightly. Julia smiled with contentment as the baby immediately took to her breast.

Julia closed her eyes, and though exhausted, she knew that she wouldn't fall asleep. Hyrum would want to see his new son soon, and he would bring Francis, and Victoria with him. She expected that Francis, aged 5, would take to his brother right away, but she wasn't so sure about Victoria, almost aged 3.

"Shall I get your husband, miss?" asked the midwife.

"Yes, of course. Thank you." replied Julia. Then she quickly added, "Give me a moment to straighten my hair." Pointing to a chest near the bed, she requested, "Please hand me that hair brush."

With her hair straightened, Julia was ready for her family to meet their new son and brother. "Please invite them in," Julia requested of the midwife.

Hyrum had been able to build a new house for his family in the few years that they had been in Africa. It was small, but considerably larger and more comfortable than the original shelter that he and Ian had constructed. The original shelter had been turned into lodging for Julia's domestic helper. The design of the shelter was similar to traditional African huts, and being native, the domestic helper found it very comfortable.

Soon Julia heard the sound of many feet ascending the stairs. She could also hear Hyrum's voice as he patiently helped little Victoria negotiate the stairs. Hearing their footsteps gave Julia a moment to take a deep breath and prepare for the excitement that was about to burst into the room.

"Mummy, Mummy," cried Victoria. She only knew a few words and it gave Julia great satisfaction that "Mummy" was one of them.

"It's a boy!" cried Francis as he bounded into the room and onto the bed.

Julia winced, and Hyrum grabbed Francis and pulled him off the bed. "Son, be a gentleman as we discussed," instructed Hyrum.

"Sorry, Mummy," Francis said as he pushed his way to the head of the bed where he could get a better look at his brother.

Hyrum smiled at Julia and bent down and kissed her forehead. "You look beautiful, my dear, and I hear it's a boy!"

"He is indeed a boy," smiled Julia. "What will you call him?"

"Luke is a strong Christian name. Don't you think?"

"A name from the Bible then?" asked Julia.

"Yes, I think it's time that we had a name from the Bible," Hyrum announced.

There were very few churches in that part of Africa and none officially in Elephant Hook. A few families occasionally met together on Sunday to read from the Bible and to sing praises, but there was no ordained minister among them. Every few months or so a minister would travel from Port Elizabeth to hold a service and to perform christenings if needed. He would presumedly also perform marriages, though there hadn't been any such need in the time that the Princes had lived in Elephant Hook. There had been a couple of funerals. Some feared that the need for funerals would rise with the tensions between the settlers and the natives.

It had bothered Julia immensely that there was no established church. The lack of a church caused her to reflect on her attitude toward church attendance while in England. She realized that her attendance had largely been motivated by a desire to wear nice dresses and to be seen by others. She supposed that Lord and Lady Hammond's motivation was based in more faith than her own, and she had largely attended at their invitation. Now that she had children of her own, she felt a strong desire to raise them in the faith of her fathers. That responsibility now rested squarely with Hyrum and herself, though Hyrum had seemed all too willing to leave it to her. The fact that Hyrum had chosen a name from the Bible filled her with hope that he would take more of a lead in the spiritual guidance of his family.

Footsteps were heard coming up the stairs and soon their domestic help was in the doorway. Julia's eyes lit up and she smiled broadly. "Oh, do come in, Subria, and see our new son!"

Subria was all smiles as she carefully approached the bed. It had been a very long time since a newborn had been a part of her life and she was instantly filled with love for the child.

"Praise the Lord, Miss Julia!" Subria declared. "He is so beautiful!"

"He's my brother, Subria," Francis announced. He hadn't yet learned to properly pronounce her name, but he loved her just the same.

Since their arrival in Africa, Hyrum had desired to secure a domestic helper for Julia. She had tried to assure him that she didn't have need of a helper. Regardless, Hyrum insisted, most probably because he had lingering doubts about his ability to provide her with the comforts that she had formerly enjoyed. He knew that he could never fully provide Julia with the comforts that she had enjoyed in England, but he felt that a domestic helper was within his reach.

Life had been hard for Subria after the Coburns had left for England. She knew little about the workings of the world of Swallows and had never worked for pay. She had gone back to the inn and asked for temporary lodging, but without means of paying for it, her request had been rejected. Discouraged and scared, she had gone to several houses to ask for food, but had been turned away immediately at each one. Without a place to stay, and afraid to sleep away from the town for fear of wild animals, she found a shed that stood apart from the other buildings of the town. Each night, just after dark, she would find her way to the shed, always being careful to arise and leave before daylight.

It was two days after the Coburns had left before Subria had been able to find food. Initially, a woman in town took pity on her and left some scraps by the backdoor of her home, but that stopped after a few days when her husband discovered the secret.

Subria's welcome in the town faded quickly, so she had been obliged to spend her days in the bush. This turned to her great advantage, as she was able to gradually remember the instructions of her mother on foraging for edible plants. She also remembered her father's description of tracking small animals and of setting snares for them. By employing these means, she eventually was able to provide food for herself. Still, she had need to belong somewhere.

After many weeks, a tribe settled near Port Elizabeth for a time. Subria hoped to join them and ventured into their camp. It was soon obvious that, other than the color of her skin, she had little in common with them. She spoke excellent English, and as a consequence, her native tongue had weakened. Despite the fact that the tribe didn't speak exactly the language of her youth, it was abundantly clear that she was primarily an English speaker.

Her manner of dress also set her apart from the natives. Whereas for years she had considered that it would be easy for her to return to the native style of dress, just being in the presence of these women who were only half clothed, made her to feel uncomfortable.

These were reasons enough for the tribe to reject her and she them, but above all else it was the apparent magic craft and superstitions of the tribe that caused Subria to reject them. She was Christian, and just being in the presence of those who were practicing the old ways, made her most uncomfortable.

In the end, she was only with the tribe a few days, then she was back in the shed near Port Elizabeth. As she lay on the hard floor of the shed on that first night back, tears filled her eyes. She had no where to belong. She wasn't a native and she wasn't a Swallow. She desperately wanted to belong somewhere. She cried in her heart to God for deliverance from a life of loneliness and subsistence. *Dear God,* she prayed, *thou that delivered me from the slave ship, please deliver me from this life of loneliness.*

It was in these circumstances that Hyrum first met Subria. He had gone to Port Elizabeth to purchase supplies that couldn't be had in Elephant Hook or Grahamstown. While there he intended to call on Mr. Barnes at the request of Amanda. Hyrum was happy to carry correspondence between Amanda and her parents on his visits to Port Elizabeth. His intention was to pop in at Mr. Barnes law office after collecting his dry goods, but Mr. Barnes saw him pass by on the street and he hurried out and called after Hyrum.

"Hyrum, my good fellow, how nice to see you. Do you have a letter from Amanda then?"

"I do indeed, sir," Hyrum replied and pulled the letter from his pocket.

Mr. Barnes took the letter and looked at it briefly before securing it in his own pocket.

"Mrs. Barnes will be ever so pleased."

Mr. Barnes' law practice was going well enough, and Hyrum took opportunity of congratulating him on his success.

"You have done very well," Hyrum stated as he looked through the window of Mr. Barnes' office. "I wouldn't have expected so much business to be had in Port Elizabeth."

"Well, my good fellow," stated Mr. Barnes, "it isn't only from Port Elizabeth that I draw my clients. It's the whole of the surrounding area, some as far as Grahamstown and other towns like it." Then he continued with a wink of his eye, "The other solicitor in town isn't fond of me, to be sure. When he was the only 'bird' in town, he could charge quite handsomely for his songs, if you catch my meaning."

"I think I do," replied Hyrum.

"And what brings you to Port Elizabeth? Apart from delivering Amanda's letter, of course," Mr. Barnes said with a smile and a hand on the pocket that secured the letter.

Neither man took note of the native woman that stood nearby in the shade.

"The handle to the pump has broken and I'm hoping to purchase a new one, among other things," replied Hyrum.

"And how is Julia then?"

"She's generally well. Truth be told, it is difficult for her with the two children. She manages well enough most of the time, but there are more times than she'd like to admit that she isn't feeling well. But she presses ahead without complaint. I would so like to hire a domestic helper for her."

"Well then, do it, man," urged Mr. Barnes. "Mrs. Barnes has two helpers and no children. You can get the help for next to nothing you know."

"Yes, I do know, but Julia and I feel that we should pay a reasonable wage and not take advantage."

"Well, there's your trouble, my good fellow," laughed Mr. Barnes. "You treat them as though they had options. Most of them don't you know."

"Quite right, but just the same, we'll not take undue advantage."

With that, Mr. Barnes turned to leave. "I wish you good fortune with that then. Oh, and do stop by before you go. I'll have a letter for you to carry back."

"Yes, sir," replied Hyrum, "I'll stop in before I go."

With that, the two men parted and Hyrum set about his chores of securing items to take back to Elephant Hook. In addition to the items that he needed for himself, he had a list of items needed by Ian and Amanda and a few other neighbors.

Subria followed at a safe distance and waited outside the dry goods store until he completed his tasks there. A number of items would be loaded into Hyrum's wagon, and as soon as the merchandise was brought outside the store, she grabbed some and started loading it into the wagon. Initially, Hyrum was startled and thought that he was being robbed in broad daylight.

"Oy!" cried Hyrum. "What are you doing?"

The woman paid him no mind as she loaded the item onto the wagon and grabbed the pump handle to load. Hyrum was amazed at the strength of this native woman.

"Very well then, I can give you a few pennies for your help, but that's all," Hyrum said.

Subria stopped loading and turned to Hyrum. "To be sure, I don't expect your pennies for my service."

Hyrum was shocked at the manner of speech used by this native woman. He had never heard a native use such fine English, and he was taken aback. Hyrum stood by and watched her return to the chore of loading, not knowing what to say.

After loading a couple more items, Subria stopped and faced Hyrum. From her graying hair and a few lines on her face, Hyrum expected that she was in her mid-forties.

"Kind sir, I desire to enter into your employment as a domestic helper for your wife. As you have witnessed, I'm strong, and as you can observe, I'm quite determined."

"Well, I," started Hyrum.

"I can cook, clean, and sew. I can also read and write."

"You can read and write?" Hyrum asked with surprise.

"Indeed, I can."

"Well…"

"Please, sir," pleaded Subria.

Hyrum thought for a moment and replied, "Very well."

Joy was clearly expressed in Subria's countenance, and she cried, "Thank you, kind sir. Your wife will be so pleased."

Subria had learned from Mrs. Coburn many important tasks of keeping a home and garden. Julia had little such training in the home of Lord and Lady Hammond, and though Hyrum's mother had tried to teach her many things, Julia and Hyrum had left England before Mrs. Prince's tutelage had yielded all the desired results. Julia had done fairly well on her own.

When Hyrum had shown the living quarters to Subria, he had done so almost apologetically.

"It's very small, and it has dirt floors," Hyrum stated.

Subria looked inside, but hesitated before stepping through the doorway. The single-roomed dwelling reminded her of the home of her childhood. She had been in few traditional huts since leaving the native village, and looking inside this hut brought back a flood of memories and emotions. Hyrum had noted that Subria's eyes were moist when she turned back from the doorway, and he assumed that the hut was a disappointment to her.

"I know it's not much," he started, but Subria interrupted him.

"It's altogether perfect. I grew up on dirt floors," she said. "It's certainly more than I deserve."

Julia initially enjoyed having the extra help very much, but when Subria started to question her methods or to do things differently, Julia bristled.

"Miss Julia," Subria said after watching her mending a pair of trousers that were torn at the knee, "the patch should always be placed inside the legging."

Julia had never been taught to patch a pair of trousers and had assumed that the patch was to be placed over the top of the torn cloth. She had done several patches for Hyrum in this manner and he had never complained.

"This patch will work very well," Julia stated through clenched teeth. *Domestic help is fine,* she thought, *but she should keep her opinions to herself.*

It was too late. Subria had taken the trousers from Julia and had begun the process of removing the half-stitched patch, ignoring Julia's attempt at protesting. After removing the patch, Subria trimmed the ripped area and turned the trousers inside out and stitched the patch inside the legging. She then turned the leg of the trousers back the right way and stitched the trimmed torn piece to the patch that had been applied beneath. Julia watched with some initial irritation, but had to admit that it was the best mending she had ever seen. Still, she was irritated.

When Hyrum came home and saw the patched trousers, he exclaimed, "A very nice job of patching indeed. Just like my mum used to do." He then kissed Julia on the top of her head in appreciation. Julia didn't look up, but kept her lips pursed.

Francis had a torn spot in his trousers, so Julia waited until Subria was busy in the garden the next day before she pulled the trousers out and tried to repeat the process that Subria had demonstrated. The result wasn't as fine as Subria's but it was the best patch that Julia had ever performed. She held up the trousers and admired them. She casually laid them out where she knew that Hyrum would see them, and that evening he did take note.

"Another fine patch job, my dear," he said with a smile. Julia beamed until Hyrum added, "Not as fine as the patch on my trousers, but fine indeed."

Soon after, Hyrum brought home the remains of a sheep that had been freshly killed by a lion. Hyrum had happened upon the kill almost immediately and had been able to kill the lion. He considered that the sheep shouldn't be wasted and had brought it home.

Julia didn't think that the meat was safe, but Subria insisted on cooking it.

"That was truly a wonderful meal," Hyrum had declared. "What a shame it would have been had we thrown out that meat." He didn't notice that Julia left the room quickly.

That night as they lay in bed, Julia couldn't get to sleep. It was clear from Hyrum's shallow, slow breathing that he was asleep. Despite that, Julia touched his side and asked, "Hyrum, are you awake?"

Hyrum groggily replied, "Yes, of course."

"I really don't need help. Perhaps we should let Subria go."

Hyrum was surprised by this declaration and awoke completely. "Let her go? Surely, you don't mean that. I thought that she was very helpful to you."

"Of course, she is, but I can manage quite well on my own."

"I don't know. You weren't feeling well last week and it was very nice to have Subria here. Wouldn't you agree?"

"Yes, quite right, but I really can manage."

Hyrum thought for a moment and said, "Francis and Victoria love her. They would miss her so."

"Indeed. Perhaps they like her too much. I'm their mum."

"We can't just turn her out," Hyrum stated. "Where would she go?"

"To be sure, I don't know. Back to her people."

"What people?"

"Her tribe. I don't know."

"Has she ever mentioned her tribe to you?" asked Hyrum.

"No, I suppose that she hasn't."

"Has she mentioned anything about her past to you?"

"No. Has she to you? You traveled from Port Elizabeth with her. She must have mentioned something."

Hyrum was quiet for a moment and then replied, "No. She really didn't say much, as I recall. She rode in the back of the wagon or walked and I drove the wagon. We really didn't talk much. She did talk about living with a family named Coburns and that they had to return to England. That's how she learned to speak English so well and to read and write."

"All that way and that's all you know of her?"

"Yes, I suppose it is."

"So we really don't know anything about this woman," Julia remarked.

"Still, I don't feel that we should turn her out. She's more English than she is native. Let's give it a little more time."

"Very well," replied Julia reluctantly. "A little more time will do no harm."

"That's the spirit, my dear," Hyrum replied. "Perhaps you should engage her and see whether she'll reveal her past to you. Perhaps if you knew her better, you'd feel differently about her."

"Perhaps," agreed Julia. "I'll try."

Julia and Subria spent most of the next day working in the garden. As they worked, Subria thought about the Coburns and where they must be and wondered whether they had made it to England. *I should have gone with them,* she thought. *Surely, I could have managed.* But just the thought of it caused her chest to tighten, and she had to admit that she couldn't have managed. She looked over at Julia. *I should be happier here. I have a roof over my head and food to eat. But Miss Julia doesn't care for me. She's so young. But even her youth doesn't account for her lack of understanding on household chores and cooking. She needs me, though she wouldn't believe it. Hyrum and the children need me.*

Julia observed that Subria was very efficient in her gardening. She didn't talk, she just worked. *Where is she from?* she wondered.

Finally, Julia cleared her throat and asked hesitantly, "Subria, where are you from?"

Subria didn't look up, but replied, "I'm from here."

"I mean, where are your people?"

Subria was quiet for a moment or two. "I have no people." Even now the very thought of the loss of her family caused her pain, and she generally chose to not think about it.

"Everyone has people," insisted Julia.

"Everyone once had people," Subria corrected her. "Where are your people?"

"In England," replied Julia.

"Will you ever see them again?"

Julia stopped and stood up. Looking into the distance, she replied, "No, I suppose not. I guess in that sense, I'm from here also."

"Did it pain you to leave your people?"

"Yes, very much."

"But you had Hyrum."

"Yes, and Francis."

"Tell me about the people you left behind in England to come to this land," Subria urged.

Julia started out hesitantly to tell her story. During the telling, she and Subria eventually sought out the shade of a tree. Julia related to Subria how devastated she felt at the untimely death of her mother. She hadn't thought that life could go on or that she could ever be happy again. She hadn't admitted it to anyone, but she had been angry at God. It was only the love of her father that helped her to begin to heal.

Tears ran down Julia's cheeks and sobs escaped her as she told Subria about the tragic death of her father, and that she had never been completly satisfied as to whether the fall from the horse had killed him or whether Katherine had suffocated him as she intended. "I thought that I had forgiven Katherine," she said, "but perhaps I'm not certain. I think that there is a part of me that is still angry with her. But she's gone also. I should forgive her. She wasn't right in the head." Subria put her arms around Julia and comforted her.

Julia cheered as she told about life with Lord and Lady Hammond and about her friendship with Princess Victoria. Julia hadn't told anyone in Africa about her relationship with the Queen and asked Subria to hold it in confidence.

"You're a princess," Subria declared.

Julia laughed and assured her that she was not. Though Julia explained in a general way, Subria had no frame of reference to really comprehend the opulence and the grandeur that had been Julia's surroundings in England.

"But you chose Hyrum and left behind your kingdom," observed Subria.

Julia smiled, "I did."

"Do you regret leaving behind your kingdom?"

Julia looked at Subria, "Not at all. I left behind riches that weren't mine and gained the love of a good man. And now you see that he has given me beautiful children."

Then Julia thought for a moment, and said with a laugh, "And Hyrum gave up a potential future with a woman that could cook and sew."

Subria also laughed. "You do very well, child. Your children are well cared for."

At the mention of her children, Julia was quiet again and her tears flowed once more. "I have another son," she said. "He's in a small grave in England." Julia told Subria about the pain she felt and the guilt that she had borne for so long regarding the passing of her oldest son.

"What causes you to feel guilt?" asked Subria.

Julia paused for several moments. What she was about to say had never crossed her lips, and now she was about to tell it to a woman that she barely knew. She realized that knowing Subria as little as she did perhaps made the telling of it easier.

Julia started to cry again. "My son was ill, but I may have killed him. I may have suffocated him," she sobbed. "I may have killed him just as much as Katherine killed my father. To be sure, it was an accident, but I may have bundled him too tightly to myself. Or maybe it was the illness. I'm not sure, and I can't forgive myself."

Subria held the trembling younger woman. "You would never bring harm to your children. I'm sure that the illness took him. You must forgive yourself. God would, even if your actions did bring unintentional harm to him."

When Julia had calmed herself somewhat, she added, "That's a major reason that I chose to leave England, to start over. England had too many sorrows for me."

Subria's eyes were moist as she considered the pain of a mother that must bury her child and the burden that she must carry.

"It must have been difficult for you to leave England just the same," Subria observed.

"Yes. Saying farewell to Hyrum's family and to Lord and Lady Hammond, and Queen Victoria, and to my brother of course, was very painful. It was as though they all died at once to us."

After a moment's reflection, Julia wiped her eyes and added with a faint smile, "So, I suppose that my people are from here."

The two women sat side by side for a few moments before Julia asked, "Where are your people?"

"My people are dead," replied Subria.

"I'm so sorry," Julia offered.

"It was a long time ago," Subria said. Then she proceeded to tell Julia about the raid on her village and her attempted escape. She told Julia about the treachery of the couple that tricked her and gave her to Shaka. She cried as she told Julia of the long march that ended on a slave ship. She didn't dare describe to Julia the complete horrors of the slave ship for fear of overburdening her sensitivities. Regardless, Julia had no frame of reference to comprehend fully the malevolent and evil nature of men who trade in human flesh. Subria told Julia of her conversion to Christianity and of her eventual forgiveness of the perpetrators of evil. She also told her about the shipwreck and the fear she experienced as she clung to the broken piece of wood from the ship, facing each moment with the possibility that she would be swept into the sea.

"Forgiving myself was most difficult," Subria confided.

"Forgiving yourself?" asked Julia.

Subria hesitated. Other than the Coburns, she had told no one how Maarku died. She started hesitantly and told Julia how in her anger, she had urged Maarku to pull the lieutenant from his own floating wood piece. She told her that because of her desire for revenge, and at her urging Maarku had reached too far and could not recover from his lost grip on the wood float.

"I felt that I had killed Maarku!" Subria declared.

Julia held her new friend as they both cried. "Oh, Subria! You must forgive yourself. You were young and it was an accident! You meant no harm to come to Maarku."

"But I did mean harm to the lieutenant!" Subria cried.

"But no harm came to him. I'm sure that God has forgiven you. Haven't you felt the love of God since that time?"

Subria replied that she had felt the love of God in her life. She shared with Julia her personal search for forgiveness, and that she felt that God had forgiven her. The two women held each other for several minutes until the tears stopped.

"You obviously made it to shore," observed Julia. "What happened after you survived the sea?"

Subria laughed as she told her about the red dress and the kindness of the Coburns. She told her about her conversion and how she learned to read English by reading the Bible. She told her about the nurturing of Mrs. Coburn and how she had been taught to sew, cook and garden. She told her about the joys of living with the Coburns for many years, and about the sadness of losing them as they boarded the ship for England. She told Julia about her prayer to be delivered from a life of loneliness and how she met Hyrum the next day.

Subria looked at Julia and smiled, "So, yes, I've felt the love of God."

"I don't think it was happenchance that brought you to us, Subria," Julia said as she smiled and hugged her new friend and mentor.

Hyrum was surprised when he returned later that afternoon to find Julia and Subria laughing and talking like they had known each other all of their lives. Julia was excited to tell Hyrum that Subria was going to teach her to preserve meat by smoking it. Hyrum was pleased, but was left wondering how the transformation had come about.

Chapter Eighteen – Uninvited Guests
March 1846
Elephant Hook, Africa

The Princes' dog raised its head and growled menacingly with teeth bared. The Princes and Subria had just sat at the table for an evening meal; the dog was laying under the table, and Luke slept on the floor nearby. Suddenly, loud banging sent the dog bounding to the door, and his growling intensified. The noise awoke Luke with a fright, and he started crying.

Irritated at the disruption, Hyrum arose from the table, stating, "I wonder who that could be." Visitors were few and always welcomed, but it was the aggressiveness of the knock that was irritating.

Subria quickly gathered Luke into her arms and handed him to Julia, then she calmed Victoria and Francis.

Hyrum held his dog by the leather collar before opening the door. Hyrum knew that if the person knocking was Ian or someone that the dog knew and liked, he wouldn't be carrying on so.

Subria cringed when she saw who was at the door, and she hoped that Hyrum wouldn't invite him in.

"Evening, Mr. Richards," Hyrum stated plainly without detectable passion.

Most people would have been invited to come inside, but the Princes were cautious when it came to Mr. Richards.

Mr. Richards stood at the door with both feet firmly planted about shoulder width apart. He wore his customary cap, despite the darkness of the night.

Subria had only met Mr. Richards a few times in the several months that she had lived with the Princes, and she didn't care for him at all. Each time that she saw him she was deeply troubled.

"I hope you're pleased!" Mr. Richards pointedly said to Hyrum.

"Do I have cause to be pleased?" asked Hyrum.

Mr. Richards' tone and approach was generally designed to put people on the defensive and to give himself the advantage. Hyrum was aware of Mr. Richards' manner and did his best to not be caught in his snares, while at the same time not antagonizing him further, if possible. Mr. Richards was considerably older than Hyrum and presented little physical threat, but he wielded an influence on the neighbors, and his temper made him volatile. Hyrum knew that he often carried a musket and a knife and rumor was that he wasn't shy about using either.

"The Xhosa are back, and I suppose you can guess whose land they've settled on."

"I wouldn't hazard a guess, Mr. Richards. But I suppose you've come here to tell me."

Mr. Richards looked past Hyrum and into the room where he caught sight of Subria. Subria immediately averted her eyes. She was careful to not lock eyes with Mr. Richards because it made her very uncomfortable. She felt that he had a strong dislike for the native people.

"They've settled on your land, sir," Mr. Richards stated with a voice filled with accusation. "And I suppose that you'll rush over there and tell them they're welcome to stay!"

Hyrum had no problem looking Mr. Richards directly in the eyes. He felt that doing so was the best way to meet the hostile behavior of an aggressor.

"I don't suppose there's any need to rush over there. They know they're welcome," replied Hyrum calmly.

"Welcome to steal our sheep, while yours are all accounted for!"

"Do you have proof of any sort that the Xhosa have stolen your sheep?"

"Their miserable presence is evidence enough. If a lion's in the area, do I need proof? No, I go and shoot the beast."

Mr. Richards' face was reddening and his voice was rising in pitch. A clear sign that his temper would flare. Hyrum thought it best to end the conversation quickly.

"If the lingering drought causes the Xhosa to need a sheep or two, it's no concern of mine. And you know, sir that the English garrison can't be too far away. If you've a problem with the Xhosa, you should knock on the garrison's door, not mine. You've disturbed my family from their meal. Now, unless this is a social call, and you'd like to join us for our meal, I'll ask you to leave this instant."

Without speaking Mr. Richards glared at Hyrum and then at Subria, turned abruptly and walked to his horse. When he was safely in the saddle, he turned and said, "I'm sure we haven't heard the end of this, Prince. You'd best decide where you're loyalties lie." Then he rode off into the night.

When the door was shut, Julia asked "Why does he frighten me so?"

"Because he's a horrible man," replied Subria.

With that comment, Julia furrowed her brow and shook her head ever so slightly and then glanced at Francis. A clear signal to Subria that Francis was within earshot and she didn't want to disturb him with such talk.

Subria also glanced at Francis and back at Julia and mouthed the words, "But, he certainly is horrible."

Hyrum called the family back to the table and they proceeded to pray before again beginning their meal. Hyrum prayed for a break in the drought and for peace in the community, with their neighbors and with the Xhosa.

"What will you do about the Xhosa?" asked Julia.

Hyrum looked at Subria and said, "Perhaps I'll take Subria with me tomorrow and visit them. Perhaps I can encourage them to leave our neighbors' sheep be and can get a sense for their plans."

"I speak so poorly," Subria protested. "Surely, one of the other workers would be a better choice."

Hyrum smiled. "Perhaps, but a woman is less threatening. Don't you think, Julia?"

"Do you think it's safe then?" asked Julia.

"Oh, quite safe, I'd say. If they meant harm, we'd know it by now," replied Hyrum.

Hyrum wasn't completely certain of his own comment. The drought had been severe, and some of the Xhosa had become nothing less than marauding bands who were raiding settlers' land. Their prey of choice was beef, but they also had a taste for mutton. It didn't help that treaties with the natives had been broken and some people of influence were encouraging settlers to move onto land that had been given back to the Xhosa after the last conflict with them.

"I hope you won't be gone long," Julia replied. "I don't know how I'll manage without Subria."

Luke had been born just a couple weeks before and Julia was finding that Francis and Victoria looked for opportunity to take advantage of her as she recuperated.

"We won't be long," Hyrum assured her.

The next day, Hyrum told Subria that he had decided to not take her to the Xhosa camp for fear that they would pressure him to keep her with them. Subria was relieved. She had felt uncomfortable about going to the camp. So Hyrum recruited one of his workers to go with him.

"Their English isn't very good, but their native tongue is still very good," observed Hyrum.

Hyrum and his worker walked the mile or so to the Xhosa camp. He would have taken the horse and wagon, but decided at the last minute that he didn't wish to present the Xhosa with temptation to steal his horse.

Their approach was noted by the Xhosa well before they reached the camp. It concerned Hyrum that the Xhosa were so close to the house. He also wondered how it was that they had moved onto his land without his observation. He had been grazing the sheep at an area in the opposite direction and supposed that accounted for him being unaware of their presence.

Hyrum wasn't enthusiastic about the presence of the Xhosa on his land, but he considered the best course to try and be friendly and establish communication with them so as to avoid conflict, if possible.

When they neared the village, they stopped and waited for an invitation to enter. When it came, they were escorted to the center of the village.

"Hyrum Prince," the chief greeted them.

Hyrum was surprised that they recognized him. It had been nearly five years since he had met them in their camp, and he hadn't expected that it would be the same group that had come back.

Hyrum greeted the chief, and his worker interpreted.

"How long will your people camp here?" Hyrum asked.

"This is not a camp," replied the chief. "This is our home."

"How long will you make this your home?"

The chief smiled, revealing a mouth with few teeth. "Perhaps until the rains come. That could be a very long time."

"I don't think that the settlers here will like that," observed Hyrum, trying to deliver the message in as diplomatic a way as possible.

Again, the chief smiled. "We mean no harm. We don't fear the settlers."

Hyrum looked about the camp. There was a significant change in their camp since he had last visited, and he was surprised that he hadn't noticed right away. Some spears were still visible leaning against the animal skin huts, but most frightening were the muskets that were also leaning against the huts. He had heard that the natives were using modern weaponry, but he hadn't realized that they had guns in so large a number. *If other tribes were as well equipped as this tribe,* he reasoned, *they could present a serious threat.* The guns were old muskets, but nevertheless, this was a major change in the way that the Xhosa might conduct themselves. *Little wonder that they didn't fear the settlers,* Hyrum thought.

"Your camp is not in accordance with treaties that have been signed with the Queen's government. And it's well known that the Xhosa have been stealing livestock," Hyrum stated, making his case as directly as possible.

Hyrum continued. "There is a regiment of the Queen's army at Grahamstown. They would come quickly if there's trouble. Even now some of the settlers may be summoning them," Hyrum stated in a serious tone. He was being more direct than he intended, but he could tell that the Xhosa's attitude had changed in the last several years. They were less intimidated by the possibility of conflict with the English. They were far more numerous than the English army, and they had experience in battles against them. Hyrum was sensing a possible shift in power favorable to the Xhosa.

The chief was unintimidated by allusions to the might of the English army. Smiling, he said, with a sweep of his arm, "See these warriors. There are many more for every one of them. Our warriors are scattered about the plains of this land and in the mountains. It's only a few days run and we can all come together."

"I understand," replied Hyrum. "Regardless, I caution you to not steal the cows or sheep of the settlers."

"The Xhosa will not take what is not ours," replied the chief with a smile.

Hyrum wasn't sure what the chief considered his, but he didn't question it.

"Very well," replied Hyrum. He bid the chief farewell, and he and his worker left the camp.

When he got back home, Ian was waiting with Julia and Subria. They were relieved to see that he was okay. Hyrum was pleased to see Ian; Ian had been in Grahamstown for several days.

After Hyrum related his conversation with the chief, Ian reported rumors he had heard in Grahamstown.

"Native raids have increased in regions north of Grahamstown. We've only been spared because Grahamstown is between us and the Xhosa country."

"Is it as bad as all that then?" asked Julia.

"It is," asserted Ian.

"What is the army doing about it?" asked Hyrum.

"There is little that they can do. Their outnumbered, and soon they'll be out gunned as well."

"But the Xhosa aren't trained in modern warfare," Hyrum stated.

"And that's just the point," Ian said raising his voice for emphasis. "Modern warfare is ineffective against a force that doesn't employee the same tactics. The Xhosa can move faster, and they don't march, they run!"

"Well, let's not discount the Queen's army just yet," Hyrum stated.

"Mark my word, brother," Ian asserted, "if things continue to get worse, if the rains don't come to ease the burden on the Xhosa, people like you and I will have to take up arms against them."

"I don't think I could do that," replied Hyrum. "I'm not a trained soldier."

"You won't need to be a trained soldier," declared Ian. Then he continued while sweeping his arm toward the hills, "You know these hills and mountains just like the Xhosa do. If it came down to defending your home and family, you'd go into the hills and drive the Xhosa back into their own lands. I know you would, because I've never known you to fear anything."

Hyrum held Julia. Francis had come outside, and Hyrum didn't want to scare him with such talk, so he put the conversation to rest with, "I hope it doesn't come to that."

"Ian's come to invite us to dinner tomorrow evening," Julia stated with a smile.

Hyrum seemed distracted, but perked up and replied, "Yes, yes. That would be capital. We'd love to. How is Amanda?"

"Amanda is well. She'd enjoy your company very much. It would cheer her so to see you." Then looking at Subria, he said, "And of course, Subria, we want you to come also."

Subria smiled, "I'd love to."

"Very well then," replied Ian. "It's settled. Tomorrow then."

After Ian left, Julia and Subria took Francis inside, and Hyrum went to feed the horse and other animals. As he did, he thought about his conversation with Ian and with the chief. *Perhaps Mr. Richards is right,* he thought. *Perhaps the Xhosa should be driven away from the settlement.*

Hyrum wasn't accustomed to conflict and hoped that everything could be worked out without resorting to violence. In his thoughts he wrestled to understand what his course should be. *Ian had a good point about defending home and family. Also, the attitude of the Xhosa is changing. Maybe that's all they are doing. Maybe they're only defending their homes and land and families. What are they to do?* he wondered. *Stand by and watch their own children starve, while there are settlers' cattle to be had for the taking? Would I act in any other fashion?*

When he finished caring for the animals, he still wasn't settled on the proper course of action.

The next day, Victoria wasn't feeling well, and was sleeping when it was time to leave for Ian and Amanda's house.

Julia was very disappointed, she hadn't seen Amanda for what seemed like weeks. "Hyrum, I'm truly disappointed, but we can't take Victoria in her present state. It wouldn't be good for her or for Amanda and her children."

"I'll stay with the child," Subria offered right away before Hyrum could respond.

"Are you quite sure?" asked Julia. "You don't mind?"

Subria was well aware of Julia's disappointment. Julia had been out of the house little since Luke had been born and it would do her well to go to Amanda's.

"Of course, I don't mind," replied Subria. And she really didn't mind, in fact, she almost relished the thought of being alone.

Julia looked at Hyrum. "Do you think that would be fine then?" she asked.

"Yes, quite," replied Hyrum. "It will do you good to get some fresh air also. Thank you Subria. We shan't be long."

Subria knew that they would be long, just not overnight. Nevertheless, she didn't mind.

While they were gone, Subria busied herself with some mending. She smiled to think how quickly a little boy could put holes in socks and trousers.

After the mending was completed, she started a fire to cook herself a meal. It was her intention, if Victoria continued sleeping, to read the Bible after her meal.

She fancied some boiled cabbage with vinegar, so while the water was coming to a boil, she walked outside to cut some cabbage from the garden. In the garden, she froze and the hair on the back of her neck bristled when she saw a footprint right next to the cabbage that she was going to cut. The print was the size of a man's foot and it was obvious that the foot had been bare. With her tracking skills it took her little investigation to realize that there was more than one person, and they weren't settlers. She also determined that the prints were fresh.

"Dear Lord," she whispered "please keep me safe."

Victoria! she thought as soon as she had whispered her prayer. Looking about quickly she was shaken to see five Xhosa warriors in the back of the house.

They must have seen the Princes leave, and they've come to steal food, she thought.

Knowing that the warriors would just as soon steal a child, she ran for the house.

"Dear Lord! What should I do?" she whispered as soon as she was in the house.

Why did they take the dog? she cried in her mind. *At least he could have warned me.*

The warriors were coming around the front of the house and Subria was frantic.

Put the child in with the mending and cover her. The thought was clear and piercing.

The mending was in a large wooden crate. Without hesitation, Subria took a few articles of clothing out of the crate. *Please stay asleep,* she thought as she picked the sleeping child up and gently placed her inside the crate. She fit perfectly! Subria loosely and gently layed a few articles of clothing atop Victoria, leaving her face uncovered. Despite the face of the child being uncovered, the other clothing was piled about her so as to render her sufficiently concealed, so long as she stayed asleep. If there were time, Subria would have liked to have put the crate with its cargo beneath a bed, but there was no time. Just as she stood and faced the door, the warriors opened it and walked into the room.

They were a frightful sight, but Subria had seen warriors before. Instantly, her mind was taken back to the day as a young girl when she had stood up to Shaka. *I've faced the most powerful man in the world without fear,* she thought. *I can face these.*

Her heart raced wildly as she sternly demanded in the native tongue, "You go. Out of this hut." Still her voice quivered ever so slightly, and her stomach ached.

The warriors laughed at her accent.

"Hear the woman Swallow try to talk," one of them laughed.

"Swallows have plenty of food. Where is it?" one of them demanded.

Subria pointed to the pantry. She was all too willing to hand over all the Princes' food to be rid of them.

The warriors walked to the pantry and started helping themselves to anything that was edible. It seemed that they would stay and eat it right there.

Subria's heart sank as they were still in the pantry and she heard a faint noise from the crate. Now she was desperate to be rid of them at almost any cost. She grabbed a nearby knife and pointed it at them threateningly.

"You go now! Take the food!"

The warriors laughed at the sight of her threatening them with a knife, but still they took the food and walked out the door. Subria quickly closed the door and bolted it. When she did, a distinct cry came from the crate. Though her energy was exhausted from fright, she hurried to the crate and scooped up Victoria and held her close. Sinking into the rocking chair, she closed her eyes and just rocked and held Victoria.

"Thank you, Lord," she whispered over and over.

When they returned hours later, Hyrum and Julia were terrified as they listened to Subria describe the encounter.

"Hyrum, we aren't safe with the Xhosa here. Something needs to be done," Julia pleaded as she held Victoria close. "The loss of sheep or food is one thing, but the loss of a child would be unbearable."

Hyrum knew she was right, something had to be done. The drought had intensified the conflict with the natives and it was only going to get worse.

"I'll take you all to Ian and Amanda's tomorrow, and I'll go to Grahamstown and notify the garrison. Surely, they'll come to our aid."

"What if they don't?" asked Julia.

"Let's not consider that possibility just yet," Hyrum urged her.

The next day, Hyrum loaded Julia and the children and Subria into the wagon and set a course for Ian and Amanda's house. He looked back at his home and land and wondered whether he would find it in the same condition when he returned, but at least his family should be safe.

Chapter Nineteen – The Patient
March 1846
Grahamstown, Africa

Hyrum left his family with Ian and Amanda and quickly made the trip to Grahamstown. The garrison was easily found in Grahamstown, since their presence had tripled its size. With a uniformed man occupying every shady spot available, Hyrum was surprised at the number of men stationed there and was pleased to see the strength the Queen had sent to defend that quarter of her realm.

They didn't appear to be in any particular state of readiness however. Many men appeared to be sleeping in the shade, others were playing cards, and the public house was well occupied.

Hyrum went with haste directly to the commander's tent that also served as his office and requested an audience with the commander.

"Wait here!" Hyrum was told by a low ranking soldier.

Hyrum waited outside the tent, but he could hear the soldier speaking with the commander.

"What is it?" asked the commander.

"A local farmer to see you, sir," replied the soldier.

"What is it, another cow stolen?" asked the commander in a voice that clearly sounded irritated.

"I don't know, sir. Probably."

"Very well, then. Show him in."

Hyrum was surprised by the appearance of the commander. He was a small man with glasses and a beard that was at least a week old. His boots were well scuffed and his braces, that should have been about his shoulders to support his trousers, hung about his waist. Only an undershirt covered his torso. Hyrum would have expected more polish in a commander of the Queen's garrison.

As Hyrum stepped to the table that functioned as a desk, the commander put aside a book that he had been reading.

"What is it then," demanded the commander in a voice bigger than his size.

"Sir, I've come from Elephant Hook. Some Xhosa have set up a village there and are causing fear among the settlers."

"Have they caused harm?"

"No, sir. But they have acted in a most threatening way. Some did enter into my own home and frightened a member of my family." Hyrum didn't want to mention that Subria was a native for fear that the commander would discount the seriousness of the situation.

"How many Xhosa are there?"

"Perhaps 200, sir."

"Two hundred warriors?"

"No, 200 total, sir. Maybe 50 men."

The commander stood up and walked to the door of the tent.

"Fifty? That's hardly enough to be concerned about, then, is it?" he said as he turned back to face Hyrum.

"Well, sir, Elephant Hook is a very small settlement. Fifty warriors are very concerning to the settlers there."

"And you want me to send men to rout them out then. Is that it?"

"Yes, sir."

The commander looked back outside his tent and surveyed his troops. "I suppose that I could spare a few men. If there are 50 warriors, I suppose that 10 of my men should do. Don't you?"

Hyrum hesitated, and replied, "The Xhosa have muskets, sir."

The commander glared at Hyrum, and said indignantly, "My men are the world's finest soldiers. There are none better trained. Would you suggest that a few natives with some old muskets are equal to them?"

"No, sir. Not at all," Hyrum assured him.

At that moment, a soldier rode into camp on a horse at full gallop, causing a commotion. The horse was wet from sweat, obviously having been ridden hard, almost to the breaking point. The rider rode directly to the commander's tent and lighted from the horse.

"Sir, the Xhosa refused to release the thief to us. They've killed all my men, and only I've escaped," he breathlessly reported.

Several days earlier, a Xhosa had been captured and was being escorted to Grahamstown for trial on charges of thievery; he had stolen an axe. The crime seemed trivial enough, but some felt that it was necessary to teach the Xhosa that there would be no tolerance. The Xhosa, weary of English dominance, attacked and killed the escorts, taking the thief back to their village.

When word of the escape reached the commander, he had sent 10 men to the village to secure the retrieval of the thief.

The commander was shocked. "All nine of your men killed?" he asked in surprise.

"Yes, sir. All nine."

The commander turned and walked back to the table and slammed both fists firmly. His head hung down for a moment and his eyes were closed.

Without lifting his head, he asked, "How did you escape?"

The soldier stood erect and reported, "Only by the hand of Providence and quick wits, sir. We stood little chance. We were ambushed before we reached the village. The Xhosa aren't very accurate marksmen, but there were many of them. My men fell almost immediately. As soon as the shots rang out, I gave command to fall back, but it was too late. My men fell quickly, and I rode hard as soon as I saw my fallen companions, and I haven't stopped till coming here, sir."

As soon as he heard it, the commander slammed his fists against the table again and turned to face the soldier. "I'll send twice as many men this time. No, 100 times as many! I'll show the Xhosa the strength of the Queen's army." His face was red and his frame shook as he spoke.

Hyrum cleared his throat. "One thousand men, sir? Do you have so many? You'll still send ten men to Elephant Hook?"

The commander appeared to have forgotten about Hyrum. When Hyrum spoke, he turned his head toward Hyrum suddenly as though he had been startled.

"Ten men will never do under the circumstances," he said as he grabbed a nearby shirt and put it on.

"Quite right," agreed Hyrum.

"I don't have any men to spare for Elephant Hook! All my men are required to secure this thief and to teach the Xhosa to respect the Queen's realm," the commander said as he left the tent abruptly.

Hyrum was shocked with the turn of events. He was too surprised to move, it seemed. He stood and watched the commander walk away, tucking in his shirt and lifting the braces to his shoulders.

The commander began barking orders, and the entire camp sprang to life in preparation to move against the Xhosa. As Hyrum watched, he became dismayed to think that he had failed entirely. *I couldn't even secure ten of the Queen's men,* he thought. *Was Mr. Richards right after all?*

Discouraged with his lack of success, Hyrum turned his back on Grahamstown and headed for home. He felt that at least he'd bear the news of the garrison's attack on another Xhosa village. Trouble with one Xhosa village often meant trouble with the whole Xhosa alliance. When the Elephant Hook Xhosa learned of the attack by the garrison on members of their alliance, as surely they would, they may leave Elephant Hook to fight with the rest of the Xhosa, or it was possible that they'd stay and cause tensions in Elephant Hook. Either way, Hyrum felt that his news was urgent.

There seemed to be no one about when he reached Ian and Amanda's house, and he entered the home immediately. Julia was sitting next to

Amanda with her arms around her shoulders consoling her. Hyrum could sense right away that the mood in the house was heavy.

"Why did he go with them?" Amanda cried.

"He felt it was the right thing to do," Julia assured her.

"Go with who?" asked Hyrum.

As soon as he spoke, Julia leapt to her feet and rushed into his arms. "Hyrum! I'm so glad you're home," she cried.

Hyrum hugged and kissed his wife and asked, "Where's Ian then?"

Julia looked somber as Amanda replied in a sad, almost desperate tone, "He's gone to the Xhosa with Mr. Richards!"

"What?" asked Hyrum with surprise. "Just he and Mr. Richards?"

"No, no. There are others," replied Julia. "Mr. Richards managed to organize a group of men. They were well armed and left this morning to force the Xhosa off the land. Ian went with them, and Amanda is fearful for his safety."

Hyrum let out a sigh. "And rightfully so," he replied. He then told the women about his experience in Grahamstown and the impending conflict with the Xhosa alliance. "Apparently, the Queen's forces will be of no help in our immediate conflict," he asserted. "Perhaps I was wrong about Mr. Richards."

Subria, who had been watching the children in a back room, entered in time to hear Hyrum's declaration about Mr. Richards.

"No, Mr. Prince," she said, "you weren't wrong about Mr. Richards. He's a bad man, I can feel it."

"Well, still I may have been wrong about his assessment of the Xhosa."

With that, Hyrum turned to leave.

"Where are you going?" asked Julia urgently.

"I'm going to find Ian and to help drive out the Xhosa."

"Please no," plead Julia.

"I really must, Julia. I can't just sit and wait while the men of the community are in danger."

"Your going will make little difference," Julia replied tearfully.

Hyrum stopped and hugged his wife. "Little difference, perhaps. But a difference, nonetheless," he replied.

Francis and Victoria were entering the room and squealed with excitement to see their father. They ran and hugged his legs as he struggled to pick them both up.

"Oh, my sweet ones!" he said as he hugged them. "Francis, you're getting bigger every day. I don't think I can pick you up."

"Where you going?" Francis asked.

"To find Uncle Ian," Hyrum replied.

"Take me!" plead Francis.

"Me too!" echoed Victoria.

Hyrum smiled and looked at Julia.

"No, your father can't take you this time," Julia told them despite their protests. "He won't be gone long, and we'll all go home together," she assured them.

"Oh, no fair," insisted Francis.

"No fair," Victoria echoed.

"Fair or not, you'll let him go," Julia said as she took Victoria out of Hyrum's arms.

Hyrum lowered Francis and then took Luke from Subria and gave him a hug and kiss before handing him back.

The women and children followed Hyrum outside; as they did, they were all surprised by yells coming from the small dirt road that led to the house. It was Ian yelling and waving.

"What's this?" Hyrum asked aloud.

Amanda ran toward Ian as soon as she heard him, falling into his welcoming arms.

"Ian, I was so worried," she cried. Then she pulled back and studied his face. "Are you injured?"

"No, dear. I'm quite alright."

Though uninjured, Ian's appearance made clear that he had been involved in a skirmish. His shirt and his trousers had rips in them as though he had run through heavy brush. His face was smudged with a mixture of blood and dirt.

Ian only held her for a moment before crying out to Hyrum, "Hitch the wagon! Mr. Richards is injured!"

"You look a terrible sight, old man," Hyrum observed with concern. "Are you sure you're uninjured?"

"Quite sure."

"What about the others?" asked Hyrum.

"Some small injuries. But Mr. Richards is in a bad way."

"Will he be okay?" asked Amanda.

"He won't die, if that's what you mean. But he's in a bad way. He took a ball to the leg, and a spear lanced his face."

Amanda and Julia grimaced to even consider such injuries. Subria's initial thought was that it was too bad that the injuries weren't worse, but she immediately reminded herself that such thoughts aren't the thoughts of a Christian.

Ian glanced at Hyrum, but looked at the women as he said, "We'll bring him back here where the women can attend to him."

"We've no experience with such things," Julia protested, and Amanda nodded in agreement.

Hyrum looked at Subria. "Subria, you probably have some experience. Can you care for him?"

Subria had seen her mother and grandmother attend to wounded warriors, and had even watched as her mother had bound up a wound on her father's arm with a bone needle and sinew thread. She had also watched Mrs. Coburn bind up small wounds for Mr. Coburn. She had no personal experience, but it hadn't seemed difficult.

More concerning for Subria was the thought that the wounded was Mr. Richards. Try as she might, she couldn't have good feelings toward the man. To think that she'd have to bind his wound repulsed her. She wanted to reject Hyrum's request, but instead she nodded her head in agreement.

"Very good, Subria," replied Hyrum. Turning to Ian, he said, "Let's get that wagon hitched."

Before they left, Ian suggested that they leave the women and children at Hyrum and Julia's home on the way to get Mr. Richards. Hyrum and Julia's home was closer to the Xhosa village. Mr. Richards could be cared for there, minimizing the distance that they would have to transport him. Hyrum agreed, and the women and children were soon in the wagon.

On the way to drop off Julia, Amanda, Subria and the children, Ian spoke of the attack on the village.

"No sooner had Mr. Richards heard that you had left for Grahamstown than he started in earnest to gather men to go against the village," Ian told Hyrum. "He didn't have to use much influence, many were willing."

"And you?" asked Hyrum.

"I was willing enough, but he assured me that we would only use force at last resort."

"And was that the case then?"

"Mr. Richards had some of these farmers so worked up as to render them incapable of control," Ian assured Hyrum. "He was offering buckets of ale

269

to the first person who shot a native. Some of the farmers were bragging that they would be the first, and they were laughing at the thought that a native warrior would even be able to operate a firearm. I should have disassociated myself from them, but I thought that I could bring some calming reason to the group."

Hyrum shook his head in disgust. He wasn't surprised that Mr. Richards could incite a group to go against the village, but he was dismayed at the apparent willingness of some farmers to offer the first strike.

"As a matter of principle, defending one's home is honorable," Hyrum stated, "but there's a fine line between being honorable and being vigilante."

Ian looked at Hyrum. "Would you accuse me of vigilantism, then?"

Hyrum returned Ian's look and replied, "I'm sorry, brother. I don't intend to reproach your actions. I'm sure they were honorable."

Ian was silent for a moment before replying, "I hope they were."

Ian went on to tell them that they hadn't even reached the village before Mr. Richards ordered one of the farmers to shoot at a warrior who was guarding the village.

"The warrior would have notified the village of course. And I suppose that would be of little consequence if the plan was to talk, but Mr. Richards had other plans," Ian told Hyrum. "The Xhosa took little notice of the noise and were caught unprepared. By appearances, it was just another day for them until we showed up."

Ian was quiet for a moment as though reluctant to continue. When he did, he said, "Women were going about their chores, and children played, until we entered the village. When we did, chaos erupted amongst the natives. Mothers gathered their children, men grabbed their weapons. Whether Mr. Richards gave the order to shoot, I couldn't say with certainty, but we certainly fired our weapons first."

Tears welled in Subria's eyes as she listened. Though many years and miles separated her from the village of her youth, listening to the account took her mind back to the night that Shaka had entered her village. *It had been "just another night"* she thought. She remembered hearing the screams of mothers for their children.

Ian told them that the Xhosa had made initial use of their muskets, but they were slow with re-loading. They quickly resorted to using their spears, but the crude weaponry was largely ineffective against the farmers' firearms.

Listening caused Subria anguish as she thought about the fathers who had been awaken abruptly in her own village as Shaka had unleashed the stroke of death. Many had died as they reached for their own weapons without being able to use them.

Ian's voice cracked a little when he continued. "I only shot once, and that was to protect one of our neighbors who was undoubtedly going to be killed by a warrior's spear."

Hyrum looked at his brother and studied his eyes and expression. *Had he killed a man?* he thought. Ian anticipated the question and responded without being asked.

"Whether my shot killed the native or not, I couldn't say. It wounded him though. And scared him enough that he ran. By the time I loaded another ball the natives were on the run."

"How many natives were killed?" Hyrum asked.

"To be sure, I don't know. Probably 10. All warriors, at least."

"Ten!" replied Hyrum in surprise. "This could bring the entire Xhosa alliance against us!"

Hyrum turned his attention to the road ahead and was silent for a moment.

"Well, maybe it won't bring the alliance against us," observed Hyrum, and he told Ian about the preparations of the British garrison to go against the Xhosa. "They will likely keep the Xhosa occupied."

Both men were silent for a short time until Ian said, "I don't know whether to be disgusted that I'm such a poor soldier, or to be ashamed that I almost killed a man. For all I know, he died of his wounds."

"You're not a trained soldier," Hyrum replied. "How many times have you even fired a weapon?"

After leaving the women and children at Hyrum and Julia's home, it wasn't long before Hyrum and Ian were passing their neighbors going in the other direction.

"Mr. Richards will be glad to see you," one of the neighbors called as the wagon neared.

"Hyrum, you should have been with us!" another called. "It was just like being in the Queen's service."

Still others bragged that they had taught the Xhosa a lesson that they'd not soon forget. Hyrum noted many were carrying souvenirs from the village in the form of spears, knives, or hides.

"Curse you, Prince," Mr. Richards moaned as the wagon halted near him. He was clearly in pain and speaking was difficult. He was alone, laying in the shade of a small tree. "You're slower than an old woman."

Hyrum was surprised that none of the neighbors had waited with him. Mr. Richards had a piece of cloth tied about his leg to slow the bleeding, and he held a cloth to his face where he had been wounded with the spear.

"We came as quickly as we could," Ian assured him, but Mr. Richards' eyes were closed and he gave no indication that he had heard.

Hyrum took Mr. Richards by the legs and Ian grasped him under the arms, and they lifted him into the wagon. Mr. Richards groaned as they did.

At the house, Subria prepared hot water, soap, clean cloths, needle and thread and a knife.

"You'd best keep the children out of the house," she advised Julia and Amanda. "It's likely to be a bloody mess, and Mr. Richards will likely use language unfit to be heard."

"Amanda can watch the children, and I'll help you," Julia offered.

Subria stopped what she was doing for a moment and smiled at Julia.

Julia watched Subria move about the kitchen. Though she did so with efficiency, it was almost in a perfunctory manner. Normally she would be laughing and speaking, but not now.

"I know you don't care for Mr. Richards," Julia observed. "It's admirable of you to care for him."

"Regardless of how I feel, we can't very well let him die," Subria stated matter of factly, as though she was trying to convince herself as much as deflecting Julia's compliment.

"He may need to convalesce here for a few days," Julia observed.

With that, Subria placed a metal bowl of water on the table with enough force as to cause much of the unsettled water to spill out.

Subria's uncharacteristic response made clear to Julia how difficult this was for her. Julia remembered the disdain that she once held for Katherine. She had felt justified because of Katherine's actions, and it had been very difficult for her to overcome the feelings of hatred toward her. *Mr. Richards has a contrary disposition,* she thought, *but he hasn't done anything to warrant Subria's disdain.*

"Has Mr. Richards harmed you in some way?" Julia ventured with concern.

Subria stopped and looked at Julia. "No more than you," she stated after a moments reflection. "He's just not a gentleman."

Julia reached out and hugged Subria. "It'll be fine. We'll get through this together."

Subria smiled and wiped a tear from her eye.

Amanda stepped into the kitchen and announced that the wagon was approaching.

Subria gave Julia a half-hearted smile and they went to meet the wagon.

"He's in a bad way," Ian said as the wagon stopped. "He's been unconscious since we loaded him into the wagon."

"Is he alive?" Julia asked.

"Yes. Where do you want him?" asked Hyrum, looking at Subria.

"Put him on the table," she replied.

The table was bare, but the women put a pillow beneath Mr. Richards' head and some folded cloths beneath his wounded leg.

With the patient on the table, Subria looked closely at the cut on Mr. Richards' face. It was deep, but hadn't pierced completely though. It would need to be sewed shut to minimize infection. As ghastly as it was, it was of secondary importance to the wounded leg.

Subria turned her attention to the wounded leg while the others watched. The wound was in the fleshy part of the upper leg. The ball appeared to still be in the wound, but probably hadn't impacted the bone. If left inside, the ball would cause certain infection and death.

"I believe that I'll take care of the animals," Hyrum announced.

"And I'll assist Amanda with the children," offered Ian.

With the others out of the room, Subria instructed Julia to pour some alcohol into the leg wound. Using a knife, she then probed inside the wound until she felt something hard. Based on the location and depth, she expected it was the ball and not a bone.

Julia averted her eyes as Subria dug inside the wound in an attempt to get beneath the ball to lift it out of the hole. She looked once when she thought it was safe, only to see Subria pull the knife out of the wound and insert her finger. Again, she averted her eyes, but thought that she'd faint when she heard sounds of air and blood escaping the hole as Subria's finger probed deeper. She was relieved to soon hear a thud as the lead ball was dropped into the bowl of water.

Julia poured more alcohol into the wound and Subria sewed it shut with a few stitches.

"Will you please shave Mr. Richards' face?" asked Subria. "I need to sit for a spell."

Julia looked at Subria. "Shave him?"

"Yes, his wound will need to be clean and clear of hair if I'm to sew it shut. May as well shave his entire face."

"He may not like that," observed Julia. "He's always worn a beard."

Subria smiled at the thought that Mr. Richards would object. "Yes, shave him clean."

Subria sat for a few moments outside the kitchen. She wasn't so tired physically as she was troubled emotionally. She had always distrusted Mr. Richards, and yet her dislike for him had intensified since he had led the raid on the native village. Despite her intense feelings toward him, she was now expected to help heal him, and the dichotomy caused her emotional distress.

Julia stepped outside just as Subria had resolved to put her feelings aside and do her Christian duty by caring for Mr. Richards.

"He's clean shaven and ready for you to stitch up, Subria," Julia said.

Subria looked at Julia and replied, "Very well then. Please get me some more clean water and heat it up, if you would."

"Yes, of course," Julia replied.

Subria walked into the kitchen. Mr. Richards lay on the table, still unconscious. *He looks to be dead already*, Subria thought. She walked to the table and put a shaky hand on his throat to feel for a pulse. She was almost disappointed when she felt the light pounding of blood moving through his veins. Turning her attention to the needle and thread, she carefully ran the thread through the eye of the needle and laid it aside.

As she stepped close to the table near his head, Subria removed the cap from Mr. Richards' head without a thought. As she did, she stood in paralyzing shock, staring at a large scar on Mr. Richards' forehead; a scar that had been covered by an ever-present cap. The clean-shaven face, the scar; it was clear now, this was the death ship lieutenant!

Subria gasped and stepped backward from the table, covering her mouth so as to not scream aloud. All the fear and hatred from her experiences on the death ship came flooding across the years as though it were the present. The hateful man, the man responsible for so many deaths, including Maarku, was before her. *Am I to save this monster?* she asked herself.

Suddenly the thought occurred to her that no one really knew whether he was dead or alive. If he were dead, it would be of little consequence to anyone, and possibly a great benefit to many.

The straight edge blade that Julia had used to shave Mr. Richards lay on the table. Subria picked it up and looked at it as she put her other hand on Mr. Richards' throat. *It would be so easy,* she thought. *No, the others would know it was me. Julia will be back soon! I'll cover his mouth and nose. No one will know!*

Slowly, carefully Subria raised her hand toward Mr. Richards' face. It would have to be done quickly and quietly! Julia would be returning with the water any moment. *He deserves this,* Subria thought. *How many deaths is he responsible for? How many death ships did he sail? If for no other reason, he deserves to die for killing the young sailor and Maarku.*

Subria lightly placed her hand on Mr. Richards's nose and lips and felt the warmth of his shallow breathing. Feeling the very air that had once expanded his lungs caused her to cringe and jerk her hand away.

Do it! she told herself. *What are you waiting for? Julia will be back!*

Again she lightly placed her hand on his nose and lips, but this time she pressed down and waited.

What am I doing? I've never killed a man! This is wrong! I'm a Christian! I must forgive.

With a start, Subria pulled her hand back and wiped away Mr. Richards' saliva that had accumulated. A great sadness and shame swept over her at the realization that she had nearly killed a man. Only brief moments had stood between who she was and who she almost became, and it frightened her. With weakened knees she sank to the floor and cried.

"What is it Subria?" asked Julia tenderly when she walked into the kitchen with the water. She sat the water down and quickly knelt beside Subria and hugged her. "I'll sew his facial wound. I'm sure I could do it. You leave the kitchen."

Julia helped Subria to her feet and walked her to the kitchen door where Subria stopped and turned back. "No. I can do this," she stated confidently. "You help me."

"Are you certain?" asked Julia.

"Yes, quite," replied Subria.

The two women returned to the table, and Subria took the needle and thread in her hand and pressed the needle gently, but firmly into the flesh of Mr. Richards' cheek. Suddenly, Mr. Richards face pulled away, and his eyes opened wide as he simultaneously grabbed Subria's wrist and began to rise from the table.

"Aaaarrrhh!" he yelled out in terror.

Subria and Julia both screamed in surprise and jumped back. Mr. Richards' sudden attempt to rise, coupled with his loss of blood proved too much, and he again blacked out. It seemed to Subria and Julia that time slowed as they watched Mr. Richards' eyes roll and then close. He then collapsed onto the stone floor, hitting his head firmly in the process.

Subria cautiously knelt beside him and felt for a pulse. She looked up at Julia. "He's alive," she said.

Hyrum had heard the screams and came running, soon followed by Amanda and Ian.

"What happened? Are you alright?" asked Hyrum urgently.

Julia hugged Hyrum and buried her face in his chest. "Yes. We're fine. Mr. Richards fell from the table in an attempt to rise," she said. Then looking at Mr. Richards on the floor, she asked, "Subria, is he breathing?"

Hyrum released Julia and knelt beside Subria and checked Mr. Richards.

"Yes, he's breathing," Subria replied.

"He has a nasty bump where his head hit the floor," Hyrum observed.

"Here, let's get him back onto the table," suggested Ian.

Hyrum and Ian lifted him back onto the table, and Hyrum said, "Perhaps Ian and I should stay until you're finished. We can hold him in the event he awakes."

"Yes, please do," replied Subria.

"His cheek is bleeding again," observed Ian.

"Best to get that sewed up," Hyrum commented.

Hyrum moved aside so that Subria could work on Mr. Richards' face. Her fingers trembled as she pushed the needle through each side of the cut. Hyrum and Ian held his arms, but it wasn't necessary. He didn't regain consciousness while Subria worked on him.

Still unconscious, Mr. Richards was moved to Francis' bed after Subria completed her work. Later that evening, he still hadn't regained consciousness.

"Hyrum, don't you think that you should go for the doctor in Grahamstown tomorrow?" Julia asked.

"Hyrum just returned from Grahamstown. Maybe Ian can go," Amanda offered.

"Yes, quite right. I'll go tomorrow," Ian agreed.

"Then you and Amanda will stay tonight," Julia insisted.

"Yes, indeed," agreed Hyrum.

The next morning, Julia was first up before the others, and she tapped lightly on Mr. Richards' door. "Mr. Richards," she said quietly, but there was no response. "Mr. Richards," she ventured again. Silence.

Julia gently opened the door and peeked inside. Mr. Richards lay on the bed in the exact position they had left him. She walked quietly to the bed and touched his hand. She expected that it would be stiff and cold. But it wasn't, and Mr. Richards opened his eyes suddenly, startling her.

"Where am I?" he demanded. Speaking pulled on the threads in his cheek and he groaned and held a hand over his wound.

"You're at Hyrum Prince's home," Julia replied as she backed out of the room and called for Hyrum, who came quickly.

"Mr. Richards," Hyrum said upon entering the room. "We weren't certain that you'd live. You took a hard blow to the head."

"I was better off with the natives," Mr. Richards said through clenched teeth so that his cheek wouldn't move. "You've tried to kill me. I'll not forget this."

Suddenly, Mr. Richards realized his cap was missing, and he demanded to have it. Julia brought it and gave it to Hyrum who handed it to Mr. Richards.

"I assure you, we meant no harm," asserted Hyrum.

Mr. Richards quickly placed the cap on his head. Subria heard the commotion and waited outside the room.

"Who's done this to me?" Mr. Richards asked, alluding to the stitches in his cheek.

"Subria," replied Hyrum.

"No doubt your native woman," replied Mr. Richards with disgust. "She's shaved me also! I demand you take me home at once. I'll not stay under the same roof with a native."

Hyrum looked at Julia and back at Mr. Richards. "Very well. I'll get Ian and we'll hitch the wagon."

Subria remained in the kitchen as Hyrum and Ian helped Mr. Richards from Francis' room and out of the house. She only dared sneak a look once, and when she did, Mr. Richards looked up and glared at her. His eyes pierced her and filled her with dread. *He recognizes me,* she worried, and she ducked back behind the door and trembled.

Chapter Twenty – Fever
Late October 1847
Elephant Hook, Africa

"Also, dear Lord, if thou canst see fit in thy tender mercies to bring rain to this parched land, we would be ever so grateful," Hyrum prayed with his family gathered about him. "Also, we pray that thou wouldst end this terrible war with the natives that has continued these many months." After a moment's silence, he added, "God bless the Queen and her garrison. Amen."

"Amen," replied Julia, Francis and Victoria in unison.

Hyrum put on his hat as he arose from his knees. He didn't notice, but Julia did, Francis mimicking his every move as he put on his own hat. Julia smiled to think that her little man was going to grow up to be every bit the man his father was.

"I saw clouds building when I was out feeding the horses this morning," Hyrum told Julia with a voice full of hope. "I'd like to think they are storm clouds."

Julia nodded and agreed.

"If we don't get rain soon, we won't have water or food for our sheep," continued Hyrum.

"A break in the drought may just put a stop to this horrible war," Julia offered. "It's heartbreaking to think that the natives have so little food."

"They might have more food if they'd made more preparations," observed Hyrum. "It's not like they haven't seen times of drought before."

Thus far, all the skirmishes with the natives had occurred many miles from Elephant Hook, but the conflicts had been steadily moving closer as the natives had become emboldened by their military successes.

Hyrum and Ian had managed to stay out of the war with the natives, but they knew if the war continued into the new year, they would be pressed into service. Ian wasn't concerned about the prospect, but Hyrum maintained that he hadn't come to Africa to be a soldier; he had come to be a sheep farmer. However, it was clear to him that assessments he had relied on prior to sailing for Africa regarding the ability of the Queen's forces to secure the land had been exaggerated. If the war continued into the new year, he would be obligated to fight the natives in defense of his home and family. Such was not something he relished, but he was willing to do so without hesitation.

Julia had worried whether the conflict with the natives would affect their relationship with Subria, but there had been no need for concern. Subria had lived with the Coburns and the Princes for so long that she had no ties to the natives. She had abandoned their way of life and superstitions, and had adopted the English way of life, dress and religion. Through Julia, Subria had also learned enough about Queen Victoria to consider the Queen as her own monarch.

The British troops suffered initial setbacks in the war against the natives. The garrison from Grahamstown had intended to confront a chief of the Xhosa alliance to obtain the release of tribesmen wanted for murder. With their three-mile wagon train of supplies in tow, the British couldn't be accused of stealth. In many respects, the British had become their own worst enemy. They lacked the knowledge of how to fight an enemy that didn't meet them openly on a field of battle, but rather attacked and then disappeared. This, coupled with an arrogance borne of a history of extending the British realm, caused them to underestimate their enemy. Their enemy was not only more numerous, ten to one, but they now had modern firepower.

It was this combination of modern weaponry, shear numbers, and a tactic of "attack and disappear" that allowed the Xhosa to strike at the middle of the garrison's three-mile wagon train and steal away supplies and weaponry intended for the garrison.

Emboldened by this victory, large numbers of Xhosa crossed imperial borders as the outnumbered English troops abandoned their posts and fell back. The natives would have marched on Grahamstown itself, but their plans had to be altered when another tribe of the alliance was defeated by the British nearby.

Eventually, it would be the third party in the conflicts, the force of nature, that would slow the pace of the war. Drought took its toll on Xhosa and British alike. Without rain, the British were incapable of finding sufficient water for the hundreds of animals that were required for long marches. Entire Xhosa villages were under threat of extinction for lack of water.

Stealing cattle might feed a tribe, but the supply of cattle was languishing, and without water, meat is of little value. The situation was becoming desperate on both sides.

Hyrum and Francis went outside to care for the animals and to repair a fence. Hyrum had waited long for Francis to get old enough that he could include him in his daily affairs on the farm. And now he was thoroughly enjoying Francis' companionship.

"Are those the blackest clouds ever?" asked Francis. Due to the length of the drought, clouds were somewhat of a novelty to Francis. Hyrum suspected that Francis had only seen rain a few times in his short life.

Hyrum thought about the difference between his own childhood in England, and Francis' childhood. *I didn't even know what drought was until we came here,* Hyrum thought. *People in England give little thought to rain, other than to complain that it rains so often. If it would just rain, I'd never complain about it again.*

"Those just might be the blackest clouds ever, Son. Let's hope there's plenty of water in them for us."

Hyrum also thought about the safety of life in England. *Any wars were in far off places, not on our doorstep. Francis and Luke may know nothing different.* Then, he thought the unthinkable. *If I have to go to war, they may grow up without a father.* Hyrum decided to put such thoughts aside and focus on his son.

Suddenly, a brilliant burst of light and the booming sound of thunder filled the sky! The lightning, so close, charged Hyrum's hair, and it seemed to stand on end. The noise elicited a scream from Francis, and he ran to his father's side. Hyrum was startled as well, but he was thrilled. Rain started falling immediately in great drops.

Hyrum looked to the sky, and with arms outstretched and heavenward, called out "It's raining!"

If the clouds had been barrels in the sky, it was as though their tops had been removed and the barrels tipped over, spilling their contents on the dry earth.

In his excitement, Hyrum called to the house with a voice full of joyous laughter, "Julia! It's raining!" He knew that she couldn't hear, and had no need of his announcement, but he wanted to share the news regardless.

By this time, both he and Francis were wet through and through, but it was a pleasantly warm, summer rain. It wouldn't have mattered whether it had been a cold winter's rain, it would have still been pleasant to Hyrum.

The rain was coming in such furious volume the ground, though parched as it was, could not absorb it as readily as it fell, and puddles were forming quickly.

"Let's get to the house, Son!" Hyrum called out. Holding his son's hand so that he wouldn't slip and fall into the many puddles, they rushed toward the house.

Julia and Subria were outside the house twirling and dancing in the rain. Their countenances beamed with joy despite being soaked to the skin. Victoria, completely unfamiliar with rain, watched in a mixture of bewilderment and fright from inside the house.

"Julia! It's raining!" laughed Hyrum.

"Indeed, I know!" laughed Julia.

Hyrum grabbed his wife about the waist and twirled her to the music of the rain. Subria held Francis' hands and they danced in circles. Another crack of thunder sent them all inside laughing and crying for joy. The roof wasn't water tight, so they hurriedly gathered all available pots and buckets, placing them to catch the water that poured through the roof.

All day, the rain poured. Gullies filled, and small rivers flowed anywhere the water gathered in lower areas. Hyrum's joy turned to concern for his sheep.

"I should go and check on the sheep," he announced near evening.

Julia looked concerned. "Surely, the sheep can find high ground," she reasoned.

Hyrum thought about it for a moment. "Yes, I suppose they will. I'm not sure that I could do anything for them anyway. Nonetheless, I feel I should go."

"Can't it wait for morning?" Julia asked.

Hyrum was looking out the window at the gathering blackness and didn't respond.

Julia let out a sigh. "Very well. Do return quickly."

"Take me," Francis urged.

"No. You aren't going," Julia retorted without hesitation.

Francis knew better than to disagree, but his disappointment was clearly visible in his expression.

"I won't be gone long, Son. And when you're older, you can go with me," Hyrum promised.

The horse was standing in several inches of water when Hyrum saddled him. As Hyrum headed out into the darkness of the coming night, the only thing clear to him was how dangerous being out on such a night could be. The mud was thick, making it difficult for the horse to maintain its footing. If he went down, it could be tragic for man and beast. It would soon be so dark as to render all visibility extinct. Under these circumstances, it wasn't long before Hyrum abandoned any plans of checking on the sheep, and he turned for home.

Julia was thrilled to see him when he came through the door.

"The mud is as thick and deep as snow in the Highlands of Scotland," Hyrum speculated, though he had no personal experience with the Highlands.

"I'm worried for Ian and Amanda," Julia replied.

"I'm sure they're as well off as we are, my dear," Hyrum assured her. "It's probably best that we get some sleep."

"If we can find a dry place in the house," Julia smiled.

The intensity of the rain let up some, but the rain continued for days. In these conditions, neither Briton nor native entertained thoughts of war. The British were miserable as they sat in canvas-walled tents, which after days of rain leaked profusely. The tents had no floors, and small rivers ran through many tents.

British supply wagons became stuck in the mud, incapable of reaching the soldiers who needed food. The few skirmishes that did occur were initiated by natives against those supply wagons as the wagons sat helpless, axle deep in mud. Being unfamiliar with the care of modern weaponry, the natives found their firearms beginning to rust soon after these raids.

Mid-November 1847
Elephant Hook, South Africa

"Dear Lord, we give thee thanks for the rains that we have received and are grateful unto thee that our sheep have largely survived. We are grateful that our well will flow with water for many months to come. We ask thee, dear God, if thou wouldst stem the rains and give way for the grasses to grow that our sheep may have food in abundance. God bless the Queen. Amen," Hyrum prayed.

"Amen," echoed Hyrum's household.

The rains soon began to subside, but left in their wake were rivers that had swollen beyond their bounds flooding vast areas where grass once grew in abundance. Both the British and the Xhosa had made liberal use of scorched earth tactics during the war, and the denuded land offered little resistance to the effects of flood waters. Large swaths of previously level ground became pocked with gullies, trenches and holes.

As the rains ceased, the warmth of the summer combined with the moist ground to yield a vast crop of mosquitos. With the mosquitos came fevers affecting the British and the natives alike. Eventually, no one had the energy or the will to wage war, and the Xhosa returned to their lands and the British to their towns and forts.

It was with great concern and sorrow that Julia noticed Luke acting lethargic one morning. Hesitantly, she reached out to check his temperature. She didn't want to know whether he had the fever, but she had to know. She touched his arm lightly, and tears began to flow. She pulled back her hand with a jerk. His skin felt as though he was sitting outside at noonday.

"Subria!" Julia cried. "Come quickly!"

Julia had an intensity in her voice that Subria had never heard, and she hurried to see what was causing the distress. "What is it?" she asked urgently.

"It's Luke!" Julia cried. "He's got the fever!"

An expression of concern settled on Subria's face. "Are you certain?" she asked.

"Feel his forehead," Julia instructed as she stepped backward and held her hands to her face in dread.

Subria felt the boy's forehead with the back of her hand, and looked at Julia with concern. "He's indeed very warm."

"What shall we do?" asked Julia urgently.

Subria wasn't ignorant to the practice of treating fevers that were so common in Africa at certain times of year, but she knew the danger that the child was in.

"Get water and cool him with a cloth," she instructed. "I'll be back."

Subria left the house immediately and was gone the rest of the morning. Julia was with Victoria when she returned. Subria knew immediately that Victoria was also afflicted. Julia's eyes were red and swollen.

"I'm so concerned," Julia cried tearfully. "Look at her, she's not responsive!"

Victoria's eyes were closed, and her skin was flushed. It wasn't clear whether she was asleep or awake. Luke was awake and crying quietly.

"Keep them cool, Miss Julia. I'll make a tonic," Subria promised, and she disappeared into the kitchen.

"I need Hyrum with me," Julia said. Hyrum and Francis were out and about the hills checking on the sheep and weren't due back before dinner.

As Julia alternated wiping a cool cloth on the two children, her mind was naturally taken back to the horrors of losing little Hyrum so suddenly. She remembered that the day she lost him had started out as an ordinary day. Little did she know at the time how completely her life would change before nightfall. And how final the change had been! The uncertainty of whether she would ever see Little Hyrum again filled her soul with anguish. Now it was happening again, but in a double portion!

Dear God, she cried in her mind, *please don't take my babies. I couldn't abide it! I couldn't go on!*

Meanwhile, Subria had started a fire and was heating water. After the water was boiling, she added several roots and berries that she had collected. The mixture needed to boil for an hour, and while it did, Subria offered comfort to Julia.

Trying to sound hopeful, Subria said, "I've seen the fever many times. It isn't always fatal. I'm sure they'll be fine."

Julia looked at Subria with tearful eyes and a faint smile.

"Try and be brave," Subria encouraged. "And have faith."

"These little ones have done nothing," Julia's voice broke as she spoke. "Why would God take them?"

Subria held Julia's hand. "He hasn't taken them. Have faith that he won't."

"I'll try," promised Julia.

"I've lived without faith in God," Subria observed, "and it's a difficult life. Faith makes it easier, regardless the outcome."

Julia smiled faintly and continued applying the cool cloth. Subria returned to the kitchen and strained the mixture through a clean cloth and took it to Julia.

"We need to get this into them," Subria directed.

The two women roused the children enough to get them to swallow a little of the mixture. Just when they had been successful, there was a rapid knock at the door and Ian burst into the room.

"It's Amanda!" he said breathlessly. "She has the fever!"

"No!" exclaimed Julia. "Not Amanda also!"

It was then that Ian realized that Luke and Victoria were ill. Grief and fear started to overtake him.

"Subria, go with Ian and help with Amanda," Julia instructed.

"Are you quite sure then?" asked Subria.

"Of course. I'll be fine here. Hyrum will be here soon."

"I'm ever so grateful," Ian assured them.

"Just give them the medicine every couple of hours. I've made enough to last a couple days," Subria instructed Julia.

"What will you do for Amanda?" asked Julia.

"I'll collect more roots and berries where I collected those."

"Very well," Julia replied. Then to Ian she said, "I'll pray for Amanda."

Ian and Subria left, and Julia continued to nurse the children. To ease her fears she sang to them songs that she had remembered her mother singing to her. After what seemed to be a long time, she heard Hyrum and Francis outside. She was filled with joy that Hyrum was home, but was afraid to let them in the house for fear they would become ill also. She met them at the door before they could enter.

"Julia, my dear," Hyrum called cheerfully.

"Please, don't come in here," Julia begged.

Hyrum could observe the concern on Julia's face and could see her reddened eyes.

"What is it, Julia?" he asked.

"It's Luke and Victoria. They have the fever."

"No!" exclaimed Hyrum as he rushed through the door despite Julia's protests. Kneeling beside them, he rubbed and kissed their foreheads.

"What's wrong," asked Francis. Julia groaned to know that both Hyrum and Francis had entered the house.

"They're ill," Julia said. "But they'll be fine."

"I don't want to get ill," Francis replied.

"I'm sure you won't, Son," replied Julia. "But you'd best go into the other room."

Julia explained to Hyrum that Subria had made a medicine for the children and had gone to nurse Amanda. Hyrum expressed concern for Amanda and her little ones.

"Subria's a Godsend, is she not?" observed Hyrum.

"She is indeed," Julia agreed.

Julia and Hyrum took turns caring for the children through the night, the next day and night. Late in the morning of the second day, Luke was beginning to show signs of improvement, but Victoria still languished. She wasn't drinking and it was near impossible to get her to swallow the medicine.

"I'm so worried, Hyrum. She's not drinking. If she doesn't drink, she'll not get better."

"Let's pray again for her," Hyrum suggested.

Julia agreed, and the two kneeled beside Victoria and poured their hearts out to God. They promised that they would seek to always know and follow his will. They expressed their confidence that they had been led to this land; not to lose children here, but to raise a family of faithful sons and daughters.

They felt more hopeful when they arose, but there was no change in Victoria's condition.

Hyrum knew that the medicine was getting low, but he was shocked on the next dosage to find that it was nearly gone. In a grave tone, he said to Julia, "There's little left."

"How much?" asked Julia.

"Two doses, maybe three," he replied.

"Will we need to send for Subria, then?"

"It would be best, before we've completely exhausted our store."

"I'll care for the children while you go for her then," Julia said.

"Very well. I'll make haste."

When Hyrum arrived at Amanda and Ian's, he found Amanda had started to improve, and Ian's spirits and hopes were high.

"It's Victoria. I've got to have Subria come with me."

"Is she not improved, then?" asked Amanda weakly.

"She hasn't, and now she's not drinking," Hyrum replied with concern.

"Yes, take Subria and go at once," Ian urged.

"Will you have sufficient medicine?" asked Hyrum.

"You take what is necessary for Victoria, and I expect that we'll have sufficient."

Hyrum and Subria passed several other farms on their way back home. Hyrum was aware that there were some in those homes who were also sick. He wanted to pass by without taking notice, but he couldn't restrain the feeling that he should share the medicine. Subria assured him that she could make more medicine if she could find the roots and berries now that she had exhausted the sources that she had found.

"What is the likelihood that other sources can be found?" he asked her.

"With your help, we may yet locate new sources before we reach Victoria."

"Even still, we'll save enough for at least one dosage for Victoria so that she won't be obliged to wait for the preparation," stated Hyrum.

The condition was worse than Hyrum expected at the third and final house where they stopped. Three children had taken ill. When Hyrum mentioned the tonic, the parents begged for an ample supply to treat their sick family. Hyrum thought of his own Victoria, but couldn't resist the fear and hopelessness on the faces of these parents that stood before him. He handed them the entire supply of medicine and wished them well.

Outside, he turned to Subria and asked, "What was I to do?"

"We'll find more supplies," Subria assured him. "But we must make haste while there's still daylight."

Hyrum and Subria began searching the hillsides for the plant that would provide the root. As they passed from one hill to another, they'd also search the gullies for the berries. They were having no success, and Hyrum feared that he would have to go home to Julia empty handed. *How will I explain to her that I had ample medicine for our daughter, but gave it away? What I've done is unpardonable.*

Hyrum expressed his fears to Subria.

"Perhaps we should try prayer," Subria suggested. Hyrum marveled that this native woman, a convert to Christianity would have more faith than he.

"Yes, we should pray. Will you please?"

They both kneeled and Subria served as voice to express their desires and their faith, and to plead that the maker of heaven and earth would show them where they might find the needed plants. Tears were running down Hyrum's face when the prayer ended. Subria was uncomfortable at the realization, not knowing whether she had ever seen Hyrum touched so. The thought occurred to Subria that this was the meaning and purpose of her life. She had been spared in her father's village, despite losing her family. Her survival of the death ship had humbled her. She had learned forgiveness from the old lady on the ship. She had been taught Christianity and faith by the Coburns. And now, she could use her faith, her knowledge of forgiveness and her knowledge of plants to save this family. In this very small way, she could act as the Savior and do what he would do. A sweet feeling swept over Subria as she raised from her knees. In her mind's eye, she could clearly see the plants that she needed.

"I know where to go," she declared with confidence. "God has shown me." And she began walking with determination to the east.

Hyrum stood in silence for a moment and watched her. He realized that her countenance had changed. She was full of determination and faith.

Following along behind her, they soon found the needed plants. When they had, they kneeled again and Hyrum gave thanks.

Julia was so overjoyed to see them that she failed to ask about their delay. Subria made the medicine and they did their best to get Victoria to swallow it. They spent an anxious night at her bedside.

The next morning Julia was awakened with a start by the sound of Victoria crying. It was a joyous sound.

"Hyrum! Subria! She's crying!" she cried out with a laugh.

Hyrum and Subria quickly awoke and joined Julia at Victoria's side.

"She's hungry!" Julia exclaimed.

"A very good sign indeed," observed Subria.

Victoria continued to make progress from that moment, and within a couple of days the entire family was relieved of the fever. There were a few deaths as a result of the fever, but most of the community was spared. The Princes gave thanks for the recovery of Luke, Victoria and Amanda.

Rivers soon receded to their traditional course taking flood waters with them. As the ground began to dry, dormant seeds sprouted to become a thick, deep carpet of grass. Hyrum and Julia gave thanks for the end of the war, for their family, and for the new crop of grass.

Chapter Twenty-one – Threats and Jealousies
Late-November 1847
Elephant Hook, Africa

Elephant Hook was full of renewed hope and enthusiasm. Grass was plentiful for the sheep and cattle. Many wild animals had returned to the area to enjoy the abundance. Hostilities with the natives were in abeyance, and the fever was under control. These favorable circumstances brought joy to the residents, and a celebratory gathering was planned. There had been no general gatherings in Elephant Hook for many months and anticipation was high, particularly amongst the women.

"What will you wear to the social?" Amanda asked Julia.

Julia smiled and with a gleam in her eye said, "I don't know really." After a brief hesitation, the kind that infers the speaker is measuring their next remark, she added, "I have some dresses that I once wore at court. I know it was terribly frivolous of me to bring them along to Africa, but I would so like to wear one. Perhaps you could wear one also."

Amanda had learned of Julia's connection to the Queen from Ian, and she seemed very pleased with the prospect of the dresses. She clapped her hands together and said, "That would be just lovely. May I see them then?"

"Of course," Julia replied, and she retrieved the dresses from a large trunk.

"How stunning!" Amanda said with her hands covering her mouth in awe when Julia had laid out the dresses. "And you'll allow me to wear one of these?"

"Of course," replied Julia.

"May I try them then?" asked Amanda.

"Indeed."

Amanda wasted no time before trying the first dress.

"Oh! You look quite lovely!" exclaimed Julia.

"Do you think so?"

"Oh yes. Ian will adore you."

"Perhaps it is a little snug," Amanda offered, not so much in looking for an affirmation as to elicit a contrary response.

"You look quite lovely dear. You'll be the most lovely woman there."

Amanda was pleased, but cautioned, "Surely, there are no dresses in Africa to compare to these. The other women will be quite jealous. They'll surely want to know how you came to have such fine dresses."

"Perhaps," Julia agreed.

Amanda smiled and countered, "But you brought them so far. They really shouldn't be left in the trunk now, should they?"

"Indeed not," agreed Julia. "I don't suppose that I can forever leave my past in that trunk now, can I?" Julia asked with a smile.

Subria walked into the room and expressed her pleasure with the dress that Amanda wore.

"Of course you'll go with us, will you not, Subria?" asked Julia.

"I don't know that it would be all together right for me to go. There would be some that wouldn't be pleased to have me there."

"Pay them no mind," Amanda offered firmly.

"Quite right, Subria. Give no heed to unkindness," agreed Julia.

Subria seemed pleased with the encouragement, but said, "I have nothing so fine to wear."

Though slender, Subria was considerably taller than either Julia or Amanda.

Julia smiled. "I have some very fine cloth from Grahamstown. If we combine our efforts, we could fashion a fine dress for you."

"Oh, yes. That would be lovely," Amanda agreed.

Subria was pleased. "Yes, that would be lovely indeed."

Over the course of the next several days, the women busied themselves with fashioning a suitable dress for Subria, and the result was stunning. At 43 years, most native women would have shown the outward signs of a life of endless toil, periods of hunger and the effects of male "ownership". Though Subria was well acquainted with hard work, she had added the years relatively lightly. Because her life with the Coburns and the Princes had been one of consistent nourishment and constant care, she was healthy, and she didn't wear the adornment of a life of chattel.

Subria blushed as Julia and Amanda gushed over her as she modeled the dress for them.

"Subria! You look stunning," Julia declared. "I do hope the years will smile upon me as they have you."

Julia was still a young woman at 28 years and quite lovely. Having witnessed the effects of the sun and wind on other immigrant women, she did worry the same would be her lot. The dry hot air and sun weathered the skin in a way that was uncommon in the cool, moist air of England.

Finally the days of celebration arrived. The renewed optimism in Elephant Hook and the longing for socialization would bring immigrants together from miles around. Along with the Princes, many would camp at the gathering location for several days.

"Is it quite necessary to bring along this trunk?" Hyrum asked as he struggled to lift it into the wagon. He of course knew the answer before asking.

"It is. Quite," replied Julia. "Amanda, Subria and I must have our dresses," she added with a smile toward Subria.

With the trunks loaded, Hyrum climbed onto the bench alongside Julia. She held Luke in her arms, while Subria, Francis and Victoria sat inside the wagon's bed.

"We'll need two wagons soon enough," Hyrum observed with a smile.

"A man of good fortune, you are," smiled Julia.

The ride to the gathering place took most of the day, but their camp was set up next to Ian and Amanda's camp by nightfall.

The next two days were spent in leisure conversation among the women while the men played cricket. Some of the men attempted lawn bowling, but the uneven ground rendered the sport nearly impossible.

Subria's presence was largely ignored though Julia and Amanda insisted that she remain at their side, and they included her in conversation.

Subria was most uncomfortable when Mr. Richards was nearby. She could feel his stares, and it appeared that he often turned to his mates and said something about her when she was near.

"I see the Princes have brought their native woman along," Mr. Richards said to one of his friends.

"She does nay belong here, does she," his friend offered.

"Of course not. She doesn't know her place," Mr. Richards said in disgust.

"You should have a word with Mr. Prince."

"I should, should I?" Mr. Richards derided. "I'll speak directly with her."

"Did she nay stitch your wounds?" asked his friend.

"She did," sneered Mr. Richards. "She gave me this scar on my face!"

Subria sat near Julia and Amanda. By appearances, she listened politely to their conversation with other women, but her attention was on Mr. Richards. She occasionally looked in his direction, and quickly averted her eyes each time that he began to look in her direction.

"Is that true, Subria?" one of the women asked, but Subria didn't respond.

"Subria?" Amanda said.

With that, Subria's attention focused back on the women.

"Pardon?" Subria asked. "I'm dreadfully sorry. Please forgive my rudeness."

Amanda smiled. "Mrs. Crawford was commenting on your nursing skills and asked whether you learned from your mother."

Subria smiled gently and said, "From my mother and grandmother."

"Are they still living in your village then?" asked Mrs. Crawford.

Other than with Julia, Subria hadn't to this point shared anything of her past. She glanced at Julia as though for guidance.

"No. They no longer live in our village," was all Subria offered.

"Is their village near then?"

"No."

Knowing that Subria was uncomfortable with the questions, Julia tried to deflect the conversation.

"Won't you just look at those farmers," she said pointing to the men playing cricket. "They're like young school lads."

The women's attention was briefly averted to the men, but Mrs. Crawford soon continued.

"Where are your people?"

Subria looked straight at Mrs. Crawford. "They are all dead."

"All?"

"Yes, all."

"How dreadful. Is that why you chose to leave your village?"

Subria sensed that Mrs. Crawford intended no harm, but was only exceedingly inquisitive. Still, Subria had little intention of revealing her past. Glancing up, she saw that Mr. Richards was looking in her direction again. The look in his eyes filled her with dread, and she briefly felt the fear and pain of the slave ship. Her hands trembled. *Will he always hold me captive?* she thought. *Why do I let him have such power over me? Surely, he doesn't know who I am. He must have seen hundreds of young girls on his death ship.*

Though she trembled inside, meeting Mr. Richards' look without aversion seemed to embolden her. Without looking away from Mr. Richards, she responded simply to Mrs. Crawford, "Yes."

Mrs. Crawford seemed satisfied with the response or bored with the conversation, and Subria was no longer the object of so much attention.

Several minutes later Julia invited Subria to walk with her.

"Subria," Julia started as they strolled toward the cricket game. "You seem quite distracted. Is everything as it should be?"

"Yes, quite. I assure you," Subria stated.

"I don't mean to pry," Julia ventured, "but I saw your hands tremble."

Subria stopped and turned to Julia. "To be sure, I'm not altogether fine. Mr. Richards fills me with dread."

"It's clear that he's objectionable, but beyond that, what is it about him that holds such power over you as to cause you to tremble so?"

"I'm sure that he recognizes me!"

"Of course he recognizes you. You've been with us for some time. Surely you don't believe he's still angry about falling from the table do you?"

Subria looked about to ensure their privacy before she continued in a hushed tone.

"He recognizes me from the slave ship!"

The full impact hadn't settled on Julia, and Subria continued, "He's the lieutenant from the death ship! And he knows that I know it!"

Julia's mouth dropped and her eyes widened. "The lieutenant that floated in the sea next to you after the storm?"

"Yes."

"The same that killed the young sailor?"

"Yes, yes," Subria whispered with a glance about the area. "And he recognizes me. I can see it in his eyes."

"He's always told everyone that he is a farmer from Wales," replied Julia. "How can you be sure then?"

"Of course you recall well the day that we stitched his cheek."

"Yes, of course."

"I removed his hat."

"Yes," whispered Julia. "Go on."

"He has a large scar on his forehead. The same scar that I saw the lieutenant receive before he killed the young sailor."

Julia held her hand to her mouth in shocked expression, and replied, "And he's been living here in anonymity, expecting that no one would discover the truth."

After a moment, Julia observed, "He never removes that hat. To be sure, I believe you, but how can you be certain? How do you know he remembers you? That was long ago, you were only a girl."

"I can feel it," replied Subria. "I can see it in his eyes. He knows."

"What can we do? Shall we inform someone?"

"No, please Miss Julia. Don't tell anyone. I just need to stay away from him."

"Yes, without any other evidence, there's no point in sharing this with anyone. They'd not believe us, and who knows but what accusations could be leveled against you by him."

"And between him and me, we know that he'd be given all the credibility."

"Without a doubt," agreed Julia. "You stay by my side, and we'll avoid Mr. Richards."

Just the sharing of it seemed to bring relief to Subria.

That evening was to be the social gathering finale, and the women had reserved their finest attire for the occasion. Grahamstown had never seen so many fine hats, hairpins, broaches and dresses gathered in one location.

Anticipation filled the air as each couple arrived. Despite their immigrant background, they understood proper decorum and courteously welcomed each person as they arrived. The women admired dresses, and the men politely engaged in conversation.

Julia and Amanda were finding it more difficult than expected to handle their children in such fine dresses. The hoops beneath the skirts made it nearly impossible to bend to pick up a child. Hyrum and Ian smiled to see their wives, appearing beautiful enough for the royal court, but unable to perform the simplest tasks. For her part, Julia realized that such attire was wholly unsuited for a woman with children, or at least unsuited for a woman that intended to care for her children.

"No worries," Hyrum smiled. "Ian and I will care for the little ones. Isn't that right, Ian?"

"Yes, quite right," Ian replied. With a laugh he added, "With Subria's help of course."

All eyes were upon Julia and Amanda as they entered. An initial hush fell over the gathering, followed by quiet whispers.

"Who is this?" one woman asked her husband.

"It's the Prince women!" another whispered.

"Are they princesses?" a young girl was overheard asking her mother.

"Dresses fit for the Queen's court," a man near Hyrum stated. "The Princes must be doing very well indeed."

"You don't obtain such fine dresses by raising sheep, I assure you. I heard that Mrs. Prince was in fact often present at court."

"You don't say?"

"Perhaps she'll start holding her own court."

"It would appear that she already does, what with Amanda and her native woman with her."

As the evening progressed Julia became increasingly aware of the whispers and looks of the other women.

Subria felt the stares of Mr. Richards often throughout the evening. Though she tried to ignore him, she couldn't shake the feeling that he was watching.

"Subria," Julia said, "will you please find a quiet place to lay the children down? They're getting so tired."

"But of course, Miss Julia," Subria stated. She was pleased for the excuse to get out of Mr. Richards' presence.

"Come with me children," Subria said to Francis and Victoria as she carried Luke in her arms away from the dancing.

The social was being held at the large home of the Crawfords' and Subria found a quiet room for the children. She hadn't noticed someone watching from the shadows.

She stayed with the children several minutes, singing quietly until Luke and Victoria fell asleep.

"You lie here quietly now and don't wake your brother and sister," she instructed Francis.

"How long do I have to stay here?" Francis asked.

"Until your parents are ready to leave. You may as well go to sleep, as it could be an extended period."

"I'm not sleepy," Francis insisted.

"None the less, lie here quietly."

Subria waited and watched to see that Francis was going to stay put and remain quiet. After a few minutes she was satisfied and turned to leave.

As she walked through the dimly lit hallway, she heard a whisper, "Maaaaarkuuuu."

The sound struck her with fear, and she seemed frozen in place.

Maarku? He's come to punish me. The thought sent shivers up her back.

"Maaaaarkuuuu," the whisper came again.

This time Subria knew the voice. She wanted to run, but her feet were frozen in place. She gasped when Mr. Richards stepped out of a dark room nearby and stood directly in front of her.

"Did you suppose I wouldn't know who you were?" asked Mr. Richards. He moved the back of his hand across the fabric of her dress. "A fancy dress doesn't disguise the slave girl that you are."

Subria couldn't move.

"I saw you push Maarku into the sea. Poor lad, he couldn't swim."

Subria looked directly into Mr. Richards' eyes. Even in the dim light she could see that they were full of darkness. Her legs felt weak and her hands shook.

He does recognize me! Is he going to kill me?

"I have no knowledge of what you refer to, sir," Subria said, hoping to placate him. There was a quiver in her voice, and she hoped that the low light would mask the fear that must have shown in her eyes. Still, facing him unyieldingly gave her strength.

This is a weak, and evil man, she thought. *Still, he can tell lies about me.*

"Well said, slave girl," Mr. Richards sneered. "If ever I hear otherwise, you'll find your place with Maarku." Then he turned and walked away.

All energy had left Subria. Her knees gave way and she fell to the floor and cried.

After several minutes, she wiped her eyes, stood and returned to the gathering. Mr. Richards sat at a table on the far side of the room, and Subria could feel his gaze as she walked to where Julia and Hyrum were standing and conversing with Ian and Amanda. Julia noticed immediately that Subria was visibly shaken and asked whether she and the children were fine.

"Yes, the children are fine," Subria assured her.

"And are you all together fine?"

"Yes Miss Julia, I'm fine also," Subria said with a faint smile that wasn't convincing.

Julia turned to Hyrum. "Hyrum, let's get the children and leave please."

Hyrum looked disappointed. "So soon, my dear?"

"Yes, I'm tired and Subria's tired."

"It really isn't necessary, Miss Julia," Subria assured her.

"Still, I insist," Julia said.

"Must you go so soon, old man?" Ian asked.

Hyrum looked at Julia and Subria. Though not as observant as his wife, he was certain that Julia's mind was firm.

"The children are fine, aren't they Julia?" asked Amanda.

"Without a doubt, they are," Julia agreed.

"Then do stay," Amanda pled.

Julia glanced at Hyrum.

"We must really be off," Hyrum said as he took Julia by the arm and moved in the direction of the room where the children were sleeping.

Subria was concerned that an abrupt departure would raise Mr. Richards' suspicions.

"The children are quite fine. We really needn't leave," she asserted as she followed Hyrum and Julia. Still, her voice quivered slightly and betrayed hidden emotions.

Ian and Amanda looked inquisitively at each other as Hyrum led Julia out of the room, followed by Subria.

When they reached the room where the children slept, Hyrum said to Julia, "What is it, Julia? Something has disturbed you."

Subria gathered Victoria into her arms while Julia picked up Luke, and Hyrum roused Francis.

Julia held a finger to her lips and whispered, "Not now, Hyrum. Not here."

No words were spoken until the family had reached their campsite, then Hyrum asked again, "What is it, Julia?"

Julia looked at Subria, and Subria took a deep breath and looked about before quietly telling Hyrum who Mr. Richards was.

"How can you be sure of this?" asked Hyrum. "It has been so many years."

"He made himself clear after I had laid the children down," Subria replied.

"Made himself clear?" asked Hyrum.

Subria exchanged looks with Julia and looked around again to ensure that no one was about. Tears began running down Subria's cheeks and her voice broke as she whispered, "He knew how Maarku died."

Hyrum looked at Julia. "Maarku?"

Subria sat on a nearby rock and buried her face in her hands and cried. Julia sat next to her and comforted her with an arm about her shoulders. After a moment, Julia looked up at Hyrum and quietly told him Subria's story. She told him about the slave ship, Maarku and the lieutenant. She told him about the knife fight between the lieutenant and the young sailor and about Mr. Richards' scar. She told him how Maarku had drowned.

Hyrum listened in stunned silence, amazed that he could know Subria so well and yet not know her at all.

"We need to leave here tonight," Julia declared.

"Tonight?" Hyrum asked in surprise.

"Yes, tonight. Mr. Richards has issued a direct threat to Subria. She can't be safe if she is near him. We must leave tonight."

"The children are asleep," Hyrum protested quietly.

"They'll sleep just fine in the wagon," Julia assured him.

"We'd need to change out of these clothes and dismantle the tents."

"Then we'd best get started," Julia insisted. "We'll not stay here tonight."

Hyrum knew that Julia's mind was firm and made no further attempt to change it. Julia and Subria were soon out of their evening gowns and dressed in traveling clothes.

As they traveled, Hyrum wondered aloud whether they should report the identity of Mr. Richards to the British garrison at Grahamstown.

"We mustn't do that, Hyrum," Julia assured him. "All we have is Subria's testimony. The testimony of a native woman would do little to persuade the authorities. Mr. Richards has friends enough. Making accusations about him would only serve to put Subria at greater risk."

Hyrum considered Julia's remarks for a moment and replied, "Yes, I see that now. What course should we follow?"

"We'll keep Subria away from Mr. Richards. Surely in time he'll cease to inflict her."

"And he goes unpunished?" Hyrum asked.

"It may appear so, but he won't escape his eternal reward," Julia promised.

Little else was said concerning the matter as they traveled home. Ian visited two days later to check on them and to ask why they had left so abruptly.

Hyrum, Julia and Subria had already agreed that they wouldn't share the information regarding Mr. Richards with anyone. Hyrum was prepared to tell Ian that one of the children had been ill. He considered it only a half untruth and was justified for the safety of Subria.

"Luke was warm and we wanted to get home so that Subria would have everything needed to care for him if he were to have the fever."

"And how is Luke today? He looks quite well," Ian observed.

"Oh yes, he's quite well. Praise God, he didn't have the fever," Hyrum assured him. "How is Amanda then?"

"She's quite well," Ian responded. Then looking down as though he didn't relish sharing the next bit of news, he said, "She had to endure some rudeness after your departure."

Julia had been listening politely, and asked, "Rudeness? Whatever for?"

Ian reconsidered and thought it better to not pursue the matter. Amanda had asked that he not speak of it. "Oh, it was nothing really," he assured them as he tried to walk the conversation backward. "It's capital that Luke is well."

"Yes, quite," Julia replied. "Rudeness isn't trivial. What happened to Amanda?"

Ian looked at Hyrum for support. "Don't look at me, old man," Hyrum said.

"Well," Ian started, "it would seem that your dresses raised the jealousies of some of the other women."

Hyrum grinned and said, "They were lovely dresses."

Julia frowned. "Perhaps we shouldn't have worn them. Poor Amanda. Rudeness really isn't necessary."

"Most of the comments were actually directed at you," Ian said hesitantly.

"At me?" asked Julia.

"Yes, some of the women said that you were putting on airs and that you wished to be in court."

"In court?" asked Julia with some surprise. "How would they know that I had been in court?"

"I surely couldn't say, but someone must have known."

Tears started to form in Julia's eyes. "Hyrum, I meant no harm. Clearly, I didn't give proper consideration to the way the dresses would be viewed. I just so wanted to wear them again."

Hyrum hugged his wife. "You were truly a lovely sight, my dear. You needn't worry about the gossiping of others."

"But they are gossiping about Amanda also. That isn't right," Julia said with tears running down her face.

Ian laughed lightly to ease the mood. "You needn't worry about Amanda," he said with a grin. "She surely can defend herself."

"All the women were lovely," Julia said through her tears. "I've never seen more lovely ladies than are in Elephant Hook. Should I apologize?"

"I don't think there is a need for that," Ian assured her.

"Then I'll use the dresses for curtains," Julia declared.

Hyrum hugged Julia again. "There's no need to make rash decisions. Don't allow the rudeness of others to guide your actions. If you do, they've succeeded in their intent."

"I shouldn't have mentioned it. Please forgive me," Ian asked.

Julia dried her eyes. "There's nothing to forgive. I should have used better judgement. Perhaps I did desire to arouse their jealousies, but surely not their disdain."

"It will soon be forgotten," Ian assured her.

Hyrum still held Julia in his arms. "The incident may be forgotten," he smiled, "but their jealousies of you will long linger."

Chapter Twenty-two – Flames of Conflict
April 1850
Elephant Hook, Africa

"Amen," Hyrum humbly said as he closed their prayer of thanks offered as prelude to their evening meal. His gaze fell upon Julia as he opened his eyes. *My, she's beautiful,* he thought. *When did the 18 year old, inexperienced girl that I married become the confident woman in front of me?*

Hyrum looked about the table and his eyes moistened as he considered his wealth. Three sons and a daughter! Francis was a willing helper on the farm. At ten years old, he'd rather go riding or hunting than read a book or practice his writing. Victoria, seven, was energetic and helpful. She loved caring for her brother, Samuel, almost two, and looked forward with anticipation to the birth of her next sibling in the coming months. Luke, four, was sensitive, but strong for his age. He loved to help his mother and was very protective of her.

"Hyrum?" Julia asked without receiving a response. "Hyrum, is everything as it should be?"

Shaken from his thoughts, Hyrum smiled and replied, "Indeed, it is. Everything is as it should be."

Life had been good since the end of the conflict with the natives, not perfect, but good.

"Some monkeys were in the garden today," Francis announced.

"You shouldn't refer to your brothers and sister in that fashion," Hyrum grinned.

Francis had developed a strong laugh and he let it out while he held onto his sides for effect.

"Hyrum," Julia replied with a tone that trailed upward at the end for emphasis.

Hyrum looked at Julia and grinned. "What?" he replied in feigned innocence.

Julia only smiled and shook her head.

"No, really, really," Francis assured them. "Some monkeys were in the garden."

"And what did you do?" Hyrum asked.

"I was going to run into the house and git…"

"Get…," Julia interrupted.

Francis glanced at his mother and continued, "…get my bow and arrows, but there wasn't time."

"So what did you do?" Hyrum asked.

"I grabbed a nearby stick and threw it at them."

"And did that scare them off then?" Hyrum asked.

"It did long enough for me to git…get my bow."

Hyrum looked at Julia and asked with a smile, "We're not eating monkey tonight, are we, my dear?"

Francis laughed aloud with his face pointed to the ceiling. Victoria and Luke thought it quite funny also.

"Nasty," Victoria said.

"Yucky," agreed Luke.

"It certainly is not monkey," Julia asserted with a pretended look of sternness at Hyrum.

"Excellent," replied a grinning Hyrum. "I'm ever so glad to hear it." Then, directed at Francis, he said, "So, what did you do next?"

"When I got back they were in the big tree. I shot a couple of arrows at them, but missed. They were too high," he sighed.

"Do you think they got the message to stay away?"

Francis looked pleased. "Indeed. I think so."

"Excellent! Good job, son," Hyrum praised.

"I want a bow and arrow!" Luke demanded with a pout on his lips.

"You're too young," Francis informed him.

With that, Luke hung his head so that his chin was in his chest and his face nearly in his food.

"I don't know," Hyrum said hopefully. "Luke is getting to be such a big boy..."

Julia eyed Hyrum, so he modified his intent. "Luke is such a big boy he'll be big enough for a bow before you know it," he said.

That wasn't very satisfying to a young boy who always considered himself every bit as big as his brother.

Hyrum reached out and rubbed Luke's head. "Come on now. Give us a smile. You really are a big helper. Isn't he, mother?"

"He is indeed," agreed Julia.

After the meal, Hyrum asked Julia whether she'd enjoy a walk in cool evening air.

"That would be just lovely," she agreed. "But we mustn't leave the children long, nor go too far," she said as she held her expanding abdomen.

As they walked they talked easily about the farm and laughed about some of the silly things that the children had said.

"Luke is sure that I'm not having a baby," Julia said with a laugh, holding her abdomen. "He's certain that I've been eating too much."

Hyrum laughed and then his voice took on a more somber tone as he said, "The news out of Grahamstown isn't good."

Julia glanced at Hyrum and asked, "Whatever do you mean?"

"You know that Governor Smith has made it his policy to take advantage of the cessation of fighting the natives. He sees it as an opportunity to push the Xhosa off the lands closest to the border and to move settlers onto the land," Hyrum said.

"Yes, I was generally aware of the governor's policies," replied Julia.

"What you may not be aware of is that his policies have caused some overcrowded Xhosa villages just over the border. I fear that these policies will destroy a fragile peace."

"Do you believe it as bad as all that then?" asked Julia.

"I do indeed," replied Hyrum. "Surely, it's shortsighted to force the Xhosa into a position where they can't possibly provide for themselves if we experience another drought."

"So, if they don't have enough land to hunt on, or to raise their own cattle, the cattle and sheep raids will resume?" asked Julia.

"Yes. And to make matters worse, any Xhosa that remain on English lands are fairly well forced to adopt a lifestyle like our own."

"Wouldn't it be desirable for them to adopt our lifestyle?" Julia asked.

"Perhaps, if they chose, but they are basically forced to do so, and many of them resent it," Hyrum asserted.

"I see," Julia agreed. "But, if they could only see how happy Subria is."

"To be sure, Subria is happy, but it must have been difficult for her initially."

Julia thought for a moment about Subria and replied, "Yes, and she was young and without a family."

Hyrum and Julia walked on for a while in silence before Julia suggested that they return to the house. As they neared the house, Hyrum said, "I haven't told you the most disturbing news."

Julia stopped and looked at Hyrum. She could see the concern in his expression. "What is it?" she asked.

"Governor Smith has also attacked and annexed the region historically held by the Dutch. The resistance leaders were hanged."

"That's awful!" Julia said in shocked surprise.

"It is awful, but it also means that if there is another problem with the natives, he's alienated potential allies."

"Let's pray that doesn't happen," Julia replied.

Subria met them at the door when they reached the house. "Miss Julia, you should take care. You're going to be a mother again."

Julia smiled. "I'll take care. I promise."

June 1850
Elephant Hook

Hyrum and Ian stood atop a small hill and surveyed a portion of Ian's land. It had been an unusually cold winter with little rain.

"I lost three sheep night before last," Ian reported.

"To the cold, or was it the lack of water?" asked Hyrum.

"I suspect neither," Ian replied. "I'm guessing it was natives. There was no sign of animals and no sign of the sheep."

"And you have a good count then?"

"Of course I have," Ian asserted.

"Have you heard whether any of your neighbors have lost animals?"

"I've heard rumor of others, but nothing definite."

"This isn't good," Hyrum said as he kicked a small stone with his boot. "The cold and the drought will undoubtedly cause the natives to start stealing animals again."

"Not good at all," Ian replied in a resolute tone that seemed to project a determination to defend his land. "And the Governor has depleted the ranks of the garrison again. The man has no foresight, I tell you."

"Or he displays a cavalier attitude toward the safety of this colony," Hyrum said.

"Well I can tell you now that if it comes to a conflict, I'll not be an idle bystander."

Hyrum looked at his brother inquisitively.

"I'll join the commandos," Ian stated plainly.

"The commandos?" asked Hyrum.

"Yes. You know that the English garrison moves too slowly, and they use outdated, or at least ineffective, tactics. The commandos aren't hampered by such archaic and burdensome methods. They move fast, and they blend into the countryside just like the natives."

"I do know that they had an impact on the success of the last war, but," Hyrum started.

"An impact?" Ian interrupted. "They were a significant contribution to the success."

"Yes, a significant contribution," Hyrum agreed. "But it is very dangerous."

"Of course, it's dangerous," Ian replied in a tone that indicated his mind was firm. "But why should we expect some kid from England who hasn't even experienced life to defend us? We belong to this land. We have families here! We should defend it!"

Hyrum was silent and looked at the ground and shuffled a foot in the dirt. He agreed with Ian, but he worried what would become of Julia and the children if he were injured or killed.

"How does Amanda feel about your intentions?"

Ian looked into the distance and replied, "She's not keen on it and she's concerned, but she agrees that we can't stand aside while others bleed for us."

"You know I'm not afraid to fight the natives?" Hyrum asked in more of a statement than a question.

"Of course I do, old man. But I also know that you have more children than I do."

In a soft tone, Hyrum replied, "Yes. Perhaps that's more cause to join the fight. If there is a fight, of course."

"Yes, of course, if," agreed Ian.

The two men were silent for several minutes, each one considering possible end courses of their decisions. Ian spoke first.

"Listen, old man, if it does come to a fight, I'll be joining. If it ends badly for me, will you care for my family?"

Hyrum looked at his brother. *I don't think I've ever feared anyone or anything,* he thought *and yet here's my younger brother more willing to defend his family, my family, than I am. How did this happen? Is this what children do? He has children? Is it because he's always been the impetous one?*

"Don't talk that way, Ian. It won't come to that," Hyrum assured him.

Ian looked earnest when he pressed, "Regardless, you'll care for my family?"

"Yes, of course, if it came to that. You know I would," Hyrum stated.

Ian seemed settled on the matter and the brothers changed the subject of their conversation.

When Hyrum returned home late that afternoon, he found Francis chopping wood.

"Excellent work, son. You swing that axe like a man."

Francis put the axe down and blew into his cupped hands to warm his fingers. When he removed his hands from his face, his broad smile indicated his pleasure with the compliment.

"Are we out of wood in the house?" Hyrum asked.

"Very near. Subria asked me to fetch more wood."

"It's this unusual cold spell," Hyrum replied as he looked at the clouded sky. "It would be helpful if these clouds had some rain in them," he said aloud, but mostly to himself.

Hyrum gathered up an armful of wood and handed it to Francis. "Take this inside, and I'll finish up."

After Francis entered the house, Subria came outside and gathered an armful of wood. Before she went back inside, she said, "I was in Elephant Hook today, and I'm concerned that the natives are going to start attacking settlements again."

"They may have already started stealing animals. Ian and Amanda lost some sheep. What have you been hearing?" Hyrum asked without slowing in chopping wood.

"There's a young warrior native that is being regarded as a prophet among the Xhosa," Subria said.

"Why is that concerning?" asked Hyrum.

"The natives tend to become very devoted to someone who espouses prophetic powers, especially if he tells them something that they want to hear."

"And what has this prophet been saying?"

"He's promising that his medicine will make the warriors invulnerable to the white man's bullets, and that the British guns will shoot out only water."

Hyrum laughed. "Surely the natives don't believe it. Shoot out only water?"

"It's a very compelling message," Subria assured him. "He's telling the Xhosa that if they will give up witchcraft and worship the sun, they will drive the white man out of their land."

Hyrum had laid the axe aside and was gathering the remaining chopped wood. "Well, giving up witchcraft is a good thing. The Xhosa already believe that this land is still their's and also anything that is on it, including the animals."

"And with a message like this from a new prophet, their cattle and sheep raids will only increase. They'll become more emboldened by the day," Subria assured him.

As Subria headed to the house, she stopped and turned back. "Oh, the Xhosa are leaving villages in large numbers and are gathering in tribal areas."

"You heard that also while in Elephant Hook?" Hyrum asked.

"Yes."

"That's concerning. How did you hear this?"

"I still understand the native tongue. There were some native workers that I overheard."

This last bit of information was most concerning to Hyrum. *If the Xhosa are amassing, it can only mean that they intend to start a campaign,* he thought.

The winter continued to be unusually cold and dry. Cattle and sheep continued to disappear and it was clear that the Xhosa were to blame. Many settlers complained to the governor without redress. When summer came without attendant rains, any expectation of avoiding conflict with natives began to dissipate. The unrest among the natives was flamed by the preaching of their new found prophet.

Ostensibly to circumvent violence, Governor Smith travelled to meet with the Xhosa chiefs, but his overtures were rebuffed when one of the higher chiefs refused to meet with him. In a rage, Governor Smith declared him a fugitive. Soon thereafter, a small detachment of British soldiers were ambushed and forced to retreat under heavy fire. They ultimately sustained 42 casualties.

That alone would have been provocation enough to escalate the tension between the British and the Xhosa to all out war, but the very next day, on Christmas eve, an atrocity occurred that left no doubt as to the Xhosa's aggression. Many presumedly friendly Xhosa had been invited into towns in the border region to celebrate Christmas Eve. At a given signal during the festivities, the Xhosa fell upon the unsuspecting settlers and killed them with great slaughter.

Christmas Day, 1850
Elephant Hook

News of the massacre traveled quickly across the region, and though Elephant Hook was not in the border region affected, the settlers were greatly disturbed. Hyrum and Julia had taken their family to be with Ian and Amanda on Christmas day and were there when their early morning celebration was interrupted by loud knocking at the door.

"Who do you suppose that is?" Amanda asked Ian as he went for the door.

"Odd that they would be out so early on Christmas morning," Julia replied.

"Perhaps it's Father Christmas," Hyrum said with a smile to the children, but he kept an eye on Ian as he opened the door. Hyrum didn't have a direct view of the visitor through the doorway, but noticed that Ian didn't greet him with the same energy as he might a friend. The visitor spoke in hushed tones and Ian stepped outside. With that Hyrum stood and approached the door.

"Who's this?" the stranger asked when Hyrum exited.

"This is my brother, Hyrum Prince. You probably already stopped at his home. It's on this same road," Ian said pointing in the direction that the visitor would have ridden.

"Yes, without a doubt, I did. You'll share with him what I told you. I must be off to warn the others."

"Warn the others?" Hyrum asked with concern.

Ian put a hand on Hyrum's shoulder, and said to the visitor, "Can we offer you refreshment before you go?"

"I'm much obliged, but there's no time. I'll get refreshment soon enough."

"Thank you, sir," Ian said. "God speed."

When the visitor had left, Ian turned to Hyrum and quietly told him about the massacre.

Hyrum grabbed a low branch of a nearby tree and shook it as though to shake off the reality of the awful news.

"So, it's started again," he said to Ian.

"Yes, but this time it's different," Ian said quietly so as to not frighten the women inside. "The garrison is smaller and the natives are more resolute now that they have a prophet telling them that they can't be injured by our guns."

"They can't very well be harmed by guns that don't exist, can they?" Hyrum said, alluding to the smaller presence of the British army in the region.

"That's why the commandos must make up the difference," Ian asserted. "The commandos will be gathering tomorrow morning, and I'll be with them. We must strike a blow to the natives right away, before they have time to gather more forces."

"Perhaps the garrison is already marching on the natives," Hyrum suggested.

"Perhaps, but the garrison is impotent!"

"That's a harsh assessment," replied Hyrum.

"Aye, it is a harsh assessment. But can you say that it isn't accurate?"

Hyrum hesitated.

"No, you can't," Ian replied.

"I can't join the commandos, Ian," Hyrum said.

"I'm not asking you to. But I am asking you to watch over Amanda and the kids and my farm."

"When will you tell Amanda?"

Ian didn't respond right away, but walked a few steps away from the house where he could look over his sheep farm. The sun was well above the horizon and it was going to be a hot day. Sheep dotted the hillside munching on the golden blades of grass that endured despite the lack of rain. Ian turned back toward the house. Through the window he could see Amanda and his children, along with Julia and her children laughing and enjoying some Christmas treats. Subria sat nearby smiling and holding

Amanda's youngest daughter. This was his world. Everything that he held dear was right here within his view. Nothing else really mattered.

"I'll tell her this morning," Ian replied quietly.

"She'll take it hard."

"She's a strong woman," Ian replied. Then, with a smile, he continued, "Did you know that she worked right alongside me to sheer the sheep this year?"

"I didn't know that," Hyrum replied. "I can't see Julia doing that," he added with a chuckle. "She's left the royal court, but some of it hasn't left her," he smiled.

Amanda could be seen standing and was looking toward the window.

"We'd best be getting inside," Hyrum offered.

"Yes, let's," agreed Ian.

Amanda and Julia both had concerned expressions when Ian and Hyrum re-entered the room.

"What was it, Ian," Amanda asked.

"I'll tell you soon, when the children aren't about," Ian replied.

"Would you two like to go for a walk and we'll watch the children?" Hyrum offered.

"Yes, that would be grand," Amanda replied.

"I'll watch the children," Subria offered. "All of you go along now."

"That's ever so good of you," Julia smiled.

Outside, the two couples walked in the bright morning sun. Amanda and Julia gasped when told about the massacre in the border towns. Ian and Hyrum held their wives while they cried, trying to comprehend the awfulness of the tragedy.

"How can this happen?" Amanda asked in tears. "The settlers have been so kind to many of the natives. They surely knew them. They invited them to celebrate Christmas Eve!"

"Are we safe, Hyrum?" Julia asked.

"I don't know that we're safe, but we aren't on the border like those poor souls who were killed."

Amanda was looking at Ian who had remained silent. She studied his face. His jaw was firm and his eyes intense.

"Ian? What are you thinking?" she asked. Ian was silent. "You're going to join the commandos, aren't you?"

Tears ran down Amanda's face, and it pained Ian to know that he was going to hurt her delicate feelings. Still, he had conviction that if the settlers did nothing to help the garrison, all would be lost.

Julia felt safe in Hyrum's arms as she awaited Ian's response.

"I must join the commandos, my dear," Ian said softly. "Something must be done."

Amanda buried her face in Ian's chest and cried. Julia stroked her hair to comfort her.

"Hyrum and Julia will be here to help you," Ian assured her.

"It's not me or the children that concerns me," Amanda said quietly through her tears.

"I'll be fine. I promise," Ian said with a mixture of care and confidence.

"I know your promise is sincere if not completely out of your control to keep," Amanda cried.

Ian kissed Amanda's forehead, but said nothing in reply.

"When will you leave?" Amanda asked.

"Tomorrow morning," Ian replied.

The news seemed almost too hard for Amanda to bear, and she lay her head on Ian's chest and cried aloud.

Julia continued rubbing Amanda's shoulders and kissed her cheek. After a few minutes Amanda looked at Hyrum and asked, "Will you be joining also?"

"I'll stay and care for the farms," Hyrum promised.

After a few minutes, Amanda dried her eyes and forced a smile. With one hand placed over Ian's heart, she looked him in the eyes and said, "I'll support your decision. I know that men as you are needed to preserve our land and lives. I'm proud of you."

Hyrum already felt guilt that he wasn't joining the commandos, and Amanda's comments did little to alleviate those feelings. Amanda must have sensed how he was feeling, because she turned to him and said, "And I assure you that men as you are needed here. If someone doesn't keep the farms thriving, there'll be nothing to stay and fight for. Will there now?"

Hyrum smiled and nodded.

Hyrum and Julia and their children, along with Subria, stayed the remainder of the day with Ian and Amanda. Nothing more was said about the massacres or Ian's plans, other than Julia taking Subria aside to tell her. Subria's reaction was one of shock, mixed with sadness and disgust.

"You'll stay the night with us, won't you?" Amanda asked Julia. "I couldn't bear to see Ian off tomorrow without you here."

"Of course, my dear," replied Julia. "We wouldn't think of leaving you so soon."

"Julia," Amanda continued hesitantly.

"Yes, what is it?"

"I'm concerned for Subria."

"Whatever for?" asked Julia.

"There will likely be some in the community that will ridicule her because of the massacre."

"Surely not. They all know her, they've known her for years," Julia replied with surprise.

"Don't forget that the settlers who were killed also knew many of their assailants. People around here will remember that also."

"I suppose you're right. What should we do?" asked Julia.

"There's probably very little that you can do. Just keep an eye on her when others are about," offered Amanda.

"I will. But I hope it's not as bad as all that," replied Julia.

The next morning, both families went outside to see Ian off. Hyrum and Julia stood aside with their children and watched as Ian held and kissed Amanda. Subria held Ian and Amanda's infant son in her arms while their two-year old daughter played nearby with Hyrum and Julia's two-year old son, Samuel.

Julia's heart was heavy as she watched the tender scene. She thought about how much she would hate to see Hyrum off to fight the natives. Tears formed in her eyes as she looked at Amanda's children, unaware that their father was leaving. Julia leaned against Hyrum's chest and felt safe, but she hurt for Amanda.

"Please be safe and don't be a hero," Amanda tearfully said to Ian.

Ian hugged and kissed Amanda. "I'm not the hero type," he smiled.

"When will you come home?" she asked.

"I don't know. But, I will come home," Ian promised. "You know that I have no wish to leave. My only desire is to stay here in your arms, I assure you."

Amanda wrapped her arms more tightly about Ian's neck and lay her face on his chest. She could feel the moisture of her tears dampening his shirt. She knew him well, and knew that he was the type to be a hero. It was the same motivation that drove him to join the fight. He was a hero. There was no changing that. *Please keep him safe, dear God,* she silently prayed.

"I must be off," Ian said as he gently removed Amanda's arms from about his neck.

Ian held both Amanda's hands as he backed away, until their fingers were no longer touching. Julia stepped forward and wrapped her arms about Amanda's shoulders as Ian backed away slowly.

"I'll send correspondence when I can," he promised.

Ian and Hyrum embraced briefly and then shook hands. "Be careful, old man," Hyrum said.

Ian smiled. "I will indeed," he said.

With that, Ian turned and walked away. He looked over his shoulder or walked backward often until he disappeared amongst the trees and around a corner.

Amanda turned and held Julia and cried. "Will I ever see him again?" she asked.

"Of course you will," Julia assured her.

Julia, Subria and the children spent the next several days with Amanda, while Hyrum traveled between the two farms to care for the flocks.

Ian had only been gone a few days when Hyrum said to Julia, "I feel that we need to be more attentive to our religious observance."

"Whatever do you mean?" Julia asked.

"While growing up in England my father and mother saw to it that we were in Church every Sunday. I can't say that I always enjoyed it; until I started going to observe you, of course," he smiled. "I think that attending was a good practice and instilled in me faith in God. I know that your experience with Lord and Lady Hammond wasn't as consistent."

"No," Julia reflected. "It is odd that there was a chapel at Brentwood Hall, but we weren't consistent in our worship."

"I think that our children would benefit if we were consistent," Hyrum replied. "I think that it would also foster good relations with our neighbors if we worshiped with them. After all, the new chapel should be fully used."

"Does Ian's situation figure into your decision?"

Hyrum thought for a moment. "Yes, it does really. We could pray for him when we attend."

"Well, I think it a grand idea. We'll start this week. I'm sure that Amanda and Subria would love to join us."

"Yes, that would be excellent," Hyrum agreed.

When mentioned to Amanda and Subria, both were agreeable, particularly Subria. The prospect that she would be required to stand in the back of the chapel did little to squelch her enthusiasm. She had made consistent Bible reading a part of her daily activities and to add consistent worship inside a church felt right to her. Amanda was initially apprehensive about wrestling with two small children, but the opportunity to pray for Ian inside the church excited her. Hyrum, Julia and Subria's promise to help her with the children comforted her.

Chapter Twenty-three – Religious Observance
January 1851
Elephant Hook, Africa

"Francis, take Samuel by the hand and go to the wagon," Julia instructed as she put the final touches on Victoria's hair.

"Ahhh, do we have to go to church?" Francis asked.

"We don't have to, but we are," Julia responded as she placed a yellow ribbon beneath Victoria's hair on the back of her head and wrapped it about her head just above the ears.

"I don't like church," Francis said as he took Samuel's hand and headed out the door.

"I don't like church either," Luke volunteered.

"Nevertheless, follow your brothers to the wagon," Julia ordered as she knotted the ribbon into a bow and pulled it tight. Addressing herself to Subria, she added, "To be sure, we should have made church attendance more of a priority. It pains me that my sons are so unfamiliar with formal worship."

Though their intentions had been good, the Princes had nevertheless attended church a precious few times over the course of the last year. They had resolved to do better in the future.

Subria cradled Rebecca in her arms. "I'm sure they'll be fine. They're good boys."

"Wagon's ready," Hyrum said as he stepped through the door. "You women are a lovely sight," he added with a smile.

"Thank you, Daddy," Victoria smiled, as she twirled her dress.

"Your boys aren't anxious to go to church," Julia commented.

"Yes, they let me know. There's no need for concern; they'll be fine. Luke's just a little boy. He'll say anything his brother says." Holding Rebecca's tiny hand, he added with a smile, "But my girls are the sweetest angels indeed."

Hyrum turned and hugged Julia as she smiled and said, "They're all angels."

"Are you ready, Subria?" Hyrum asked. "We've a ways to go and had best be off."

"I and Rebecca are ready," Subria smiled.

The sun was rising well into the sky as the wagon creeped along the dusty road. The hills were dry for lack of rain, and only a few sheep foraged the gentle, rolling slopes amongst the golden patches of dry grass. Most of the sheep that the wagon passed by were bedded down in the shade of trees against the approaching heat of the day. Travel time to the church would be spent singing and listening to stories that Hyrum would tell of his childhood in England. Subria would also tell stories from the Bible. Francis, more particularly, enjoyed the stories of battles and liked to hear a re-telling of David fighting Goliath.

"Now why do you suppose God included the story of David killing the giant Goliath?" Subria asked Francis after he requested her to tell it again.

"To teach us that we can kill giants," Francis responded.

Julia smiled to think that after having heard the story several times Francis was finally able to start grasping its meaning. She was hoping that he would eventually be able to apply it to his own life, thereby increasing his faith in God. She hoped he would do the same with other Biblical stories as he learned them. Knowing that her oldest child would set a powerful example for her other children, she was particularly interested in the development of his faith and character.

"That's correct indeed," Subria assured him. "What kinds of giants might we face?"

"Big ones," Luke offered.

"I don't think we have giants here," Victoria volunteered.

Hyrum laughed and Julia smiled. *This is why we travel together to church,* she thought. *We're all together laughing and learning.*

"We don't have big, people kind of giants," Hyrum agreed. "But I think Subria is referring to a different kind of giant."

"I am indeed," Subria smiled. "We all have giants. Some that we face every day. The drought is a giant that your father is facing. Your auntie Amanda is facing the giant of your uncle Ian being gone. Isn't that a big giant to face?"

"And the natives that Uncle Ian is fighting are giants," Francis offered.

"Some of them are truly giants," Hyrum agreed.

"Are you a native?" Luke asked Subria.

"I am indeed," Subria said.

"Then why isn't Uncle Ian fighting you?" Luke asked.

"Uncle Ian isn't so much fighting the natives," Julia offered, "as he is fighting to keep us safe."

"He's still fighting the natives," Francis insisted. "But he's not fighting Subria because she lives with us."

Subria smiled and hugged Luke. "I am a native, but I live with you, and I don't agree with some of the things that the other natives are doing. So, Ian doesn't have to fight me."

"You're a good native," Luke offered.

Subria smiled. "Yes, I'm a good native. But remember, there are lots of good natives."

"That's right, son," Julia said. "There are lots of good natives. They have families that need food just like we do. They have mommies and daddies that love their children very much, just like we love you."

"Well, I don't know why they have to steal our sheep and kill the settlers," Francis commented.

"It's difficult to explain, son," Hyrum said. "When someone's family is hungry, they'll feed them pretty much anyway that they can. Hunger is a powerful motivator. So really, it's the drought that is the bigger giant for the natives and for the settlers. In our own way, we are battling the same giant."

"Wouldn't it be better to battle him together instead of battling each other?" Francis asked.

"I suppose it would be better," Hyrum agreed. "But I don't think that the settlers and the natives know how to do that."

Julia thought again about the two worlds that Subria was sandwiched between. She wondered whether Subria even considered herself a native any longer. Her English was better than her native tongue. She had long ago adopted the English dress style. If she held any of the superstitious beliefs of the natives, it wasn't evident. But her devotion to Jesus Christ was evident. And yet, the color of her skin must be a constant reminder of the conflicting societies. *What's the key to Subria's successful transition to our society?* Julia asked herself. *Is it the adoption of our religion?*

"Subria," Julia ventured, "you've been with us so very long, and with the Coburns so very long before coming to us. And yet, I'm puzzled."

"After such a long time, what puzzles you?" Subria asked with a smile.

"How is it that you can live so contentedly in our society without the regular association of your own people? Is it the adoption of our religion?"

Subria smiled and looked into the distance. This was her land. Her ancestors had been on this land since the beginning of time itself. Yet, they were ignorant to the ways of Christianity. *Truly, the religion of the settlers made it easier to live in a society that wasn't mine from birth,* she thought. *But that's not the key.*

"Love came first," Subria said still looking into the distance. "Without love, there is no religion." Subria looked at Julia and smiled. "Love opens hearts and transcends culture and skin color. When the natives feel loved by the settlers in all things, then they'll live in peace. Love doesn't let children starve. When children are fed, and parents are loved, only then are their hearts open to receive God."

"Is that what the Coburns did for you?" Julia asked quietly, almost reverently.

"Yes. They clothed me, fed me and loved me," Subria said with tears in her eyes.

Julia was quiet for a few moments. She looked at the baby in her arms. Rebecca, so fresh from God's presence, yet totally dependent on her mother for food and love. She looked at Hyrum, strong and tanned. She realized again her dependence on him for food and love. Her dependence on him, and the love and care she felt from him, increased her love and faith in God.

"I suppose it was much that way for me with Lord and Lady Hammond," Julia said. "Without them, I may have been lost in the world, not much different from the poor, hungry children that I saw whilst traveling with Princess Victoria. I wonder sometimes whether they knew how much I loved them."

"I'm sure they did," Hyrum offered.

"I'm not sure that we English confess our love openly enough," Julia observed.

"Still, they knew," Hyrum assured her.

"I do hope so," Julia said.

Subria cast her mind back to the last moments she spent with the Coburns. "Love casts out all fear," she said aloud.

"Indeed," Hyrum agreed.

"Perhaps I should have let my love for the Coburns cast out my fear of the ship," Subria said. "Then they'd know how much I loved them."

Julia placed a hand on Subria's arm. "They know. I assure you. That aside, if you had gone with the Coburns, you wouldn't be with us and that would be dreadful."

Subria smiled and placed her hand atop Julia's own.

The church house was a small wooden structure in serious need of a coat of paint. Many had arrived in advance of the Princes, most having also traveled by wagon. Amanda had made significant effort to hitch her own wagon and drive herself and her children there. She had arrived very shortly before Hyrum and Julia.

"Good morning, Amanda," Hyrum called.

"Oh, how wonderful to see you. Good morning," Amanda replied.

"Won't you sit with us?" Julia asked.

"But of course," Amanda replied.

The two families walked toward the building just as Mr. Richards also approached.

Looking at Subria with some scorn, Mr. Richards said, "So, Mr. Prince, you didn't join your brother to fight the natives?"

Hyrum considered not responding, but said, "No. I didn't. I've two farms to care for now."

"You'd best keep an eye on your domestic help. Your family may receive the same treatment that the border settlers received," Mr. Richards sneered.

Julia held Subria by the arm and pulled her closer as they walked toward the church. "Pay him no mind," she urged Subria.

"We don't allow her kind in here," Mr. Richards' companion said as Subria approached the doorway.

"She's with us," Hyrum insisted.

"She'll stand in the back then," Mr. Richards said in disgust.

Mr. Richards and his companion grumbled something about there being no safety when a native was about, but protested no further.

Subria was shaken, but not surprised. She hadn't expected a warm welcome. Standing in the back of the church with a few other domestic helpers didn't bother her terribly, she was accustomed to being treated poorly by some settlers. At least, she felt, she would be worshiping inside the church.

"Why must Subria stand in the back?" Victoria asked aloud after the Princes were seated.

"Because some people are afraid," Julia whispered.

"Afraid of what?" Victoria asked.

"Afraid to love everyone as God has commanded," Hyrum said quietly.

Though she pretended to not notice, Subria was aware that Mr. Richards glared at her several times during the service.

On the way home following the service, Victoria said to Subria, "I'm sorry that you couldn't sit with us."

Subria smiled and hugged her. "Not to worry, child. I could hear just fine," she replied.

Chapter Twenty-four – The Eighth War
February 1853
Near Fort White, Africa

Ian dug his heels into the sides of his horse. At full gallop, while holding his heavy rifle, it was only the strength of the grip he had with his legs that kept him in the saddle. After just over two years of battling the natives, much of it on horseback, Ian had complete trust in his horse. Once nothing more than a farm animal, a beast of burden, his horse had become battle hardened. The noise, smoke and chaos of a battlefield no longer frightened the animal. It almost seemed that the horse anticipated each charge.

A thick blanket of dust filled the air, choking man and beast alike. Ian's horse was wet with lathered sweat; a muddy layer of dust had attached itself to the horse's neck and back. The horse's nostrils flared wide with each breath, and his hooves pounded the dusty earth.

Ian and the commandos were closing the gap between themselves and a band of natives that had attacked Fort White the night before. The commandos expected that they would encounter the natives just beyond the stand of trees at the bottom of the hill. Suddenly the horse just in front and to the left of Ian went down and fell into the path of his own horse. Ian pulled the reins hard to the right, and his horse reacted instantly to avoid the fallen animal and rider.

In that moment, time seemed to slow to a crawl for Ian. He saw the side of the other horse's head gaped open having been hit with a ball. *The natives have stopped in the trees!* he thought. *We're being ambushed! A stupid mistake, caused by our haste!*

The movement to avoid the other horse and rider had been so violent it caused the ankle of Ian's horse to buckle under the force. Ian lost grip of his gun as he flew from the saddle. He landed hard on his side, and winced in pain when his ribcage struck a rock with the full force of his weight.

Ian tried to rise, but fell back to his knees enveloped in pain so severe that for a moment he couldn't breathe. Chaos was all about him as other horses and riders pounded by or also fell to the ground. His own horse was struggling to rise, but fell with each attempt.

Shots rang out, and Ian heard the whistling sound of balls flying past him.

He spotted his rifle a few paces away, and staying low to the ground, he carefully made his way to it and lay behind a dead horse. Using the horse as cover, he looked in the direction of the trees. Small clouds of smoke erupted from the trees with each round fired by the natives; and there were many of them, many more than the commandos had believed possible. *Have they received reinforcements?* Ian wondered.

As he lay behind the dead horse, Ian couldn't help but think of Amanda. *Two years and now I get hurt,* he thought. *Amanda's not going to be happy to hear this.*

Ian was happy that this war, the eighth with the natives, was possibly winding down. Despite heavy initial losses by the British, or perhaps because of them, the Crown had sent additional troops to defend the colonies. Sadly, one of those ships of reinforcements sunk to the depths of the sea taking 300 souls with it. But other reinforcements had arrived which boosted morale greatly.

A turning point in the war had come a year earlier when the British Government had finally decided that Governor Smith was inept, and that his heavy hand had been responsible for much of the violence. After he was replaced by George Cathcart, the British fortunes began to turn for the better. Reportedly, the natives were nearing defeat, and their attempts to attack were largely futile.

Nearly two years earlier

January 1851
My Darling Amanda,

We have not yet been apart a month and already my heart aches for you, to hold you and to feel the warmth of your body against my own. My love for you grows more tender with each passing day. I almost repent the day that I decided to leave you and to join this horrible fight. But repent I must not, for it is only in putting my love for you and the children first that brings me here and gives me the courage to be separated from you for a time.

Make no mistake, we face a formidable foe, a foe that would burn our homes and destroy our families if we did not stand against them. But stand against them we shall. I shall not share with you the burdens of war, for I would not wish to weigh your heart down with sorrow. Your words, "Don't be a hero," ring in my ears, and I am striving to follow your command. My only desire is to come to you again.

Hold our sweet children for me. I miss them more than words can express.

Faithfully yours,
Ian

February 1851
My Dearest Ian,

Your letter brought unspeakable joy to my heart. I could hear your voice as I read it aloud to the children. Like me, they love and miss you more than I have capacity to express. But I know that you are engaged in a just and honorable cause.

Hyrum feels that he should join you in the fight, but I and Julia have assured him that he is needed here. Some natives have attacked as far south as Winterberg, so it is good to have some men here should the natives manage to push farther south still.

I know that you must be worried about the sheep. They are doing well. Hyrum is so good to come and care for them regularly.

I pray to God every night for your care and safety. I trust your care to him.

With all my love and care,
Amanda

Life was difficult for Amanda in Ian's absence. There was nothing about it that pleased her. Caring for the children night and day, without the support of another person was taxing. Hyrum couldn't come every day, so she also helped to care for the animals between his visits. Though she saw Hyrum every few days, and Julia nearly weekly, loneliness gnawed at her. She longed for Ian's company. She missed his voice, his laugh and his embrace. Though she waited with great anticipation for each letter, she decided that the time would pass more quickly if she didn't think of him every moment of every day. She made an effort instead to think of him only during the evening meal.

April 1851

My Sweet Amanda,

I have read your recent letter 100 times if I have read it once. I would have written earlier, but there is no paper, and we are constantly on the move. We have engaged the enemy several times and are making our worth known to the British garrison. We travel light and swift. They travel heavy and slow. We've been able to come to their aid many times. They are outnumbered and outmaneuvered and have suffered many losses. The commandos have been very fortunate indeed to have suffered few losses, but we mourn each one. We not only fight the formidable native foe, but hunger and fatigue are constant enemies. And now, with the encroaching cold, we have another enemy to battle.

Your love and prayers sustain me. I think of you and the children constantly. I would give anything to just hold you for a moment and to kiss you. I trust that right will prevail in this conflict and I will be home soon.

Please express my warmest regards to Hyrum and Julia.

Faithfully, your husband,
Ian

April 1851

My dear husband, Ian,

I am in possession of your recent letter, and I cannot express my joy when I contemplate your safety. Words escape me such that I also cannot adequately express my love for you.

I and the children pray for you every day, and my tears water my pillow by night. But I trust that I will see you again soon.

I hesitate to tell you this for fear that I will cause you undue concern, but there has been greater anxiety recently regarding marauding bands of natives. They are hopeful to take advantage of a community that has sent several of its men away to fight. We regularly post guards to watch for any approaching bands. Francis and other young boys like him have often shouldered the burden of this important responsibility.

I've written you several times since I was in receipt of your last correspondence, but it would seem that my letters do not always find you. Please know that I will continue to send to you my love regularly in hopes that some of the letters will find you.

I send you my love, 'till we meet again,
Amanda

If Ian had expected to find a well-organized group of commandos when he first joined, he would have been disappointed. The commandos had played a decisive role in the earlier Xhosa wars, but because they were comprised entirely of settlers, they had disbanded following the cessation of fighting in the earlier conflicts. Any organizational authority occurred naturally, as settlers with prior fighting experience, coupled with leadership skills, rose in rank and command. Ian had no plans to lead, he only wanted to play a role in defending his adopted country and his family.

It took Ian two days riding to arrive at the gathering place for commando volunteers. Two settlers had joined him from Elephant Hook and on the morning of the second day they were joined by five more men on horseback. More men still joined them as they drew closer to the designated gathering point for commandos. Though small in numbers, it gave Ian hope that they would eventually be strong in numbers when they had all assembled.

These commandos weren't foot soldiers, and each man was to provide his own horse. Ian knew that his horse wasn't much more than perhaps a plow horse, but he was a far sight better than some of the other horses. As volunteers arrived, it didn't take long for the commando leaders to size them up, eliminating those that were too young or those with unsuitable steeds from their fighting ranks. Those without suitable horses could join the foot commandos or join the supply ranks. Regardless of their capacity, every willing man was put to some use. Boys were sent home.

There was already a group of about 100 men gathered before Ian arrived.

"What's your name, sir?" asked a captain.

"Ian Prince, sir."

"Where are you from?"

"Elephant Hook, sir."

It was difficult for Ian to determine how old the captain might be, but it appeared that he had spent a considerable portion of his life outdoors. He had a thin beard that hung below his chin. He wore a sweat-stained hat with a broad brim. His long-sleeved shirt was rolled up to the elbows against the heat of the day. When he spoke, Ian could see that he was missing several teeth. It occurred to Ian that he had smelled the captain before he had seen him.

"Can you ride?"

"Yes, sir."

"Can you shoot?"

"Yes, sir."

"Can you shoot and ride at the same time?"

"Yes, sir, though I've never done so," replied Ian.

The captain and some of the other seasoned veterans laughed loudly, causing Ian's face to redden.

"You'd best learn quick," snapped the captain. "Reloading on horseback can be tricky indeed."

"Yes, sir," Ian replied.

"You've got a fine horse there. Have you ever shot a gun near him?"

"No, sir."

With that, the captain pointed his long gun into the air and pulled the trigger. Ian was startled, but managed to hold tight to his horse's reins when the horse attempted to bolt. The strong horse nearly pulled Ian off his feet, but with a firm grip on the reins, Ian managed to control the horse's head and thus his movement; keeping himself from being dragged. The horse reared up and beat the air with his hooves attempting to free himself from the reins.

"Whoa, boy! Whoa!" Ian called.

When the horse lowered its front legs to the ground, Ian patted his head and spoke softly to him. The horse's eyes were wide with fright and he blew loud puffs of air from his nostrils.

Ian was furious. "Why'd you do that?" he snapped at the captain.

"The battlefield is a loud and confusing place," the captain yelled back. "It's no place for a horse to hear the sound of shot above its head for the first time. You'd best get your horse accustomed to it." Then to all the new volunteers he yelled, "You'd all best do the same. Join up in groups to conserve powder. Get to it."

Though Ian knew that the captain was right, it angered him that no warning was given.

Ian started to join several other men to train their horses to the sound of gunshot, but the captain called him to stay.

"Does it anger you that I treated you so?"

"It does, sir," replied Ian straightly, but with some contempt.

"Yet you obey?"

"Of course I obey. I came here to fight natives, not to fight with you."

The captain smiled. "I need more men like you," he said. "I need men that will execute commands without question and with exactness."

"Yes, sir."

"Does that describe you?" asked the captain.

"Yes, sir."

"Good. Now go and lead those men in the drill."

"Yes, sir."

From that day, Ian was trusted with the command of 20 men. One of those men was an older man of about 40 years of age, named Harold. Ian had met Harold on their way into camp the first day. Ian hadn't cared for him much; he talked too much and in his suit and tie, he seemed like an unlikely soldier. Having Harold assigned to his group didn't please Ian.

"How old are you?" Harold had asked Ian shortly after they met.

"I'm nearly 30," Ian had replied. "And you?"

"I'm a fair sight older, to be sure," was all that Harold had offered regarding his own age. "But I hope to live still longer. I'm hoping that we won't engage the enemy anytime soon."

Ian was confused. "Why are you here then?"

"I've never done much outdoors, and I thought this would impress my wife."

"How long have you been married to this woman?" asked Ian in surprise.

"Twenty years."

"Twenty years and you haven't impressed her yet?" Ian asked, but then apologized for what seemed like a rude remark.

Harold hung his head. "No need to apologize, sir. Truth is, nothing that I can do would impress her. She's beyond that. I actually volunteered so that I'd have reason to be away from her."

Ian was surprised that a near stranger would speak so openly about the shortcomings of his relationship with his wife. He wasn't so naive as to believe that all relationships were as satisfying as his with Amanda. Still, he was curious.

"You surprise me, sir. I'd give anything to be with my Amanda right now. Yet, you wish to be away from your wife. I'm speechless."

"Perhaps if you knew my wife, you'd be less astounded. She certainly isn't speechless, especially when it concerns me and my abilities. The woman has an unrelenting tongue. I'd rather face the natives than bear her tongue lashings longer."

"Meet the natives? Do you know how to ride a horse, or shoot a gun?"

"I ride well enough," Harold replied. "And you've seen my fine horse."

"Aye, you do have a fine horse," Ian agreed. "Can you shoot?"

"I own a gun."

"You own a gun?" Ian laughed. "Can you shoot a gun?"

"I certainly can shoot," replied Harold. Then with a grin, he added, "Whether I can hit a target or no, it remains to be seen."

"You'll get us all killed," Ian replied. "We can't have that. I'll teach you to shoot."

Ian made it a point to spend time teaching Harold every day for the next several days.

"Excellent shot, Harold!" Ian exclaimed after Harold successfully hit the target. "Now if we can just get the natives to hold still like that target, you'll do just fine," he laughed.

Harold was obviously pleased with the praise. There was an unmistakable catch in his throat when he replied with a grin, "Thank you, kind sir. Your praise is received most gratefully."

The new commandos spent the next week practicing shooting while riding. It was difficult even for Ian to master. It was hard enough to ride while holding onto the gun, let alone raising it to the firing position. Reloading was near impossible. Many recruits fell from their horse during the drills. Ian found that his inner thighs burned with pain from gripping the sides of his horse so firmly, but with practice he had mastered the new skill.

In the late afternoon near the end of the week, the captain called Ian and the other group leaders to his tent.

"We've received our command to go against a band of natives that have been spotted inside the borders near Fort Alice. It's believed that they will attack the fort, knowing that its ranks are depleted."

"How many are there, sir?" asked one of the others.

"300."

"300? Can we go against so many? We're only 120."

"We have little choice. The natives are without horses. We'll hit them fast and hard. Can we leave the few in the fort without hope? There are women and children inside that fort I remind you," replied the captain firmly.

"Yes, sir."

"Good," said the captain. Then surveying his other leaders, he asked, "Are all in agreement?"

"Aye," came the unanimous reply.

"Good. Fort Alice is almost a day's ride. We'll send a forward party tonight to scout ahead. The rest will leave before first light. Be ready."

Ian gathered his men to tell them their orders; as he did he saw two men ride quickly out of camp. "God speed," Ian whispered to the scouts.

With the exception of Harold, his men cheered when they heard the news. After they had been dismissed, Ian called Harold aside.

"You are under no obligation to accompany us," Ian said. "This is a volunteer garrison. There's no shame in going home."

Harold looked straight at Ian and replied, "I'll not go home. I'd never hear the end of it."

"As you wish, but don't charge in recklessly," Ian smiled.

"No, sir. And I'll not be a burden."

Ian was pleased with Harold's willingness, and he was surprised that his initial dislike of Harold had nearly dissipated. He actually enjoyed his company.

Before sun up, the company was on the move. Each commando was responsible to take along only the provisions that he would need to sustain himself for four-day's time. The horses would eat grass as they had opportunity at night, and man and beast would drink from any streams or holes that they could find.

We truly do travel light and fast, Ian thought. *The British garrison would be marching in rank, followed by many wagons full of supplies and tents. Little wonder then, they can't win this war without us.*

Though this would be the first encounter with the enemy for many of the commandos, there was an excitement in the air that increased the unity they felt in their purpose.

At mid-day, they encountered the scouts returning at high speed. With great excitement, they rode straight to the captain and called out, "The natives are already at the fort, and the fort doesn't look like it can repel the attack much longer!"

"How far is the fort?" the captain asked urgently.

"Two hours! One if we push the horses hard."

"Dear God, save them!" whispered the captain. Then turning to his men, he called, "Ride hard men! We've no time to lose! We'll engage the natives, taking one or two shots each. Then we'll pull back before we hit them again. We'll keep hitting them in this fashion until we've freed the fort."

A cheer went up from the men as they kicked the sides of their horses. Soon, they were surrounded by a thick cloud of dust. *We probably won't have surprise on our side,* Ian thought.

Ian was surprised to see that Harold was riding neck-to-neck beside him. He was leaning into the ride, so much so that his upper torso was nearly atop his horse's neck. His horse's mane whipped his face with each stride. Harold had an intense look on his face and seemed quite determined.

"Harold!" Ian called over the pounding of the horses' hooves. Harold looked at Ian briefly and then back to the trail. "Are you ready, Harold?"

Without looking in his direction, Harold yelled back, "I'm ready! I've never felt so alive!"

Ian couldn't help but grin. Ian felt alive as well, but he hoped he would still be alive at the end of the day.

Ian had never ridden so far, so quickly and the pounding was starting to jar him. He marveled that Harold was still in the saddle. Just when Ian felt he could take no more, the fort was sighted.

With loud yells, the commandos descended upon the natives. The Xhosa were now faced with resistance on two sides. Ian could see fear in their eyes as the commandos rode by them firing their guns. Ian was able to get off two shots before the commandos pulled back to re-group. Again, the commandos descended upon the natives. Bodies were starting to scatter the ground. Ian was aware of three commandos down. One tried to run for the shelter of nearby trees, but was gunned down by native fire.

Again, the commandos pulled back to re-group. *Where's Harold?* Ian thought. With relief, he caught sight of Harold. It didn't look like the same Harold he had met just days before. This Harold was confident and determined.

A third time the commandos roared toward the natives. There were far fewer this time and less resistance. Many of the remaining natives turned to run, but other commandos chased them down with their horses and shot them dead. Ian was shocked. *Why are they shooting retreating natives?* he cried in his mind.

With a sigh of relief, Ian realized that his first battle was over. The fort was liberated! The sound of cheers could be heard coming from inside the fort. Soon the gate of the fort was thrown open and soldiers and other men poured out, followed by a few women and children. They greeted the commandos with joyous cheers.

As Ian surveyed the battlefield with its sad display of the fallen from both sides, his heart ached knowing that he was partially responsible. But he knew that he had done only as he had been called upon to do. He wasn't the aggressor.

The commandos that had chased and killed the fleeing natives returned and joined the celebration of victory. *If there's a stain on the day, this was it,* Ian thought.

Later Ian was able to find the captain alone and asked him how it was justified that the fleeing natives had been killed. The captain responded that he would speak with the men involved, but he assured Ian that if the natives hadn't been killed, they would only join with other natives and take the battle somewhere else.

"Such a thing can't be demonstrated beyond doubt," Ian insisted.

"Perhaps not," agreed the captain, "but, what is done is done. I'll not speak of the matter more."

"Well, I'll have no part of it. Such a thing isn't the English way. The English fight with honor."

"You needn't have any part in it, but the commando way will always be less inhibited by honor than that of the garrison," the captain retorted. "That's part of what makes us so effective. If you wanted to fight with honor, you should have joined the garrison."

Ian considered his options. He could quit and return home, but that would only leave his family and country a little less secure. Or, he could stay and fight with honor and encourage others to do the same. He chose the latter.

Elephant Hook
June 1851

Francis sat on the highest hill in the vicinity of the scattered homes of Elephant Hook and surveyed the surrounding area. He had the important job of watching for a possible attack. He was aware that other boys were stationed on similar hills nearby, but he had no way of communicating with them. He had initially enjoyed the assignment, it made him feel grown up and responsible, but the luster had long since faded. The cold winter wind blowing up the hillside from the east didn't do anything to increase his enthusiasm.

The fact that he had the assignment was a testament to the number of men who had left the area to join the commandos. The remaining men were needed to work the farms during the day, and they rotated the assignment to guard the village during the night hours.

Francis was glad that he didn't have the assignment to watch at night. The boredom and loneliness of the daytime watch was difficult to endure, but if the cold darkness were added to the mix, it would be challenging beyond anything he wished to experience. Wild animals weren't much of a concern in the area, but if there were a concern, it would be at night.

That evening at the table, Hyrum quizzed his son on his assignment to ensure that it was being filled appropriately.

"Are you vigilant to stay awake and keep watch during your assignment?" Hyrum asked.

"Yes, sir."

"I know that the hours can seem long and without stimulation, but it is an important task you've taken on," Hyrum assured him.

"Yes, sir, but it's very cold," Francis replied.

Julia looked at Francis sitting across the table and for a moment she was startled. She didn't see a boy before her, but a young man. Her initial reaction of surprise was quickly replaced with satisfaction. She smiled with pleasure and thought, *He's becoming a fine young man.* When did this happen? *He'll be a good man like his father.* A tear formed in her eye as she contemplated the "loss" of her little boy.

"Perhaps it's too cold for the lad to be on that hill for so long?" Julia offered.

"Quite right," agreed Subria. "I can take part of his time."

Hyrum put down his fork and knife and rested his hands on the table as a clear indication that what he was about to say was intended to be taken in all seriousness.

"We're raising a man here. He's quite capable of performing this important assignment. There's no need for anyone to take his time," Hyrum stated. Then he turned to Francis and asked, "Is there, son?"

"No, sir," Francis agreed.

The next afternoon Hyrum was working near their home when a man on horseback rode up quickly. Hyrum recognized the man as a settler who lived farther to the east and closer to Elephant Hook. The man pulled his horse up short and, without getting out of the saddle, told Hyrum that natives had been seen not more than 10 miles distant.

"You should move your family to town temporarily," the messenger stated with some urgency. "You'll be in a better position to defend your family there."

"Is that really necessary?" asked Hyrum.

"It's your choice, sir, but I've already moved mine. If the natives come this direction, you don't want your family left in a vulnerable position."

"And what about the house, and the sheep?" Hyrum asked.

"You'll have to leave those in the good Lord's hands. You've got precious little time to concern yourself with those matters. You'd best to get into town."

As he rode off to warn others, Hyrum thanked the messenger and assured him that they would go to Elephant Hook.

"Julia! Subria!" Hyrum called urgently as he entered the house.

"What is it?" Julia asked as she entered from the next room.

"Gather the children! Natives have been spotted not ten miles distant. We need to get to Elephant Hook for safety."

"Oh my!" Julia gasped.

"Where's Subria?" Hyrum asked.

Julia placed her hand over her mouth and exclaimed, "She left for the Johnson's this morning. She's not due back until evening."

"Hopefully, the Johnson's have gotten the message and she'll go with them to Elephant Hook," Hyrum stated.

"Or perhaps we'll see her on the roadway."

"Perhaps, but the Johnson's are not exactly on our way to Elephant Hook," Hyrum observed.

"If we don't see her along the way, or if she's not at Elephant Hook, will you please find her?"

"I will if at all possible," Hyrum promised. "But right now, I've got to get Francis off that hill. Throw some food in the wagon and some blankets! I'll be right back," Hyrum said as he headed back outside.

Hyrum grabbed his horse's mane and swung himself onto the horse's back. It wasn't often that he rode without a saddle, but there was little time now to concern himself with saddling the horse. Holding tightly to the mane and gripping firmly with his knees and feet, he rode quickly to the nearby hill. While remaining on the horse's back he called to Francis.

"Hurry, son. The natives are about and we must get to Elephant Hook. Grab my hand!"

Grabbing Francis hand, he pulled him onto the horse behind himself and kicked the horse's sides to spur him back down the hill. Julia was loading the other children into the wagon as Hyrum and Francis arrived.

"Francis, come with me. Let's get the old tent," Hyrum ordered.

Francis followed Hyrum, but asked, "What old tent?"

"An old tent that we lived in for a short time while we built our first permanent structure," Hyrum replied.

The tent was large and constructed of thick canvas. It weighed nearly 200 pounds and almost proved too heavy for Hyrum and Francis to drag. By exerting great effort, they managed to drag it from its resting place in the barn.

At the barn door, Hyrum said, "Let's hitch the wagon and bring the wagon to the tent. This tent is heavier than I remember."

Francis readily agreed, and the two hurried to hitch the horse to the wagon. Soon, the wagon was loaded with food and supplies to last several days. Hyrum instructed his family to hold tight because he was going to push the horse and wagon harder than he usually did. It soon became clear that he wasn't exaggerating.

Julia kept scanning the roadway ahead for sign of Subria, but she wasn't to be found. Soon, they came to the point where the road to the Johnson's farm departed from the road to Elephant Hook. Still, Subria wasn't in sight.

"Hyrum, I don't see Subria," Julia cried.

"I'm sure that the Johnson's have been warned and will go to Elephant Hook. I'm sure she'll go with them," Hyrum replied. "We can't divert from the road to go to Johnson's."

"What about Amanda? We must check on her on our way. She's only a short distance from the road," Julia insisted.

"Yes, of course, we'll go by her place, but we must hurry."

It wasn't far out of the way to check on Amanda, but they found her house empty. Her horse and wagon were missing also.

"She's surely received word and is gone for Elephant Hook," Hyrum said breathlessly after he had run through the house and barn yelling for Amanda.

"Oh, I do hope so," Julia cried.

"We must hurry now," Hyrum stated. "No further delays."

The excitement had upset the younger children and they were crying. Francis didn't seem concerned. "Did you bring the gun?" he asked.

"Yes, of course," Hyrum replied as he shook the reins to encourage the horse to keep up the pace.

"Can I use it?" Francis asked.

"Of course not," Julia declared emphatically. "You'll do no such thing," she insisted.

"No, son. You aren't old enough," Hyrum replied. Defending his family with a gun was not something that he had considered when they left England. He hoped instead that his children would grow up in peace. "I hope you're never old enough," Hyrum added.

The settlers were gathering in the small church and the general store. The Princes went straight to the church and were overjoyed to see Amanda already there.

"Amanda!" Julia cried as she pushed her way through the assembled families.

"Julia! I was so worried!" Amanda exclaimed as the two women hugged tightly. "I didn't know whether you got word!"

Tears of joy coursed the women's cheeks as they hugged and kissed each other's children.

"Have you seen Subria?" Julia asked with hopeful concern.

"She's not with you?" Amanda asked in surprise.

"No, she left for the Johnson's and hadn't returned."

"Perhaps she's in the general store," Amanda suggested.

Hyrum and Francis had tied the horse and unloaded the wagon and had joined the family.

"Hyrum," Julia urged, "do check the store for Subria."

"She's not here then?" Hyrum asked with disappointment.

"No, please do hurry?" Julia replied.

Hyrum didn't find Subria at the general store and soon returned.

"She's not there," he said, and urgently added, "but it's too late to look for her. The natives have been seen closing in on us."

Julia and Amanda both gasped. "No!" Julia exclaimed.

"All women and children get in the middle of the room and sit or lay on the floor," a man called out. "Men, get to the windows!"

Francis wanted to join Hyrum at the window, but Hyrum wouldn't hear of it, and Francis sat on the floor next to Victoria and Luke.

Hyrum's heart raced as he saw a large group of natives come over the rise. They were running directly toward the small town, yelling and waving guns in the air. "God help us," Hyrum whispered.

"How many are there," the man next to him asked.

"Must be a hundred," Hyrum replied.

"Seems like more," the man said.

Using the butts of their guns, Hyrum and the other men broke all the glass out of the windows so that it wouldn't fly inside and onto the women and children when shot out by the natives. Hyrum then took his place at a window and waited breathlessly.

"Don't waste your shot!" a man yelled. "Make every shot count. Don't shoot until their close enough to ensure a kill!"

"Ensure a kill!" The words rang in Hyrum's ears. Though he knew that he must apply all his energies to the task at hand, he couldn't help but wish that Ian was beside him. *What horrors must Ian be facing daily?* he wondered.

Hyrum saw a puff of smoke from the group of natives moments before he heard a whooshing sound through the window above him followed by a thud as a shot sank deep into the wood in the wall behind him. Gasps and cries went up from the women and children at the sound of the shot piercing the wall.

Filled with anxiety, most of the men lowered their weapons through the window to take aim.

"Hold your fire!" came the order. "Take courage! Don't waste your shot!"

Hyrum realized that his hands were sweaty and his finger trembled as it rested lightly on the trigger.

Without so much as slowing, the natives suddenly released a volley of shots at the town. Many puffs of smoke were seen, followed immediately by small rushes of wind and thuds. A cry went out when a man took a shot in the shoulder and dropped back from his window. Immediately, his place was taken by a woman.

Dear God! Hyrum thought. *Don't let Julia stand at this window!*

The natives didn't stop or slow to reload. Hyrum watched as they poured fresh powder into the barrels of their guns; gun butts dragging on the ground as they held the barrels steady. Then they reached into their pouches and retrieved ball and wad which they pressed into the barrel a short way with a thumb. Then out came the ramming rod and with a couple of quick pounds with the rod, the gun was ready to fire again. Hyrum wasn't certain that he could accomplish the same task as quickly while stationary. The realization struck him with fear.

I've never felt such fear! he cried to himself. He realized that he had never felt such fear because the stakes had never been higher. *Give me strength, dear God! I must protect me family.*

A calmness rested on Hyrum, and the fear left him. In his mind's eye, he saw his family sitting across from him at the dinner table, heads bowed in reverent recognition of God's goodness. The image gave him courage.

Forgive me dear God! I wouldn't shoot if they'd turn around and leave! But, I must defend my family!

"Fire, men!" came the cry, and Hyrum's shaking finger ceased its trembling and pulled on the small metal trigger. The gun recoiled violently and smoke from its barrel obscured his vision momentarily.

Chaos erupted all about Hyrum as other guns fired and the women and children screamed loudly. Strangely, all was rather quiet for Hyrum. The noise of the guns fell to the background and his entire concentration was on keeping his gun loaded after each shot.

The natives were so close that several had stopped to take up positions of defense. *At least it makes them stationary targets,* Hyrum thought.

Earlier that day at the Johnson's, Subria waited at the door with the Johnson's domestic helper as Mr. and Mrs. Johnson spoke with a messenger who had ridden up with some urgency.

"We won't be leaving!" Subria heard Mr. Johnson declare.

"Suit yourself," replied the messenger.

"Josiah, we should go to Elephant Hook," Mrs. Johnson ventured.

"I'll not hear of it, woman. Me mind is firm," Mr. Johnson declared more emphatically. "I'll not leave me home unprotected for a bunch of natives to burn to the ground!"

Subria turned to her friend. "I've got to get home," she said.

"You can't go home. You need to go to Elephant Hook," her friend insisted.

"I must check on the Princes."

"Surely, they've been warned."

Subria ventured outside her third class societal role and asked the messenger, "Have you been to the Princes'?"

The messenger's horse spun about in a high-spirited fashion, anxious to continue the run. The messenger looked at Subria, surprised that she would address him so boldly. Still, he answered, "Aye, I've been to the Princes'."

"Will they go to Elephant Hook?" asked Subria.

"Aye, they will."

With that, Subria turned to her friend. "I must go," she said. "Come with me."

"I mustn't," her friend replied quietly while looking in Mr. Johnson's direction.

"Goodbye, my dear," Subria said as she reached out a hand.

Her friend took her hand momentarily and gave it a squeeze; then Subria was off, walking briskly in the direction of Elephant Hook.

Mr. Richards' house lay in a direct line between the Johnson's farm and Elephant Hook. Subria resolved to make a slight detour around his farm. She was glad for the cool weather as she walked quickly up one hill and down another. A chilly breeze blew across the hills and pulled at her dress and shawl. Subria leaned into the wind and pulled her shawl more tightly about her chin and face.

As she began a detour around Mr. Richards' farm, she stopped atop a small rise and looked back toward the Johnson's farm. The farm lay behind a small hill in the distance. To her horror, she saw a large plume of smoke rising above the hill. Subria gasped. "No! Not the Johnson's," she exclaimed aloud.

Subria stood atop the crest of the hill for a few moments, looking with disbelief on the scene before her. She cried softly, knowing that her friend and the Johnson's were likely dead and their home burned. Thoughts of Shaka and the night her family was attacked and killed raced through her mind. She was momentarily transported back over the years, and she stood shaking in the cold breeze. Suddenly, she realized that the natives would be moving quickly and they wouldn't wait to watch the Johnson's house burn. They'd be pressing toward Elephant Hook burning and killing along the way.

Turning toward Elephant Hook she could see Mr. Richards' house not a 1/2 mile away to the left.

"Should I hide, or seek refuge at Mr. Richards' farm?" she exclaimed aloud. *He's probably not even there,* she thought. But then she saw several of his farm workers running from the barn. *They are there,* she said to herself.

Subria quickly started down the hill, but stopped short when she saw the barn going up in flames.

"What? No!" she cried aloud.

She watched momentarily, wondering how it was possible that Mr. Richards' own men set the barn ablaze. The blaze quickly spread to the grass surrounding the barn, and began traveling up the nearby hill. But the blaze didn't travel to the house as the area about the house had been cleared of grass.

Then it struck her. "They've set the barn ablaze as a deterrent! The natives will think that another group already set it ablaze!" she exclaimed aloud.

Again, she continued her quick descent of the hill and toward the house. It seemed to take an eternity to reach the house and she wondered whether she'd be allowed inside. *I don't know that I even want to be inside,* she thought. *What is safer, facing the natives, or facing Mr. Richards?* Her choice was made, she would importune Mr. Richards for protection.

Soon she was nearing the house, and her approach had been observed. Mr. Richards stepped outside before she was near the door.

"Away with you, slave girl," he ordered.

"Please, sir, the Xhosa are coming! They've attacked the Johnson's."

"You belong to them! Go to them!" Mr. Richards exclaimed.

Subria fell to her knees and cried, "Please, sir. I need your protection."

"How do I know you won't try to cut my throat?"

"You know I wouldn't do so, sir. How do you know your own workers won't? They're Xhosa," Subria reasoned.

Mr. Richards hesitated. Then he looked back toward the house and yelled, "They're coming!" And he rushed inside.

Subria didn't wait for an invitation, but followed quickly behind Mr. Richards. Inside the house she found a dark corner and sat quietly.

After attacking the Johnson's, the Xhosa had noticed the smoke coming from the direction of Mr. Richards' farm. Thinking that other Xhosa had already attacked the farm, the main body of natives proceeded toward Elephant Hook, but a small group of warriors were sent to be sure. Eventually, 9 natives approached Mr. Richards' house.

"Don't be seen until they're very close," Mr. Richards ordered, hoping to surprise the natives with their presence.

Mr. Richards and each of his four farm hands gripped their guns, but stayed concealed. Subria thought the farm hands looked terrified while Mr. Richards appeared to await the engagement with anticipation.

"Now!" exclaimed Mr. Richards and the five men broke the glass and began shooting.

Subria had never been around gun fire and the noise was deafening. She buried her head between her curled up knees.

Three natives fell immediately, while six ran around the sides of the house. Mr. Richards and his men ran to the back of the house, making an attempt to reload as they went. Subria could hear shots that originated outside the back of the house, and Mr. Richards yelling orders at his men.

Suddenly, the front door flew open and a native burst through the doorway. His eyes were wide as he surveyed the room quickly. Fear filled Subria's heart and her chest felt heavy. Still the native didn't seem to see her. *His eyes aren't accustomed to the dark room,* she thought.

The native crept quietly toward the back room where he could hear Mr. Richards and the others. With that, Subria jumped up and grabbed a metal poker from near the fireplace and rushed to follow the native. Just as he leveled his gun toward Mr. Richards, Subria struck him hard across the side of his head with the poker. The native hesitated for a moment before dropping his gun and falling face first to the floor. The sound of the gun hitting the floor startled Mr. Richards, and he whirled about nearly discharging his weapon at Subria. Subria jumped backward and screamed.

Mr. Richards was shocked to see the fallen native and Subria standing over him with the poker in her hand. To ensure the native was dead, Mr. Richards sank a knife deep into his back. Subria gasped and felt sick. She quickly returned to her hiding place.

When Mr. Richards turned back toward the window, a ball struck his chest, and he fell backward to the floor with a groan. Subria heard his fall and came back into the room and saw him bleeding profusely and writhing in pain. She quickly removed her apron and packed the hole to stop the bleeding. Mr. Richards initially protested her assistance, but was too weak to resist.

The battle was soon over, as Mr. Richards' farm workers managed to kill the remaining natives.

With Mr. Richards still on the floor, Subria used a finger to remove the ball. Mr. Richards yelled out in pain as she did.

"Don't touch me!" yelled Mr. Richards.

"I'll not harm you," Subria assured him.

"I'll not have a slave girl for a doctor," sneered Mr. Richards.

"Very well then. I must be off to Elephant Hook regardless," Subria responded.

"The natives will kill you before you get there."

"Perhaps, but I'll not stay here with you another minute," Subria responded as she stood and straightened her dress.

"I hope they do kill you," Mr. Richards yelled as Subria walked out the door and away from the house.

Subria hadn't walked thirty minutes before she heard the first sound of gun fire coming from the direction of Elephant Hook. Initially, the volleys came in rapid succession, but soon they stopped altogether.

"Dear Lord," she exclaimed aloud, "please let it be the settlers who are victorious."

She wasn't certain as to whether to stay or go on. *If the Xhosa have prevailed, I shan't wish to walk into their trap,* she thought. She hesitated, but ultimately decided to cautiously approach the town.

Cheers went up at the church when the few remaining natives disappeared into a stand of trees. Women and children jumped from their prone positions and hugged each other and the men. Only one man had been mortally wounded, which brought sadness to all, but the fact that the natives had withdrawn brought irrepressible joy.

Only Hyrum remained at the window. *Why have the natives gone into the trees?* he wondered. *Why wouldn't they just disappear over the hill?* He wasn't left wondering long. The natives soon reappeared, and Hyrum was shocked that several carried flaming clumps of dried grass. When the natives lowered their torches the dried prairie grass greeted the flames like an old friend and spread quickly. The wind was blowing in the direction of the town and pushing the flames before it.

"Fire!" Hyrum yelled. "Fire! The natives have set the grass ablaze!"

The celebrations stopped and the cheering turned to screams when the women and children saw the swift moving flames. In a body they moved toward the door.

"Stop!" a man cried out. "That's just what the natives want you to do! If you go out there, they will surely shoot some of you!"

"So we just stay in here and burn?" yelled another man.

Shots from outside rang out, startling those in the church, but no balls hit inside the church.

"The others must have left the general store and are being shot at," the first man yelled out.

The smoke was too thick to make it possible to effectively shoot at the few natives, but the natives might be successful in killing settlers if they left the safety of the buildings. If the settlers didn't leave the buildings, the flames would either kill them or drive them out to the waiting natives.

"There's only a few natives out there, I'm sure of it," Hyrum called out. "The flames can't be very wide. Who'll run through the flames with me and attack the natives?"

There was no response.

"Will you stay here and die?" Hyrum yelled. "We don't have long. The flames will be here soon."

"How many natives are there?" someone asked.

"There can't be more than four, I'm sure of it," replied Hyrum. "Who'll go with me?"

Julia and Amanda's terrified children clung to their mothers. Julia wasn't surprised by what she was hearing, but she said, half to herself and half aloud, "Hyrum, don't go! Don't leave us here." She knew he would go.

"I'll go," came a cry.

"I'll go," came another and then another, followed by two more.

"I'll go," Francis yelled, and Julia grabbed him and pulled him to herself.

"Hush, son," Julia said. "You'll do no such thing."

Julia watched as Hyrum and five men jumped from the windows and bolted toward the flaming grass.

"They'll be ablaze when they emerge," a man nearby Julia muttered.

Julia started crying and Amanda glared at the man.

Subria was still a way off when she saw clouds of smoke in the direction of Elephant Hook. She realized the column of smoke was too wide to be only a building.

"The natives have set the prairie ablaze," she exclaimed. She slowed, but continued her approach toward Elephant Hook.

Hyrum expected that they would have an advantage, because the natives weren't likely to anticipate their action. Because the wind was blowing toward them, they would have to pass through a thick cloud of smoke, then they would encounter the flames. If they weren't completely ablaze they would engage the natives.

Hyrum coughed and struggled for breath as he ran through the smoke. Soon he could feel the heat of the flames. He couldn't see his companions and hoped they hadn't fainted or turned back. In an instant he was in the flames running for his life. Heat from the flames made breathing even more difficult, but he ran on.

If the flames didn't catch his clothes on fire, he still had to be concerned whether his powder pouch would explode. Suddenly he broke through the flames and saw a native not 50 yards away. As anticipated, the native hadn't expected their approach and was completely surprised. Almost instinctively Hyrum leveled his gun and pulled the trigger. The gun's recoil kicked his shoulder hard, but the native fell back and didn't rise.

Other shots rang out and the remaining natives fell to the ground. Only then did Hyrum realize his trousers were ablaze. He felt the intense heat of the flame and smelled his burning flesh. Without a thought he began to run, but one of the others pushed him to the ground and threw dirt on his flaming trousers.

From inside the church Julia looked on as the flames approached. Smoke inside the building was gathering thick as a cloud, and Julia was concerned that they would soon be out of air to breathe. She looked at her frightened children and knew that something must be done.

Horrified, Amanda exclaimed, "How long shall we stay in here?"

"The gun fire has ceased," Julia cried. "Hyrum's either been successful or he hasn't. Either way, we must leave."

"But how?" asked Amanda.

"If they shan't open the door, we'll use the windows away from the flames."

The two women pushed their way toward the door.

"Open the door," Julia cried. "There's been no further gun fire. If we don't leave at once, we'll all burn."

Other women echoed Julia's cries, and the man at the door opened it to them, allowing the women and children to pour out into the street. The road between the church and the store was dirt, so there was no immediate fear of the approaching flames. As much as possible, they stayed behind the church and away from possible view of the natives. The men followed after the women and children were out of the church.

"The church is going to go up in flames if we don't do something," one man exclaimed.

"What can we do?" asked another.

"There haven't been any shots fired for a while. We need to get water and wet the grass about the church."

Suddenly, several figures emerged at a full run through the smoke, startling the settlers such that some men lowered their guns at them.

"Hold! It's Prince and the others," a man yelled out.

Hyrum's clothing was black from rolling in the sooty dirt to douse the flames. Regardless, Julia, with Rebecca in her arms, ran to him and threw her free arm about his neck, buried her face in his chest and cried.

Amanda and the other children quickly followed, and the group hugged and cried and laughed together to know that their father, uncle and brother-in-law was safe.

"Prince, is it safe now?" asked a man.

"Yes, quite," replied Hyrum.

The man turned to the others and yelled, "Grab all the buckets and shovels you can find. We've got to wet that grass and dig about the church."

"There'll be extra buckets and shovels in the general store," someone offered.

"Quite right," replied the first man. "Get them."

Using the water and shovels, the men dug up or wet the grass closest the church, and then stood by and beat the flames with burlap and canvas if they threatened to cross the fire line. It was soon clear that the church and the store would be saved, and a great sense of relief and joy settled over the assembled group. Their joy was only dampened by their sadness for the few who had been killed in either the church or the general store. With reverence, they kneeled as a group in prayer of thanks for their safekeeping.

"You'd all be wise to stay here in Elephant Hook a few days," a man called out to the settlers who had come in from the countryside for protection. "There may still be marauding bands of natives about. If you don't have accommodation, some can stay in the church," he offered. "We'll post watches throughout the night."

"Hyrum, I'm so concerned for Subria," Julia said.

Hyrum turned his gaze toward the gently rolling hills that lay in the direction of their home as though he might see Subria.

"Yes, as am I," Hyrum agreed. "It's going to be dark in a few hours, and it's going to be cold."

"I can't bear the thought of her out there alone in the cold all night," Julia replied.

"If she is out there," Hyrum said.

"Please, don't even suggest that she's come to harm," Julia replied.

"You're right. I'm sorry," Hyrum offered. "I must get the tent set up, and then I'll go and search for her."

"Oh, shouldn't you go right away?" Julia implored.

"I can't leave my family without shelter against the cold tonight. It won't take so long to put the tent up and then I'll go right away," Hyrum promised.

Julia reluctantly agreed, and Hyrum started putting up the tent with the help of some other men.

Just as they had nearly finished, Julia jumped up and yelled out, "Subria! Subria!"

"Where?" asked Hyrum and Amanda at the same time.

"There!" Julia said pointing toward a nearby hill.

Julia was already running, with a baby in her arms, toward Subria. Subria saw her and started running down the hillside. Overjoyed, they fell into each other's embrace, and were soon joined by Hyrum, Amanda and the children.

"We were so worried for you!" Julia exclaimed.

"And I you," Subria replied.

"We're so glad you're safe!" Amanda said.

"Praise the Lord, we're all safe!" Subria declared.

Francis was excited to tell his version of the natives' attack, aided by Victoria and Luke. After hearing of their frightful experience, Subria related her own experiences at Mr. Richards'.

"Truly, I couldn't be happier than I am right now!" Julia exclaimed later as the two families prepared to go to sleep in the tent.

"Is it the fine tent then?" a grinning Hyrum asked.

Julia kissed his cheek. "Yes," she replied with a smile, "it's the finest bedroom I've ever encountered. It's a little crowded, to be sure. But no finer accommodation could be found in all of the Queen's palaces. Of this I'm certain."

Chapter Twenty-five - Farewell
June 1851
Elephant Hook, Africa

The Princes were among the fortunate settlers who had a tent available and the forethought to bring it with them when they evacuated their properties. Some settlers were able to spend the night in the church and others in the general store, but some spent the night outside in the cold.

Hyrum was anxious to check on their home as soon as they had arisen the next day. Julia would like to have accompanied him, but he didn't think it safe.

"Is it possible that the burning grass could have threatened our house?" Julia asked.

"Well, anything's possible, I suppose," Hyrum replied. "It would depend on the prevailing winds and where the fire was set. I wouldn't expect that this fire had reached our property. But the natives could have set other fires, or even have burned abandoned structures."

"Oh, don't say that," Julia replied.

"They are at war, my dear, and they'll stop at nothing. But, I'm sure that our place is fine. It's far enough removed from Elephant Hook that the natives probably gave it little heed."

"I do hope so," replied Julia. Then she added, "Since we're likely to be here in Elephant Hook for some time, please bring more clothing and bedding. A table and some chairs would be nice as well."

Amanda also asked that Hyrum go to her property and bring some additional bedding and clothing.

"May I go also?" Francis asked.

Hyrum hesitated. It wouldn't be all that long before the boy would be a man, and he had already been entrusted with a man's task in standing guard on the hillside. Hyrum looked at Julia. He expected to read a negative signal in her expression, but there was none.

"Yes, son," Hyrum said, "I believe that you are man enough to go with me."

Francis was ecstatic, but Luke pouted that he wanted to go also.

"No, son," Julia said, "you stay here with mum. I need you here."

Luke wasn't very happy with that prospect, but he wasn't going to change his mother's mind.

Hyrum and Francis soon had the horse hitched to the wagon and were off. They expected to be gone the better part of the day.

Much of the countryside was devoid of grass from the fires set by the natives. In place of the golden grass, the hillsides were blackened. Some tree trunks were also scorched, though most of the trees had survived. Still, the countryside looked unlike anything Hyrum had seen. They occasionally saw dead sheep that hadn't been able to outrun the fires. The dead sheep made a gruesome sight. Their wool had been entirely burned off, and all that remained were blackened carcasses that the vultures would likely have little interest in.

It all caused Hyrum concern for his own property, but soon the scorched areas thinned, and it became apparent that the winds must have been driving the fires away from their own property.

"This is a very good sign, son," Hyrum observed as they left the scorched area. "Perhaps our sheep and farm were spared."

"Why would the natives burn everything anyway?" Francis asked his father.

"They're desperate, son. They'd do almost anything to drive the settlers away. I suppose that the Queen's soldiers have also used fire against the natives."

"Maybe that's where they got the idea," observed Francis.

"Perhaps, but they've likely been using fire as a weapon in this land for a very long time. I doubt that they learned it from the English."

As they neared the last bend in the road before coming to their property, Hyrum said to Francis, "Now, son, don't let me forget that table and a few chairs for your mother. You know she'd be awfully disappointed if I were to forget. I also wouldn't wish for her to send me back to get them."

Francis promised to help his father remember.

As they rounded the last bend in the road, the horse quickened his pace in anticipation. Hyrum was elated also to be home, though he had been away only one night.

Suddenly, Hyrum's heart sank, and Francis exclaimed, "It's gone! Our house is gone!"

Their house was gone, burned to the ground. Most of the house was nothing more than a pile of charred rubble. The fireplace and chimney stood erect, and a portion of one wall remained. All else was lost.

Hyrum wanted to cry, but he didn't speak and didn't show any emotion. Francis did cry. The horse seemed to sense the loss and slowed his approach until he stood directly in front of the charred remains.

Hyrum slowly climbed down from the wagon and stood on what was once the front step. Small trails of smoke found their way out from under some embers and were swept away by the gentle breeze.

Hyrum's stomach ached as he looked at the remains of his house. It looked smaller than he imagined. He thought of the joys and disappointments that they had experienced as a family inside this small space. He knew that it didn't define who his family was, but so much of who they were happened within the walls that it felt as though their family had suffered a loss of monumental proportions.

"What will we do?" Francis asked.

"Well son, there isn't much else for us to do, but to start again."

"Build another house?"

"Yes, build another house."

"Will we build it here on the foundation?" asked Francis.

"I don't know. We'll have to decide whether it's worth the effort to clear the foundation of the rubble, and whether the foundation is sound."

"Where will we live until it's built?"

"I don't know, son, but we'll figure something out."

"I hate the natives."

Hyrum looked at his son and put an arm on his shoulder. "It's easy to hate, son, and harder to love. But taking the easy course will generally bring less reward."

Francis looked at his father inquisitively, and Hyrum continued, "You should try to love everyone, your life will be easier if you do."

"Why is Uncle Ian fighting the natives then? He must hate them."

"No, I don't think he hates them. But he has to protect his family. Once the natives back down, he'll not fight them any longer." Then in a voice barely audible, Hyrum added, "Perhaps I should join him."

Hyrum looked across his property. The grass hadn't been burned and sheep grazed on the golden blades. It was clear to Hyrum that his house had been deliberately torched.

"I suppose that the natives rode by here on their way to Elephant Hook and set the house ablaze. It seems that we were wise to leave before they arrived," Hyrum observed.

The two walked about the charred remains for a little longer before Hyrum patted Francis on the back and said with feigned cheerfulness, "We'll build again, only bigger and better. At least the barn is intact and the sheep are fine. And the most important thing is that our family is safe."

"Do you suppose that Aunt Amanda's house is burned as well," Francis asked.

"Let's ride over there and find out," Hyrum replied. "Let's pray not."

When they arrived at Amanda and Ian's house, they were thrilled to see that it was untouched and that sheep dotted the hillside.

"This is a grand sight, son!" Hyrum declared. "This is a very grand sight!"

"Mum's going to be sad though," Francis replied.

"Yes, but she'll be happy for Amanda, to be sure. I'll not enjoy sharing the news with your mum though."

Subria saw Hyrum and Francis returning early in the evening and called to Julia and Amanda. The women walked along the road away from Elephant Hook to meet the two.

When they were near, Julia noticed that there was no table and chairs inside the wagon.

"Please tell me that you forgot the table and chairs," she said hopefully.

Hyrum climbed from the wagon and hugged his wife. "No, dear," he said solemnly, "I didn't forget. There were no chairs or table to be had."

Julia studied his face, and with a quiver in her voice asked with anticipation, "Were they stolen then?"

"No, they weren't stolen," Hyrum responded slowly. He really didn't want to tell his wife that her house was gone.

"The natives burned the house to the ground," Francis finally blurted out.

"What?" cried Julia. "Burned? All of it?"

Hyrum couldn't look at his wife and instead looked at his feet. "Yes, all of it, except for the barn."

"The barn?" Julia asked.

"Yes, the barn was untouched."

Julia covered her face with her hands and cried. Amanda and Subria put their arms about Julia to comfort her.

"Did you go to my house?" Amanda asked hesitantly.

"Yes, your house is fine. I've brought the bedding and clothing that you requested," replied Hyrum.

After a few minutes, Julia dried her eyes with her skirt and said with a forced smile, "Well, we're all safe, and that's the important thing."

"Indeed it is," Hyrum agreed. "And we'll re-build, only better. I promise."

That night after the children were in bed, Hyrum took Julia by the hand and suggested that they walk in the cold evening air. As they walked side-by-side, with Hyrum's arm around Julia's shoulder for warmth, Hyrum said, "I've given our situation considerable thought, and I feel that I must join with Ian and the commandos."

Julia stopped and looked at Hyrum. "Join the commandos?"

"Yes. I feel that I need to do more to drive the Xhosa out of our land."

"What if they attack Elephant Hook again?"

"You'll be safe here whether I'm here or not. We sent the natives a strong message, and they aren't likely to return."

"I don't want to stay here without you," Julia insisted.

"And I don't want to leave, but I feel I must. You'll have Amanda and Subria with you."

"It isn't the same," Julia said.

Hyrum noticed a tear on her cheek and wiped it off.

"When will you leave?" Julia asked.

"Before the end of the week. I'll make certain that you have a supply of wood, and I'll kill a couple of sheep."

"How long will you be gone?"

"I don't expect I'll be gone more than a year."

"A year? That's so long!"

"Perhaps less than a year."

Julia was quiet for a while, then asked, "What if you don't come back?"

"I'll come back," Hyrum promised.

Julia tried to smile. "You won't be a hero?"

Hyrum hugged and kissed her. "No. I won't be a hero. I'll come home again."

Julia lay her head on Hyrum's chest. Though she made no sound, Hyrum could feel from her breathing that she was crying and he felt the wetness of her tears through his thin jacket.

Early on the morning of the third day, Hyrum strapped his gun and a blanket roll to his horse. Each breath the horse took in the cold morning air sent out plumes of condensation.

"Good morning, boys," Hyrum said as Francis walked up followed closely by Luke. Their arms were folded against the cold, and their hair had the appearance of a restless night.

"When will you leave?" Francis asked.

"Right after we eat a morning meal."

Hyrum lay a blanket across the back of his horse and picked Luke up and sat him on the horse. Though still sleepy, Luke smiled with pleasure.

"You look good up there, son. When I get back, I'll teach you to ride."

"I already know how to ride," Luke asserted.

"Well, I suppose you do," Hyrum agreed.

"You can't ride by yourself," Francis reminded him.

Julia was out of the tent by that point, holding Samuel's hand and carrying Rebecca in her arms. Hyrum held her and kissed her.

"Will you leave before we eat?" Julia asked.

Hyrum smiled and squeezed her a little tighter. "Not on your life, my dear." Then he reached down and picked up Samuel and also took Rebecca in his arms. "Let's go and fix a meal," he said.

With that, Luke exclaimed, "Don't leave me up here."

Hyrum smiled, put Samuel down and with one hand still holding Rebecca, offered a hand to Luke and alighted him gently on the ground.

After eating their meal, the family, along with Amanda and her children and Subria, prepared to say goodbye to Hyrum. Julia, Victoria and Luke cried, which greatly disturbed Samuel and Rebecca. Tears also flowed from the eyes of Amanda and Subria. Hyrum felt his chest tighten and also felt a lump in his throat.

Giving them each a final hug and kiss, he declared, "I'll be back before you know it."

"Please give my love to Ian," Amanda tearfully requested.

"Of course I will," Hyrum promised as he climbed atop the horse. "Subria, please look after this lot while I'm gone," he added.

"I will, Mr. Hyrum," she promised.

With that, Hyrum pulled on his horse's reins to spin him about, gently kicked his sides and the horse leapt forward into a trot.

Julia stood and watched as Hyrum rode away. She didn't move for some time even after he was out of sight. She had never felt so alone. He had taken short trips to Grahamstown, leaving her for a few days, but this was different. She didn't know when, or if, he would return, and it frightened her.

Amanda put her arms around Julia and hugged her tightly. "He'll come back," she promised.

"I know," Julia said tearfully as she tried to dry her eyes. "But I know now that I've never been alone. Never in my whole life. Someone's always been with me. Now I'm alone."

"You've got Subria and myself. You're not alone," Amanda said softly with a concerned glance at Subria.

Through tears, Julia replied, "True, but it's not the same." She dried her eyes a little and recanted with the slightest of smiles, "To be sure, you know better than I."

Chapter Twenty-six – Ian, the Commander
June, 1851

It took Hyrum the better part of three days to find Ian and the commandos. When he rode into camp, he asked the first person he saw where he might find Ian Prince.

"He's just there with the captain," the man stated with a motion in the direction of some tents.

There were three men speaking together near the farthest tent, but Hyrum didn't recognize any of them. Hyrum dismounted and approached the group on foot. He hadn't taken but a few steps when a commando with shoulder-length hair bolted from the group and called, "Hyrum! Hyrum! What are you doing here?"

The commando was nearly sprinting toward Hyrum, and though he knew the voice, he didn't know the bearded face.

"Ian?" Hyrum called. "Ian!"

The two men greeted each other with a strong hug and slap on the back.

Stepping backward for a better look, Hyrum said, "I hardly recognize you, what with the long hair and beard."

Ian smoothed his beard and ran a hand through his hair. "We've no time for such niceties out here, mate," he replied with a wink and a grin. Then he grabbed Hyrum by the shoulders and said, "How's Amanda? She and the children are fine, right?"

"Indeed they are fine," Hyrum assured him.

"Why have you come?"

Hyrum related to Ian the details of the attack by the natives and the news that he and Julia's house had been burned. "There's plenty of men in Elephant Hook to defend in the event of another attack, so I've decided to come and help push the natives back to their own lands," Hyrum assured Ian.

Ian frowned and said, "That's a hard turnabout for you that your house burned. But, it's capital that our families are safe. Thank you for protecting them." Then Ian smiled and grabbed Hyrum's hand and shook it. "I'm glad to have you with us, brother," he declared. "Aye, but I should reject you and send you back home."

"You can do that?" Hyrum asked in surprise.

"Aye, I can. The captain would do it if I said so."

"But you won't," Hyrum ventured.

Ian hesitated for effect. "Of course not! I'm thrilled to have my brother with me, fighting by my side. Let's meet the captain."

Ian led the way to the captain and announced Hyrum's arrival with an introduction to the captain.

"Welcome, Hyrum Prince," the captain said with a smile. "If you're half the soldier your brother is, we'll drive the natives back to their lands for good before spring!"

"Thank you, sir," Hyrum said, "but I've only ever been in one battle. I'm quite sure I'm not half the soldier that my brother is."

"Aye, but you will be," the captain assured him. "We've been making real progress in these parts, and with your help and with the help of others like you that are joining from day to day, we will be successful."

"Excellent to know, sir," Hyrum stated.

Speaking to Ian, the captain said, "He must be hungry. See that he gets something to eat."

Taking their leave from the captain, Ian led Hyrum to tie his horse, then to a tent where he could get something to eat. As Hyrum was eating, a commando approached and Ian jumped up to greet him.

"Harold! Meet my brother, Hyrum!"

Hyrum stood to shake hands with Harold.

Offering his hand, Harold said with a broad smile, "I am so pleased to meet the brother of my commander. You must be a great man if you're the brother of such a great soldier!"

Hyrum was somewhat embarrassed with the undeserved praise, but knew it was only lavished out of respect for his younger brother. He looked at his brother with new eyes. He had always considered him to be impetuous and maybe lacking a little direction, but here he was in his element. *Have I misunderstood who he is?* Hyrum wondered. *Is he the leader that I'm being told?*

"I can only shoot because your brother taught me. I'm alive because he taught me to ride, shoot and load all at the same time. And he's provided cover for me more than once," Harold declared.

Still looking at Ian, but barely recognizing his physical appearance or the declaration of the soldier that he had become, Hyrum said, "Ride, shoot and load? All at the same time? I can't do that."

Harold slapped him on his back and said to Ian, "May I have the honor of instructing him, sir?"

"Without a doubt!" Ian stated. "He'll be instructed by the best then."

Sir? Hyrum thought. *Am I to call him sir?*

"Harold is perhaps the finest soldier that I have," Ian declared. "Not much of a soldier when he arrived, mind you, but time and experience and fearless determination have molded him."

Hyrum looked more closely at Harold. *How old is he?* he wondered. Harold too had a full beard and shoulder-length hair that poured out beneath his hat. His beard and hair were almost entirely gray.

"I know what you're thinking," Harold declared. "Yes, I'm probably too old to be a soldier, but I've got a few battles left in me." Then stroking his hair, he continued with a smile, "Perhaps the grayness you see is the result of following your brother into battle."

Hyrum felt his face flush at the recognition that his thoughts were so obviously expressed on his face.

"You'd better get started with his instruction after he's eaten," Ian said. "We'll be going against the natives in a few days' time." Looking at Hyrum, he added, "We've heard that the natives are likely to push east and we'll be there to cut them off."

Harold sat with the brothers and listened as Ian asked about his family and farm. It was evident to Harold that Ian had a great love for his wife, Amanda. He hadn't spoken of her often, but with his brother near his side, his guard seemed to drop a little, and his hunger for news of his dear wife and little ones was almost unquenchable.

"They pray for you nightly," Hyrum assured him.

Ian sat quietly for a time, but ran a sleeve across the base of his nose. Placing a hand on Hyrum's arm, he said, "Thank you, brother. I'm so glad you're here."

Hyrum spent the next two days under the instruction of Harold, riding and going through the motions of shooting and reloading. He didn't fire the gun during these practices due to the need to conserve gunpowder.

When the day arrived that they would go against the Xhosa, Ian called his men together and gave them instructions. The instructions were particularly for the benefit of the new men who had arrived since their last battle.

"We don't rush into battle, men," Ian declared. "Remember, the enemy isn't going to be marching in file and rank like the British do. They'll be hiding behind trees and will be moving like a ghost across the landscape."

Several of the men audibly agreed with Ian.

"When we approach the natives' location, we'll not cross open meadows," Ian reminded them. "We'll stay in the trees. Remember, the natives may employ stratagem. They may be in separate groups. One group may attempt to draw us in, while another group hides in the trees."

Hyrum looked about at the men. They stood at attention and listened intently. It was clear that the men who Ian had been leading respected him and that the recent arrivals saw only a battle-ready leader in front of them, not a younger brother.

"If we aren't careful, the natives may see the dust from our horses as we approach. If warranted, we'll slow our approach, or even walk the horses," Ian instructed.

Ian then stopped and looked at the ground for a moment as though he was searching for the right words. When he continued, his voice was a little quieter. "Most of you have families at home. I expect that those families are praying for you, for us. I hope they are." Then looking directly at Hyrum, he finished with, "Always remember those who love you and are anticipating your return."

After Hyrum had secured his gun to the side of his horse and mounted, he noticed Harold beside him also mounted on a horse.

"Are you nervous?" Harold asked.

Hyrum patted his horse's neck and replied, "I don't think so."

"You are, and it's okay," Harold assured him.

"I guess that I never anticipated that I'd be following my little brother into battle," Hyrum confided.

"Indeed, the proverbial older brother struggles to see that his little brother has come into his own," Harold replied with a smile.

Hyrum thought for a moment and motioned his horse forward with the others. Ian was at the front of the group of men. He sat erect in the saddle and appeared to be moving fearlessly, perhaps resolutely, toward the enemy.

Turning to face Harold, Hyrum said, "Yes. Perhaps you're right. Perhaps he's been this way all along, and I haven't noticed."

Harold smiled. "Birth order and age have little to do with leadership, courage and skill," he observed. "The glorious thing is, though, that his achievements don't distract or detract from your own."

Hyrum smiled and replied, "You know, I think you're right."

"I know I'm right," Harold said with a smile, and added, "If you follow your brother completely, you'll be more likely to come through this without a bullet in your head."

Hyrum laughed, "Now that I can do."

Early the next morning while the commandos were finishing their morning meal the scouts, who had been sent ahead to watch the movement of the

Xhosa, rode quickly into camp with word that the natives were only a few miles distant and were moving quickly toward Colesburg.

"Do you suspect that they are aware of our position?" Ian asked the scouts.

"No sir. If they were aware, they'd likely be moving further to the north. As it is, their path will bring them within a mile of where you are now."

The news seemed to please Ian, and he called the commandos together.

"Men," he said after they had assembled, "the Almighty has been kind to us today. The enemy has been located and they're apparently moving on an unsuspecting town. We're in the right position to head their march. I'll take the bulk of you and we'll cut them off before they reach Colesburg. Harold will take the remainder and will cut off their retreat." Then looking at Hyrum, he added, "You'll go with me."

"Yes, sir," Hyrum found himself saying.

After they had mounted and were riding quickly in the direction of Colesburg, Hyrum rode alongside Ian and asked, "Will they see our dust?"

"Perhaps, but it will make little difference now. If we don't hurry, Colesburg is in danger. If we do hurry and the Xhosa see our dust, they'll do one of two things. They'll either quicken their pace toward Colesburg, or they'll retreat. If they retreat, Harold will be there to greet them and we'll come up on their rear. If, instead, they quicken their march toward Colesburg, our pace will allow us to cut them off before they get there."

"So, surprise is not a consideration today?" asked Hyrum.

Ian looked at Hyrum and smiled. "Oh, they'll be surprised to see us. They'll just get their surprise early."

The group soon mounted a hill and Ian slowed to a stop. From the top of the hill, the group had a good view of the valley below.

"There they are, sir," one of the commandos reported while pointing to the far side of the valley.

"Excellent!" Ian said.

Looking to the head of the valley on their left the group could see Harold and his commandos behind the natives. Colesburg was visible in the distance on their right.

"Men," Ian called, "we'll take our positions in that rock outcropping just there," pointing to a sizable mound of boulders just outside of Colesburg. "We'll leave the horses on the Colesburg side. Let's go men," Ian called. With that, the commandos' horses thundered down the hill.

Hyrum kicked the sides of his horse and it sprang forward with the rest. Hyrum noticed that his heart raced and his mouth was dry. He didn't relish the thought of taking the fight to the natives, but still there was a certain excitement building within him. He wasn't a stranger to that feeling, having recently felt it when they defended their families at the church. He had also felt it when they rescued the girl in Casa Blanca, and when he had occasionally defended his sheep from predators.

As the commandos charged down the hill, the natives quickened their march to a run in anticipation of reaching the outcropping before the commandos. In this they were disappointed. The commandos reached the outcropping and were in position just as the natives reached the bottom of the outcropping. It wasn't the ideal situation for the commandos, as it meant that the natives were able to take significant advantage of the lower rocks.

Fighting ensued immediately with each side firing their guns at the other, and the gray smoke of spent gunpowder quickly filled the air. The noise was deafening, making the entire scene disorienting. Hyrum looked about for his brother and caught sight of him behind one of the rocks nearest the natives.

The commandos were superior shots, and the natives soon began to fall. Still the natives held their position, and returned volleys of fire to counter the commandos. Hyrum occasionally heard the frightening sound of a ball splitting the air above his head.

The fighting continued for almost an hour before a cry went up amongst the natives when they saw Harold and his commandos approaching from their rearwards. Harold was soon upon them and took position in a small stand of trees. Surrounded on both sides, and without the opportunity of complete coverage, the natives who had not fallen ultimately laid down their guns and surrendered.

As they made way down the hill through the boulders, Hyrum asked Ian, "What will we do with the natives now?"

"I'll send some men to guard them to the garrison."

"Won't that be a difficult task?" Hyrum asked.

"It will be a dangerous task, to be sure, but there aren't very many of them, and the garrison is only a couple days' march beyond Colesburg, so it won't be impossible."

As they tied the hands of the Xhosa, and also tied short lengths of rope between their legs to slow any attempt at running, Ian asked one of his men to take a count of the commandos. The man soon came back and reported that all were accounted for.

"Excellent!" Ian replied. To his men he called, "The hand of God has looked favorably upon us today. God save the Queen!"

To which, all the men returned the call, "God save the Queen!"

Chapter Twenty-seven - Letters

July 1851
Elephant Hook, Africa

My dear Hyrum,

A moment does not go by that I don't think about you and the hardships that you must endure. The cold must be unbearable. I thank God daily for your safekeeping.

The children miss their father terribly. Francis has been such a wonderful helper. He will be a fine man someday.

Please do not think less of me, without intention to complain of my circumstances I tell you that I've been ill. But I gained the strength last week to visit the remains of our home with Subria. The reality of the loss struck me deeply when I finally laid eyes on it. I couldn't help but think of the wonderful times that we had there for several years, memories that cannot be burned by fire.

Despite the tears that streamed from my eyes, I found amongst the debris the broach that Queen Victoria had given to me. What joy filled my heart as I saw it laying amongst the charred remains. It too was blackened, but it cleaned up beautifully, and I have worn it daily since.

What would I do without Subria? Ever strong and courageous, she works tirelessly to help care for our children and Amanda's children. If she has regrets, she has not shared them. She inquires about you regularly.

My love for you is constant and sure. I leave you in God's care.

God speed, my love,
Julia

August 1851
Fort Hare

My dearest Julia,

It seems so long since I last held you in my arms, and yet it hasn't been two months. As of this writing, I am well and think of you every day. I pray that you are cared for and lack for nothing. I am cheered with the news that you have regained strength.

How is Francis? Is he becoming a man? Give my love to Victoria, Luke, Samuel and Rebecca.

Since my last writing we have been against the Xhosa several times and have pushed them farther back into their own territory. Ian is a true leader. I'm honored to follow him into battle.

It is unfortunate that we have lost a few of our good soldiers, but all fight willingly to preserve their homes and families. God willing, this war will likely end soon enough.

The cold winter months have given way to a promising spring and our hardships are easier to bear.

My fondest hope is to hold you in my arms soon. I'll write again soon if I have paper and opportunity.

Yours truly,
Hyrum

January 1853
Near Fort White

My dearest Julia,

The months drag on and with each one I feel the hope that you will be in my arms soon. I cherish each of your letters and read them time and again until I have committed them to memory and written them in my heart.

I am distressed to hear that your strength is still weakened from your illness. Perhaps to know that we are winning in this conflict and that it will soon be over will bring you strength.

We are receiving strength to our numbers almost daily. It would seem that our successes are just the encouragement needed to bring more men to the fight. News travels slowly, but we've received word that a ship of British troops has been lost to the sea. If we are to win this fight, it will be won by our brave neighbors who will fight for the preservation of their families and homes. The fight is real and must be won.

I would not wish to harrow up your mind with the brutalities of the natives, but we will press on in this fight until we are successful.

With all my love,
Hyrum

January 1853
Elephant Hook

My dearest husband,

What joyous news I have to share with you! Queen Victoria has received an inventory of the destructions here and when she heard of the loss of our home, she was deeply moved. She has sent to us the means needed to re-build! She will also send another rocking chair! I am so grateful to her. She has been such a devoted friend.

The children are doing wonderfully. You will scarcely recognize them. Francis may be as tall as you. It is quite difficult to clothe him. Victoria is quite the young lady. Luke asks about you continually, but I fear that Samuel and Rebecca will need to reacquaint themselves with you.

Oh, how I pray for the cessation of these hostilities and for you to come home to us. I would live in a tent for the rest of my days if I could only have you here with me again.

God speed, my love,
Julia

January 1853
Near Fort White

My Darling Amanda,

How I miss you! It has been nearly two years since we parted, and I long
for the day when we will be together again. I almost repent the day that I
left you and the children to join this awful fight. Yet, I cannot in good
conscience say that I entirely regret my course. The fight had to be taken to
the natives, for that was the only sure way to secure a future for you and the
children in this land. I almost feel for the natives, for they too have families.
However, treaties were made long before we arrived on this land, treaties
that the natives have not altogether abided by. This is the Queen's land now
and they remain on it at her will and pleasure. We would not take the battle
to them, if they would but abide by the treaties that have been in
agreement.

The men at my command are undaunted in their desire to end this conflict
and to return home to their families. We remember you always! It has been
a Godsend to have Hyrum fight alongside me, but I know that he does so
at great cost to not only Julia and her family, but also to you. I trust that
there will be something of a sheep farm to return to, and return I will in the
not too distant future.

Our successes in battle are encouraging more and more men to join with us
and we receive strength to our forces daily. We welcome the additional
forces, but the bond of love and companionship is strongest amongst these
brave men who have fought alongside me for these many months.

My heart yearns for your companionship. War is an ugly thing, but its
ugliest side is the unseen sword that severs the wife from the husband and
the husband from his wife and children. But that won't be the case for long
my love.

We are about to succeed in this conflict, and I will be home within two
months. I'm sure of it. What a joyous reunion it will be!

Give my love to our sweet children for me. My heart aches for want to hold
them.

Sincerely, with all my love,
Ian

January 1853
Elephant Hook

My Dearest Ian,

My heart leapt with gladness when I read your latest letter! To think that you'll be home within two months fills my soul with joy! You are my love, and I need you beside me. The two years that we have been apart will be as a fleeting moment once you hold me again.

I've often thought of the young man that I met by the sea, and I smile to think that he has become a brave soldier and commander of men. As wonderful as that is, it is more wonderful still that you are mine and the father of our children. That will never change! Don't be a hero, and come home to me soon.

Faithfully yours,
Amanda

Chapter Twenty-eight – End of the Conflict
February 1853

"Harold! A letter for you," Ian said with a smile. "You've not had many letters, have you?"

"Indeed not!" Harold replied. Taking the letter from Ian and examining the handwriting, he said, "I don't recognize the penmanship." Then with a smile, he added, "Still, a letter's a letter."

"Without a doubt. Just the same, read it quickly. I'd like to gather the men. We go out soon against the Xhosa."

"Very well, Sir," Harold said.

A short time later, Ian called the men together and told them that they would be moving out later that afternoon. The natives had suffered many setbacks, and the English, supported by the commandos, had pushed them back into their own territories. With any luck, and with the support of the Almighty, there would be few skirmishes before the English could be declared victorious in the Eighth War against the natives.

After speaking with his men, Ian noted that Harold seemed quiet, which was against his nature.

"Harold, you seemed disturbed," Ian noted after approaching him. "Don't you wish to go against the natives?"

"No, Sir, it isn't that," Harold assured him.

"Then what is it?"

"It's my wife, Sir. She's passed away by fever."

Ian hesitated, then he put a hand on Harold's shoulder. "I'm sorry, Harold. Do you wish to go home and see to your affairs there?"

Harold was looking at the ground and without looking up replied, "No, Sir. Her burial has been attended to. There's nothing for me there since she's gone. The natives burned my house and carried off my cattle months ago."

"Still, this has been a shock for you...."

Harold looked Ian in the eye. "No more than others have endured. I'm honored to fight alongside you, and I'll follow you into battle tomorrow."

Ian placed a hand gently on Harold's back and replied, "Excellent then. We're undoubtedly going to need you."

The commandos left camp later that afternoon as planned and rode hard toward the area that they had been told the natives would be attacking. The grassland that they covered was relatively flat, with few trees. The flatness and the openness increased their visibility, giving Ian confidence that they wouldn't be riding into a trap. The grass kept the dust down, ensuring that there wouldn't be a large cloud of dust that could be seen for miles. So, they made good progress.

Before stopping for the evening, they entered hilly terrain. Ian saw to it that their camp was situated between two small hills that would keep the light of their fires from being seen beyond the nearest hills. He also posted guards on the two hilltops.

That night, as they prepared their evening meal, Ian noted that many of his men bragged about their successes in prior skirmishes. Ian listened, but it concerned him that such apparent arrogance would lead to a certain carelessness in battle. Hyrum and Harold sat beside him.

"I hope these men are alert tomorrow," Ian stated. "We can't afford too much arrogance. It's dangerous."

"The men are just excited to end this conflict. Don't you think?" Harold asked as more of a statement than a question.

"Perhaps you're right. Still it's concerning," Ian said.

"If it bothers you, perhaps you should say something to them," Hyrum offered.

Ian didn't respond immediately, but kneeled beside their small fire and added wood. Satisfied with the fire, Ian stood, but continued to gaze at the flickering blaze. "What is it about fires that make them so irresistible to watch?" he asked with a smile.

Looking about the camp at the men sitting around other small fires, he continued, "I suppose their chatter will die down. They're just excited, as you say, to end this thing." Then looking at Hyrum and Harold, he said with a reflective tone, "I hate to even think it, but some of them may die tomorrow."

Hyrum and Harold nodded their agreement.

"Let's pray not," Ian stated, and nothing further was said on the subject.

The group broke camp before sunrise, but didn't ride as hard as the previous day. Ian thought it prudent to exercise some caution as the natives were reportedly not far distant. The hills would naturally slow their approach, as would the occasional stand of trees.

After several miles, their trackers started picking out signs that indicated a group had been there ahead of the commandos.

"They've been this way, Sir," a tracker said as he studied the trail. "It hasn't been long either. Maybe yesterday, maybe this morning."

"How many?" Ian asked.

"I can't say how many, but it was more than a few, and they were moving fast."

"If they were moving fast, they must know that we're coming," Ian stated to Harold.

"Perhaps so. Any attack target is still too far off to justify a fast approach," Harold stated.

"Yes, that may be so, but the Xhosa are able to travel far at a running pace," Ian observed.

"Perhaps they're headed to Fort White," Hyrum suggested.

"Fort White?" Ian asked. "These natives are headed east. Fort White is to the north of us and heavily guarded."

"It was heavily guarded," Harold stated.

"Is there any reason to think it is not still?" Ian asked.

"Not that I've heard, but the garrison may have gone out on a campaign," Harold suggested.

"Let's follow these tracks. If the natives are intent on hitting Fort White, we should know soon enough. The tracks will have to turn north at some point," Ian directed.

With that, Ian gave the command to head out at a quicker pace than before. The natives' tracks followed a singular trail, and because of the terrain, the commandos were also required to stay in a line. They soon came to a fork in the trail at the base of a prominent hill. One set of tracks took the trail that headed north toward Fort White. Another sizable portion of the tracks continued on the eastern trail around the base of the hill in the opposite direction.

"Harold, what do you make of this?" Ian asked.

Harold thought for a moment and then said, "I don't like it. Why would they split up?"

"Exactly," Ian responded. "Hyrum, what do you think?"

"It could be some sort of a trick. They may just want you to believe that they are attacking Fort White, but have intent farther east."

"Do we stay with the east trail and ignore a possible threat on Fort White?" Harold asked.

"How far is Fort White," Hyrum asked.

"Maybe ten miles," Ian responded. "Harold, take 20 men and carry on toward Fort White. If you have reason to believe it's a trick, circle around the north of this hill and join back up with us. We'll carry on around the east. If we determine it to be a trick, we'll proceed to Fort White. Either way, we haven't lost too much time."

With that, Harold called out 20 men and proceeded north, while Ian and Hyrum took the remaining men and headed around the south side of the hill and proceeded east. Nearly 30 minutes later, after Ian and his men had circled about the south of the hill, they discovered that the hill dropped into a large valley. Various stands of trees dotted the valley floor.

"Look, Sir," a soldier called out. "Xhosa are just beyond the first stand of trees."

Ian saw a small number of Xhosa warriors exiting the stand of trees and moving fast.

"Let's go men," Ian called out, and the entire group began a charge down the hill.

"Shouldn't we wait for Harold and his men?" Hyrum called out.

"No!" called Ian. "The natives have surely split up to split us up. There are only a few here. We'll take care of them and then ride to Fort White to help Harold."

Hyrum was slightly behind Ian in the charge down the hill. He watched as Ian dug his heels into the sides of his horse. He was quite a sight holding his heavy rifle in one hand while riding at full gallop. It was only the strength of the grip he had with his legs that kept him in the saddle.

The charging horses kicked up a thick blanket of dust that soon caught in the throats of man and beast. Their horses were wet with lathered sweat, and a muddy layer of dust had attached itself to the horses' necks and backs.

As they closed the gap between themselves and the natives, they didn't realize that the natives had attacked Fort White the night before with great success. The Xhosa scouts had also seen the commandos coming the previous day and made certain to leave tracks that could not only be found, but would have the appearance of going in the direction of Fort White.

Ian expected that the commandos would encounter the natives just beyond the stand of trees at the bottom of the hill. Suddenly the horse just in front and to the left of Ian went down and fell into the path of his own horse. Ian pulled the reins hard to the right, and his horse reacted instantly to avoid the fallen animal and rider.

In that moment, time seemed to slow to a crawl for Ian. He saw the side of the other horse's head gaped open having been hit with a ball. *Some of the natives have stopped in the trees!* he thought. *We're being ambushed! A stupid mistake, caused by my haste!*

The maneuver to avoid the other horse and rider had been so violent it caused the ankle of Ian's horse to buckle under the force. Ian lost grip of his gun as he flew from the saddle. He landed hard on his side, and winced in pain when his ribcage struck a rock with the full force of his weight.

Ian tried to rise, but fell back to his knees enveloped in pain so severe that for a moment he couldn't breathe. Chaos was all about him as other horses and riders pounded by or also fell to the ground. His own horse was struggling to rise, but fell with each attempt.

Shots rang out, and Ian heard the whistling sound of balls flying past him.

Hyrum was behind Ian and had watched in horror as Ian's horse went down. He also became aware of small bursts of smoke erupting from the trees. *Some of the natives have stopped in the trees and are firing on us!* he thought. There seemed to be many more natives than the commandos had believed possible.

Hyrum jumped from his horse not far from where Ian had gone down and took cover behind a rock.

Ian spotted his rifle a few paces away. Though the pain in his side was great, he stayed low to the ground, and carefully crawled to it and then took cover behind a dead horse. With some level of safety provided by the dead animal, Ian looked in the direction of the trees. He was surprised at the number of shots being fired from the trees. *Have they received reinforcements?* he wondered.

As he lay behind the dead horse, Ian couldn't help but think of Amanda. *Two years, and now I get hurt,* he thought. *Amanda's not going to be happy to hear this.*

His thoughts were turned back to his current situation when he heard his name called over the battlefield noise.

"Ian!" Hyrum called.

In the confusion, Ian had lost track of Hyrum's location and was glad to see that he was okay.

"Hyrum! Are you injured?" Ian yelled to his brother.

"No! I'm fine."

"I've made a grave miscalculation leading my men into this trap!" called Ian.

"You need better cover. That dead horse is wholly inadequate as cover!" Hyrum called out, ignoring Ian's admission of guilt.

"Your rock isn't much better," Ian called with a smile.

Hyrum looked about and saw a small boulder behind Ian's position. "Can you make that boulder?" Hyrum called.

Before Ian could reply, a ball struck the dead horse, passed through the horse's bowels and struck Ian in his back just beneath his shoulder blade, penetrating his lung. Ian let out a groan and lay back against the dead horse.

"Ian!" Hyrum called out and started to rise to run to him. "Ian!"

Hyrum feared Ian was dead, but was greatly relieved when he saw Ian raise a hand to him. Leaving his gun at the small boulder, Hyrum pulled himself on his forearms and belly until he reached Ian.

"Ian!" Hyrum said loudly as he shook his brother.

Ian didn't open his eyes or move, other than to grin slightly and grimace. "I'm still here," he said.

"I've got to get you to that rock," Hyrum said urgently.

"No, it's too dangerous. You shouldn't have come over here."

"Hold on! I'm going to drag you back," Hyrum said, but ducked his head quickly when he heard the whoosh of air created by a ball that flew past them.

"Leave me here and crawl back to the rock. You'll get yourself killed," Ian insisted.

Ignoring the commands of his leader, Hyrum grabbed Ian by the wrists and pulled him across the ground from behind the horse. Ian grimaced with pain as Hyrum pulled him to the relative safety of the rock. A ball hit the rock and ricocheted through the air just as they were covered.

"You don't take orders well, do you," Ian said through a forced smile.

Hyrum grabbed his gun and took aim into the trees and fired.

"I guess I'm not good at taking orders," Hyrum said as he quickly reloaded his gun. With the ball rammed into the barrel, he took aim again and fired.

"Tell Amanda that I wasn't being a hero," Ian said quietly.

Hyrum looked at his brother. He lay on the ground with an arm across his chest, his eyes closed, struggling for breath. A small pool of blood was gathering to his side.

"Ian!" Hyrum said as he shook his brother gently. "Ian, you'll tell Amanda yourself."

"No. I don't think so," Ian said weakly.

Another ball hit the rock and chips of stone flew into the air and landed on Hyrum and Ian.

"Be careful, Hyrum," Ian whispered. "You've got to make it home. We're almost done with this war!"

Hyrum lay his gun aside and kneeled next to Ian. Cradling his brother's head in his hands, he said, "Ian, we're all going to make it home."

Ian tried to speak, but coughed blood. "I shouldn't have left Amanda," he managed.

"You did the right thing. You protected your family," Hyrum assured him.

Ian opened his eyes slightly. "I'm glad you came, Hyrum," he said quietly. "I'm glad you came." He coughed again, grimacing with each cough. Then he closed his eyes.

Ian's breathing became more labored and he coughed more blood. Hyrum's sight was blurred by tears that formed in his eyes. It seemed that all was quiet around them. The noise of the battlefield was pushed into the background. Hyrum stroked his brother's hair.

"I love you, Ian," Hyrum whispered. "I love you."

Ian smiled faintly. "I love you, brother."

Ian lay motionless, except for shallow, but labored breathing interrupted by coughing.

"Tell Amanda that I love her and that I'm sorry to leave her," Ian whispered.

Hyrum's chest was tight and there was a lump in his throat when he replied quietly, "I will. I promise."

Ian's face relaxed and his arm slipped off his chest and fell down to his side. He was gone. Hyrum held his brother's head close to his own chest and cried. Hyrum wasn't sure how long he stayed with his brother. Though the fight raged on for a time, it was as though they were alone. Eventually, a shadow fell across Ian's face and Hyrum felt a hand on his shoulder.

"It's over, Hyrum."

Hyrum recognized Harold's voice and looked up. "He's gone!" Hyrum said quietly.

"Yes, I know," Harold said softly.

"He didn't want to be a hero, but he was."

"Yes, I know," Harold repeated quietly.

"Why would he go and get himself killed now?"

"I'm sorry, Hyrum. He was a good man."

Hyrum stood and took a deep breath and let it out slowly. "I don't want to tell Amanda."

"Truly, this is a sad day," Harold said. "I've never met a finer man."

Hyrum nodded agreement.

Several of the commandos had gathered and stood quietly by with heads bowed.

"We'll give our commander and the others a proper burial," one of the commandos stated.

Hyrum looked up at the commando in bewilderment. He hadn't considered burying his brother on the plains of Africa. He had assumed that he would take him back to Elephant Hook for burial. Harold sensed Hyrum's feelings.

"We can't take the bodies back with us, Hyrum. I'm sorry," he said. "It's too far, and there's still the chance of native attack."

Hyrum bowed his head again. "I understand."

Digging shallow graves was difficult without proper tools. The commandos had brought along one small shovel that eventually accomplished the task.

Hyrum carefully lowered his brother into the grave. Before pushing dirt into the grave, he placed Ian's hat over his face. Tossing the first fistful of dirt onto the body was the most difficult. Hyrum held the dirt inside his clenched fist over the body and slowly let the dirt slip between his fingers. Much of the finer dirt was caught by the breeze and floated away. Eventually, Hyrum and Harold pushed dirt and rocks into the grave until the body was covered.

"I've lost my father and a son," Hyrum said, "but I never expected to lose my brother."

"I don't think that we ever expect to lose anyone," Harold observed. "If Amanda really expected that she'd lose Ian, she would have compelled him to stay."

Hyrum looked Harold in the eye and asked, "Do you believe in life after death?"

Harold averted his gaze. "I don't know anymore. I once did, but I'm not sure."

"I suppose I'm not sure either," Hyrum replied.

"Part of me wants to think that there must be more to existence than the toil and strife that we go through here."

"Though that's a compelling thought," Hyrum replied, "why would God allow such pain to exist?"

"To be sure, I don't know."

To ensure that animals wouldn't dig the body up, Hyrum and Harold stacked an ample number of rocks atop the grave.

Following the burial, Hyrum bowed his head and prayed for Ian and Amanda. Afterward, he mounted his horse, turned to Harold and stated, "I guess that you're our leader now. Where will we go?"

Several commandos were near on their horses and they all looked at Harold and waited.

"I suppose you're right," Harold said in a quiet tone. After a moment's reflection, he added, "We'll ride to Fort White and see what condition they're in."

"That sounds like the right thing to do, Sir," Hyrum replied. "I'm sure Ian would agree."

The commandos found the Union Jack flying above Fort White, but smoke still wafted in the breeze from buildings inside the fort. A British garrison had arrived at the fort that morning, too late to help repel the native attack. As the commandos rode into the fort, they sensed an attitude of excitement despite the destruction.

"What's the meaning of this celebratory atmosphere?" Harold asked a soldier.

"The war's over! Chief Sandile and all the other chiefs have surrendered."

Harold looked at Hyrum in surprise. Shouts of joy went up amongst the commandos, and for a moment Harold and Hyrum were caught up in the celebrations. Suddenly the irony of Ian's death struck them, and they hung their heads. Tears filled their eyes at the realization that Ian had died during the last skirmish of the war, after the chiefs had surrendered.

"Such a tragedy," Hyrum said, "to die in the last battle."

"It is a tragedy," Harold agreed. "But if he had died in the first battle, the result would be the same. Don't dwell on the timing. Just remember his sacrifice."

After a moment's hesitation, Hyrum turned his horse about and started riding toward the fort's gate.

"Where're you going?" Harold called after him.

Hyrum pulled his horse up and turned back to face Harold. "Elephant Hook. The war's over. What will you do?"

"I don't know. There's nothing left for me at home," Harold said.

"Come to Elephant Hook with me."

"What would I do in Elephant Hook?" Harold asked.

"Help me re-build my house and work Ian's farm. It's too much for one man. The children would love having you around," Hyrum assured him.

After a few moments consideration, Harold looked about and then back at Hyrum and replied with a smile, "Doesn't look as though I've any better offers. I accept."

"Jolly good. Let's go," Hyrum smiled.

It was a three-day ride to Elephant Hook, and as they neared, Harold asked, "When will you tell Amanda?"

"I've thought about that for the last three days," Hyrum replied. "To be sure, I'd rather not tell her. But I must."

"Sooner is probably better than later," Harold suggested.

"Without a doubt," Hyrum agreed.

Francis saw two men on horseback nearing Elephant Hook as he and another boy were playing near the church. Julia and Amanda had continued living in the tent near the church for safety during the many months that their husbands had been gone. They had considered moving into Amanda's home, but decided that three women and several children alone in the countryside wasn't safe while the natives were resisting the settlers. Several other families had also continued on in Elephant Hook.

Francis initially didn't pay much attention to the two riders, but as they neared, one of them called his name, and he immediately recognized his father's voice.

"Mum!" he called out. "It's Pa and Uncle Ian!"

Julia was inside the tent with Amanda, Subria and the other children.

"Hyrum?" she said aloud to Amanda.

"And Ian!" Amanda exclaimed.

Both women rushed from the tent in great anticipation as they simultaneously ran fingers through their hair and straightened their dresses. Subria and the children followed close behind with great excitement.

"Hyrum!" Julia called as Hyrum alighted from his horse and took her in his arms. Francis, Victoria and Luke joined them in the embrace, but Samuel and Rebecca stood aside uncertain about the situation.

Subria put her arms around Samuel and Rebecca and said, "It's your father! Give him a hug." Instead of joining the embrace, they buried their faces on her shoulders.

"Oh, Hyrum! I've missed you so!" Julia declared with a smile and laughter.

"I love you, Julia. It's so good to be home!" Hyrum replied joyfully.

The arrival of the two men and the warm welcome of Hyrum home had caused a small crowd of villagers to gather. Some called greetings to welcome Hyrum home.

"Where's Ian?" Amanda asked hesitantly.

Julia, still in Hyrum's arms, leaned backward and looked at Harold and then into Hyrum's eyes and asked, "Yes, where is Ian?"

Hyrum felt very uncomfortable. He wished that he had come into Elephant Hook with more discretion so that he could have found Amanda alone and shared his awful news to her privately. Now there was little opportunity to save her the discomfort of a public display.

Hyrum looked at Amanda. She was so young. He had always considered her to be strong willed and daring, but now there was uncertainty and perhaps fear in her eyes. It was obvious that she expected the worst news possible.

Hyrum broke from Julia's embrace and hugged Amanda. Then, taking her by the arm, he said, "Come with me," and led her toward the tent.

Tears filled Amanda's eyes and she covered her mouth with her hands. "No!" she cried. "Not Ian!"

Hyrum put his arms around her and supported her as her energy gave way.

"He was a brave man," Hyrum assured her. "You can be proud of him, but he isn't coming home."

Amanda fell to her knees and sobbed. Julia kneeled beside her and held her trembling body. Amanda's children were distressed to see their mother so distraught, and they too started to cry. Subria brought them to their mother's side, and they hugged their mother along with Julia and Hyrum.

"He loved you very much," Hyrum assured her. "His only concern was for you and the children."

The small crowd that had gathered whispered amongst themselves and word of Ian's death spread quickly through Elephant Hook.

Julia and Subria helped Amanda into the tent where she could lay upon a cot. They tried to console her, but they knew that their words of love and encouragement could do little to mend the hole that had formed in her heart.

Harold was quite uncomfortable, and went about caring for the horses.

Toward evening Amanda arose and asked Hyrum to walk with her outside.

"Tell me how Ian died," she asked him.

Hyrum cleared his throat. He didn't even wish to utter the words, but what could he do when asked directly by Amanda?

"He was a great commander, Amanda, and loved by his men. They would follow him and execute his commands with exactness," Hyrum said.

Hyrum then told her of Ian's bravery, and skill as a soldier. He told her about their successful campaigns, and then he told her how they had been led into a trap by the natives and surprised.

"Was he trying to be a hero?" Amanda asked with a nervous laugh and a feigned smile. "I told him to not be a hero."

"He was never careless," Hyrum assured her. "He didn't have to try and be a hero. He was always a hero. Just ask any of the men who served with him."

Amanda sighed and smiled slightly. "Ian," she whispered. "Ian. I miss you so much."

After a few moments Amanda asked, "Who's the man that came with you?"

"Oh, that's Harold. If anyone knew Ian, it's Harold. He was Ian's right hand man. He loved Ian."

Amanda smiled.

"If you ever want to know more about how great a commander Ian was, Harold's the one to ask." Hyrum assured her.

"What will Harold do now that the war is over? He must have a family."

"No. He really doesn't have anyone," Hyrum said. "His wife died of fever not long ago and they had no children. So, he'll stay in Elephant Hook for a while and help with both our farms and re-building Julia's house."

Amanda looked at Hyrum. "I can't pay him."

"There's no need to concern yourself. The Queen sent more than enough to re-build our house, and we'll have wool from the sheep soon enough. We'll do fine."

Amanda was satisfied and gave Hyrum a gentle hug. "You're so good to me. Thank you."

Chapter Twenty-nine – The Dream
April 1853
Elephant Hook, Africa

Hyrum and Harold spent the remainder of February and March and into early April clearing the burned-out rubble from the foundation of Julia's home. The foundation was solid and it was Hyrum's intent to re-build on the foundation and extend additional foundation as needed for the new home. Francis had been very helpful in the clean-up effort.

The weather was mild, but winter would soon approach. Hyrum didn't relish the thought that Julia and the children would spend another winter in the tent, but it was clear that he wouldn't have their home re-built in time to avoid it.

"I'd like to ask Amanda whether you and the children might be welcome to stay with her for the winter," Hyrum suggested to Julia. "I can't bear the thought of you and the children suffering another winter in the tent."

Julia's brow furrowed. "I don't wish to stay there without you."

"I'll be there at least on Saturdays and Sundays," Hyrum promised her. "Harold, Francis and I will work on the house most of the week. Harold will have to work Amanda's farm in the later part of the week, but then Francis and I will join you all on Saturdays and Sundays."

"I suppose it would be nice to keep Amanda company, so that she's not on the farm entirely alone," Julia observed. Then, with her arms folded across her chest as though trying to keep warm, she added, "It was awful cold last winter in the tent."

Hyrum smiled and hugged Julia as though to keep her warm. "Very well," Julia said, "we'll stay at Amanda's, that will be nice."

"It's settled then. I'll speak with Amanda," Hyrum replied with his arms still about Julia.

When Hyrum did speak with Amanda a few days later, she was thrilled. It was just as she wished, and she would have liked to have Julia, Subria and the children move in right away.

"It will be so wonderful to have them here," Amanda assured Hyrum with a broad smile. Her countenance changed to one of sadness when she added, "I get so lonely without Ian."

"I'm sure it's terribly lonely for you," Hyrum agreed. "I'm so sorry."

With that, tears started to flow down Amanda's cheeks. "I'm sorry," she said as she wiped her tears with her apron. The memory of Ian was fresh and the wound created by losing him was still open, and she began to cry freely.

Hyrum put his arms around her neck and held her head on his shoulder. "I miss him as well. He was a fine man. I still think of him often."

Amanda cried for several moments, then wiped her tears and feigned a smile. "It does get easier with time," she tried to assure Hyrum.

"I'm sure it does," Hyrum agreed, "but it doesn't mean that we love him any less, does it?"

Amanda wiped her eyes again and replied, "No, of course not."

With a change of subject, Hyrum asked, "How's it working out having Harold here?"

Amanda's eyes surveyed the nearby hills with sheep gently grazing. "It's been good," she said with a smile. "He's a very hard worker."

"Indeed, he is," Hyrum agreed. "I've known few men better. He's very loyal."

"Loyal?" Amanda asked.

"Yes. He has a long memory for those who've cared for him. He'll stand by them regardless the circumstances. And he's a man of high moral character." After a brief pause, Hyrum added, "He's the only man I can think of that I'd allow to stay here with you and the children."

"Well, his accommodations out in the shed can't be very comfortable. How long do you suppose he'll stay?" Amanda asked.

Hyrum reached down, pulled a grass shoot out of the ground and put it between his lips. "As long as he's needed, I suppose. Ian meant a great deal to him; really made him the man he is today. And I wouldn't worry too much about his accommodations, he's had far worse, I assure you. Perhaps after the house is built, we can improve his circumstances."

"I hope he doesn't feel obligated," Amanda said.

The barn was visible from where they stood and at that moment Harold was seen exiting the barn and walking toward them.

"I'm confident that he wouldn't refer to it as an obligation, but rather a gift. A gift to Ian, if not to yourself. He really doesn't have anyone else, or anywhere to go really. So, he'll stay until he's no longer needed, or maybe until he decides to get his own place again."

Harold was nearing them, and they smiled and greeted him.

"Hello, Harold," Hyrum said with a hand extended as he discarded the grass shoot.

"Good morning, Hyrum," Harold smiled. Then, removing his hat, he added with a smile at Amanda. "And good morning to you, Amanda."

Amanda smiled and offered her hand, which Harold gently took and held for a moment.

"Can you watch over the farms for a few days while I go to Grahamstown for building supplies?" Hyrum asked Harold.

"I'd be happy to," Harold assured him.

"I'll take Francis with me."

"Yes, he'll enjoy that very much," Harold replied. "When will you leave?"

Hyrum squinted and looked at the sun. "It's too late to start out today. We'll leave tomorrow morning."

"It will be so nice for Julia to have a house again," Amanda smiled.

"It will indeed," Hyrum agreed, "but it will be several months yet." Then looking at Harold, he added, "It would be several years, I'm sure, without Harold's help."

"I'm glad I can help," Harold assured him. "The good Lord willing, we'll have it up before the end of summer."

"That would be grand. Or at least to have enough up that she and the children can move back in to before next winter," Hyrum agreed.

The next morning, Julia, Subria, and the children all stood outside the tent to see Hyrum and Francis off. Despite mild protests from her son, Julia hugged Francis and kissed his forehead.

"You be a good boy and help your father," Julia instructed. Then looking at Hyrum, she added with a smile, "Keep track of your son now."

Hyrum messed his son's hair and replied, "He's a big helper, and I'm certain that he'll keep track of me."

Hyrum then hugged and kissed Julia. "We'll only be gone a few days, then when I return, we'll move you and the children to Amanda's."

Julia smiled and squeezed Hyrum. "I'd like that very much," she replied. "Will Amanda be fine until we move in with her?"

"Oh, I think so," Hyrum assured them. "Harold's there to keep an eye on things." Then, looking at Subria, Hyrum smiled and added, "And you'll keep an eye on these here?"

Subria smiled. "Of course," she replied as she scooped Rebecca into her arms.

After hugging the children and kissing Julia again, Hyrum climbed onto the wagon next to Francis, and shook the reins. As the wagon pulled away, Hyrum and Francis waved and called out goodbyes to the others.

The long ride to Grahamstown would be spent in light conversation between father and son, punctuated by opportunities to see wildlife. But it also left long timespans where each was left to his own thoughts. During those periods, Hyrum's thoughts invariably returned to Ian's death and questions about life and death that had occupied his mind often since that time.

Hyrum had always believed in God, and in a life after death, but he had little understanding about either. He realized that his faith in God was fairly shallow. He wasn't sure whether God knew who he was, or whether God was interested in his circumstances. *Surely, God is too busy to be concerned with me,* he often thought. Another persistent concern was why a loving god would allow a good man like Ian to be killed in such a meaningless fashion. *God must have had the power to stop Ian from being killed, but he didn't. Does he not care about Amanda and her children?* he wondered. *Will the natives go to hell, or can they be saved? What about Subria?*

Hyrum tried to push such thoughts from his mind, because he noticed that they sometimes caused him to be angry at God. But the thoughts persisted.

Hyrum thought that he had long ago come to terms with the death of his first son, but these intrusive thoughts had opened old wounds. This time doubts were creeping in alongside those wounds. As much as he hated to admit it, the doubts had affected his relationship with God. Julia had noticed that Hyrum wasn't praying as often as he should. Her encouragement hadn't affected much of a change in his patterns.

That evening after they had eaten their evening meal, cooked over an open fire, and after they had cared for the horses, Hyrum and Francis retired to their bedrolls. Francis' breathing indicated that he was soon asleep, but Hyrum lay awake staring at the stars. His mind replayed over again the last battle with the natives. In his mind, he could see Ian, and he could almost feel him in his arms as he lay dying. Hyrum's chest was tight, and tears formed in his eyes, blurring the night sky.

Soon Hyrum found himself on his knees quietly praying to God. He prayed until his knees hurt, then he lay down and was soon asleep. Sometime during the night he dreamed that two men in white came to him. Initially, he was afraid, but soon learned that there was nothing threatening about them. They walked directly to him and told him to have faith, that God was indeed aware of him and his family, that Ian was fine. The two men additionally told him that two other men would find him in the coming days and would bring to him additional knowledge about the nature of God's dealings with his children. The messengers showed to Hyrum the other two men that would come to him, and told him that he would recognize them when they came to him.

The dream was so vivid that Hyrum wasn't certain the next morning whether it was a dream or an actual heavenly visitation. Either way, the impact on him was profound. From that moment, he felt a renewed assurance in his heart that God was aware of him and his family and that everything would be alright. With this added confidence, he was anxious to complete their errand and return in haste to his family in Elephant Hook.

Hyrum and Francis continued to Grahamstown where they loaded the wagon with a supply of building materials. This was the first of many such trips that would be required for rebuilding the house, and with the wagon loaded, they headed for Elephant Hook.

"I'm going to have to teach you to drive a team if we're ever going to haul enough materials," Hyrum said to Francis as they pulled away from Grahamstown.

"I can drive a team," Francis asserted. "Let me drive now, and I'll show you."

"Hmm, I don't know," Hyrum said. "Driving a team with a full load can be a bit tricky."

"I could do it," Francis replied with confidence.

There was something in his expression and tone that reminded Hyrum of Ian and his confidence. Hyrum looked at his son. He was definitely becoming a young man.

"Very well, son. Let's see how you do then," he said as he handed the reins to Francis.

Francis took the reins with confidence and kept the wagon moving steadily toward Elephant Hook. It wasn't long before the warmth of the sun and the rocking of the wagon had put Hyrum to sleep.

Soon after reaching Elephant Hook the next day, Hyrum found opportunity to share his dream with Julia.

"What do you suppose it means?" Julia asked.

"I believe it was more than just a dream. It left a significant impact on me. So, I don't know how or when, but I believe we will receive servants of the Lord. And when they come, we'd best listen to them."

"How will we recognize them?" Julia questioned.

"The men in my dream said that I would recognize them. So, I trust that will be the case. If not, I suppose that we'll recognize their message."

"Have you shared your dream with Amanda?" Julia asked. "I think that she'd find comfort knowing Ian is fine."

"I haven't yet, but soon will," Hyrum assured her.

Chapter Thirty – The New House
February 1855
Elephant Hook, Africa

It had been several weeks since Julia had seen the house that Hyrum and Harold were building, and her excitement was mounting by the day. Hyrum had purposefully kept her from seeing the house so that it would be a grand surprise once completed, and today was the day. Hyrum had pronounced it completed the day before. Today, he and Harold were taking Julia, Subria, Amanda and the children to see it.

"You're going to love it, mum," Francis declared. "It's the grandest house in the whole world, and I helped build it!"

Julia smiled and hugged Francis. Having been raised in Brentwood Hall and also having been a frequent visitor to the royal palaces and residences in England, Julia had known grand houses. But she also knew that her home would indeed be the grandest in the world because her family would be there.

"I'm certain that it is the grandest," Julia assured him. "Thank you ever so much for helping to build it."

"I'm so happy for you, Julia" Amanda said.

"And Subria has her own apartment in the main house!" Francis said.

Hyrum gave Francis a look of feigned sternness for going on about the house before the ladies had seen the finished product.

"If we wait here long enough, there won't be any surprises remaining when you see the house," Hyrum stated.

"Let's be off then," Harold said offering his arm to Amanda as they walked to the wagons.

Amanda took Harold's arm with a smile. Her two children ran ahead and climbed into the wagon. At the wagon, Harold aided Amanda into the wagon and sat beside her.

Everyone was dressed in their Sunday-best clothing and the atmosphere was quite festive as they rode toward the Princes' farm and their re-built home.

"You look quite lovely, my dear," Hyrum said as they rode along.

Julia smiled.

"Did I just see you blush?" Hyrum asked with a smile and a tease in his voice.

Julia smiled and lowered her head so that her hat covered her blushing face.

Julia looked at her children seated behind herself and Hyrum. At 12 years, Victoria was already as tall as her mother and quite lovely. Her light colored hair hung in long, loose curls, well below her shoulders. Because she had brothers, she wasn't required to do many outside chores, leaving her hands soft and gentle. Julia liked it that way. In many ways, Victoria mirrored Julia's own ladylike demeanor. Julia felt that she was raising a young lady, and not a farmhand. Victoria would never have the opportunity of a 'finishing' instructor. Regardless, Julia was doing her best to raise her daughter in a fashion similar to the way she had been raised by Lady Hammond.

At nearly 15, Francis was taller than his father. The hard work on the farm and building the house had rendered him physically strong. He had also retained the enthusiasm of his youth, and was always willing to help.

Luke was almost nine. He had a more reserved disposition than did Francis. He was also very sensitive and readily took note of his mother's needs. It wasn't uncommon for him to leave his play and rush to her aid if she needed something lifted or moved. Subria secretly favored Luke and was fond of calling him her 'little man'.

Four-year-old Rebecca was so solicitous of Hyrum that it almost seemed at times she was in competition with Julia for his attention. Julia enjoyed the fact that Rebecca loved her father so much.

Julia noticed Subria watching her as she surveyed her children. The two women smiled knowingly. Julia loved Subria. Julia wasn't entirely certain how old Subria was, and apparently Subria wasn't sure either. They guessed that she was just over 50 years. She was such a part of the family that Julia couldn't imagine life without her. She wondered whether Subria regretted not marrying and not having children. If she did, she hadn't mentioned it. Julia did all she could to ensure that Subria felt part of the family and could rejoice with her in having children in the home.

Anticipation caused the pace of the wagons to seem even slower than normal.

Rebecca bounced in her seat and exclaimed, "When will we be there?"

"We're almost there, I assure you, my dear," Hyrum exclaimed.

"Two more bends in the road and five more dips," Francis declared. "I know this road probably better than anyone," he smiled.

"You do not," declared Victoria. "Father knows it better than you. Don't you Father?"

Hyrum looked at Julia and smiled. "I expect I do, child, but Francis does know it very well. He's traveled it about as much as anyone else."

"Humph," Victoria muttered with scorn.

"Be nice to your brother, young lady," Julia said in mild reprimand. "A lady keeps accusations to herself."

"Yes, Mum," Victoria said, but her eyes fired a glare at Francis.

After two more bends and five dips in the road, Victoria counted them, the house came into view.

"Wow!" Luke exclaimed.

Julia and Victoria sat speechless, each with a hand covering her mouth.

"It's wonderful!" Amanda declared.

Tears had formed in Julia's eyes, and with a catch in her throat she agreed, "It is wonderful! Hyrum, it's beautiful!"

"Didn't I tell you that it was grand?" Francis bragged.

Julia hugged Hyrum and said, "It is grand. It's the grandest."

"When can we move in?" Rebecca asked excitedly.

"We'll start tomorrow," Francis offered.

Hyrum smiled and agreed. "It shan't take long either, since we have so little following the fire."

The family was out of the wagon and walking into the home. Julia stopped and wrapped her arms about Hyrum's neck. "We have plenty, my dear," she said.

Francis gave the group the grand tour, making certain to point out the straight corners, the smooth plaster, and the well-fitted doors.

"I hit my thumb while driving this very nail," he offered as they entered Subria's apartment.

Subria smiled and ruffled his hair. "I shall think of you every time that I see that nail then," she grinned.

Amanda was very happy for Julia, and she was particularly excited about the water pump next to the kitchen sink.

"No more going for water in the cold morning air," Amanda said.

"Isn't it wonderful!" Julia said. Then she put an arm around Luke and added with a smile, "I actually haven't had to get water in the cold morning air ever since Luke was old enough to carry the pail. Have I Luke?"

Luke smiled and blushed without a word.

"Don't worry Amanda, you'll not be fetching water in the cold morning air," Hyrum promised.

Amanda smiled and blushed. Julia and Subria exchanged looks with slight smiles.

Chapter Thirty-one – The Prophetess
February 1857
Elephant Hook, Africa

Hyrum's expression was one of obvious concern when he walked in with Francis and Luke after having been away at Grahamstown for several days. Julia didn't have to ask what troubled him, Francis let her know right away.

"Well, it's started," Francis declared with an air of having news to share, but wanting to string it out.

Julia looked quizzically at Hyrum, as Francis continued, "The Xhosa have started killing their cattle!"

"Please, no!" Julia exclaimed with a hand over her mouth in surprise. "I honestly didn't expect it to come to this. Why?"

"Because they labor under superstitions, without a knowledge of the true and living God," Subria offered as she entered the room.

Hyrum was hanging his hat near the door. "This isn't good, not good at all," he said, stating the obvious.

May 1856
Xhosa Territory

The old warrior stood at the doorway of his round, mud-covered hut and listened to the conversation of a small group of women nearby. What he heard wasn't new, and until the last several days seemed nothing more than idle chat, without substance. It had been repeated so often recently that he feared it was taking on substance and would be heeded.

"The prophetess says that we must be ready for the ancestors' return by mid-summer," one woman stated.

The listening women agreed enthusiastically.

"Everyone must do as she says, or the ancestors will not come," another warned.

The prophetess of which they spoke was a 16 year old girl named Nongqawuse. In the last few weeks she had declared that she was the oracle through which the ancestors were communicating from the afterlife.

Life had long been difficult for the Xhosa. They had suffered untold misery from conflicts with other native tribes. They had been pushed from their traditional lands by Swallows. Their nomadic way of life had been hampered by the restriction of their movement across land now held by Swallows. Coupled with drought and pestilence, their cattle had often been decimated. This had led them to seek food from any source available, including stealing from the Swallows.

The message of the young prophetess was an alluring message of endless bounty of cattle, horses, sheep, goats, crops and great amounts of cloth and food. All to be brought back from the afterlife by the ancestors. The ancestors would also return in large numbers to drive the Swallows into the sea.

The old warrior had initially wanted to believe the stories of the prophetess, but he had been alive long enough to have seen others prey upon the weakness of the people by appealing to their greed and to their desire for prosperity. One message of the prophetess was particularly appealing to him. She had promised that the ancestors would also restore the elderly to youth. His old frame yearned to be restored to the strength and flexibility that had many times made it possible for him to escape death in battle.

His eagerness to believe the young prophetess was hampered by one thing. She had declared that the ancestors would only return from the afterlife with these bounties if the Xhosa were to first destroy all their sources of food and clothing, and all meant all sources. They were to kill all of their cattle and burn all of their crops. After some consideration, this made no sense to him. *If that were the case, why shouldn't we all just kill ourselves and be with the ancestors in their supreme society,* he reasoned.

There were few who initially paid any attention to the babbling of the young girl. It seemed to them that she only wanted attention. But people were starting to listen, and her fame was growing among many villages.

The old warrior looked across the open grassland and saw five of his 20 grandchildren running through the tall grass chasing an errant cow. He had tried to influence his family to ignore the prophetess, but his wife was amongst the believers. She was the real influence in their family. As a result, all of his children were willing and prepared to destroy their animals.

"You must have faith in the prophetess," his wife had declared.

Faith in the prophetess, he wondered. *How is faith in the prophetess possible? What proof was there?*

When he had questioned his wife she had emphatically declared that the very desire for proof was an indication of his lack of faith.

"And what if she's wrong," he had asked her. "Are you prepared to watch your grandchildren starve?"

"If the Swallows aren't driven into the sea, our grandchildren are likely to starve regardless," she had declared, alluding to the many conflicts over the years.

In the interest of keeping peace in his home, the old warrior had chosen to hold his tongue. *Besides,* he reasoned, *the plan is so ridiculous it will never be put into effect.*

January 1857
Xhosa Territory

"The appointed day is less than one cycle of the moon," The old warrior's wife declared with some excitement. "The ancestors will return and we will be restored to youth!"

The old warrior looked about at his family. Six beautiful daughters, four strong sons, all with husbands and wives and children. They were all enthusiastic about the prospect of the ancestors' return. The old warrior held his tongue. He had been the object of much ridicule amongst other members of the tribe in recent days for his antagonistic view of the prophetess. His objections had been met with much contention. Some members of the tribe had also threatened physical violence upon him.

The Swallows' government was greatly concerned about the prophecies. They knew that if the words of the prophetess were heeded, it could result in an economic and social collapse amongst the Xhosa. In an effort to quell the influence of the prophetess, she was arrested. Her arrest only served to legitimize her declarations and solidify her influence.

Early February 1857
Xhosa Territory

The rhythmic chant of the drums grew louder and faster, and the dancers leapt and twirled about the large fire. Chief Sarhili, the main chief of the area, had begun killing his animals and had already burned his crops. The villagers in the old warrior's village had declared that they would begin the destruction of their crops and animals the next day. Tonight was a night of celebration.

The old warrior watched from the village edge. The drums he had heard all of his life were quite compelling and seemed to be calling for him to come and join with the villagers in their revelry. He was only able to resist by physically distancing himself from the group. He watched the long shadows of the dancers move about the fire, and he discovered his own feet were tapping to the rhythm. To further distance himself, he climbed a small hill nearby and sat down. Eventually, weariness overtook his old frame, and he rested his head on his knees as they were drawn up to his chest, and fell asleep.

When he awoke, the sun was just beginning to illuminate the eastern sky. Low, thin clouds stretched into the horizon, and as the rays of the sun began to pierce them, the clouds were draped in vibrant orange and red. It was a magnificent sunrise, but the scene in the village below was one of chaos.

Villagers yelled and screamed and drums echoed loudly as cattle, sheep, goats, dogs and any other beast on four legs was rounded up to be killed. When the killing began, the excitement of the villagers mounted. Blood flowed freely while the tribe members cheered and sang and danced.

The juxtaposition of the beautiful sunrise against the scene of carnage was not lost on the old warrior. A tear rolled down his cheek until it hesitated momentarily on his chin, eventually dropping to the earth to form the smallest of puddles.

Someone had set fire to the crops and grassland, and the smoke was rising against the sky, obscuring the brilliance of the sunrise. The old warrior thought that the dirtiness of the smoke was befitting the slaughter.

Eventually, all of the animals were dead. Their bodies strewn about the village, laying where they had been overtaken by the villagers. Vast amounts of blood had turned the dirt to mud.

Villagers, drained of energy from their night of revelry, and exhausted by the chase and killing of their domestic beasts, began to return to their huts or to lay in a dry spot of earth, and go to sleep.

The old warrior arose from his seated position. His back ached and he walked with a slight hunch as he slowly descended the hill. In the village, he didn't bother to avoid the blood-soaked mud, there was too much of it to avoid conveniently. He had rarely cried in his life, but this battle-hardened warrior felt a lump form in his throat as he walked amongst the dead animals. The carnage of the battlefields he had known didn't often match the destruction that he was witnessing in his own village. His heart sank.

"Why have you done this?" he cried aloud to no one.

The villagers didn't stir all that day, or night, until the early hours of the next day. They seemed a little less enthusiastic when they arose, and many were hungry. They considered eating some of the dead animals, but decided that they were unfit after sitting all day in the hot sun.

"The appointed time for the ancestors' return is tomorrow," their chief eagerly reminded them. With that, the dancing and drumming of the previous night began again, albeit with less energy; and it only lasted minutes, not hours.

The villagers spent most of the day laying in the shade. The drums started in the early evening and there was a renewed energy. Despite their hunger, the tribe members danced well into the night.

Smiles were on all faces the next morning as they gathered in the center of the village, anticipating the ancestors' return.

"We're going to be young again!" the old warrior's wife declared.

The old warrior smiled wearily. He felt the pangs of his old enemy, hunger, gnawing at his stomach.

There was considerably less enthusiasm when the ancestors hadn't returned by midday. By evening, the night air was filled with the hunger cries of young children. Tempers started to flare, and villagers made accusations of others as they sought reasons for the ancestors' delay.

"Perhaps they've gone to another village," someone suggested.

"Maybe we're to meet them there," another agreed.

"Such was never declared by the prophetess," yet another insisted.

"We must have patience," urged the tribal chief.

The next day, the chief sent groups out to other villages to determine whether the ancestors had come. He also sent others out in search of wild beasts. They would find few. Because of the continuing drought few wild beasts were in the area. Though warned against it, some villagers began to eat the rotting flesh of the dead animals.

A few flies became great swarms as maggots began crawling out of the dead animals in the following days. The people were greatly troubled by the stench of the rotting flesh and by the persistent torment of the flies. Those who had feasted on the rotting flesh a few days earlier, had become violently ill. Vomiting and diarrhea were their constant companions until dehydration overtook them as they slowly died.

The living were too weakened by hunger to effectively keep the flies at bay, and the vile insects freely crawled in and out of ears, nose, mouth and eyes at will, effectively spreading disease from person to person.

In these desperate circumstances, the Xhosa had little choice, but to begin raiding the cattle and sheep of the Swallows once again.

Chapter Thirty-two – The Messengers
February 1857
Elephant Hook, Africa

Elephant Hook wasn't as near the borders of Xhosa territory as other villages, so the Princes were spared the initial effects of cattle and sheep raids after the Xhosa had killed their own cattle. Still, they were well aware of the brewing conflict and also of the suffering amongst the native people.

The prospect of yet another series of battles with the Xhosa cast Hyrum's thoughts back to the death of Ian, and he began again to contemplate the nature of life and its transient state. He also thought often of his dream from four years previous. In some ways, the dream seemed so long ago. *Was it real? Did it really have meaning?* he sometimes wondered. Yet in other ways, it was so vivid and real, like it had been yesterday. *Will there really be messengers?* he wondered.

He could tell that the continuing conflict with the natives was wearing on Julia. She wanted to be brave, but she worried whether he would be pulled into another war. Worse yet, Francis was old enough to be called into action, or to volunteer. Julia could almost not bear the thought of her son, so young, on a battlefield. Hyrum suspected that Julia's preference would be to move to a safer location, such as Cape Town. He also knew that Julia had concern for the future of her daughters and whether they would easily find acceptable suitors when they came of age.

It was in these difficult circumstances that Hyrum and Julia determined to pray together with more earnestness. They desired to know God's will for their lives and to supplicate him for his protection and blessing.

One evening, just about dusk, as they sat on their front porch enjoying the cool evening air, they observed two men approaching the house on foot from the dirt road that ran in front of the house. The men were strangers and were obviously not from Elephant Hook.

Before the men had reached the gate, Hyrum turned to Julia and said with some excitement, "These are the men from my dream."

"Can you be sure?" Julia asked.

"Without a doubt!" Hyrum declared. "I recognize them."

Hyrum stood as the men entered through the gate and approached the porch.

"Good evening, sir and madame," one of the men greeted them. "I'm Elder Walker and this is Elder Wesley. God has sent us here with a message for you."

Julia thought it odd that they had the same first names. She would later realize that it was a title borne by official representatives of their church.

Hyrum offered his hand and said, "We've been waiting for you. Do come in."

The two men briefly looked at each other and smiled.

Hyrum and Julia escorted their guests inside their home and called their family, including Subria.

When the family had gathered, Hyrum told them, "These are the men from my dream. We'll listen to what they have to say."

With the realization that the men were the men from their father's dream, the children's interest was piqued, and they sat and listened intently.

Elder Walker asked whether they could pray, and Hyrum readily agreed. After praying, Elder Walker declared, "God has again spoken to man and has set up His kingdom on the earth. He is calling for all people to repent, be baptized and to gather to Zion."

The boldness of the message startled Hyrum, but at the same time he felt something stir inside him, and he also felt of the messengers' sincerity.

The messengers went on to tell the Prince family that God was not only speaking to men again, but that He had appeared to one, Joseph Smith, and had used him as an instrument to set up His kingdom on earth.

God has appeared to a man? Hyrum thought. *Is that possible?* Hyrum knew that there was record of God's dealings with man recorded in the Holy Bible, but wasn't sure that it was possible, or even necessary for God to speak to men today. *What is the proof of this?* he wondered.

As though to read his thoughts, Elder Wesley stated, "A message of such importance would not come without some evidence of its veracity. We have a book here to loan to you. If you will read the book with sincerity, God's Holy Spirit will witness to your soul the truthfulness of our message." Then he cautioned, "The Holy Spirit will only witness to you if you are willing to accept this truth and join God's kingdom through baptism."

Elder Walker looked deep into Hyrum's eyes and asked, "Are you willing to do that, to read with sincerity and accept baptism when the Holy Spirit convicts your heart with the truthfulness of our message?"

The intensity of Elder Walker's gaze startled Hyrum, but something stirred deep within him, and he knew that their message was indeed true. Without hesitation, Hyrum responded, "Yes!"

Elder Wesley smiled and handed a book to Hyrum and said, "We'll return for the book before noon one week from today."

Hyrum took the book and looked at its cover. *The Book of Mormon,* he read to himself. *An odd name, to be sure.*

After the men had gone, Julia asked Hyrum, "What do you think of their message?"

Hyrum looked at the book in his hands and slowly turned a few pages. "I'm going to read their book. If there's error in it, it should be easy to spot." Then looking at Julia, he added, "I felt something stir inside me when they spoke. I believe that they are speaking the truth, or at least they believe what they are saying and are not trying to deceive."

The next day was the Sabbath and the family went to church as was their custom. Julia told Amanda about the messengers and the book. Amanda had heard nothing of the messengers or the book and seemed to have little interest either.

The minister's sermon spoke strongly of God's dealings with man, stating that God has spoken and has done His work. The minister declared that God's word is recorded in the Holy Bible and there would be no further word from God until He came again to the earth. He stated that God does not need a spokesperson on the earth today, He has already spoken. Then the minister declared boldly, with a raised voice, "The devil has sent messengers amongst us to deceive us! Anyone that listens to them, and those who read their book, will be damned! They are liars and thieves!"

Hyrum looked in astonishment at Julia. Julia and Amanda were exchanging glances. Hyrum leaned near to Julia and whispered, "Liars and thieves? I certainly didn't sense that. Did you?"

Julia replied quietly, "No, but you'd best be careful. We've known our minister for a long time. Why would he say such things if there wasn't merit?"

"I don't know," whispered Hyrum. "But, I'm going to read their book and find out for myself."

After the service, Harold approached Hyrum and asked about the book. "Amanda mentioned to me that you've accepted the Mormon's book."

"The Mormon's book?" Hyrum asked.

"Yes, that's what they're called. I heard about them years ago, but I know little about them. I can tell you that nothing I heard was good," Harold asserted. "I'd advise against reading the book."

"What harm could come from reading the book?" Hyrum asked. Whereas he had been quite interested in reading the book since receiving it the previous day, all the fuss surrounding it had caused his curiosity to mount considerably.

"I just think that you'd be best served by not stirring controversy."

"How about I read the book and then loan it to you," Hyrum smiled.

Harold smiled. "I think not, friend."

It was customary, due to the distances traveled, for the congregants to linger after services and to share a meal together. As the women prepared the meal, one woman related that the Mormons had approached their farm in the previous week.

"My husband ran them off before they could so much as set foot on the porch," she declared.

Another woman said that Mr. Richards had fired a weapon at them.

Julia listened, but didn't mention that she and Hyrum had a Book of Mormon. She exchanged a glance with Amanda in hopes that Amanda wouldn't make mention of it either.

Mrs. Crawford walked nearby at that moment, and the first woman who had spoken said to the others with a lowered voice and a sneer, "I hear that the Crawfords are reading their book."

A short time later, after the group had sat down to eat their meal, a woman sitting directly across from Hyrum and Julia stated loud enough for others nearby to hear, "Mrs. Prince, my Sally told me that you and Mr. Prince have entertained those Mormon missionaries and have their bible. Is that true?"

Julia's face flushed as she searched her mind for a response. *Why is there so much interest in these missionaries?* she wondered. *Do these people feel threatened by them? Victoria must have told Sally that the missionaries were at our home.*

Julia looked at Hyrum, and then responded, "Yes, we entertained the Mormons, and we do have their book."

The minister's wife spoke next. "Why would you entertain those Mormons?" she stated with a thinly veiled attitude of accusation. Then, looking about the table, she added for the entire group, "They should be run back to America from whence they came."

Many voiced their agreement at the suggestion. Hyrum had no interest in allowing his wife to be verbally abused, nor did he see any point in accusing the missionaries for doing nothing more than spreading the Gospel as they saw fit.

"Might I remind you that God asks us to be tolerant of all," he stated calmly, "and that includes the Mormons. Everyone has always been welcome at our home and that is still the case."

There were a few that mildly expressed their agreement, but most grumbled at his apparent willingness to stand up for the missionaries.

Then, to drive home his point, he added, "The Jews rejected Jesus, and where did that get them?"

The minister walked up to the tables at about that moment and overheard Hyrum's last comment.

"Are you suggesting that the Mormons are like Jesus then?" The minister asked in an incredulous tone.

Hyrum didn't take the bait, but calmly stated, "Sir, I was only making reference that we shouldn't reject someone based on gossip and hearsay, but we should hear their message and then decide. What harm could come of that?"

The minister's face reddened, and a vein in his neck bulged just above his starched collar. "Perhaps this congregation would be better served if the Princes didn't worship here in the future," he stated firmly.

Hyrum stood from the table and reached out for Julia's hand. Taking her hand, he helped her to rise. "Perhaps you're right," he said. He then called for his family and they walked away from the tables and toward their wagon.

Amanda watched in shock, and she reached out her hand to Julia as Julia walked past.

Harold jumped up from the table and followed the Princes to their wagon.

"Hyrum," he said, "I'm sure that he doesn't mean it. You'll come again next week I hope."

Hyrum smiled at Harold and offered his hand. "Oh, I do think he means it. We'll have to see what next week brings."

"Just so long as you know that not everyone feels as he does," Harold stated. Then with a smile, he added, "Most people probably do, but not everyone."

Hyrum smiled and turned to climb into the wagon, but he was stopped by Harold.

"I would like to speak with you briefly," Harold stated.

Hyrum got back down from the wagon and followed Harold a few paces.

"What is it then?" Hyrum asked.

Harold looked at the ground and kicked the dirt. "It's awkward for me, old man, but I don't know when I'll see you again."

"And?" Hyrum asked.

Harold looked Hyrum in the eye. "I thought it only right that I ask you for Amanda's hand in marriage," Harold said with a smile and some nervousness.

Hyrum smiled broadly and slapped Harold's shoulder. "That's first rate, old man! Of course, I approve." Then Hyrum added with a wink, "But will Amanda agree?"

"I think she will," Harold smiled.

"When will you marry then?"

"Soon. At least before winter," Harold replied.

"Of course you have my blessing," Hyrum said, offering his hand again.

Hyrum was all smiles when he approached the wagon where Julia, Subria and the children waited. His jovial countenance surprised Julia and Subria given the exchange that had occurred at the tables.

No one asked Hyrum about his exchange with Harold until the wagon was moving away from Elephant Hook toward their farm, then Julia asked, "And what was it that you and Harold were conversing about with such enthusiasm?"

Hyrum looked at Julia and Subria with a broad grin. "Harold is going to ask Amanda to marry him."

Julia and Subria laughed. "Well it's certainly about time," Julia said.

"What?" replied Hyrum.

"Amanda's all but given up on him ever asking," Subria said with a laugh as she and Julia exchanged smiles.

Hyrum just shook his head at the unexpressed thought that men are the last to know.

They were filled with joy that Harold would be joining the family, but most of the conversation as they traveled home centered on the rudeness they had experienced at the church lunch. They were hurt by the fact that, though they had known their fellow congregants for many years and considered them close friends, they had turned on them so readily.

"It doesn't change the command of the Lord for us to love our neighbors," Hyrum instructed.

"I'm never speaking to Sally again," Victoria threatened.

"Now young lady," Julia said in mild reprimand, "that isn't how we treat others."

"That's how I treat them," Luke ventured.

Subria reached over and touched his arm. Her eyes were moist when she replied in tenderness, "By their fruits, ye shall know them. We should always respond in love and kindness. Even when we are treated poorly."

Luke lowered his head and kept silent for a while. He knew that Subria had been on a slave ship, and he felt badly that he had caused old feelings to surface within her.

After he had cared for the animals, Hyrum spent the remainder of the day reading the Book of Mormon. He was surprised at the feeling of joy that filled his heart as he read. His knowledge of God's dealings with man and of a Savior expanded as he read, and he knew that it was the word of God. The things that he read clarified biblical truths and enlarged his understanding of them.

Toward evening, he called his family together and declared to them his belief that God had again established his kingdom on the earth, and that they should accept baptism at the hands of the missionaries.

The children seemed excited, but he could tell that Julia and Subria were hesitant. As they dressed for bed, he and Julia spoke.

"Hyrum, this seems so sudden. How can you be so certain?" Julia asked.

"I can feel it, Julia. I've never been so certain of anything in all of my life," Hyrum replied.

"People around here won't take kindly to us joining with the Mormons," Julia warned.

Hyrum held his wife and smiled. "Since when do we choose our course based on the expectations of others?" he asked.

Julia was quiet for a moment and rested her head on his shoulder. "You're so certain, Hyrum, and this could bring big changes for our family. It worries me that I don't feel the same as you."

Hyrum kissed Julia's forehead. "Of course you don't feel the way that I do, yet. But you can, and you will if you'll read the book."

"I read the Bible every day. Why would I need to read the Book of Mormon?"

"Because it's so plain and clear to understand, and it speaks so powerfully of Jesus Christ as Savior of the world," Hyrum declared. "If you'll read it, you'll understand why you should read it."

Again Julia was silent and rested in his arms.

Hyrum looked down at her and asked quietly, "Will you do that?"

After a moment's hesitation, Julia responded with a slight smile, "Yes."

The next day, Julia sat near a window and began to read. She was surprised that she started to feel joy and increased happiness almost immediately. Her initial reluctance was swept away, and she read with eagerness.

By the next day, Subria, Francis, Victoria and Luke were reading the book also. There was so much demand that Hyrum began reading to the family in the evenings, and by the end of the week the entire family was eagerly anticipating the return of the missionaries so that they could learn more about this restored gospel and God's dealings with man.

Saturday came and the family was disappointed that the missionaries hadn't returned by noon as they had promised. Near sunset, Luke let out a call that he could see them approaching on foot along the dirt road.

"Good evening, Elder Walker and Elder Wesley," Hyrum called out.

"Good evening," the missionaries called out.

"We had hoped to see you much earlier in the day, but we're glad you're here now," Hyrum said.

"And the Lord has blessed us with a warm welcome," Elder Wesley observed.

"You're in time for our evening meal. Won't you join us?" Julia asked.

The missionaries gladly accepted the invitation.

After the meal, the missionaries continued teaching the family. The Princes readily accepted their teachings about a living prophet and the eternal nature of the family. The children were excited to tell the missionaries that they had been reading the Book of Mormon and that they desired baptism. Rebecca was disappointed to learn that she was too young to be baptized.

"The Lord has declared eight years old as the minimum age for baptism," Elder Walker informed her. "Prior to that time, baptism isn't needed."

"The Savior's atoning sacrifice saves little children without baptism," Elder Wesley assured her.

It was agreed that they would be baptized in the coming week along with the Crawfords and a few other families that had recently accepted the Gospel.

"It's much too late for you to leave this evening," Hyrum said after they had finished discussing the Gospel. "Won't you stay with us tonight?"

The missionaries traveled without money, as did the apostles of old, so they readily accepted the offer of a room for the night. When Hyrum learned that they were dependent on others for their welfare, he insisted that they lodge in one of the outbuildings for as long as they desired and that they should take their meals with the family. Elders Walker and Wesley expressed thanks, but said that they had suitable accomodation at the Crawfords' at present.

The next day was the Sabbath and the Princes prepared to attend church as was their custom. During the morning meal, the missionaries asked them instead to meet with them, the Crawfords and a few other families in the area round about. They would be meeting at the Crawfords'.

Hyrum readily accepted their offer, but Julia looked perplexed.

"What is it my dear," he asked her.

"I had agreed to bring three loaves of bread for the meal after church today," she said.

"And you daren't ignore your responsibility. Isn't that right, my dear," Hyrum asked.

"Of course that's right," Julia replied. "We've always met our responsibilities, and we shouldn't change that now."

Hyrum smiled. "Of course not. We'll send Francis by horseback. He'll enjoy the ride and he can meet us at the Crawfords'."

Julia smiled and put her arms about Hyrum's neck. "Yes, that would be lovely. Thank you."

Subria soon had the three loaves wrapped carefully in a cloth, and Francis was off.

The family enjoyed meeting with the other believers at the Crawfords'. Francis returned soon after they had arrived, and he still had the loaves.

"Francis," Julia said with concern when she saw the loaves, "didn't you go to Elephant Hook?"

"Yes, ma'am, I did," he replied as he handed the loaves to his mother.

"Then why do you still have the loaves?"

"They wouldn't accept them from me."

"Who wouldn't," Hyrum asked.

"The minister's wife."

Hyrum and Julia exchanged a look of confusion between themselves.

"Why wouldn't she accept them? Did she forget that I had said that I would bring them?" Julia asked.

"She remembered," Francis assured her. "She said that she wouldn't accept bread from a Mormon."

"A Mormon?" Julia was shocked and looked at Hyrum with surprise. "Is that what we are, Mormons?" she asked.

Hyrum looked at the missionaries. "That's what people call those who are baptized into the Church of Jesus Christ of Latter-day Saints," Elder Walker offered. "We'd prefer to be called saints, but because we believe in the teachings of the Book of Mormon, we are derogatorily called 'Mormons'."

"So, rather than fight it, we accept the moniker," Elder Wesley added.

Julia felt her eyes moisten and her face flush. "But are we such pariahs that they can't accept our bread?"

"It's intended to punish and intimidate you," Elder Wesley stated.

Elder Walker placed a hand on Hyrum's shoulder. "You need to decide where you stand in this. The rejection of a loaf is a trifle compared to the hate that can be unleashed on the saints of God by the unbelievers."

"The saints in America have already been driven from place to place like animals," Elder Wesley offered. "They've had their homes burned and worse. Are you prepared to meet such opposition?"

Francis then related that he had learned that the missionaries no longer had a wagon because it had been tossed into the river by Mr. Richards and his men the day before. That's why the missionaries had been late in arriving at the Princes' home.

Julia looked at Hyrum for an indication of what they should do, but it was Subria that spoke. "I know what it's like to be driven and hated, to be shackled and starved," she said boldly. "I know what it's like to have a home burned and family members killed. And none of it because I stood for God and His Gospel. But rather, because of the color of my skin." Julia looked at Subria. She stood erect, with a determined look about her. There was no arrogance or malice in her voice as she continued. "I have no fear about what men can or might do. I've lived too long and have seen too much hate to fear men any longer. If I'm a Mormon, so be it, I'm a Mormon. I know what I know, and I've felt what I've felt!"

"I agree," Hyrum added. "Can we be baptized today?"

Julia nodded in agreement, as did the children.

"Very well," Elder Walker replied with a smile. Turning to Mr. Crawford, he asked, "Mr. Crawford, you have a pond, do you not?"

"I do indeed. A very nice pond."

"Who here desires baptism today?" Elder Walker asked the assembled group.

All hands went up, and with that they assembled at the water's edge where all who were eight years and older were baptized.

Hyrum and Julia felt overjoyed when they came out of the water. Tears flowed freely from Subria's eyes and she immediately began to sing praises and clap her hands for joy.

Chapter Thirty-three - Persecution
July 1857
Elephant Hook, Africa

Winter had come with a vengeance. It was much colder than the Princes could remember since they had been in Africa. The Xhosa were especially feeling the strain. Many had died for want of food, and out of desperation they had begun attacks on many settlements beyond their own territory. The British forces were doing what they could to contain the violence, but had been losing ground. In as much as local commandos had made a decisive difference in previous conflicts with the natives, and also because many felt that local battles should be fought with local forces and not just those sent by the Queen, pressure was mounting for commandos to join the fight.

"Julia," Hyrum said with concern in his voice, "I know that this isn't what you want to hear, but I feel that I should form a commando unit."

Julia didn't want to hear that, but it didn't surprise her. "Why would you do that? You're too old to fight."

Hyrum grinned. "I'm not so old yet. There's plenty of fight in me yet," he said with a smile. "After all, I'm not yet 42."

Julia frowned. "And will you take Francis with you?"

The smile disappeared from Hyrum's face. "Francis is a man now, my dear. He'll have to make his own decision in this fight."

"And how long will these fights last? Is this going to be the end? Can you assure me of that?" Julia asked with a voice hinting of accusation.

Hyrum looked down and quietly responded, "I can't assure you of that, but what can we do? You wouldn't have us just turn this land over to the Xhosa, would you?"

"Of course not," Julia quietly replied. "But this won't be the end of it, I assure you. Settlers have been fighting the natives for two hundred years in this land. What will the next two hundred years bring?"

"I don't know. I'm just trying to get us through the next two years," Hyrum replied with some firmness. "Remember, it's not you that the natives would be shooting at," he added, but regretted it as soon as the words escaped his mouth.

Julia was visibly hurt. With tears in her eyes, she replied, "You may not be concerned for the next two hundred years, but your children, grandchildren and great-grandchildren will be here, and they'll be concerned." Then with a choke in her voice, she added, "No, it isn't me that the natives would be shooting at, but if something were to happen to you, it would be a dangerous world for the children and myself."

Julia started to cry softly and Hyrum sat beside her and hugged her. "I'm sorry, that was careless of me. Let's give it some more thought and prayer before we decide what we should do."

Julia dried her eyes and looked at Hyrum with a forced smile. "Are you certain that anyone would follow a Mormon captain anyway? Some might just as soon shoot you as to wait for the natives to do it."

Hyrum knew that Julia was right. He had thought of those possibilities, but had not wanted to take them seriously. He and his family had never been happier since they had been baptized, but life had never been harder. Within the walls of their home, they felt safe and had more joy in each other's company than they had before experienced. They felt that God was aware of them and was caring for them. Still, outside the walls of their home they had come under increased persecutions from their neighbors and former friends.

Five months earlier, March 1857

"I'll be going in to Elephant Hook to purchase some feed," Hyrum announced during the morning meal. "I'll also take some of the young lambs to sell. They should fetch a fine price. Luke, you'll go with me. Francis, I need for you to stay and work on the fence near the barn."

"Do check at the dry goods store for any new cloth that may have come in," Julia asked.

"Of course," Hyrum agreed.

"A flower print would be best, but solid blue or light green is fine also," Julia added.

Because they hadn't been attending the local church, this would be his first trip into Elephant Hook since being baptized. Once in Elephant Hook, he was fairly certain that people were staring at him and Luke. He tried to dismiss his concern with the thought that Elephant Hook wasn't very big and so they had little else to look at. Still, their stares made him feel odd. Hyrum had also tipped his hat to a few people, but they had not returned a salutation.

"Those men are talking about us," Luke said with a nod in the direction of three men who stood near the dry goods store.

Hyrum recognized two of the men from his previous church congregation, and he had seen the other man occasionally while in Elephant Hook.

"How can you be sure that they're talking about us?" Hyrum asked Luke as he pulled the wagon to a stop near the store.

"Because they keep looking in our direction and one pointed."

"Well son, you can't be too sure. Besides, no harm is done if they are," Hyrum assured him. "Let's get these lambs sold."

Second year lambs that had been weaned shouldn't be too hard to sell. There was generally someone who was looking to add to their own flock, especially those who lived closer to Xhosa territory and who had suffered recent losses. Or there were others who would like very much to take them to Grahamstown or Cape Town were they could bring a fine price.

Hyrum approached the three men with an offer to sell the lambs.

"Morning Sam, Charles," Hyrum nodded as he approached the men. He received a cold welcome, but he continued. "I've some fine lambs here for sale. Any interest?"

"We don't want no Mormon lambs, Prince," one of the men retorted.

Hyrum was somewhat taken aback, but replied with a smile, "They've not been baptized, I assure you."

The man that Hyrum wasn't familiar with stepped forward aggressively. "We don't want your lambs. Off with you."

Hyrum was offended by the unprovoked aggression, and he clenched his fists and stepped forward. The two men stood face to face for a moment.

"Don't bother with him, James," Sam said with a hand on James' arm.

"He'll be gone soon enough," Charles added with a snort.

Hyrum decided that the better course would be to move on, so he and Luke went on to the dry goods store.

As soon as they were a few steps away from the three men, Luke asked, "Why did you let those men talk to you like that?"

Hyrum was still sore, but he measured his response. "It wouldn't be right to get into a fight over words, now would it?"

"Just because we're Mormons, people think that they can be rude to us?"

Just before they stepped into the store, but out of hearing of the three men, Hyrum stopped and turned to his son. With a hand on his son's shoulder, he replied, "People feel threatened by those that are different than themselves. You've seen how some people treat the natives. Well, they see us as different than most folks now, so they feel that it is fine to treat us poorly. It'll pass though. I'm sure of it. They'll soon see that we are no different than we've always been."

Luke looked puzzled. "I don't think it will pass so quickly," he replied.

"Why so?" asked Hyrum.

"The missionaries said that the saints in America had been driven from their homes."

Hyrum glanced up at the three men who still stood several paces away, but continued to look in his direction. Looking back into Luke's eyes, Hyrum replied, "Let's pray that's not the case here."

Hyrum wasn't entirely certain whether it was his imagination, or whether the few people inside the store glared at he and Luke when they entered, but he walked directly to the store owner and asked whether there was new cloth available.

"Will Mrs. Prince be making a new dress then?" the store owner asked with a chuckle.

"Actually, I'm not really certain whether it's for herself or for one of the girls," Hyrum admitted with a grin.

The owner showed Hyrum some recently arrived cloth and asked, "How much will you be needing?"

Hyrum shrugged his shoulders. "I don't rightly know."

"She wants two yards," Luke offered. "She mentioned that just before we left."

Hyrum smiled and grabbed Luke about the shoulders and pulled him close. "I guess I didn't hear that," he laughed. "Good thing I've got Luke with me."

"It is indeed," the store owner agreed.

As he cut the cloth and rolled it into a bundle, the store owner peered over his glasses to glance about the store and said quietly, "Not everyone around here feels threatened by new ideas."

Hyrum glanced about the store casually and saw that the few others in the store seemed to be whispering amongst themselves.

"I appreciate that," Hyrum replied quietly to the store owner. "I would have thought that we had been in this area long enough that people wouldn't turn so quickly against us."

"Well, people don't like change. It makes them feel threatened," the store owner whispered.

"I can't imagine why. But, I suppose that's the truth," Hyrum agreed.

"It'll blow over. Seasons always change," the store owner tried to assure him.

Hyrum paid for the cloth, thanked the store owner, and he and Luke left the store.

Mr. Crawford was passing on his horse just as Hyrum and Luke climbed onto their wagon and he called out to them.

"Where are you headed with these fine lambs?" Mr. Crawford asked.

"Well, we were going to sell them, but there doesn't seem to be a market today," Hyrum smiled.

"Oh? Those are fine lambs. They shouldn't be difficult to sell."

"I would have thought so, but they're evidently Mormon lambs."

Mr. Crawford smiled and said with a laugh, "Oh, I understand. Elephant Hook only wants Gentile lambs."

Hyrum and Luke both laughed and agreed.

"I'm headed to Grahamstown in the next few days. Drop those lambs at my place and I'll fetch a good price for them. The folks in Grahamstown don't seem to care what religion the sheep are," he smiled.

"That would be much appreciated," Hyrum said. "I'll stop off at your place on my way home."

After they parted company with Mr. Crawford, Hyrum said, "See son, the Lord provides a way."

"Didn't you buy your first sheep from Mr. Crawford?" Luke asked.

"I did indeed," Hyrum smiled, a little surprised that his young son recalled having been told that fact. "You should always be kind to people. You never know how important they may be in your life someday."

"Even Sam, Charles and James?" Luke asked.

Hyrum hesitated. "Yes, even Sam, Charles, and James," he agreed with a smile.

August 1857

Hyrum threw a few articles of clothing into a small bag and tied it to the saddle on his horse. Rebecca was at his side, questioning him as to why he had to leave, and when he'd be back, and who was in charge of the farm while he was away. Hyrum had already discussed all of these things around the family table for the last week, but his curious seven-year-old daughter demanded answers.

Hyrum smiled and picked her up and placed her on his left shoulder as he walked back into the house to tell Julia goodbye.

"Elder Walker needs for me to go to Grahamstown with him to do some preaching," Hyrum patiently explained. A chapel had been built in Grahamstown several years early, and Elder Walker had written to the minister and had received permission to preach a sermon.

"Why? Where is Elder Wesley?" Rebecca asked.

"Elder Wesley is still recovering from the fall he took."

"You mean that he's still recovering from the rock that hit him in the back," Rebecca corrected him.

"Well, yes," Hyrum replied slowly.

Elder Wesley had been hit by a rock that had been thrown at the missionaries as they passed through Elephant Hook recently. He had been in considerable pain, but the result could have been deadly had the rock hit him in the head. It wasn't clear who had thrown the rock, but it was likely Sam, Charles or James. They had been very outspoken against the missionaries and Mormons in general and were in Elephant Hook at the time. Mr. Richards had also been nearby, but it was not likely that he would have actually thrown the rock himself. Of all the people in the surrounding area, Mr. Richards without doubt spoke in the most inflammatory tone about the missionaries and the Mormons. He could have easily incited someone to throw the rock.

"So why does Elder Walker need to preach in Grahamstown anyway?" Rebecca inquired.

"Because he's a missionary and that's what missionaries do, they preach. Elder Walker and Elder Wesley left their homes and families in America to come all the way to Grahamstown to preach. So, they should preach," Hyrum said.

Hyrum and Rebecca had entered the house, and Hyrum lowered Rebecca to stand on her own feet.

"You're not a missionary," Rebecca reminded her father. "Why will you preach?"

"I don't know whether I will preach. I have no intention of preaching at least," Hyrum replied with a smile toward Victoria. Victoria had recently turned 14, and she liked to display how much older and wiser she was than her little sister.

"Missionaries always travel in pairs," Victoria interjected.

"So?" Rebecca replied.

"Father needs to go so that there will be two of them. That way, he can protect Elder Walker," Victoria offered.

Rebecca looked at her father. "Is that what you are going to do, protect Elder Walker?"

Julia had just walked into the room, and Hyrum held her by the hand for a moment.

"And who's going to protect us?" Julia asked with a smile.

"Yes, who?" Rebecca asked.

"Francis and Luke will be here. You'll be fine," Hyrum assured them.

"Of course we will," Julia said with a smile and a kiss on Hyrum's cheek. "Don't ask your father so many questions," she added to Rebecca.

Hyrum hugged and kissed his daughters. "I'll miss you, but I'll be back soon," he added.

"I wish that I could go and preach!" Subria said as she also walked into the room from outside. "I'd give those heathens something to think about."

Julia and Hyrum both smiled. "You'd do a fine job of preaching," Hyrum assured her. "You take care of this family now while I'm away," he added.

"Of course," Subria replied.

With that, Hyrum left the house and mounted his horse. He then rode to the place on the road to Grahamstown where he had agreed to meet Elder Walker.

On the way to Grahamstown, Elder Walker related to Hyrum that he had received word that the saints were to gather to Zion in the American West.

Hyrum was surprised. "Are you suggesting that I sell my farm and move my family to America?" Hyrum asked.

"I'm not suggesting it," Elder Walker stated plainly, "but the Lord has stated it through His prophet and it becomes incumbent on all saints to obey."

Hyrum rode in silence for a time before responding. "I just don't think that I could do that. We've established ourselves quite well here in Africa. My children don't know anything different."

"The saints are gathering from Sweden, Denmark, England, France, Germany and lots of other places. If you don't gather with them, you'll end up losing the gospel that you've accepted. A coal removed from the fire can't glow long on its own," Elder Walker said.

Hyrum looked at Elder Walker as the two rode along the dusty road. "It exacted a large toll on my Julia when we left England. She left a buried child there and people that loved her. We have my brother's grave here in Africa now. I just can't imagine pulling up our roots and making such a long and difficult trip. And I don't know how Subria would feel about such a move. I don't think she'd agree either."

Elder Walker looked at Hyrum and said, "You'll have to decide soon. I and Elder Wesley have been called back to Utah. As soon as he's able to travel, we'll be on our way. I really think that the Lord would have your family join us."

"If you're leaving so soon, why are we seeking new converts in Grahamstown?" Hyrum asked.

Elder Walker smiled. "Because we're missionaries and we've been called to teach. We'll preach until we reach Utah. The Lord has prepared people to hear us, Brother Prince, and He'll prepare a way for them to do as He says, and that includes you and your family."

Hyrum looked away from Elder Walker and focused on the road ahead. No more was said on the matter, but it had left Hyrum with much to consider. He knew that his family had never been happier than they had been since their baptisms. But now the Church that they had come to love was going to leave them abandoned in Africa, and that bothered him.

August 1857
Grahamstown, Africa

The small chapel was filled to capacity, and though a cold winter breeze blew, windows had been left open so that those gathered outside could also hear the Mormons preach. It had been noised about for days that the Mormons would be preaching, and anticipation had been growing as a result. Until recently, local people had heard nothing of the Mormons, but once the missionaries had started performing baptisms, word of their arrival had spread quickly. Some were intrigued by this sect which had recently started in the Americas. It proclaimed to be the only authorized agent of God on earth. Further, they claimed that God Himself had visited a young boy and had told him that he would be used to establish again the Kingdom of God on the earth, and the Mormons regarded him to be a prophet similar to Moses or Isaiah.

Such teaching generally incensed the good, church-going people of other religions. They scoffed at the thought that God would bypass the great churches of the day and their leaders to instead start His earthly kingdom from scratch, using the most unlikely of servants as a young boy. After all, they contended, what does a young boy know of God and of religion?

Some had heard that the Mormons actually had horns under their hats, or that they were really there to steal young girls away to America to become their wives. Some believed that the Mormons had extended their underground tunnel. Though no one had actually seen the tunnel, it was rumored to reach from Liverpool to Utah. And now the story was that it extended from Cape Town to Utah as well.

Elder Walker was under no illusion that the congregation he faced was friendly, but he also knew that in every unfriendly crowd there was one or two individuals who had been prepared by God. It was those one or two people who would be touched by the Spirit of the Lord and would accept the message. It was those few people that he had been sent by the Lord's prophet to gather in, and he wouldn't be deterred by rumors and lies, or by bigotry.

The appointed time to start the meeting soon arrived and the local minister arose and told the assemblage that the Mormon elders would speak. Many in the congregation raised their voices to protest allowing Elder Walker and Hyrum to speak. Hyrum hadn't expected a warm welcome, but this welcome approached hostility. He turned to Elder Walker to see whether they should depart, but Elder Walker seemed unconcerned. He actually seemed serene.

When the most vocal of the congregants had quieted, Elder Walker stood at the podium. Hyrum felt anxious for him. He wondered how Elder Walker would manage the hostile crowd. Other than feeling anxious for Elder Walker, Hyrum was otherwise quite calm until he heard Elder Walker say, "We'll first hear the testimony of Brother Prince of Elephant Hook."

Hyrum froze in place. His feet felt nailed to the floor. His chest tightened and his mind went blank.

Elder Walker turned from the podium and sat next to Hyrum. Hyrum still didn't move. Elder Walker placed a hand on Hyrum's knee and said, "Hurry, before they get angry."

Hyrum looked at Elder Walker and asked, "What do I say."

"Start by telling them how you feel about Joseph Smith and Jesus Christ. The Spirit will take over from there," Elder Walker promised.

Hyrum stood at the podium. He glanced at the congregation and then at Elder Walker. Elder Walker's eyes seemed to tell Hyrum to begin. Hyrum looked back at the congregation, some of whom were calling for him to say something. He didn't notice Sam, Charles and James standing in the shadows outside the rear window on the right.

Hyrum eventually took a deep breath and began, "Good men and ladies of Grahamstown. Some of you know me as Hyrum Prince of Elephant Hook. I think that you know me as a man of solid representation."

Some of the congregants acknowledged verbally that they knew Hyrum, and he continued.

"I have read the Book of Mormon and have asked God whether it is His word and whether Joseph Smith was His chosen mouthpiece today, and He has shed forth His Spirit upon me and my family in marvelous ways to affirm these things."

As Hyrum spoke, he suddenly realized that he wasn't afraid and that he wasn't at a loss for words. Despite the audible grumblings of many of those assembled, he boldly continued.

"The Holy Bible plainly teaches that God would establish His word by the mouth of two or more witnesses. That is exactly what He has done. And why should He not? Is anything too hard for the Lord?"

Hyrum spoke at length, and when he sat down he was satisfied that he had taught the word of God by the power of His Spirit. When he had said "Amen" however, there were many who were visibly agitated, who stood and loudly protested his testimony.

"We'll not listen further to these Mormon devils," someone yelled.

Someone called through the open window, "Send them out to us. We have hot tar and feathers ready." The reference was to the barbaric practice of stripping the clothing from someone and applying hot tar and feathers directly to their naked skin. Humiliating at the least and potentially lethal, the practice was reserved only for the most hated individuals.

Despite the cool breeze blowing through the windows, Hyrum felt sweat beading on his forehead and his chest tighten as he looked at the angry crowd.

Elder Walker stood and with both hands raised above his head, called loudly, "Brothers and sisters in the body of Christ, we come in peace and only wish to share with you our testimony of Jesus, the Prince of peace. Will you not hear us?"

The irony was lost on the revengeful crowd, and they had heard enough. Several rushed forward and were on the raised speaker's platform before Hyrum or Elder Walker could make an escape. Elder Walker was seized upon immediately by several strong men and was roughly hauled toward the door in the back of the chapel.

Hyrum looked about quickly for an escape. There were few options and none of them good. The open windows were clogged both inside and outside by hostile congregants. The main door was in the back of the chapel and completely inaccessible to him without fighting his way through the crowd. Hyrum knew that there was a door behind the altar, but to access it, he would have to fight his way off the speaker's platform.

Several angry men were almost upon him, and he rushed them with his head down, hoping to force his way through. Their strength was too much, and they seized upon him. Their grasp was firm, rendering escape completely impossible. Hyrum yelled out loudly at them, but they didn't scare. That's when the blows started, first to his side, and then to his head.

Hyrum fought back as best he could, but the blows increased. Despite the pounding, he didn't immediately feel pain. Soon a strike to his head caused his head to spin, and blackness settled in. Hyrum fell to the floor, but the beating didn't immediately stop. Some of the men continued the beating until it was obvious that he was unconscious. They didn't want to necessarily kill him, so they quickly dispersed, leaving Hyrum in a heap on the floor.

Elder Walker had been carried outside the church house into the cold night air where he was stripped of most his clothing. He tried to free himself, but couldn't. In his desperation, he called out to God for protection and was mocked by the angry mob.

He cried out in excruciating pain when a piece of wood, covered with hot tar, was slapped against his chest and scraped down his torso, spreading the tar across his body. More tar was spread across his back, burning him badly, but not severely. Fortunate for Elder Walker, the angry mob had quickly assembled the tar and feathers without sufficient time to heat it properly. If it had been heated thoroughly, it would have burned completely through the skin and down to the muscle. Few would have survived such brutal treatment.

The crowd cheered when feathers were thrown against his tarred body. In pain and humiliation, he was strapped to a beam and paraded through the streets by the light of torches. Eventually, the mob tired, and he was left by the side of the road that led out of Grahamstown.

Elder Walker didn't know how long he lay in pain and exhaustion, but eventually someone cut him loose of the beam and loaded him into a wagon. He didn't know what the intentions were of whoever it was that had loaded him into the wagon, but he felt that they meant him no harm. The wagon hadn't gone far before he heard a groan next to him. Startled, he painfully looked in the direction of the sound. In the darkness, he could make out the form of a man laying next to him.

"Brother Prince?" he groaned.

The person groaned again. Even though the sound was barely audible, Elder Walker was certain that it was Hyrum.

"Brother Prince," he repeated with effort.

"Elder Walker?" Hyrum groaned.

"Yes, it's me."

"I thought you were dead," Hyrum whispered.

"I thought you were dead," Elder Walker assured him.

"I'm not," Hyrum quietly groaned with a hint of humor in his voice.

"I don't think they liked your preaching. You really need to work on that."

Hyrum quietly laughed, but the laughter turned to groans, and he held his sides in pain.

"Whose wagon are we in?" Hyrum whispered.

"I don't know," Elder Walker whispered back.

Each uneven spot in the road sent a jolt of pain through Hyrum's chest.

"I recognized some of our attackers," Elder Walker eventually said.

"Without a doubt?" Hyrum groaned.

"There's no doubt in my mind."

"Who?" Hyrum whispered in pain.

"Mr. Richards' men. Sam, Charles and one other who's been keeping company with them."

"James."

"Yes, James," Elder Walker agreed.

After at least thirty minutes in the back of the wagon, it pulled to a stop and the driver turned and asked, "Are you two alright back there?"

"We're alive," Elder Walker replied quietly.

"Very good. Very good indeed," came the reply.

The voice was that of an older man. He climbed from the wagon and stood next to the side that Elder Walker was on.

"You're safe now. You both took a terrible beating, and I wasn't certain that you'd live. But praise be to God, you have."

The man disappeared, but was soon back with a lantern and a native farm worker.

"We'll be as gentle as we can be, but this is going to hurt," he assured them.

The older man and his farm hand then carefully helped Hyrum from the wagon and into the house, where they laid him on a small bed. Hyrum groaned with pain at every step.

Because of the tar, Elder Walker couldn't be brought directly into the house. Instead, the older man instructed his wife to heat water. Using kerosene and warm water with strong soap, they cleaned Elder Walker up. Hyrum could hear groans from Elder Walker as the tar was pulled from his tender skin. It seemed to take a very long time, but eventually, Elder Walker was also brought inside and laid on a bed.

As bad as his wounds were, infection was the real concern. Consistent with traditional tribal medicine that she had long used, the farmer's wife gently applied crushed sugar cane to the most severe of Elder Walker's wounds. She also covered them with rendered animal fat.

"Please rest now," the farmer's wife instructed them. "You'll be safe. Mr. Allen, my husband, was worried that this would happen when he heard that you were coming to preach in Grahamstown. He was certainly right."

Elder Walker tried to thank Mrs. Allen, but the pain was too much.

"Shhh," Mrs. Allen demanded. "Sleep, we'll talk when you wake."

Hyrum and Elder Walker had trouble sleeping because of pain. Hyrum's ribs ached so badly that he could lay only on his back and not on his sides. Fortunately, most of the tar had been applied to Elder Walker's chest and arms, so he was able also lay on his back, but not his side or stomach.

By midday, they were each able to get out of bed for short durations, but neither left the house.

"We're ever so grateful to you for all you've done," Hyrum said to Mrs. Allen.

"It's nothing," replied Mrs. Allen. "Anyone would have done the same."

"No. I assure you, good woman," replied Elder Walker, "not everyone would have done the same. I think that many wanted to see us dead."

"Well, most are good people," Mrs. Allen said. "But there are some bad apples."

Hyrum was looking out the window and remarked with some excitement, "Mr. Allen even fetched our horses!"

Elder Walker looked out the window and smiled.

"How did Mr. Allen come to be in Grahamstown last night?" Elder Walker asked.

Mrs. Allen was heating water to use in cleaning Elder Walker's sores. After adding more wood to the fire, she said, "It's no surprise that we're from England. Before coming to Africa we were aware of the Mormons. They created quite a stir in our area. Many accepted their message." Then for emphasis, she added, "We of course did not."

Mrs. Allen added some water to the pot and continued, "We witnessed firsthand the persecutions that sometimes awaited Mormon elders as they preached."

Elder Walker shook his head in understanding.

"Of course we never took part in such brutality," Mrs. Allen quickly added. "But when we heard that some people were planning mischief against you, Mr. Allen went into Grahamstown in hopes of warning you if he could, or to help you if he couldn't warn you."

Hyrum bowed his head and said, "We owe our lives to you and Mr. Allen. We are very grateful."

"We try to be Christians," Mrs. Allen replied with a smile.

"We won't be a burden long," Hyrum promised.

"Oh, you're no burden," Mrs. Allen assured him.

"Even still, we'll be leaving tomorrow," Hyrum asserted.

"You'll do no such thing. You're in no condition to ride," Mrs. Allen protested.

"She's right," Elder Walker added. "You'll need a week at the very least."

Hyrum felt his ribs with one hand and grimaced. "I'll give it two days, but then I really must return to Elephant Hook. Julia will be concerned, to be sure."

"You'll be in no condition to ride in two days," Elder Walker said.

"We'll see," Hyrum smiled.

When Hyrum was alone with Elder Walker, he confided, "I've been concerned ever since you told me that you recognized your attackers. It's Mr. Richards who's calling the shots here. I know it. He's a dangerous man."

"I can understand your urgency to get home then," Elder Walker replied.

"There's no telling just what Mr. Richards is capable of. I really need to get home."

Chapter Thirty-four – The Rescue
August 1857
Elephant Hook, Africa

Julia began to worry when Hyrum hadn't returned by the morning of the fourth day, and she debated whether to send Francis to Grahamstown to find him, or to ask Francis to go for Harold. Francis had assured her that he knew the way to Grahamstown, and that he should go looking for his father. Julia wasn't entirely convinced that he would know how to get there or what to do once there.

"He's almost 17," Subria reminded her. "He's a man now."

Julia looked at Subria, pursed her lips and then looked away. She knew Subria was right. Francis was quite capable. He had been working on the farm for years with his father. He was obedient and had a good head on his shoulders. Nevertheless, he was her son, and she was nervous about sending him.

"I suppose you're right," Julia said at last. "If Hyrum isn't home tomorrow, I'll send Francis."

When Hyrum hadn't returned by noon the next day, Francis approached his mother and said, "I've got my horse saddled, and I'm ready to go look for Father. May I go?"

When Julia hesitated, he added, "I know the way. It will be fine. He should have been back by now."

Julia sighed. "Yes, he should have been back by now. Maybe we should ask Harold to go with you, or perhaps Elder Wesley is feeling better."

Francis was respectful, but insistent. "Elder Wesley surely isn't up to riding. I'll fetch Harold if that's what you wish, but it really isn't necessary. He's in the opposite direction and I'll lose valuable time."

After brief consideration, Julia held out her hand to her son, and he placed his hand in hers. Holding his hand and looking at him closely, she said, "You're right. Go and get your father. Something must not be right. Hurry now, and God speed."

Francis gave his mother a quick kiss on the forehead and was out the door before she could change her mind.

On the morning of the fifth day since leaving home, Hyrum announced that he would be leaving for Elephant Hook.

"You're in no condition to ride," Elder Walker replied.

"I agree," added Mr. Allen.

Hyrum rubbed a hand across his ribs. "I feel fine enough. I'm overdue getting home. Julia will worry." Then to Elder Walker, he added, "Can you ride?"

"I think I can ride, but I'm more concerned for you. Let's give it another day," Elder Walker urged.

"That won't do. I dreamed last night that my family could be in danger. I need to get home."

"At least let Mr. Allen take you in the wagon," Mrs. Allen urged.

"Yes. Of course. I'd be happy to," Mr. Allen agreed.

"No, the wagon's too slow. I'll take my horse."

"You'll at least have something to eat before you go," Mrs. Allen said as more of a question than a statement.

Hyrum smiled. "Yes, I'd like that. You and Mr. Allen have been so kind to us."

Elder Walker echoed the gratitude expressed by Hyrum.

After eating, the two men went outside to saddle their horses. Elder Walker saw Hyrum grimace when he picked up his saddle and threw it over his horse's back. Elder Walker knew that it was useless to try and dissuade Hyrum from riding. Elder Walker had his own concerns with riding. The sores on his chest and arms were still very raw, and every movement caused the coarse material of his shirt to rub painfully against them. Mrs. Allen insisted that he take along some animal fat to reapply as needed.

Riding was even more painful than Hyrum had expected. Any pace quicker than a walk was impossible. It seemed that each placement of the horse's hooves shot straight to Hyrum's chest. He found that he could get some relief by leaning forward over the horse's neck.

"You appear as though you'll fall from that horse," Elder Walker chided him.

"It would probably hurt less if I did," Hyrum replied with a faint smile.

After a couple hours Hyrum realized that trying to ride so soon after their injuries was not good for either man. They rode as long as they could stand the pain, then they stopped and rested.

"At this pace, it's going to take us two days to get to Elephant Hook," Elder Walker observed.

"I suppose you're quite right," Hyrum admitted. "But we've gone too far to turn back. There's nothing to do but press ahead."

There were a few spots of red dotting Elder Walker's shirt where tender sores had been rubbed raw and were bleeding.

"We really should put something on those wounds," Hyrum suggested.

Elder Walker reapplied some fat to the wounds, hoping that it would provide some relief to the constant rubbing.

Hyrum looked about at the rolling hills that the road they were on passed through. He knew the road well, having traveled it many times.

"If we keep a slow, steady pace, with rests evenly spaced, we'll be fine," Hyrum offered.

"Do you suppose we'll see anyone else along the road?" Elder Walker asked.

"Undoubtedly," Hyrum replied.

"Perhaps they'll want to finish the job that our friends in Grahamstown started," Elder Walker smiled.

Hyrum chuckled, but held his ribs when the laugh caused him pain. "I'm sure the good people of Grahamstown have calmed down by now," he replied assuredly. "Although, if it's Mr. Richards' men that we encounter, God help us."

The two men soon remounted and resumed their slow pace toward Elephant Hook, continuing their pattern of resting every hour or two. To their surprise, they didn't encounter anyone along the road throughout the day.

After they had stopped for the evening and were preparing to build a fire, Elder Walker spotted a lone rider coming from the direction of Elephant Hook. Nudging Hyrum gently on the shoulder, he pointed at the approaching rider. The two stood silently and watched the rider's approach. He was moving fast, pushing his horse harder than Hyrum thought prudent. When the rider and horse were nearly upon them, he pulled the horse up short.

"Pa? Elder Walker?" Francis called out, with some surprise in his voice.

Hyrum recognized his son and horse at about the same instance.

"Francis," he called out with joy. "Francis!" Pain shot through his chest at the exertion.

Francis turned his horse about and dismounted.

"Pa," he said as he started to hug his father.

Hyrum pulled back and, with an outstretched arm to keep Francis back, said, "Careful, son. It's great to see you, but don't touch me."

Several days earlier
Elephant Hook, Africa

"I hate those Mormons! Do you hear me?" Mr. Richards exclaimed to Sam, Charles and James who were standing nearby.

"Yes, sir," Sam replied.

"Did you think that one little rock in the back would drive them off?" Mr. Richards snorted.

"No, sir," Sam agreed quietly.

"Of course not. They need to be taught a lesson!" Mr. Richards declared.

"What would you have us do?" Charles asked.

Though he was smaller than the other men and considerably older, Mr. Richards was a commanding presence. Sam and Charles had worked on his land off and on for several years, whereas James was a relative newcomer to the area. All three men were paid by Mr. Richards to "protect his interests".

Mr. Richards got right in Charles' face. "I don't care what you do, but I want those Mormon missionaries driven out of Africa."

"What about Prince, Crawford and the other converts?" Sam asked.

Mr. Richards paced for a moment. "I don't care much about Crawford, but we may still need Prince to lead the commandos if the natives continue their campaigns. Still, he and the others need to be taught a lesson."

"I could lead the commandos," Sam asserted.

With that, Mr. Richards struck Sam on a leg with his walking stick. "You, lead the commandos? What do you know about leading anyone? Have you ever been in a battle with the natives?"

Sam rubbed his aching leg. "No," he replied in a cowering manner.

"I didn't think so," Mr. Richards sneered. "No, we may still need Prince. It's those Mormon missionaries that we need to get rid of. If they're gone, Prince and the others will soon forget their foolishness."

James had remained quiet, but now stepped forward and spoke. "I hear that the Mormon elders will be preaching in Grahamstown in the coming days," he said in a manner almost as to bait Mr. Richards.

Mr. Richards looked down and rubbed the stubble on his chin. "Will they now?" he replied. "In Grahamstown no one will suspect us." Then looking at James, he said, "Yes, go to Grahamstown and teach these Mormons a lesson. I'm not asking you to kill them, yet. But make the lesson stick."

Sam, Charles and James left for Grahamstown the next morning. The road took them near the Princes' home. Victoria and her younger brother, Luke, were near the roadway when the men passed nearby.

As they approached, James took note of the pretty girl with long, blonde hair, and he tipped his hat to her as they passed. Victoria smiled and blushed and looked away.

Luke glared at the men.

Still looking backward from his saddle after they'd passed, James commented, "Now that's a pretty, little wench."

"That may be so," Charles retorted, "but she's also Prince's daughter. You'd best leave her be."

James turned back to a forward-facing position on his saddle. "Is that so now," he grinned at Charles, his smile revealing the absence of his two front teeth. "Maybe I'll have to call at the Prince home when we return."

"Suit yourself, but leave me out of it," Charles replied emphatically.

After the men were gone, Luke turned to his sister and said with a voice full of disdain, "Those are Mr. Richards' men. You shouldn't even be looking in the same direction as men like that."

Victoria was mildly annoyed to receive correction from her little brother. "I did no harm," she said and walked toward the house.

"Men like that aren't to be trusted," Luke insisted.

Once in Grahamstown, the men were initially disappointed to hear that Hyrum had accompanied Elder Walker and that Elder Wesley wasn't there.

"We'll just have to teach Prince that he shouldn't keep company with the Mormons," Sam declared.

"If Prince is here in Grahamstown," James grinned, "he isn't in Elephant Hook watching over his daughter."

"Keep your mind on why we're here," Charles snapped. "There'll be time enough to visit Prince's daughter."

James smiled eerily. "I think that you'd like Prince's daughter for yourself."

Charles glared at James. "Maybe I would," he snarled. "But then I think there's plenty of girls in Grahamstown. Maybe I'll just take one of them back to Elephant Hook."

"When you two are done arguing over 15 year old girls, we can make some plans," Sam growled.

The next evening, Sam, Charles and James gathered at the church with many others to hear the Mormons preach. They made certain to place themselves outside where they wouldn't be noticed, and also near to others who hated the Mormons as they did. They had intended to subject both men to a severe beating, but soon learned that still other men had prepared hot tar and feathers. Sam, Charles and James exchanged evil smiles as they contemplated the fun awaiting them. The fire warming the tar could be seen near a building about 100 yards distant and the faint smell of hot tar wafted through the air.

Sam, Charles and James made certain to mock and jeer as Hyrum and Elder Walker spoke, in an effort to encourage the angry crowd. Little encouragement was needed, however. When it became clear that the crowd would soon rush the podium, the three men quickly made their way through the back door and were among the first to encounter Elder Walker. Elder Walker struggled, but was no match for the three.

"Tar and feather him!" James yelled as they carried Elder Walker outside.

Elder Walker was able to momentarily free himself, managing to strike his attackers several times before they lay hold of him again, and beat him to the ground.

"Take his shirt off!" someone yelled.

Elder Walker felt the cold night air against his chest just before he felt the sting of hot tar being applied with the end of a stick. Though he screamed in pain, his attackers laughed and cheered.

James had secured a beam and, with the help of others, had strapped Elder Walker to it. Hanging like a dead animal from the beam, Elder Walker was paraded through the streets. The sounds of the cheering crowd echoed in his ears until he was eventually left by the side of the road that led to Elephant Hook.

Sam, Charles and James disappeared into the night and headed toward Elephant Hook without delay. If questioned, Mr. Richards would maintain that they had been on his farm the entire time. The three rode a couple of hours outside of Grahamstown before stopping for the night. They continued their ride to Elephant Hook early the next day and reported to Mr. Richards by mid afternoon.

After the joyous reunion of Francis, Hyrum and Elder Walker, Francis quickly started a campfire to warm the other two men against the cold winter night. As they sat around the fire, he listened as the two men shared with him the circumstances of their injuries. Francis was shocked. He had never heard or considered that people could be so brutal over something that he considered so benign.

"I thought that the people of Grahamstown were Christian," Francis declared with some surprise in his voice.

"Oh, they most certainly do consider themselves Christian," Elder Walker assured him. "That might be one motivation for doing what they did."

Hyrum looked his son in the eyes and said, "Wars have been fought through the ages over religion, son."

"But that doesn't make it right," added Elder Walker.

"Some people feel threatened by new ideas, and they act out against them," Hyrum said.

Each of the men stared into the flames. Sitting next to a small fire has a calming effect, even when the conversation is unsettling.

After a few silent moments, Elder Walker reminded Francis that the Mormons had been slain and driven from Ohio to Missouri, until they had found safety in the mountains of the West.

Hyrum looked at his son. "Elder Walker tells me that the Lord would have us join the saints in Utah. He and Elder Wesley will be leaving us soon."

"Utah?" Francis replied. "Where's that?"

"It's in the mountains of the West. In America," Elder Walker replied.

Francis looked at his father. "Are we going to America then?"

Hyrum didn't look away from the fire when he responded. "No. Africa has everything we need. The people here also need our help in fighting the natives. It would pain them for us to leave now. Besides, I've already traveled halfway around the world once to establish a new home. I just can't imagine doing it again at my age and with a family in tow."

Elder Walker looked closely at Hyrum. "You say that Africa has everything that you need? It doesn't have a prophet of God. Without a prophet of God, you've got nothing."

Francis looked earnestly at Elder Walker. "I'll go with you."

Hyrum looked up from the flames prepared to rebuke his son. To his surprise, he didn't see a boy. Instead, he saw a man. He suddenly saw an image of himself in his son's expression.

Francis looked expectedly at his father, anticipating a retort.

Hyrum hesitated, and replied, "If you feel that's right son, that's what you should do. But remember, it's a long way, and there's no return."

"I do feel it's right," replied Francis.

The three sat in silence for several minutes staring at the flames as though held spellbound by the flickering orange and yellow light. Hyrum eventually broke the silence.

"Francis, you'd best ride ahead of us tomorrow. At the pace we're traveling, it'll take us another two days to reach Elephant Hook. I'd hate for your mother to worry unnecessarily."

Francis resisted, stating that given their physical condition, he should stay with them to ensure their safety, but Hyrum insisted. Francis departed for Elephant Hook right after daylight the next morning, and by pushing his horse hard, he was able to reach home just before dark.

"Oh Francis, you're back! Thank the Lord," Subria welcomed him as soon as he'd entered the house. "Where's your father?" she asked urgently.

Julia entered the room at that moment, and Francis knew right away that she was distressed. She clasped a white handkerchief with both hands close to her breast, and her eyes were red from crying.

"Where's Father?" Julia asked expectedly.

"I left him and Elder Walker this morning. Pa insisted on account that they are riding slowly," Francis responded.

"Riding slowly?" Julia asked calmly, but with a catch in her voice. "Is something wrong?"

"Pa insisted that I ride ahead to assure you that they are fine."

"Then where are they?" Julia asked.

"Pa doesn't want you to worry, but they were beaten by a mob in Grahamstown. That's the cause of their delay. They're forced to ride slowly due to the pain caused by riding."

With that, Julia collapsed onto a chair and began to cry freely.

Francis looked at Subria in confusion. He had expected that his mother would be relieved at the news, but she seemed all the more distressed.

Luke walked in from outside at that moment. "She isn't in the pasture," he declared.

"Who isn't?" Francis asked.

"Victoria's missing!" Subria said as she walked to Julia's side and put an arm around her.

"Victoria's missing?" Francis asked in a confused tone. "How long has she been missing?"

"We're not certain. Maybe a couple of hours," Subria replied. "Your mother was anticipating Hyrum's return so that he could find her. The news that he's injured and won't be arriving anytime soon is distressing. She was just about to send Luke to get Harold."

"Luke?" Francis asked in surprise with a glance toward Luke.

Luke had recently turned 11, and he was quite sure of himself despite his tender years.

Julia dried her eyes and, while choking back sobs, quietly said, "Please, both of you, go get Harold. He'll know what to do."

"We can find her," Luke assured his mother.

"No, get Harold, and go quickly," Julia urged.

"Yes ma'am," Luke replied.

A few hours earlier
Elephant Hook

James lay stretched out in the shade of a tree with his hat over his eyes. By appearances, he was asleep. As Sam and Charles walked passed, Charles kicked James' boot and chided, "Still dreaming of that Prince wench, are you?"

James removed his hat and glared at Charles. "I don't have to dream."

"Oh, really?" replied Charles. "I don't see her."

James jumped up and walked quickly toward his horse.

"What're you gonna do? Go and get yourself a Mormon girl?" Charles called after him.

James swung into the saddle and spun his horse about. "That's right. Maybe I'll have two or three," he snarled.

"You'd best leave Prince's daughter be," Sam warned.

James grinned. "I don't think we'll have to worry about Prince anytime soon now. Do you?" he snarled. "Besides, I'll be leaving Elephant Hook real soon. Maybe I'll take her with me. It's a big country. What's one commando going to do about that?"

Sam took the comment about commandos as an insult to himself, after having been told by Mr. Richards that he wasn't fit to lead them. It was too late to issue a retort, as James kicked his horse in the sides and the animal leapt into action.

James rode near to the Prince farm and tied his horse in a gully. He then watched the farm from the crest of a hill, secluded behind a tree. He noted that a young lad left in the company of a dog, and that there didn't appear to be other dogs on the property. He watched as the lad passed over a hill on the opposite side of the farm.

James' heart began to pound when he saw a teenage girl leave the house with a basketful of clothing to hang on a line. James hurried to his horse, and staying below the crest of the hill, he rode to the back of the house and put the barn between himself and the house. Using the barn as a blind, James rode to the barn and dismounted. From inside the barn, he watched Victoria shake out each article before pinning it to the line.

"Victoria," Subria called from the house.

Victoria continued her chore, but called out, "Yes?"

"When you're finished with those clothes, your mother would like your help with dinner."

James' heart raced. He knew that he didn't have much time. He expected that his best opportunity was to lure her into the barn. He picked up a pebble and tossed it in Victoria's direction.

Victoria was startled when something small hit one of her father's shirts. She looked about for the cause, but didn't notice anything unusual, so she returned to her chore.

James picked up another pebble and tossed it in her direction.

"Luke!" Victoria exclaimed as she looked about. "That's not funny! If you get these clothes dirty, you're going to wash them yourself."

James tossed another pebble from inside the dark barn.

"Alright! That's it, Luke," Victoria called, and she stomped toward the barn.

Victoria hesitated just inside the entrance as her eyes began to acclimate to the low light of the barn. In that instant, she felt a strong arm grab her about the waist. A scream instinctively began to escape her throat, but a rough hand covered her mouth, and all that escaped were muffled cries. Her first thought was that her father or Francis were playing games, but then they would never treat her in such a rough manner. Though she couldn't see her attacker, she could smell his foul breath.

Despite her kicks and struggles, James easily carried Victoria to his horse and tried to force her on its back.

"Keep quiet you little wench, or I'll slit your brother's throat," James growled. "I've got him tied up just over that hill."

Victoria's eyes were wide with fright and her nostrils flared as she struggled for each breath. She tried to bite James' hand, but he kept her mouth too tightly closed.

"Oh, you think to bite, do you? I bite too," James snarled with a toothless grin.

Victoria squirmed all the more, but James held her tight, releasing her only momentarily to slap her across the face and then covered her mouth again.

"I'll release you right now and go and slit your brother Luke's throat if you don't keep quiet," James whispered loudly directly into Victoria's ear.

Shocked that he knew Luke's name, Victoria stopped trying to scream.

"There. That's better," smiled James, and he threw her up onto the horse.

"Don't kill my brother," Victoria said quietly between sobs that forced their way out despite her efforts to hold them in.

"Shut up," replied James angrily.

James quickly climbed onto the horse behind Victoria and spurred the horse to a run, and they were soon over the hill. After several minutes, with tears filling her eyes and sobs escaping her mouth, Victoria realized that James didn't have Luke tied up, or at least that they weren't going to go to free him as she'd expected. At the realization, she started screaming.

"Scream!" James laughed. "Go ahead and scream! No one will hear you out here."

After Francis and Luke left to ask for Harold's assistance in searching for Victoria, Luke said, "I'm sure it's Mr. Richards' men!"

"How can you be certain?" Francis asked.

"I was with Victoria when they passed on their way to Grahamstown. One of them just stared at her. I know it's them."

"That's excellent," Francis replied. "We'll tell that to Harold, he'll know what to do."

"By then it might be too late!" Luke insisted. "We'll pass near Mr. Richards' place on the way to get Harold. Let's go straight there and see if she's there."

"And what if she is, then what?" Francis asked. "What would we do?"

Francis nudged his horse to a gallop and Luke followed close behind on his horse.

"We won't know until we find her," Luke called over the pounding of the horses' hooves.

Francis didn't reply.

After riding at a quick pace for nearly 30 minutes, the glow of lanterns through the windows of Mr. Richards' place came into view. His house was still a considerable way off the road, so their approach wouldn't likely have been noticed. Luke pulled his horse up and looked as though he would change his course and go to Mr. Richards' place. Francis pulled his horse about and stopped alongside Luke.

"Let's just take a look," Luke urged.

Francis hesitated. "I don't know Luke. Even if she was there, Mr. Richards' and his men aren't just going to hand her over."

"Listen, if we just go and take a peek it will save time later. If she's there, we can tell Harold that we found her there. If she's not, then Harold can search elsewhere."

"And what if there's dogs? They'll give us away."

"That's a chance we'll have to take," Luke ventured. "Of course there's dogs. Everyone has dogs, but the dogs may be gone. Our dog was with me, so if someone took Victoria, he wasn't around to notice."

When Francis didn't respond right away, Luke kicked his horse and raced toward Mr. Richards' house. Not wanting to lose a brother as well as a sister, Francis followed close behind.

Before getting too close, Luke stopped and tied his horse to a tree. Francis did the same.

"Fine, we'll take a quick look, but then we're off to get Harold," Francis whispered forcefully.

Luke smiled. "That's fine with me," he whispered in reply.

The two boys approached the house cautiously, listening and watching carefully for any sign of dogs. They froze when they saw the front door open. Mr. Richards stepped out onto the covered porch that surrounded the house. The boys' hearts seemed that they would fail, and though it was only moments, it seemed an eternity that Mr. Richards stood looking into the darkness.

"What's he doing?" Francis whispered barely audibly.

"Shh," Luke replied.

"Maybe he's seen us!" Francis whispered.

Luke didn't bother to respond audibly, he only reached out and squeezed Francis' arm as though to command silence.

After a moment, Mr. Richards whistled and called for his dogs. They soon came running from behind the house and bounded through the front door where they would then settle beside the warm fire.

Francis let out a sigh of relief. "See, there were dogs!" he whispered forcefully.

Luke turned and smiled at him. "There aren't now," he whispered in reply.

The two waited momentarily before Luke began creeping toward the house. Francis was close behind. Luke stopped just before the house and grabbed Francis' arm again. Startled, but silent, Francis froze.

"What is it?" Francis whispered.

"Listen."

The two didn't move or make a sound.

"There, did you hear that?" Luke asked quietly.

"Yes. What is it?"

"I don't know, but it's coming from the barn."

"There it is again. It sounds like crying," Francis whispered.

"It is crying," Luke whispered in reply. "Come on. It's Victoria!" And he started to tiptoe toward the barn, but stopped when he felt Francis tug on his jacket.

"Careful. We don't know that she's alone."

The two boys made their way carefully to the barn and listened. They could hear the unmistakable sound of a girl's soft crying just on the other side of the barn wall from where they had kneeled.

"Victoria," whispered Francis quietly.

The soft crying stopped and there was sound of a quick movement from the other side of the wall.

"Victoria," whispered Luke. "Are you alone?"

With relief evident in her quiet voice, she replied, "Yes! Hurry! I'm tied. He'll be back."

Francis and Luke hurried inside the barn, being certain to stay quiet and not disturb the few animals that were inside. Victoria was joyous to see them, but contained her emotions. She had been tied hand and feet and efforts to undo the knots proved fruitless. Francis always carried a small knife with him, which he now used to cut the ropes. With her hands freed, Victoria threw her arms around her brothers and cried.

"Shh. We've got to go," Francis urged her.

Victoria dried her eyes on her skirt, and the three quietly, but swiftly left the barn and hurried to the horses. As they mounted, they saw someone with a lantern walking toward the barn.

"Let's go!" Francis ordered, and the two horses were spurred into action.

They were soon on the road toward home, when Francis called for Luke to slow.

"You take Victoria home. I'm going to get Harold. If they come looking for her tonight, I think that mother would want him there," Francis said.

Luke agreed, and he and Victoria sped for home. Julia was beside herself with joy to get her daughter back.

When James discovered Victoria missing, he called out in anger. Sam heard him hollering and stepped out to see what was the cause.

"She's gone!" James yelled.

"Who's gone?" Sam asked.

"That Prince girl! And I'm going to get her back!"

James was headed for a saddle when Sam grabbed his arm and roughly turned him around.

"The Prince girl? What do you mean the Prince girl is gone?" Sam ordered.

"You heard me," James snarled, and shook himself loose from Sam's grasp. "And I'm gonna get her back!"

"You had better not have had the Prince girl here! Mr. Richards don't want no trouble with Mr. Prince."

"Well I did, but now she's gone. I'll track her with the dogs."

Sam grabbed James' arm, then landed a blow directly into James' stomach. James doubled over, holding his stomach with both hands. But then he was up, both arms swinging in the low light of the lantern. Sam dodged all of his attempts, and hit James again across the face, knocking him to the ground. James jumped to his feet and in the process knocked the lantern over spilling fire and lantern oil across the hay strewn floor.

The two men took little notice of the toppled lantern and the small flickering yellow glow. As they continued to focus their energies and attention on beating each other, the fire quickly grew and spread to the walls and the loose stacks of hay. The men took their fight outside the barn as the flames soon climbed the walls and encroached on the roof.

Realizing the eminent danger to the animals inside, Sam called out, "Stop! We've got to get the animals!" And he started to run back inside the burning barn.

James kicked his legs tripping him and Sam went down hard. Mr. Richards and Charles had seen the flames and were outside in time to see James first trip Sam and then hit him as he tried to rise.

"What's going on here?" Mr. Richards yelled. "Get some water. Get those animals out of there."

The horse and cow were greatly distressed by the flames and were frantically attempting to break through their stalls without success. Charles and Sam tried to go inside, but it was just too hot. Then pieces of the roof started to fall.

"My barn! My animals!" Mr. Richards cried. "Who's responsible for this?" he demanded.

Sam pointed at James.

"You? Of course you! You fool!" Mr. Richards screamed. "I've had enough of you!"

With that Mr. Richards lowered the gun that he was carrying.

"No! Wait!" James pled. "I'll pay for the damage."

"With what? You aren't worth a shilling!"

"I'll get it! I promise!"

"He had the Prince girl in there!" Sam yelled over the noise of the crumbling barn.

Mr. Richards was furious. The light of the flaming barn cast dancing shadows across Mr. Richards' face, yet James could see that his eyes were full of rage. James began to run into the darkness. He hadn't taken more than a few steps before a thunderous explosion emanated from Mr. Richards' gun. James fell on his face and lay motionless in the dirt.

"Fool! I'm so tired of him. I should have done that long ago. Throw him in the barn!" Mr. Richards demanded. "He should be more careful than to fall asleep drunken in a barn with a lantern."

Sam and Charles hurriedly grabbed James' body and dragged it to the barn where they threw him in as best they could.

"What's this about a Prince girl?" Mr. Richards demanded of Sam.

"I only know that he said he had her here, but now she's gone."

"Gone? Did someone come and get her?" Mr. Richards asked emphatically.

"I couldn't say. He was going to try and track her with the dogs."

Mr. Richards walked about the area for a few moments searching in the dirt. Soon he pointed to footprints still visible. "Dogs? I don't need no dog to tell that there's been someone here."

Sam and Charles studied the prints.

"Do you suppose that Hyrum was here?" Charles asked.

Mr. Richards looked up and surveyed the surrounding darkness, a little concerned that someone may have seen him shoot James.

"No," he said slowly. "Hyrum wouldn't sneak around like a thief. He'd have come pounding on the front door." Mr. Richards looked at Sam and Charles. "You worked Hyrum over good, didn't you?"

"We did," Sam assured him.

"If that's so, he's probably not even in Elephant Hook," Mr. Richards observed.

Studying the prints further, he added, "One of the prints is the girl, and one is another child, but this set could be a man. Hyrum has an older boy." Again, he stopped and looked into the darkness. "I think Mr. Prince's boys were here," he said. "Still, if they saw the thief try to run, they'll know he got what he deserved."

"Should we get the dogs and go after them?" Charles asked.

"To what end, you fool? I don't need no dog to know that they're at the Princes' place!" Mr. Richards yelled. "We don't need to find them. Hyrum will find us!"

"Yes, sir," Charles replied submissively.

The three men watched the barn burn for a while in silence, then went back into the house after the barn had caved in onto itself and James.

As Francis and Harold raced along the roadway toward the Prince home they could see a large fire in the distance. The two pulled their horses to a stop and watched for a moment.

"That's got to be Mr. Richards' place," Francis observed.

"It is indeed," Harold agreed. "What do you make of that?"

"I don't rightly know."

"Was there a candle or lantern in the barn when you were there?"

"No, sir."

"How very odd," Harold replied. "Well, the Lord works in mysterious ways," he added and spurred his horse on.

It was a joyous reunion at the Prince home when Francis and Harold burst through the door. Julia was almost overcome with relief to know that all of her children were safe. As Julia hugged and kissed Francis, Subria cried, "Praise the Lord! Praise the Lord for His miraculous goodness!"

Harold stayed that night and the next to keep watch over the family.

Chapter Thirty-five - Decision
August 1857
Elephant Hook, Africa

Hyrum and Elder Walker heard about Victoria's ordeal and her rescue as soon as they had arrived at the Prince home. While he was relieved and thankful for Victoria's safe return and for his family's safety, Hyrum was furious that one of Mr. Richards' men would capture and imprison his daughter. He had long ago accepted the dangers associated with living near or amongst the native people, but to be harassed in such an offending manner by one of his own countryman made him feel especially violated.

Julia looked on with a beaming smile as Hyrum hugged Victoria and said to his sons, "Boys, you did well."

"They did do well," Harold agreed. "What will you do now?"

Hyrum hesitated. He looked at Elder Walker and at Julia. He wanted to get his gun and pay Mr. Richards a visit, but he also knew that acting out of anger and in haste could only make matters worse. Still, to leave something as egregious as this without a response didn't seem adequate.

When he didn't respond right away, Julia said, "Let it go dear. Victoria's safe now."

"Yes, let it go," agreed Elder Walker. "I think the Lord would have you forgive and move on."

"I don't know," Hyrum replied. "To just let it go doesn't exactly sit well with me. If there's no justice, what's to stop this man from stealing someone else's daughter, and with more harm than has come to our own?"

"Very well then, turn it over to the authorities," Elder Walker offered.

Harold chuckled. "Authorities?" he said with a feigned laugh. "The nearest authorities are in Grahamstown. We're about as much authority as these parts have. What did the 'authorities' do to those who dumped your wagon into the river, or where were the 'authorities' when you were beaten?" he asked with some excitement. And then added, "And in Grahamstown no less?"

Hyrum put a hand on Harold's arm to calm him a little. "Elder Walker only means well Harold," he said gently.

Harold smiled. "Right," Harold said. Then to Elder Walker, he added, "Sorry, old man."

"No harm done," Elder Walker smiled.

"I'll leave my gun home then, but I'm going to pay Mr. Richards a visit," Hyrum insisted.

"Take Harold with you," Julia said with concern in her voice.

"No. It's better if I go alone. The more men I have with me will unnecessarily increase the likelihood that Mr. Richards will use violence. If it's just me, he can't feel too threatened," Hyrum replied.

"I don't know whether that's wise, Captain," Harold said. "You know that I'd be happy to accompany you."

"Yes, friend, I know that, but there're some things that a father has to take care of on his own."

Julia looked Hyrum in the eyes. Her eyes were moist when she replied, "Don't be stubborn Hyrum. I almost lost you in Grahamstown, I don't want to lose you now."

Hyrum hugged Julia and said with a smile, "You'll not lose me. I'll be in the Lord's care." He then looked at Elder Walker and asked, "Don't you agree?"

Elder Walker nodded. "You'll be in the Lord's care."

Later that day, Mr. Richards was dozing in a chair on his front step with his dog nearby when he heard his dog's low growl. When he opened his eyes he saw a lone rider on horseback coming up his roadway.

"Charles," he called into the house, "bring my gun."

Charles stepped onto the porch with gun in hand.

"Get back inside," Mr. Richards ordered. "You and Sam get your guns and guard from the house."

"It's Prince, isn't it? Let me just finish him off now," Charles offered.

"Get into the house fool, and don't attempt nothing. We still need Prince," Mr. Richards asserted.

Mr. Richards carried his gun, and with his dog at his side, went to meet Hyrum.

"Mr. Richards," Hyrum acknowledged when he approached.

"Mr. Prince," Mr. Richards returned. "You've come alone."

"Should I not come alone?" Hyrum asked.

"No, of course you may come alone."

Hyrum could see the burned out barn from where he spoke with Mr. Richards.

"Tragic that you've lost your barn. Must have been recent."

"Dang fool, James. Fell asleep in a drunken stupor and burned the barn down after he kicked the lantern. He's still inside."

"Still inside?" Hyrum asked.

"He never awoke. But then you didn't come all this way to check on my barn nor on James now, did you?"

"No, to be sure, I did not," Hyrum agreed. "I understand that one of your men brought my daughter here against her will. Is this true?"

Mr. Richards feigned surprise. "If your daughter was here against her will, I have no knowledge of it. Those are serious accusations, Mr. Prince."

"I don't make them lightly," Hyrum insisted. "Nevertheless, I'm making the accusations."

"Sir, you offend me," Mr. Richards asserted. He lowed his gun and added, "I ought to shoot you right here."

Hyrum didn't flinch. "If you do, you shoot an innocent man. Ask your men whether they have any knowledge of my daughter being held here. You can see that I brought no weapon. If your men are to blame, I'll notify the authorities and let them handle it."

Mr. Richards turned toward the house. "Charles! Sam!" he yelled. "Get out here!"

Sam and Charles soon walked out of the house, each holding a gun.

"Mr. Prince says that his daughter was held here against her will. Do you know anything of this?"

Sam and Charles looked at each other inquisitively. Eventually, Sam ventured, "James did hold her here, but no harm came to her."

"Can you be certain of this?" Mr. Richards demanded.

"Yes, sir. He told me himself," Sam assured him.

Mr. Richards turned back toward Hyrum. "There you have it, sir. She was here, but justice has already been served upon him. No need for the authorities." Mr. Richards then motioned toward the burned out shell of the barn. "His bones are still in the rubble if you want to sort through it."

Hyrum turned his horse about as though he would leave. "I have no need to sift through for his bones. Your word is all I need."

"Will you be leading the commandos then?" Mr. Richards asked.

Hyrum turned his horse back toward Mr. Richards. "No, sir. I'll not be leading the commandos."

"This community needs you to lead the commandos!" Mr. Richards demanded. "Who else has the necessary experience?"

"Harold does."

"Harold's too old," Mr. Richards growled. "I'd do it myself if I were younger."

"Have your men lead the commandos then," Hyrum offered.

Mr. Richards spit on the ground. "If you won't lead the commandos, we've got no use for you or your kind, Mormon!"

"Harold can lead the commandos just fine. You won't miss me."

"That's right, Mormon! We won't miss you. Nobody will miss you. Get off my property before I decide to shoot you right here."

Hyrum turned his horse about and kicked its sides and left without saying another word. Mr. Richards watched in disgust as he rode away.

"Why didn't you shoot him?" Sam asked.

"For trespassing," Charles added.

"Shut your mouths, fools. I've got my reasons. If Mr. Prince doesn't change his mind about the commandos, I'll be the first to burn him and the other Mormons out."

At home, Hyrum reported that justice had already been served to James, but that they should still be very careful and not leave Victoria or the little ones out of their sight.

Soon after he had arrived home, Hyrum took Julia aside in their front garden. While the younger children played nearby, he related to her that Elder Walker had advised them to take their family and join the saints in America. He expected that Julia would resist such a huge undertaking. Her response surprised him.

With some excitement in her voice, Julia said, "Hyrum, I feel this is right! I've been concerned since we were baptized. Even you know that our neighbors are getting more bold in their persecutions. It's not just some idle tale. And with the natives raiding again, we need to leave."

"It's not so bad as all that," Hyrum demurred. "Surely it isn't."

Julia placed a hand on Hyrum's face. "Yes, it is. You know that. After all, it's you that was beaten. Next time they may do worse. And what of the children? Can we keep such a close eye on them forever? Are they never to experience the carefree life that you and I experienced as youth?"

Hyrum was silent, and Julia continued. "What kind of life does Francis have to look forward to? Is he going to have to go on in fighting the natives? Will he end up like Ian? Even if he were to survive, would he find a decent woman to wed?"

"Maybe we should go back to England then," Hyrum ventured.

Julia's eyes moistened. "England? My how I've dreamed of going back over the years." Julia held her shawl closer about her shoulders. "See this shawl that our Queen sent to me last year?" she continued. "It's a near constant reminder of the life we left in England, but that's not our life anymore. We've accepted the call of a prophet to be baptized, and now this same prophet calls us to America. If we don't heed his call, it will be just as Elder Walker stated, we and our children will soon give up the joy of the Gospel. I remember also Elder Wesley saying that a lump of coal left out of the fire for long can't sustain itself and will grow cold. While the same lump of coal left in the fire will glow with the same heat as the rest of the fire."

Hyrum looked into Julia's eyes. "Do you know what it would mean to leave this land?" he asked. "We would leave our home and most all of our belongings. It would be a hard ocean voyage and then a long trek by wagon across most of America, with children in tow."

"I do know what it means," Julia assured him with a voice to urge him to understand.

"We aren't as young as we once were," Hyrum smiled.

"But we're not as old as we'll yet be either," Julia grinned.

Hyrum held Julia close and looked beyond her. The children ran about inventing games amongst themselves. Beyond the front garden some sheep grazed on rolling hills. The cold weather hadn't yielded much grass, but the sheep somehow managed. Hyrum thought about his sheep and other animals. He thought about his barn and house. After these many years, he was starting to accumulate some wealth that would secure their old age, and now they were being asked to leave it. He almost bristled at the thought.

Hyrum felt the warmth of Julia's breast against himself and felt her heart beating ever so gently. Suddenly, he had the unmistakable impression that this was his wealth. He was holding his only true wealth, and her offspring was his promise of a future. Then his heart burned as he remembered the Elders teaching them that to hold onto this true wealth required covenants to be made with God, but that those covenants could only be made in the House of the Lord. There was no such house in Africa. The only House of the Lord worthy of such covenants was in America with the prophet of the

Lord. Hyrum knew that this man was a prophet, the burning witness of the Spirit had told him so. It was clear what must be done.

Hyrum released his embrace on Julia slightly so that he could look into her beautiful eyes.

"You're right," he smiled. "We've been called by a prophet to leave home and to join the saints. We mustn't lose any time. No cost is too great to gather to the House of the Lord. I'll speak with the Elders."

Hyrum's response elicited joy from Julia and tears coursed freely down her cheeks. All she could do was smile and bury her face against Hyrum's chest. After a moment, she replied, "Speak with Mr. Crawford as well. Perhaps they've determined to go also."

The next day, Hyrum spoke with the Elders and with Mr. and Mrs. Crawford. They received with joy the news that the Princes would go to America. The Crawfords had already determined that they would leave as soon as arrangements could be made.

October 1857
Elephant Hook, Africa

"Julia!" Hyrum called as he walked into the house. "Julia!"

Julia hurried in from the kitchen. "Yes? What is it?" she replied with concern.

"We've sold the farm! And for a good price!" Hyrum declared.

Julia clapped her hands together and held them to her mouth. "How wonderful! Subria! Hyrum sold the farm."

Subria also walked into the room from the kitchen. "That's wonderful," she stated, but with considerably less excitement than Julia had expressed.

"Who are the purchasers?" Julia asked.

"A family fresh from England," Hyrum smiled. "They wanted to come to a land with more opportunity, and they have money!"

"Oh, how wonderful," Julia exclaimed.

Julia and Hyrum conversed for a moment about the exciting news that would allow them to join with the saints. But the whole while, Julia kept a watch on Subria and could tell that Subria was uncomfortable.

After Hyrum had left the house, Julia said to Subria, "Subria, is something bothering you? You've seemed disturbed ever since we determined to go to America. You're going with us, right?"

Subria had made herself busy folding some clothing, and she didn't look up as she responded. "I can't go with you," she whispered without looking up.

"What do you mean, you can't go with us?" Julia asked with concern in her voice.

Subria still didn't look up, but replied as though unconcerned. "Look at me. I'm too old for such a relocation."

"Oh, Subria," Julia replied with a smile, "you certainly aren't too old. You'll be fine. You'll be on a large ship, and then ride in a wagon. It won't be too difficult. It will be exciting to see America. Don't you agree?"

Subria smiled faintly. "Oh yes, it would be exciting indeed."

"Then you'll go?"

Subria put down the clothing that she had been folding and turned toward Julia. Julia saw tears in Subria's eyes when she said, "It's not that I don't wish to go, child. I love this family. I don't know what I'll do without you. But I can't go to America. Slavery is still very much a part of their society, and I'll not be a slave."

Julia put her arms around Subria and held her. "You'll not be a slave! What a ridiculous notion. You're part of our family."

"Others don't know that. To them, I'll be a slave."

Julia released her embrace of Subria. "We'd pay no mind to what others might think," Julia said with deep emotion. "You're like my mother. You're my dearest friend. My children need you. They don't know life without you."

Tears ran down the length of Subria's cheeks and dripped onto her dress. "When you leave, it will be as a piece of my soul has been ripped out. But I can't go. It's not just that there's slavery in America. I can't get on a ship. I've been on a ship, and I'll never be on another. If I were to get onto another ship, my breath would escape me and my heart would stop. I wouldn't last three minutes and certainly not three months."

Julia listened intently, but tearfully. She had just assumed that with the passage of time, it would have been easier for Subria to board a ship, but that was obviously not the case.

Subria continued, "This land is my land. It runs through me. If I were to leave it, it would miss me. The owls would miss me. The elephants and the lion would miss me. I would miss them." Then with a catch in her voice that mustered no more than a whisper, she added, "This is where I'll die and be laid to rest."

"I'll speak with Hyrum, and we won't go either then," Julia said sincerely.

Subria stood up straight; her expression was one of maternal authority. "You'll do no such thing, child! You're going to take your family to the House of the Lord! Not me, nor an ocean will keep you from doing that."

"I'll miss you so much," Julia said tearfully.

Subria held her and patted her head. "I know. I know."

Julia looked at Subria. "What will you do?"

"Well, I've been thinking that maybe Amanda would like some help."

Julia's countenance brightened somewhat and she replied, "Oh yes! That would be quite lovely! May I speak with her for you?"

"Of course, my dear. I'd like that."

"But to be sure, I don't know how we'll get on without you," Julia added.

Chapter Thirty-six – Port Elizabeth
April 1858
Port Elizabeth, Africa

Julia stood at the bow of the ship and looked out to sea. The ship's mooring was secured by large hemp ropes, but they would be removed soon enough. The sea was calm on the horizon, and Julia wondered whether it was a sign of a smooth voyage to America.

Rebecca stood next to Julia and rubbed her mother's gently bulging abdomen. Julia had only recently told her children and Hyrum that she was with child. Hyrum and the children were overjoyed. Rebecca was particularly pleased after seven years of waiting for a sibling. She was certain that it was a girl. For her part, Julia was happy enough for the addition to their family, but at 39 years old, she knew that carrying the child would be more difficult than before, especially aboard a ship. In her prayers, she had good-naturedly asked God about His timing, but had committed to being as cheerful as possible.

As she stood at the railing, Julia couldn't help but think of the first time she had boarded a similar ship. She was young and fair then, her skin so light that she now wondered whether she had appeared sickly. She looked down at her hands. They were bronzed by the sun and roughened by the labor required of a farmer's wife. She smiled to realize that no one would mistake her for a princess's companion now. At the time that they had first left England, she had felt that she had given up so much to follow Hyrum's dream. The marble walls of the great houses that she had known were gone, as were the finely laced dresses. In England, she had been sought out by many because of her association with Princess Victoria, but she had chosen a different path. Her's wasn't to be a path of luxury and idleness, but rather a path whose companions were often hardship, and toil. She realized now that she hadn't fully appreciated the difference between these two lives at the time of her choosing. But she was satisfied with her choice.

At that moment Luke, ever mindful of his mother's needs, approached bearing a yellow fruit and said, "Mum, look what I have!"

Julia smiled. "A monkey fruit! Wherever did you find it?"

"The captain gave it to me!"

Julia looked about to see whether the captain was nearby that she might thank him. Not seeing him, she turned her attention to Luke. "How wonderful! Did you thank him properly?"

"Yes, of course." Then holding it out for her to take, he added, "It's for you."

Julia took the fruit and kissed her son on the forehead. Though he liked the affection, anything more than a quick peck on the forehead would have obliged him to protest.

"I want some too," Rebecca added hopefully.

Julia smiled. "Yes," she thought, "I'm indeed satisfied with my choice."

They had said goodbye to their home in Elephant Hook several months earlier. Leaving Subria and Amanda pained Julia nearly as much as leaving Lord and Lady Hammond, and she vowed that these would be her last such goodbyes.

Harold and Amanda had come the morning of their departure to tell them goodbye and to move Subria to their home.

"What will I ever do without you?" Julia asked Subria as she gave her a farewell hug.

Subria feigned a smile and through her tears said, "Child, you'll always be in my heart. I thank God that He brought us together."

"You'll be fine with Amanda and Harold then?" asked Julia.

"Of course I will," Subria assured her.

Amanda and Harold were standing nearby.

"We love Subria," Amanda assured her. "She'll be our family now."

"Quite right," Harold agreed.

Subria wiped tears from Julia's face and asked, "Will you be quite alright?"

"Yes," Julia replied through a half-smile.

Harold held out a hand to Hyrum and said, "Well, I guess this is goodbye old man."

Hyrum smiled as he shook Harold's hand. "Yes. I never expected this day to come, to leave Africa, I mean."

"Life can be strange," Harold offered.

"Yes," Hyrum agreed with a smile. "If you ever decide to leave Africa, join us in Utah."

"Oh, I think this is where my bones will be laid, Captain," Harold smiled.

"Goodbye, my dear," Amanda said as she hugged Julia. "I'll miss you so."

"I love you, Amanda," Julia said tearfully.

"Will you be meeting the Crawfords and the Elders in Port Elizabeth?" Harold asked.

"We actually will be meeting them on the road tomorrow. We'll also be meeting quite a number of other families in Port Elizabeth," Hyrum replied.

"So many converts?" Harold asked in surprise.

"Indeed. That's what the Elders tell me," Hyrum answered. Then to his family, he added, "We'd best be off if we're going to catch the ship."

"Indeed, you wouldn't want to miss it," replied Harold. "It would be quite a wait for the next one."

The family climbed into the wagon with the few belongings they would be able to take. They waved until Amanda, Harold, Subria and the house were out of sight.

Traveling by wagon was slow, but they had made reasonable progress. Hyrum expected that they could reach Port Elizabeth in six days. That would be a thin margin for catching the ship, but Hyrum expected there was an extra day built into their schedule.

They were overjoyed to meet up with the Crawfords and the Elders the next day just as they had planned. Excitement for the trip seemed to build after joining with them. Elder Walker and Elder Wesley had been away from their families for nearly five years, so their anticipation was particularly high.

On the third day, Hyrum experienced some difficulty controlling the speed of the wagon as they descended a steep hill. Julia held tightly to her children and feared that the wagon would flip. Near the bottom of the hill, just when they expected that all would be well, the wagon hit a large rock. Julia and the children screamed and there was a loud cracking sound. Hyrum managed to stop the wagon without an upset.

"Hold, hold," Hyrum called out to the team of horses as he pulled the wagon to a halt. As the wagon came to a stop, Hyrum surveyed his family. "Is anyone hurt?" he asked.

"We're all fine," Julia breathlessly replied. "What was that sound?"

As he climbed from the wagon, Hyrum replied, "It sounded like a wheel."

The wagons carrying the Crawfords and the Elders, slowly approached.

"What seems to be the trouble?" Mr. Crawford called.

Hyrum stood beside his wagon and shook his head. "The brake wasn't working as it should, and we hit that rock back there a little hard."

"More than a little hard by the looks of things," Mr. Crawford commented.

Hyrum looked up at Julia sitting in the wagon with the children. "Yes. This is going to be a problem."

"We can get the wheel off easily enough, but how will we mend it? There isn't much wood around here to fix it with," Elder Wesley observed.

"I'm not certain that I have the necessary tools for a break such as this regardless," Hyrum lamented.

"Well, let's see what we can do," Mr. Crawford said.

The metal band that circled the wheel was caved inward at the point where it had encountered the rock. The metal band encircled a ring of wood that connected with the spokes, and the ring of wood was completely shattered at that point. Two spokes were also badly cracked. When the wheel was removed from the wagon, the broken wood fell to the ground and the spokes extended uselessly from the hub.

"Well, to be sure, it's every bit as bad as I expected," Hyrum lamented.

"I've some wire," Mr. Crawford said. "We can try bandaging it together. It might get us as far as Port Elizabeth."

Hyrum removed his hat and scratched his head. "It's worth a try. If we proceed slowly, it may just work."

"And let's be sure to proceed with prayer this time," Elder Walker suggested.

"Capital idea," Mr. Crawford agreed.

It took several hours and considerable wire to band the wheel together, but eventually they felt that the wheel was ready for traveling. By this time, the sun was low in the sky.

Mr. Crawford surveyed the setting sun and said, "We'd better stay right here tonight. It'd do no good to travel in the dark."

"I'm really sorry about this," Hyrum offered. "We can't afford much more delay. If we continue to have trouble tomorrow, you all go and catch the ship. We'll just have to catch the next one."

Mr. Crawford put a hand on Hyrum's shoulder. "We'll not be leaving you. We'll all make it to the ship, or we'll all wait for the next."

Mr. Crawford was a big man and several years Hyrum's senior. He had also been the wealthiest resident of Elephant Hook and an influential citizen. So it was natural that Hyrum yielded to his authority.

"Yes, sir. But all the same, I'd feel awful if you were to miss that ship," Hyrum replied.

Mr. Crawford smiled. "We aren't going to miss it."

The next morning the group was happy to be on their way after eating a morning meal and having said a prayer. Before they started, they also transferred a few items from the Princes' wagon to the Crawfords' wagon to lighten the Princes' load. But they hadn't gone very many miles before the wheel failed again.

Hyrum swallowed hard and used care to reply patiently when Victoria asked, "We prayed before we left. Why didn't God keep our wheel together?"

"Perhaps He's trying to teach us patience," he replied.

"Doesn't He want us to go to Zion?" Rebecca asked.

"Of course, He does," Julia assured her.

"Then did He not hear our prayer?" Victoria asked.

"Of course, He heard our prayer," Julia responded. "He always hears our prayers."

"It doesn't seem as though He did," Samuel chimed in. Hyrum had climbed from the wagon to study the damaged wheel, but he stopped and looked up at Samuel sitting in the wagon. As the fourth child, and third son, ten-year-old Samuel didn't usually get an opportunity to speak, so he generally didn't have much to say. When he did speak, it seemed to catch people by surprise and they took note.

"You must have faith, son," Hyrum replied. "Perhaps God's trying to teach us something."

Hyrum then turned his attention to the wheel. It was shattered worse than before.

The Elders and the Crawfords had stopped alongside the Princes' wagon.

"Looks like we'll have to find some wood to fix that wheel after all," Elder Wesley said.

"How many more of these delays can we afford?" Hyrum asked.

"Well, not many," Mr. Crawford replied. "Let's not dwell on that though. Let's figure out how to fix this wheel."

"Listen," Hyrum said, "I'm thinking that God doesn't want us to leave Africa just yet. Please, go on ahead. It's your only chance to make the ship."

"We aren't leaving you," Mr. Crawford insisted.

"We'll stay with the Princes," Mrs. Crawford said. "But you Elders need to go on ahead and catch that ship. You've already been away from your families nearly five years."

"Oh no," Elder Walker replied. "We're not leaving you."

"You're absolutely right, Mrs. Crawford," Mr. Crawford said. "You Elders need to go on ahead. If you miss that ship, it could be months before the next ship. There's no point in making your families wait any longer than needful."

Elder Walker and Elder Wesley exchanged looks before Elder Walker replied, "If you're certain that you'll be fine without us, I suppose that we could agree to go on ahead."

"We'll be fine," Hyrum assured them. "Please do go on ahead." Then he also pled for the Crawfords to go on ahead.

"We'll not be leaving you, son," Mr. Crawford replied emphatically.

Julia asked Hyrum to come and speak with her. After they had conversed privately, Julia said to the Elders, "Will you consider taking Francis with you?"

The Elders seemed confused at the request.

"I'll not have him conscripted to fight the natives," Julia insisted.

"Is that possible?" Elder Wesley asked.

"Possible," Mr. Crawford replied. "The fighting is escalating, and it is possible that the Queen's garrison would conscript young men into their ranks."

"Well, we can certainly take him with us. He'd be no trouble," Elder Walker replied.

Francis seemed excited about the prospect of traveling with the Elders, but mildly protested. "Are you quite certain that I should leave with the Elders then?"

"Yes, son. You're a man now and I don't want to take any chances that you'll join this awful war. If you were conscripted, you may never leave Africa," Julia replied.

"Very well then," Elder Walker said, "gather your things and let's be off."

"Let me go with them also," Luke urged. "I could be conscripted also."

"No, son, you're staying with us," Hyrum replied. "You'll not be conscripted."

Luke's disappointment showed in his face. Victoria and Rebecca started to cry when Francis hugged them goodbye and climbed onto the Elders' wagon. The Elders' wagon was very small, not meant for more than two people, so Francis sat on the back with his feet dangling.

The family called goodbye and waved until the Elders and Francis were out of sight. Only then did Julia begin to cry.

"What have we done?" she asked Hyrum. "Will we ever see him again?"

Hyrum hugged his wife. "I'm sure we will. He'll be with Elder Walker in Salt Lake City. And like you said, he's a man now. We've taught him well. He'll be fine."

Hyrum's words did little to console Julia.

As Julia, Victoria and Rebecca consoled each other, Hyrum and Mr. Crawford turned their attention to fixing the wheel, their every movement shadowed by Luke and Samuel. At one point, Hyrum went off in search of suitable wood that might be fashioned for the fix. He didn't get back until after dark. Mr. Crawford and Hyrum worked by lantern late into the night trying to fashion the wood appropriately for the fix. Eventually, they retired to bed in exhaustion.

Early the next morning, they started again on the fix, but it didn't go well.

"By the looks of things, I may need to leave you here with your family and Mrs. Crawford while I go on to Port Elizabeth to purchase a wheel," Mr. Crawford advised.

Hyrum looked at the wheel and shook his head. "I suppose you're right. We apparently have little choice."

Julia was standing nearby, and said, "I and the girls have been praying. We surely thought that God would answer our prayer."

"Well, don't give up the faith," Mrs. Crawford replied encouragingly.

"What's this?" Hyrum said, looking back up the road from the direction that they had come.

In the distance the group could see a wagon coming quickly.

"They're in a mighty hurry," Mr. Crawford observed.

"Perhaps they can be of service," Mrs. Crawford replied hopefully.

"It's not very likely, unless they're carrying an extra wheel," Hyrum smiled.

As the wagon neared, it became clear that there were only two people in the wagon, a man and a woman.

"They must not have a load with the pace they're keeping," Hyrum observed.

As the wagon drew quite near, it began to slow, and Julia called, "Subria?"

In surprise, Hyrum called, "Harold?"

"What in the world is this?" Mr. Crawford said with a smile.

Harold stopped the wagon and nearly bounded off, and thrust his offered hand to Hyrum and Mr. Crawford.

"Praise the good Lord, we caught up with you," Subria said as she climbed from the wagon.

"Yes, praise the Lord," Harold chuckled. "I didn't think that there was any possibility of catching you, but Subria assured me that we would."

"I prayed that we would," Subria smiled.

Julia and Hyrum had concerned looks on their faces, and Hyrum asked, "Is everything fine? Is something wrong with Amanda?"

"Amanda's fine," Subria and Harold replied simultaneously.

"Then why are you here?" Julia asked.

Subria smiled. "I'm going with you!" Subria declared.

Julia caught her breath and tears formed in her eyes. "You're going to America with us?"

"I am!" Subria declared with a joyful voice.

"Splendid!" Hyrum replied.

Julia threw her arms about Subria's neck and said through tears of joy, "What's changed your mind?"

"Hyrum holds the priesthood, and I know that if I receive a priesthood blessing, I can get onto the ship," Subria responded with confidence.

"Oh, Subria," Julia declared joyfully, "I'm so very happy. Yes, Hyrum will give you a priesthood blessing!"

Mrs. Crawford and the children each expressed their joy that Subria would be joining them.

"Of course, I'd be delighted to give you a priesthood blessing," Hyrum agreed, "and Mr. Crawford would be happy to assist. Isn't that so, Mr. Crawford?"

"Without a doubt, it would be a privilege," Mr. Crawford assured her.

Hyrum gave Subria a hug. "This is most excellent, Subria," he declared. "We'll give the blessing tonight after dinner then."

It was then that Harold turned their attention to the damaged wheel.

"That's a bad break, Captain," Harold replied.

"Yes, and it's cost us the better part of two days," Hyrum said.

"Well, maybe we know the reason for the broken wheel," Julia smiled as she hugged Subria again. "God wants Subria to go to America!"

"Listen, Captain," Harold said with confidence, "you don't have a moment to spare, and that wheel isn't going to get repaired with the materials out here. Let's transfer everything into my wagon. It'll be tight, but we can manage. Then let's get you to Port Elizabeth. We'll leave your wagon here, and I'll deal with it later."

Hyrum was pleased. "Harold, God did send you to us. Let's hurry, we don't have a moment to spare."

Before long, the Princes' belongings had been transferred to Harold's wagon. One of Hyrum's horses was harnessed to Harold's wagon with Harold's horse, and Luke rode the other horse.

After three days of travel, they caught sight of the sea, and it was beautiful to behold. The sun was high in the sky, and the light piercing the surface gave it a brilliant azure hue.

The approach to Port Elizabeth was from a prominent hill, and the town and its harbor could be seen in the distance below.

"Hyrum," Julia said excitedly, "there's a ship at dock. Could it be our ship?"

"God willing," Hyrum replied. "Let's hope so."

With that, Harold shook the reins to encourage the horses on more quickly.

Before the group reached Port Elizabeth, they watched in disbelief as the sails on the ship were unfurled. The sails quickly filled with a breeze and the ship began moving out to sea.

"Hyrum," Julia cried, the ship's leaving port."

Hyrum didn't reply right away.

"Looks like a stroke of bad luck, Captain," Harold said.

"What will we do?" Julia asked.

"There's little we can do," Hyrum replied resolutely. "I suppose we knew this was a possibility."

The approach to Port Elizabeth widened and Mr. Crawford brought his wagon alongside that of Harold's wagon.

"It appears we've missed the ship, old man," Mr. Crawford said to Hyrum.

"It does indeed," Hyrum replied. "I'm sorry that we've inconvenienced you and Mrs. Crawford so."

"Oh, not at all," Mr. Crawford replied good-naturedly. "We're in no particular hurry."

The group slowed their approach into Port Elizabeth and said little the remainder of the way in.

Eventually, Julia said to Hyrum, "I suppose that I'd hoped to catch up with Francis and to be on that ship with him."

Hyrum put an arm around Julia. "I'd hoped the same, but he'll be fine."

"When might we see him again?"

"Perhaps a couple years," Hyrum replied.

"As long as that?" Julia asked in surprise.

"Maybe not that long."

Tears had formed in Julia's eyes, and there was a catch in her voice when she replied, "He may be married by the time we see him again?"

Hyrum smiled and gave his wife a squeeze. "Now, wouldn't that be wonderful."

Once in Port Elizabeth they went directly to the dock and inquired about the ship that had just left and whether another ship would be arriving in the coming days. They were disappointed to hear that there wouldn't likely be a ship for many months, as there wasn't a significant demand for travel to America.

Mr. Crawford had ample funds to find lodging for Mrs. Crawford and himself, and other than being an inconvenience, the wait for the next ship would be little else.

Hyrum knew that he would have to find lodging for his family and that he would need to find work. It was uncertain whether there would be any temporary work.

"Harold, we're grateful to you for getting us this far, but you'd better take the wagon and find a wheel," Hyrum said.

"Yes, Amanda will be looking for my return," Harold replied. "Will you be quite alright then?"

"We'll be fine," Hyrum assured him. "We've got the horse, and we'll camp near town until we can find something better. Finding work may be the first order of business."

"You'll not camp anywhere," Mrs. Crawford asserted. "Mr. Crawford will pay for your lodging until you can find work."

"Quite right," Mr. Crawford agreed.

Hyrum tried to protest, but the Crawfords would hear nothing of it.

"We're grateful to you," Julia assured them.

"Well, Amanda can wait until we find lodging for you," Harold said. "We can't just dump your belongings along the road now, can we?"

The Princes gratefully accepted the help and were soon moving their few belongings into a small rented house. The children thought it a great adventure to be living in a new location for the first time of their lives.

"God speed to you," Harold said after the wagon was emptied.

Julia tearfully expressed her thanks and hugged Harold goodbye.

"Goodbye, old man," Hyrum said as he extended his hand to Harold. "Give our love to Amanda."

Harold was soon on his way, and Hyrum left the family to seek employment. He was fortunate to find work on the docks. Though he was unfamiliar with such work, he wasn't afraid to apply himself to learning.

Subria also found work as domestic help for one of the prominent families of Port Elizabeth. So, with these resources, the family found that they could live quite comfortably. Without concern of native attack, the days passed pleasantly enough.

As the weeks and months passed, the Princes and Crawfords were thrilled to become acquainted with several other families of their new-found faith who were also gathering to Port Elizabeth in anticipation of the next ship to America. They soon developed a strong bond with these would-be immigrants who would be gathering to Zion with them.

An added benefit was that some of these newly arrived saints were authorized to hold religious services for the gathering saints.

In these pleasant circumstances, the months passed quickly. The family was thrilled when Julia announced that she was with child. Hyrum's initial concern was whether Julia was up to making such a long and arduous trip while pregnant. It was quite conceivable that she would give birth somewhere along the way. He knew that others had done the same, but worried for Julia and the baby.

"We'll wait for the next ship after this one," Hyrum offered.

"No, my dear, we'll do no such thing," Julia asserted straightly. "That would only delay the time that we'd be reunited with Francis. Can you even imagine how Francis would feel if we weren't to arrive next year as expected? No, I won't do that to him."

Concern still showed on Hyrum's face.

"Let's not forget," Julia said cheerfully, "I'll have Subria with me."

Hyrum reluctantly agreed, but he marveled at the strength and determination of the girl that he had married so many years before. Yes, they would press forward as a family and put their trust in the Lord.

Soon the word went out that the next ship bound for America was due to arrive at port. Hyrum was at the dock when someone called out that the top of the mast could be seen on the horizon. Hyrum stopped his work and held a hand above his eyes to shield the sun as he watched intently. His heart leaped when he caught the first glimpse of the top sail. He watched in great anticipation until he could see the entire ship on the horizon. Laying his work aside, he ran to tell Julia.

Julia and Subria and the children were beside themselves with excitement. Despite her joy, Julia wondered whether Subria was concerned about getting on the ship. Since having received a blessing, Subria had spoken nothing of such concern. Now that their departure was only days away, Julia worried whether Subria still maintained her determination.

"Subria," Julia asked quietly as she took hold of Subria's hand, "are you still resolved to join us on the ship?" Though she asked, she wasn't certain she wanted an answer.

Subria smiled with confidence. "Yes, my dear, I'll be on the ship with you. The Lord has heard my plea, and I'll be fine."

Julia hugged Subria and knew that her own prayers had been answered.

Two days were required to re-stock the ship and to prepare it for the next voyage, and the crew needed a few additional days for a well-deserved holiday on land.

Finally, in mid-April, the Princes and the other immigrants walked aboard the ship. Luke and Samuel, who had spent much time in the preceding months on the docks watching their father and the other workers, were quite excited to point out to their mother and Subria all the parts of the ship and to declare the uses for many of the knots that were visible in the ropes. Julia walked arm-in-arm with Victoria and Rebecca. She smiled as she watched her sons vie for her attention. She and her girls listened intently to their narrative.

Julia kept a close eye on Subria, watching for any sign of distress, but there was none. At one point, Subria found herself away from the others and was approached by a native man of about her age. As Julia watched, she thought that she saw in Subria something that she'd never noticed before. Subria seemed to glow, and obviously was enjoying the attention very much. Julia smiled at the thought that Subria would find the attentions of a man flattering.

When Subria did rejoin their family group, Julia took her by the arm and said with a smile, "Subria, who was that gentleman that you were speaking with? He's quite pleasing to look upon."

It was clear that Subria was blushing when she replied, "To be sure, I don't know to whom you are referring?"

Julia smiled as the two women walked on arm-in-arm.

The deck was getting crowded and excitement was building when it became clear that the captain was going to give the order to lower the sails and to release the tethers. Julia kept a close eye on her children, but leaned into Hyrum's chest and wrapped his strong arms about herself. As the sails dropped into position and the ropes tethering the ship to the dock were released, Julia thought of the first time that she set sail aboard a ship. She was so young, and she now realized that, in some way, she may have been running away; running away from the painful memory of her son's death. Though she dearly missed her baby who remained buried in English soil, and her heart longed to visit that graveside, she knew that they had made the right decision. Despite its wildness, or because of it, Africa had been good to them. They had been blessed beyond measure. Their children and their newly found faith were evidence of those blessings, and she wouldn't change it. Though they had lost a brother, they had gained a dear friend in Subria.

The wind soon filled the sails and the ship began to silently move from the dock. Subria stood at the railing and watched. Though both hands held tightly to the wooden top rail, she wasn't afraid. She closed her eyes and smelled the salty air. A gentle breeze caressed her face. She opened her eyes and watched her beloved homeland slipping away. Tears formed in her eyes, and for a moment her breathing shallowed and her chest tightened as she considered her first experience aboard a ship. She hadn't been above deck on that occasion to watch the shoreline and the memory of her experiences grieved her. Just when she thought that she might sink into despair, she felt the African breeze return against her face. She felt that it was the Holy Spirit whispering to her to remain calm and to have faith in God. *"You can do all things through Me,"* it seemed to say to her mind.

Smiling, Subria turned her face away from Africa and toward the sea. When she did, her gaze fell upon the entire Prince family. *How I love them,* she thought. It was a confirmation to her that all her experiences, though harsh as some of them were, had brought her to this moment and place. She wouldn't have wished for Shaka's destruction of her own family, or to have experienced the brutality of the slave ship. *But without those experiences, I may not be here,* she remembered.

Subria thought of an old woman that she had met on the slave ship so many years before. The old woman had told her that there are many seasons; some good, some bad, and some very bad, but that seasons change. The good turn to bad and the bad turn to good. Subria smiled to think that this was now a very good season.

The old woman had encouraged her to choose to be free in her own mind regardless of her circumstances. But to be free, she must forgive all, even the Swallows. It had taken Subria a very long time to forgive Shaka and the Swallows. But she had forgiven them, even Mr. Richards. Forgiveness had opened her heart to freedom and love.

The old woman had encouraged her to believe in God, but before she could believe in God, she must love. Subria thought of the Coburns and how they had taught an angry, young girl to love. *They truly loved me,* she thought with a smile. *It is because of their love, that my heart was opened to God.*

I'm just a simple soul, Subria thought. *Yet, God had a plan for me.*

Joy filled her heart and she released her grip on the wooden rail and placed a hand on Julia's. "I love you, Julia," Subria said. "Thank you."

Tears were coursing Julia's cheeks as she smiled back at Subria. "I love you, Subria," she said.

Hyrum kissed Julia's cheek and held her more tightly. "America!" he said confidently with a wink and a smile to his children. "Here we come."

The end.

ABOUT THE AUTHOR

This is the third novel by EH Lorenzo. In addition to this novel, his first, *The Remembered*, and his second, *Facing the Wind 1: Brentwood Hall* are available on Amazon. EH Lorenzo has an interest in English history and lived in England for two years. He is fascinated by the lives of ordinary people who have gone before, particularly his ancestors.

He is husband to Dana, father of four daughters, sons-in-law, and 20 grandchildren.

If you enjoyed this book, please provide a review on Amazon.

www.ingramcontent.com/pod-product-compliance
Lightning Source LLC
Chambersburg PA
CBHW071630260626
47170CB00001B/34